THE WYVERN MYSTERY

J. SHERIDAN LE FANU

THE WYVERN MYSTERY

SUTTON PUBLISHING

First published in 1869

First published in this edition in 1994 by Alan Sutton Publishing Ltd,
an imprint of Sutton Publishing Limited
Phoenix Mill · Thrupp · Stroud · Gloucestershire

Reprinted 2000

British Library Cataloguing-in-Publication Data

A catalogue record for this book is available from the British Library.

ISBN 0 7509 0687 1

Typeset in 10/11 Bembo.
Typesetting and origination by
Sutton Publishing Limited.
Printed in Great Britain by
Cox & Wyman Limited,
Reading, Berkshire.

CONTENTS

INTRODUCTION

JOSEPH SHERIDAN LE FANU was born on 28 August 1814, in Lower Dominic Street, Dublin. He was the second of three children born to Thomas Le Fanu, a Church of Ireland clergyman, of Huguenot descent, and his wife Emma, herself the daughter of a cleric, Dr William Dobbin. The first child, Catherine, was born in 1813; the third, William, in 1816.

In *Seventy Years of Irish Life* (1893), William Le Fanu recorded the boyhood adventures he shared with Joseph, centred on Dublin's Phoenix Park. The family had moved to the Park in 1815, when Reverend Le Fanu took up a post as chaplain to the Royal Hibernian Military School.

There were notable literary practitioners among Joseph's ancestors. His paternal grandmother was a sister of Richard Brinsley Sheridan (1751–1816), dramatist, best-known for *The Rivals* and *The School for Scandal*, and skilled parliamentary orator. Their mother, Frances Sheridan, was a friend of Samuel Richardson, who had written novels in the mid-eighteenth century, at Richardson's behest. It is, however, difficult to gauge the extent of the Sheridan influence on Joseph, for the literary Sheridans had their triumphs in London, and died too early for him to have known them.

The Le Fanu children enjoyed a relatively comfortable upbringing, but it is unlikely that the young Joseph could have remained entirely unaware of the divisions and hardships within Irish life. In 1826 his father became Dean of Emly, and the family moved from Dublin to rural County Limerick, which was stricken with poverty on account of economic and agricultural depression, resulting in violent and sustained social unrest. The contrast to the ordered world of Phoenix Park and the Military School must have been both dramatic and unsettling.

After education by his father and various tutors, Le Fanu went to Trinity College Dublin in 1833, studying law. He was called to the Bar in 1839, but never made a career in legal practice. He had received favourable attention after publishing some Irish ballads, and, like his English contemporary Wilkie Collins, he preferred to channel his legal knowledge into the creation of fictions. For a while it seemed that he was headed for a career in politics. He stood unsuccessfully as a prospective parliamentary candidate in 1852, and belonged to the Irish Metropolitan Conservative Society throughout the 1840s and 1850s. But this too was abandoned once it became clear that he would not get the party's nomination.

From 1840, Le Fanu became increasingly involved with Irish journalism. He bought into several newspapers, largely to promote his political views. His interest in the Irish Tory paper, *The Warder*, lasted until 1870, but overall his involvement proved unfortunate and expensive. More happily, he had, since the late 1830s, been publishing short stories and tales in the *Dublin University Magazine*, (which in the early seventies gave Oscar Wilde some of his first opportunities in print). He had joined the magazine's staff in 1837, and eventually became its editor and proprietor. Le Fanu's initial publications were adventure stories and historical romances, in the style of Sir Walter Scott and William Harrison Ainsworth. Although often derivative, the literary quality evident in his later writing was at times apparent in the early work. No less an authority than M.R. James rated the supernatural tale 'A Strange Event in the Life of Schalken the Painter' (1839) as 'one of the best of Le Fanu's good things'.

On 18 December 1843 Le Fanu married Susanna Bennett, the daughter of a prominent barrister, and settled in the suburbs of Dublin. Their marriage appears to have been a very contented one, producing four children, and when Susanna died in 1858, Joseph was inconsolable. He became a virtual recluse, and in Dublin was nicknamed 'the Invisible Prince', so rarely was he to be seen in company. He took to going out only at night, making infrequent visits to old bookshops where he sought out old tomes that fuelled his fascination with ghosts and the occult.

This withdrawal bore fruit of a curious kind. It was only after the death of his wife that Le Fanu properly began the career as a novelist for which he is now justly famous. It seems that most of his writing was done from the safe haven of his bed, committing his imaginings to scraps of paper that happened to be lying around. In 1861, following the additional blow of his mother's death, he bought the *Dublin University Magazine*, and began to use it as a vehicle for the publication of his own novels in serial form. In rapid succession, a series of ingeniously plotted novels appeared, including *The House by the Churchyard* (1863), *Wylder's Hand* (1864), *Uncle Silas* (1864), *Guy Deverell* (1865), *The Wyvern Mystery* (1869), *The Rose and the Key* (1871), and *Willing to Die* (1873), which he finished just a few days before his own death, still at the height of his considerable literary powers.

Le Fanu's novels were immensely popular on publication, and he ranked with Wilkie Collins (whose themes and preoccupations he shared) as one of the bestsellers of his day. Like Collins, he both helped to create and benefited from the Victorian taste for the Gothic novel and the novel of sensation. In the year before his death he published a remarkable collection of short stories, *In a Glass Darkly*, pervaded by that skilled rendering of the supernatural which has ensured the volume's continued popularity. His reputation as a great writer of tales of suspense remained high throughout the nineteenth century. 'There was the customary novel of Mr Le Fanu for the bedside; the ideal reading in a country house for the hours after midnight', wrote Henry James in a short story of 1888. Although his fame declined somewhat at the turn of the century, it was easily revived when in 1923 *Madame Crowl's Ghost and Other Tales of Mystery* appeared. This collection of neglected short stories was edited by M.R. James, who affirmed that Le Fanu 'stands absolutely in the first rank as a writer of ghost stories'.

As a boy, Joseph had encountered in his father's library such diverse classics of psychological abnormality as Ann Radcliffe's *The Mysteries of Udolpho* (1794), and Thomas de Quincey's *Confessions of an English Opium Eater* (1823), alongside less enduring indicators of a taste for the strange and the sensational, bearing titles like *The Mummy* and *The History of the Devil*. From the pages of these books sprang images and figures to embody the 'fears of childhood', the phantoms and 'ghostly terrors of the nursery' to which he later referred.

His adult projection of these fears and terrors into fiction, undoubtedly produced works of lasting power. Especially worthy of note are *Uncle Silas*, with its concentrated menace, and 'Carmilla', the concluding story of *In a Glass Darkly*. This story is a signal work in the literary history of the vampire, an influential antecedent to Bram Stoker's *Dracula* (1897). The thinly veiled eroticism of such a work may allow us a suggestive glimpse into the turbulent inner world of Le Fanu, the Victorian male, trying to come to terms with the traumatic loss of a wife to whom, as his brother recorded, 'he was devotedly attached'. More generally, isolation, guilt, and the eruption of violent passions, tearing through the fabric of the ordinary and familiar, characterize his particular contributions to the literature of the Gothic, and the novel of mystery, suspense and sensation.

It is tempting to discover a direct connection between Le Fanu's recollection of isolation and anxiety in the glebe-house of his Limerick boyhood, and the large isolated houses that feature in his later fiction, the focal points for fear and grim foreboding. Carwell Grange, in *The Wyvern Mystery*, is one such edifice. For Alice Maybell, the novel's heroine, it is literally the childhood home to which she returns. In 1834, the Anglo-Irish novelist Maria Edgeworth observed that 'It is impossible to draw Ireland as she now is in a book of fiction – realities are too strong, party passions too violent. . . .'. Arguably, Le Fanu's heightening of violent passion, and stylized presentation of realities infused with lurid imaginings, is a means of accommodating that historical situation.

But *The Wyvern Mystery*'s rural landscape of 'forest-darkened glens' has resonance beyond the particulars of geography and biography. Venturing into the Vale of Carwell, one enters what Le Fanu termed the 'moral and mental darkness of suspense'. *The Wyvern Mystery* appeared during the period between those peaks of achievement, *Uncle Silas* and 'Carmilla'. It belongs to a lesser range, but has suffered excessive neglect. There are stock figures here – the genteel heroine, who is an orphan, the austere squire, his dashing son, and the sinister older woman – but it is by playing variations on the familiar and the known that the novelist effects the sensational. For the reader who pursues the lure of the mystery, there are chilling pleasures in store at Carwell Grange.

DR JULIAN COWLEY
University of Luton

CHAPTER 1

ALICE MAYBELL

In the small breakfast parlour of Oulton, a pretty girl, Miss Alice Maybell, with her furs and wrappers about her, and a journey of forty miles before her – not by rail – to Wyvern, had stood up to hug and kiss her old aunt, and bid her goodbye.

'Now, do sit down again; you need not be in such a hurry – you're not to go for ten minutes or more,' said the old lady; 'do, there's a darling.'

'If I'm not home before the sun goes down, aunt, Mr Fairfield will be so angry,' said the girl, laying a hand on each shoulder of kind old Lady Wyndale, and looking fondly, but also sadly, into her face.

'Which Mr Fairfield, dear – the old or the young one?'

'Old Mr Fairfield, the squire, as we call him at Wyvern. He'll really be angry, and I'm a little bit afraid of him, and I would not vex him for the world – he has always been so kind.'

As she answered, the young lady blushed a beautiful crimson, and the old lady, not observing it, said:–

'Indeed, I don't know why I said young – young Mr Fairfield is old enough, I think, to be your father; but I want to know how you liked Lord Tremaine. I told you how much he liked you. I'm a great believer in first impressions. He was so charmed with you, when he saw you in Wyvern church. Of course he ought to have been thinking of something better; but no matter – the fact was so, and now he is, I really think, in love – very much – and who knows? He's such a charming person, and there is everything to make it – I don't know what word to use – but you know Tremaine is quite a beautiful place and he does not owe a guinea.'

'You dear old auntie,' said the girl, kissing her again on the cheek, 'wicked old darling – always making great matches for me. If you had remained in India, you'd have married me, I'm sure, to a native prince.'

'Native fiddlestick! Of course I could if I had liked, but you never should have married a Mahomedan with my consent. Never mind though; you're sure to do well; marriages are made in heaven, and I really believe there is no use in plotting and planning. There was your darling mamma, when we were both girls together, I said I should never consent

1

to marry a soldier or live out of England, and I did marry a soldier, and lived twelve years of my life in India; and she, poor darling, said again and again she did not care who her husband might be, provided he was not a clergyman, nor a person living all the year round in the country – *that* no power could induce her to consent to, and yet she did consent, and to both one and the other, and married a clergyman, and a poor one, and lived and died in the country. So, after all, there's not much use in planning beforehand.'

'Very true, auntie; none in the world, I believe.'

The girl was looking partly over her shoulder, out of the window, upward towards the clouds, and she sighed heavily; and recollecting herself, looked again in her aunt's face and smiled.

'I wished you could have stayed a little longer here,' said her aunt.

'I wish I could,' she answered slowly, 'I was thinking of talking over a great many things with you – that is, of telling you all my long stories; but while those people were staying here I could not, and now there is not time.'

'What long stories, my dear?'

'Stupid stories, I should have said,' answered Alice.

'Well, come, is there anything to tell?' demanded the old lady, looking in her large dark eyes.

'Nothing worth telling – nothing that is ——' and she paused for the continuation of her sentence.

'That is what?' asked her aunt.

'I was going to talk to you, darling,' answered the girl, 'but I could not in so short a time – so short a time as remains now,' and she looked at her watch – a gift of old Squire Fairfield's. 'I should not know how to make myself understood; I have so many hundred things, and all jumbled up in my head, and should not know how to begin.'

'Well, I'll begin for you. Come – have any visitors looked in at Wyvern lately?' said her aunt.

'Not one,' she answered.

'No new faces?'

'No, indeed.'

'Are there any new neighbours?' persisted the old lady.

'Not one. No, aunt, it isn't that.'

'And where are these elderly young gentlemen, the two Mr Fairfields?' asked the old lady.

The girl laughed, and shook her head.

'Wandering at present. Captain Fairfield is in London.'

'And his charming young brother – where is he?' asked Lady Wyndale.

'At some fair, I suppose, or horse-race; or, goodness knows where,' answered the girl.

'I was going to ask you whether there was an affair of the heart,' said her aunt. 'But there does not seem much material; and what was the subject? Though I can't hear it all, you may tell me what it was to be about.'

'About fifty things, or nothings. There's no one on earth, auntie, darling, but you I can talk anything over with; and I'll write, or, if you let me, come again for a day or two, very soon – may I?'

'Of course, *no*,' said her aunt gaily. 'But we are not to be quite alone, all the time, mind. There are people who would not forgive me if I were to do anything so selfish, but I promise you ample time to talk – you and I to ourselves; and now that I think, I should like to hear by the post, if you will write and say anything you like. You may be quite sure nobody shall hear a word about it.'

By this time they had got to the hall door.

'I'm sure of that, darling,' and she kissed the kind old lady.

'And are you *quite* sure you would not like a servant to travel with you; he could sit beside the driver?'

'No, dear auntie, my trusty old Dulcibella sits inside to take care of me.'

'Well, dear, are you quite sure? I should not miss him the least.'

'Quite, dear aunt, I assure you.'

'And you know you told me you were quite happy at Wyvern,' said Lady Wyndale, returning her farewell caress, and speaking low, for a servant stood at the chaise door.

'Did I? Well, I shouldn't have said that, for – I'm *not* happy.' whispered Alice Maybell, and the tears sprang to her eyes as she kissed her old kinswoman; and then, with her arms still about her neck, there was a brief look from her large, brimming eyes, while her lip trembled; and suddenly she turned, and before Lady Wyndale had recovered from that little shock, her pretty guest was seated in the chaise, the door shut, and she drove away.

'What can it be, poor little thing?' thought Lady Wyndale, as her eyes anxiously followed the carriage in its flight down the avenue.

'They have shot her pet pigeon, or the dog has killed her guinea pig, or old Fairfield won't allow her to sit up till twelve o'clock at night, reading her novel. Some childish misery, I dare say, poor little soul!'

But for all that she was not satisfied, and her poor, pale, troubled look haunted her.

CHAPTER 2

THE VALE OF CARWELL

In about an hour and a half this chaise reached the 'Pied Horse,' on Elverstone Moor. Having changed horses at this inn, they resumed their journey, and Miss Alice Maybell, who had been sad and abstracted, now lowered the window beside her, and looked out upon the broad, shaggy heath, rising in low hillocks, and breaking here and there into pools – a wild, and on the whole a monotonous and rather dismal expanse.

'How fresh and pleasant the air is here, and how beautiful the purple of the heath!' exclaimed the young lady with animation.

'There now – that's right – beautiful it is, my darling; that's how I like to see my child – pleasant-like and 'appy, and not mopin' and dull, like a sick bird. Be that way always; *do*, dear.'

'You're a kind old thing,' said the young lady, placing her slender hand fondly on her old nurse's arm, 'good old Dulcibella: you're always to come with me wherever I go.'

'That's just what Dulcibella'd like,' answered the old woman, who was fat, and liked her comforts, and loved Miss Alice more than many mothers love their own children, and had answered the same reminders, in the same terms, a good many thousand times in her life.

Again the young lady was looking out of the window – not like one enjoying a landscape as it comes, but with something of anxiety in her countenance, with her head through the open window, and gazing forward as if in search of some expected object.

'Do you remember some old trees standing together at the end of this moor, and a ruined windmill, on a hillock?' she asked suddenly.

'Well,' answered Dulcibella, who was not of an observant turn, 'I suppose I do, Miss Alice; perhaps there is.'

'I remember it very well, but not *where* it is; and when last we passed, it was dark,' murmured the young lady to herself, rather than to Dulcibella, whom upon such points she did not much mind. 'Suppose we ask the driver?'

She tapped at the window behind the box, and signed to the man, who looked over his shoulder. When he had pulled up she opened the front window and said:–

'There's a village a little way on – isn't there?'

'Shuldon – yes'm, two mile and a bit,' he answered.

'Well, before we come to it, on the left there is a grove of tall trees and an old windmill,' continued the pretty young lady, looking pale.

'Gryce's Mill we call it, but it don't go this many a day.'

'Yes, I dare say; and there is a road that turns off to the left, just under that old mill?'

'That'll be the road to Church Carwell.'

'You must drive about three miles along that road.'

'That'll be out o' the way, ma'am – three, and three back – six miles – I don't know about the hosses.'

'You must try, I'll pay you – listen,' and she lowered her voice. 'There's one house – an old house – on the way, in the Vale of Carwell; it is called Carwell Grange – do you know it?'

'Yes'm; but there's no one livin' there.'

'No matter – there is; there is an old woman whom I want to see; that's where I want to go, and you must manage it – I shan't delay you many minutes – and you're to tell no one, either on the way or when you get home, and I'll give you two pounds for yourself.'

'All right,' he answered, looking hard in the pale face and large dark eyes that gazed on him eagerly from the window. 'Thank ye, Miss, all right, we'll wet their mouths at the Grange, or you wouldn't mind waiting till they get a mouthful of oats, I dessay?'

'No, certainly; anything that is necessary, only I have a good way still to go before evening, and you won't delay more than you can help?'

'Get along, then,' said the man, briskly to his horses, and forthwith they were again motion.

The young lady pulled up the window, and leaned back for some minutes in her place.

'And where are we going to dear Miss Alice?' inquired Dulcibella, who dimly apprehended that they were about to deviate from the straight way home, and feared the old squire, as other Wyvern folk did.

'A very little way, nothing of any consequence; and Dulcibella, if you really love me as you say, one word about it, to living being at Wyvern or anywhere else, you'll never say – you promise?'

'You know me well, Miss Alice – I don't talk to no one; but I'm sorry like to hear there's anything like a secret. I dread secrets.'

'You need not fear this – it is nothing, no secret, if people were not unreasonable, and it shan't be a secret long, perhaps – only be true to me.'

'True to you! Well, who should I be true to if not to you, darling? and never a word about it will pass old Dulcibella's lips, talk who will; and we are pretty near it?'

'Very near, I think; it's only to see an old woman, and get some information from her – nothing, only I don't wish it to be talked about, and I know you won't.'

'Not a word, dear. I never talk to anyone, not I, for all the world.'

In a few minutes more they crossed a little bridge spanning a brawling steam, and the chaise turned the corner of a by-road to the left, under the shadow of a group of tall and sombre elms, over-topped by the roofless tower of the old windmill. Utterly lonely was the road, but at first with only a solitariness that partook of the wildness and melancholy of the moor which they had been traversing. Soon, however, the uplands at either side drew nearer, grew steeper, and the scattered bushes gathered into groups, and rose into trees, thickening as the road proceeded. Steeper grew the banks, higher and gloomier. Precipitous rocks showed their fronts, over-topped by trees and copse. The hollow which they had entered by the old windmill had deepened into a valley and was now contracted to a dark glen, overgrown by forest, and relieved from utter silence only by the moan and tinkle of the brook that wound its way through stones and brambles in its unseen depths. Along the side of this melancholy glen, about half way down, ran the narrow road; near the point where they now were it makes an ascent, and as they were slowly mounting this an open carriage − a shabby, hired, nondescript vehicle − appeared in the deep shadow, at some distance, descending towards them. The road is so narrow that two carriages could not pass one another without risk. Here and there the inconvenience is provided against by a recess in the bank, and into one of these the distant carriage drew aside. A tall female figure, with feet extended on the opposite cushion, sat or rather reclined in the back seat. There was no one else in the carriage. She was wrapped in grey tweed, and the driver had now turned his face towards her, and was plainly receiving some orders.

Miss Maybell, as the carriage entered this melancholy pass, had grown more and more anxious; and, pale and silent, was looking forward through the window as they advanced. At sight of this vehicle, drawn up before them, a sudden fear chilled the young lady with, perhaps, a remote prescience.

CHAPTER 3

THE GRANGE

The excited nerves of children people the darkness of the nursery with phantoms. The moral and mental darkness of suspense provokes, after its sort, a similar phantasmagoria. Alice Maybell's heart grew still, and her cheeks paled as she looked with most unreasonable alarm upon the carriage, which had come to a standstill.

There was, however, the sense of a great stake, of great helplessness, of great but undefined possible mischiefs, such as to the 'lookout' of a rich galleon in the old piratical days, would have made a strange sail, on the high seas, always an anxious object on the horizon.

And now Miss Alice Maybell was not reassured by observing the enemy's driver get down, and, taking the horses by the head, back the carriage far enough across the road to obstruct their passage, and this had clearly been done by the direction of the lady in the carriage.

They had now reached the point of obstruction; the driver pulled up. Miss Maybell had lowered the chaise window and was peeping. She saw a tall woman, wrapped up and reclining, as I have said. Her face she could not see, for it was thickly veiled, but she held her hand, from which she had pulled her glove, to her ear, and it was not a young hand nor very refined – lean and masculine, on the contrary, and its veins and sinews rather strongly marked. The woman was listening, evidently, with attention, and her face, veiled as it was, was turned away so as to bring her ear towards the speakers in the expected colloquy.

Miss Alice Maybell saw the driver exchange a look with hers that seemed to betoken old acquaintance.

'I say, give us room to pass, will ye?' said Miss Maybell's man.

'Where will you be going to?' inquired the other and followed the question with a jerk of his thumb over his shoulder, toward the lady in the tweed wrappers, putting out his tongue and winking at the same time.

'To Church Carwell,' answered the man.

'To Church Carwell, ma'am,' repeated the driver over his shoulder to the reclining figure.

'What to do there?' said she, in a sharp undertone, and with a decided foreign accent.

'What to do there?' repeated the man.

'Change hosses, and go on.'

'On *where*?' repeated the lady to her driver.

'On where?' repeated he.

'Doughton,' fibbed Miss Maybell's man, and the same repetition ensued.

'Not going to the Grange?' prompted the lady in the same undertone and foreign accent, and the question was transmitted as before.

'What Grange?' demanded the driver.

'Carwell Grange.'

'No.'

Miss Alice Maybell was very much frightened as she heard this home question put, and relieved by the audacity of her friend on the box, who continued:–

'Now then, you move out of that!'

The tall woman in the wrappers nodded, and her driver accordingly pulled the horses aside, with another grin and a wink to his friend, and Miss Maybell drove by, to her own great relief.

The reclining figure did not care to turn her face enough to catch a passing sight of the people whom she had thus arbitrarily detained.

She went her way toward Gryce's Mill, and Miss Maybell, pursuing hers towards Carwell Grange, was quickly out of sight.

A few minutes more and the glen expanded gently, so as to leave a long oval pasture of two or three acres visible beneath, with the little stream winding its way through the soft sward among scattered trees. Two or three cows were peacefully grazing there, and at the same point a converging hollow made its way into the glen at their right, and through this also spread the forest, under whose shadow they had already been driving for more than two miles.

Into this, from the main road, diverged a ruder track, with a rather steep ascent. This by-road leads up to the Grange, rather a stiff pull. The driver had to dismount and lead his horses, and once or twice expressed doubts as to whether they could pull their burden up the hill.

Alice Maybell, however, offered not to get out. She was nervous, and like a frightened child who gets its bedclothes about its head the instinct of concealment prevailed, and she trembled lest some other inquirer should cross her way less easily satisfied than the first.

They soon reached a level platform, under the deep shadow of huge old trees, nearly meeting overhead. The hoarse cawing of a rookery came mellowed by short distance on the air. For all else, the place was silence itself.

The man came to the door of the carriage to tell his 'fare' that they had reached the Grange.

'Stay where you are, Dulcibella – I shan't be away many minutes,' said the young lady, looking pale, as if she were going to her execution.

'I will, Miss Alice; but you must get a bit to eat, dear. You're hungry, I know by your looks; get a bit of bread and butter.'

'Yes, yes, Dulcie,' said the young lady, not having heard a syllable of this little speach, as, looking curiously at the old place, under whose walls they had arrived, she descended from the chaise.

Under the leafy darkness stood two time-stained piers of stone, with a wicket open in the gate. Through this she peeped into a paved yard, all grass-grown and surrounded by a high wall, with a fine mantle of ivy, through which showed dimly the neglected doors and windows of out-offices and stables. At the right rose, three storeys high, with melancholy gables and tall chimneys, the old stone house.

So this was Carwell Grange. Nettles grew in the corners of the yard, and tufts of grass in the chinks of the stone steps, and the worn masonry was tinted with moss and lichens, and all around rose the solemn melancholy screen of darksome foliage, high over the surrounding walls, and out-topping the grey roof of the house.

She hesitated at the door, and then raised the latch; but a bolt secured it. Another hesitation, and she ventured to knock with a stone, that was probably placed there for the purpose.

A lean old woman, whose countenance did not indicate a pleasant temper, put out her head from a window, and asked: 'Well, an' what brings *you* here?'

'I expected – to see a friend here,' she answered timidly; 'and – and you are Mrs Tarnley – I *think?*'

'I'm the person,' answered the woman.

'And I was told to show you this – and that you would admit me.'

And she handed her, through the iron bars of the window, a little oval picture in a shagreen case, hardly bigger than a pennypiece.

The old lady turned it to the light and looked at it, saying, 'Ay – ay – my old eyes – they won't see as they used to – but it is so – the old missus – yes – it's all right, Miss,' and she viewed the young lady with some curiosity, but her tones were much more respectful as she handed her back the miniature.

'I'll open the door, please'm.'

And almost instantly Miss Maybell heard the bolts withdrawn.

'Would you please to walk in – my lady? I can only bring ye into the kitchen. The apples is in the parlour, and the big room's full o' straw – and the rest o' them is locked up. It'll be master I know who ye'll be looking arter?'

The young lady blushed deeply – the question was hardly shaped in the most delicate way.

'There was a woman in a *barooche*, I think they call it, asking was anyone here, and asking very sharp after master, and I told her he wasn't here this many a day, nor like to be – and 'twas that made me a bit shy o' you, you'll understand, just for a bit.'

'And is he – is your master?' – and she looked round the interior of the house.

'No, he b'aint come; but here's a letter – what's your name?' she added abruptly, with a sudden access of suspicion.

'Miss Maybell,' answered she.

'Yes – well – you'll excuse me, Miss, but I was told to be sharp, and wide-awake, you see. Will you come into the kitchen?'

And without waiting her answer the old woman led the way into the kitchen – a melancholy chamber, with two narrow windows, darkened by the trees not far off, that over-shadowed the house.

A crooked little cur dog, with protruding ribs, and an air of starvation, flew furiously at Miss Maybell as she entered, and was rolled over on his back by a lusty kick from the old woman's shoe; and a cat sitting before the fire bounced under the table to escape the chances of battle.

A little bit of fire smouldered in a corner of the grate. An oak stool, a deal chair, and a battered balloon-backed one, imported from better company, in a crazed and faded state, had grown weaker in the joints, and more ragged and dirty in its antique finery in its present fallen fortunes. There was some cracked delf on the dresser, and something was stewing in a tall saucepan, covered with a broken plate, and to this the old woman directed her attention first, stirring its contents, and peering into it for a while; and when she had replaced it carefully she took the letter from her pocket, and gave it to Miss Maybell, who read it standing near the window.

As she read this letter, which was a short one, the young lady looked angry, with bright eyes and a brilliant flush, then pale, and then the tears started to her eyes, and turning quite away from the old woman, and still holding the letter as if reading it, she wept in silence.

The old woman, if she saw this, evinced no sympathy, but continued to fidget about, muttering to herself, shoving her miserable furniture this way or that, arranging her crockery on the dresser, visiting the saucepan that sat patiently on the embers, and sometimes kicking the dog, with an unwomanly curse, when he growled. Drying her eyes, the young lady took her departure, and with a heavy heart left this dismal abode; but with the instinct of propitiation, strong in the unhappy, and with the melancholy hope of even buying a momentary sympathy, she placed some money in the dark hand of the crone, who made her curtsey and a thankless 'Thankee, Miss' on the step, as her eye counted over the silver with a greedy ogle, that lay on her lean palm.

'Nothing for nothing.' On the whole a somewhat mercenary type of creation is the human. The post-boy reminded the young lady, as she came to the chaise door, that she might as well gratify him, there and then, with the two pounds which she had promised. And this done, she took her place beside old Dulcibella, who had dropped into a reverie near akin to a doze, and so, without adventure, they retraced their way, and once more passing under the shadow of Gryce's Mill, entered on their direct journey to Wyvern.

The sun was near the western horizon, and threw the melancholy tints of sunset over a landscape, undulating and wooded, that spread before them as they entered the short, broad avenue that leads through two files of noble old trees to the grey front of many-chimneyed Wyvern.

CHAPTER 4

THE OLD SQUIRE AND ALICE MAYBELL

Wyvern is a very pretty old house. It is built of a light grey stone, in the later Tudor style. A portion of it is overgrown with thick ivy. It stands not far away from the high road, among grand old trees, and is one of the most interesting features in a richly wooded landscape, that rises into little hills, and, breaking into rocky and forest darkened glens, and sometimes into dimpling hollows, where the cattle pasture beside pleasant brooks, presents one of the prettiest countries to be found in England.

The old squire, Henry Fairfield, has seen his summer and his autumn days out. It is winter with him now.

He is not a pleasant picture of an English squire, but such, nevertheless, as the old portraits on the walls of Wyvern here and there testify, the family of Fairfield have occasionally turned out.

He is not cheery nor kindly. Bleak, dark, and austere as a northern winter, is the age of that gaunt old man.

He is too proud to grumble, and never asked anyone for sympathy. But it is plain that he parts with strength and his pleasures bitterly. Of course, seeing the old churchyard, down in the hollow at the left, as he stands of an evening on the steps, thoughts will strike him. He does not acquiesce in death. He resents the order of things. But he keeps his repinings to himself, and retaliates his mortification on the people about him.

Though his hair is snowy, and his shoulders stooped, there is that in his length of bone and his stature that accords with the tradition of his early prowess and activity.

He has long been a widower – fully thirty years. He has two sons, and no daughter. Two sons whom he does not much trust – neither of them young – Charles and Henry.

By no means young are they – the elder, now forty-three, the younger only a year or two less. Charles has led a wandering life, and tried a good many things. He had been fond of play, and other expensive follies. He had sobered, however, people thought, and it might be his mission, notwithstanding his wild and wasteful young days, to pay off the debts of the estate.

Henry, the younger son, a shrewd dealer in horses, liked being king of his company, condescended to strong ale, made love to the barmaid at the 'George,' in the little town of Wyvern, and affected the conversation of dog fanciers, horse jockeys, wrestlers, and similar celebrities.

The old squire was not much considered, and less beloved, by his sons. The gaunt old man was, however, more feared by these matured scions than their pride would have easily allowed. The fears of childhood survive its pleasures. Something of the ghostly terrors of the nursery haunt us through life, and the tyrant of early days maintains a strange and unavowed ascendancy over the imagination long after his real power to inflict pain or privation has quite come to an end.

As this tall, grim, handsome old man moves about the room, as he stands, or sits down, or turns eastward at the Creed in church – as he marches slowly toppling along the terrace, with his gold-headed cane in his hand, surveying the long familiar scenes which will soon bloom and brown no more for him – with sullen eyes, thinking his solitary thoughts – as in the long summer evenings he dozes in the great chair by the fire, which even in the dog-days smoulders in the drawing-room grate – looking like a gigantic effigy of winter – a pair of large and soft eyes follow, or steal towards him – removed when observed – but ever and anon returning. People have remarked this, and talked it over, and laughed and shook their heads, and built odd speculations upon it.

Alice Maybell had grown up from orphan childhood under the roof of Wyvern. The old squire had been, after a fashion, kind to that pretty waif of humanity, which a chance wave of fortune had thrown at his door. She was the child of a distant cousin, who had happened, being a clergyman, to die in occupation of the vicarage of Wyvern. Her young mother lay, under the branches of the two great trees, in the lonely corner of the village churchyard; and not two years later the vicar died, and was buried beside her.

Melancholy, gentle vicar! Some good judges, I believe, pronounced his services admirable. Seedily clothed, with kindly patience visiting his poor; very frugal – his pretty young wife and he were yet happy in the light and glow of the true love that is eternal. He was to her the nonpareil of vicars – the loveliest, wisest, wittiest, and best of men. She to him – what shall I say? The *same* beautiful first love. Never a day older. Every summer threw new gold on her rich hair, and a softer and brighter bloom on her cheeks, and made her dearer and dearer than he could speak. He could only look and feel his heart swelling with a vain yearning to tell the love that lighted his face with its glory and called a mist to his kind eye.

And then came a time when she had a secret to tell her Willie. Full of a wild fear and delight, in their tiny drawing-room, clasped in each other's arms, they wept for joy, and a kind of wonder and some dim unspoken tremblings of fear, and loved one another, it seemed, as it were more desperately than ever.

And then, as he read aloud to her in the evenings, her pretty fingers were busy with a new sort of work, full of wonderful and delightful interest. A little guest was coming, a little creature with an immortal soul, that was to be as clever and handsome as Willie.

'And oh, Willie darling, don't you hope I may live to see it? Ah, Willie, would not it be sad?'

And then the vicar, smiling through tears, would put his arms round her, and comfort her, breaking into a rapturous castle-building and a painting of pictures of this great new happiness and treasure that was coming.

And so in due time the little caps and frocks and all the tiny wardrobe were finished; and the day came when the long-pictured treasure was to come. It was there; but its young mother's eyes were dim, and the pretty hands that had made its little dress and longed to clasp it were laid beside her, never to stir again.

'The Lord gave and the Lord hath taken away – blessed be the name of the Lord.' Yes, blessed be the name of the Lord for that love that outlives the separation of death – that saddens and glorifies memory with its melancholy light, and illuminates far futurity with a lamp whose trembling ray is the thread that draws us toward heaven. Blessed in giving and in taking – blessed for the yearning remembrances, and for the agony of hope.

The little baby – the relic – the treasure was there. Poor little forlorn baby! And with this little mute companion to look at and sit by, his sorrow was stealing away into a wonderful love; and in this love a consolation and a living fountain of sympathy with his darling who was gone.

A trouble of a new kind had come. Squire Fairfield, who wanted money, raised a claim for rent for the vicarage and its little garden. The vicar hated law and feared it, and would no doubt have submitted; but this was a battle in which the bishop took command, and insisted on fighting it out. It was a tedious business.

It had lasted two years nearly and was still alive and angry, when the Reverend William Maybell took a cold, which no one thought would signify. A brother clergyman from Willowford kindly undertook his duty for one Sunday, and on the next he had died. The Wyvern doctor said the *vis-vitæ* was wanting – he had lived quite too low, and had not stamina, and so sank like a child.

But there was more. When on Sundays, as the sweet bell of Wyvern trembled in the air, the vicar had walked alone up to the old grey porch, and saw the two trees near the ivied nook of the churchyard wall, a home-sickness yearned at his heart, and when the hour came his spirit acquiesced in death.

Old Squire Fairfield knew that it was the bishop who really, and, as I believe, rightly opposed him, for to this day the vicarage pays no rent; but the proud and violent man chose to make the vicar feel his resentment. He beheld him with a gloomy and thunderous aspect, never a word more would he exchange with him; he turned his back upon him; he forbade him the footpath across the fields of Wyvern that made the way to church shorter.

He walked out of church grimly when his sermon began. He turned the vicar's cow off the common, and made him every way feel the weight of his displeasure.

Well, now the vicar was dead. He had borne it all very gently and sadly, and it was over, a page in the past, no line erasable, no line addible for ever.

'So parson's dead and buried; serve him right,' said the squire of Wyvern. 'Thankless rascal. You go down and tell them I must have the house up on the 24th, and if they don't go, you bundle 'em out, Thomas Rooke.'

'There'll be the vicar's little child there; who's to take it in, squire?' asked Tom Rooke, after a hesitation.

'You may, or the bishop, d—— him.'

'I'm a poor man, and, for the bishop, he's not like to——'

'Let 'em try the workhouse,' said the squire, 'where many a better man's brat is.'

And he gave Tom Rooke a look that might have knocked him down, and turned his back on him and walked away.

A week or so after he went down himself to the vicarage with Tom Rooke. Old Dulcibella Crane went over the lower part of the house with Tom, and the squire strode up the stairs, and stooping his tall head as he entered the door, walked into the first room he met with, in a surly mood.

The clatter of his boots prevented his hearing, till he had got well into the room, the low crying of a little child in a cradle. He stayed his step for a moment. He had quite forgotten that unimportant being, and he half turned to go out again, but changed his mind. He stooped over the cradle, and the little child's crying ceased. It was a very pretty face and large eyes, still wet with tears, that looked up with an earnest, wondering gaze at him from out the tiny blankets.

Old Dulcibella Crane had gone down, and the solitude, no doubt, affrighted it, and there was consolation even in the presence of the grim squire, into whose face those large eyes looked with innocent trust.

Who would have thought it? Below lay the little image of utter human weakness; above stooped a statue of inflexibility and power, a strong statue with a grim contracted eye. There was a heart, steeled against man's remonstrance, and a pride that would have burst into fury at a hint of reproof. Below lay the mere wonder and vagueness of dumb infancy. Could contest be imagined more hopeless! But 'the faithful Creator,' who loved the poor vicar, had brought those eyes to meet.

The little child's crying was hushed; big tears hung in its great wondering eyes, and the little face looked up pale and forlorn. It was a gaze that lasted while you might count four or five. But its mysterious work of love was done. 'All things were made by Him, and without Him was not anything made that was made.'

Squire Fairfield walked round this room, and went out and examined the others, and went downstairs in silence, and when he was going out of the hall door he stopped and looked at old Dulcibella Crane, who stood curtseying at it in great fear, and said he:–

'The child'll be better at home wi' me, up at Wyvern, and I'll send down for it and you in the afternoon, till – something's settled.'

And on this invitation little Alice Maybell and her nurse, Dulcibella Crane, came to Wyvern Manor, and had remained there now for twenty years.

CHAPTER 5

THE TERRACE GARDEN

Alice Maybell grew up very pretty; not a riant beauty, without much colour, rather pale, indeed, and a little sad. What struck one at first sight was a slender figure, with a prettiness in every motion. A clear-tinted oval face, with very dark grey eyes, such as Chaucer describes in his beauties as 'ey-es grey as glass,' with very long lashes; her lips of a very brilliant red, with even little teeth, and when she smiled a great many tiny soft dimples.

This pretty creature led a lonely life at Wyvern. Between her and the young squires, Charles and Henry, there intervened the great gulf of twenty years, and she was left very much to herself.

Sometimes she rode into the village with the old squire; she sat in the Wyvern pew every Sunday; but except on those and like occasions the townsfolk saw little of her.

''Tain't after her father or mother she takes with them airs of hers; there was no pride in the vicar or poor Mrs Maybell, and she'll never be like her mother, a nice little thing she was.'

So said Mrs Ford of the 'George Inn' at Wyvern – but what she called pride was in reality shyness.

About Miss Maybell there was a very odd rumour afloat in the town. It had got about that this beautiful young lady was in love with the old Squire Fairfield – or at least with his estate of Wyvern.

The village doctor was standing with his back to his drawing-room fire, and the newspaper in his left hand lowered to his knee – as he held forth to his wife, and romantic old Mrs Diaper – at the tea-table.

'If she is in love with that old man, as they say, take my word for it, she'll not be long out of a madhouse.'

'How do you mean, my dear?' asked his wife.

'I mean it is not love at all, but incipient mania. Her lonely life up there at Wyvern would make any girl odd, and it's setting her mad – that's how I mean.'

'My dear sir,' remonstrated fat Mrs Diaper, who was learned as well as romantic, 'romance takes very whimsical shape at times; Vanessa was in love with Dean Swift, and very young men were passionately in love with Ninon de l'Enclos.'

'Tut – stuff – did I ever hear!' exclaimed Mrs Buttle, derisively, 'who ever thought of love or romance in the matter? The young lady thinks it would be very well to be mistress of Wyvern, and secure a comfortable jointure, and so it would; and if she can make that unfortunate old man fancy her in love with him, she'll bring him to that, I have very little doubt. I never knew a quiet minx that wasn't sly – smooth water.'

In fact, through the little town of Wyvern, shut out for the most part from the forest grounds, the old grey manor-house of the same name, it came to be buzzed abroad and about that, whether for love, or from a motive more sane, though less refined, pretty Miss Alice Maybell had set her heart on marrying her surly old benefactor, whose years were enough for her grandfather.

It as an odd idea to get into people's heads; but why were her large soft grey eyes always following the squire by stealth?

And, after all, what is incredible of the insanities of ambition? or the subtlety of women?

In the stable-yard of Wyvern Master Charles had his foot in the stirrup, and the old fellow with a mulberry-coloured face, and little grey eyes, who held the stirrup-leather at the other side, said, grinning:–

'I wish ye may get it.'

'Get what?' said Charles Fairfield, arresting his spring for a moment, and turning his dark and still handsome face, with a hard look at the man, for there was something dry and sly in his face and voice.

'What we was talking of – the old house and the land,' said the man.

'Hey, is that all?' said the young squire, as he was still called at four-and-forty, throwing himself lightly into the saddle. 'I'm pretty easy about that. Why, what's the matter?'

'What if the old fellow took it in his head to marry?'

'Marry – eh? well, if he did, I don't care; but what the devil makes you talk like that? Why, man, there's black and white, seal and parchment for that; the house and acres are settled, Tom; and who do you think would marry him?'

'You're the last to hear it; any child in the town could tell you, Miss Alice Maybell.'

'Oh! do they really? I did not think of that,' said the young squire, first looking in old Tom's hard grey eyes. Then for a moment at his own boot thoughtfully, and then he swung himself into the saddle, and struck his spur in his horse's side, and away he plunged, without another word.

'He don't like it, not a bit,' said Tom, following him with askance look as he rode down the avenue. 'No more do I; she's always a-watching of the squire and old Harry does throw a sheep's eye at her, and she's a likely lass; what though he be old, it's an old rat that won't eat cheese.'

As Tom stood thus, he received a poke on the shoulder with the end of a stick, and looking round saw old Squire Harry.

The squire's face was threatening. 'Turn about, d——n ye! What were you saying to that boy o' mine?'

'Nothin' as I remember,' lied Tom, bluntly.

'Come, what was it?' said the hard old voice, sternly.

'I said Blackie'd be the better of a brushin'-boot that's all, I mind.'

'You lie; I saw you look over your shoulder before you said it, and while he was talkin' he saw me a-comin', and he looked away – I caught ye at it, ye pair of false, pratin' scoundrels; ye were talkin' o' me – come, what did he say, sirrah?'

'Narra word about ye.'

'You lie; out wi' it, sir, or I'll make your head sing like the church bell.'

And he shook his stick in his great tremulous fist, with a look that Tom well knew.

'Narra word about you from first to last,' said Tom; and he cursed and swore in support of his statement, for a violent master makes liars of his servants, and the servile vices crop up fast and rank under the shadow of tyranny.

'I don't believe you,' said the squire irresolutely; 'you're a liar, Tom, a black liar; ye'll choke wi' lies some day – you – fool!'

But the squire seemed partly appeased, and stood with the point of his stick now upon the ground, looking down on little Tom, with a somewhat grim and dubious visage, and after a few moments' silence, he asked:–

'Where's Miss Alice?'

'Takin' a walk, sir.'

'*Where*, I say?'

'She went towards the terrace garden,' answered Tom.

And towards the terrace garden walked with a stately, tottering step the old squire, with his great mastiff at his heels. Under the shadow of tall trees, one side of their rugged stems lighted with the yellow sunset, the other in soft grey, while the small birds were singing pleasantly high over his head among quivering leaves.

He entered the garden, ascending five worn steps of stone, between two weather-worn stone urns. It is a pretty garden, all the prettier though sadder for its neglected state. Tall trees overtop its walls from without, and those grey walls are here and there overgrown with a luxuriant mantle of ivy; within are yew trees and wonderfully tall old myrtles; laurels not headed down for fifty years, and grown from shrubs into straggling, melancholy trees. Its broad walls are now overgrown with grass, and it has the air and solitude of a ruin.

In this conventual seclusion, seated under the shade of a great old tree, he saw her. The old-fashioned rustic seat on which she sat is confronted by another, with what was once a gravel walk between.

More erect, shaking himself up as it were, he strode slowly toward her. Her head was supported by her hand – her book on her lap – she seemed lost in a reverie, as he approached unawares over the thick carpet of grass and weeds.

'Well, lass, what brings you here? You'll be sneezing and coughing for this; won't you – sneezing and coughing – a moist, dark nook ye've chosen,' said Squire Harry, placing himself, nevertheless, on the seat opposite.

She started at the sound of his voice, and as she looked up in his face, he saw that she had been crying.

The squire said nothing, but stiffly scuffled and poked the weeds and grass at his feet, for a while, with the end of his stick, and whistled low, some dreary old bars to himself.

At length he said abruptly, but in a kind tone:–

'You're no child now; you've grown up; you're a well-thriven, handsome young woman, little Alice. There's not one to compare wi' ye; of all the lasses that come to Wyvern church ye bear the bell, ye do, ye bear the bell; ye know it. Don't ye? Come, say lass; don't ye know there's none to compare wi' ye?'

'Thank you, sir. It's very good of you to think so – you're always so kind,' said pretty Alice, looking very earnestly up in his face, her large tearful eyes wider than usual, and wondering, and, perhaps, hoping for what might come next.

'I'll be kinder, maybe; never ye mind; ye like Wyvern, lass – the old house; well, it's snug, it is. It's a good old English house: none o' your thin brick walls and Greek pillars, and scrape o' rotten plaster, like my Lord Wrybroke's sprawling house, they think so fine – but they don't think it, only they say so, and they lie, just to flatter the peer; d—— them. They go to London and learn courtiers' ways there; that wasn't so when I was a boy; a good old gentleman that kept house and hounds here was more, by a long score, than half a dozen fine Lunnon lords; and you're handsomer, Alice, and a deal better, and a better lady, too, than the best o' them painted, fine ladies, that's too nice to eat good beef or mutton, and can't call a cabbage a cabbage, I'm told, and would turn up their eyes, like a duck in thunder, if a body told 'em to put on their patterns, and walk out, as my mother used, to look over the poultry. But what was that you were saying – I forget?'

'I don't think, sir – I don't remember – was I saying anything? I – I don't recollect,' said Alice, who knew that she had contributed nothing to the talk.

'And you like Wyvern,' pursued the old man, with a gruff sort of kindness. 'Well, you're right; it's not bin a bad home for ye, and ye'd grieve to leave it. Ay – you're right, there's no place like it – there's no air like it, and ye love Wyvern, and ye *shan't* leave it, Alice.'

Alice Maybell looked hard at him; she was frightened, and also agitated. She grew suddenly pale, but the squire not observing this, continued:–

'That is, unless ye be the greatest fool in the country's side. You'd miss Wyvern, and the old woods, and glens, and spinnies, and, mayhap, ye'd miss the old man a bit too – not so old as they give out though, and 'tisn't always the old dog gives in first – mind ye – nor the young 'un that's the best dog, neither. I don't care that stick for my sons – no more than they for me – that's reason. They're no comfort to me, nor never was. They'd be devilish glad I was carried out o' Wyvern Hall feet foremost.'

'Oh, sir, you can't think———'

'Hold your little fool's tongue; I'm wiser than you. If it warn't for you, child, I don't see much my life would be good for. You don't wish me dead, like those cubs. Hold your tongue, lass. I see someone's bin frightenin' you; but I'm not going to die for a bit. Don't you take on; gi'e us your hand.'

And he took it, and held it fast in his massive grasp.

'Ye've been cryin', ye fool. Them fellows bin sayin' I'm breakin' up. It's a d———d lie. I've a mind to send them about their business. I'd do it as ready as put a horse over a three-foot wall; but I've twelve years' life in me yet. I'm good for fourteen years, if I live as long as my father did. He took his time about it, and no one heard me grumble, and I'll take mine. Don't ye be a fool; I tell you there's no one goin' to die here, that I know of. There's gentle blood in your veins, and you're a kind lass, and I'll take care o' you – mind, I'll do it, and I'll talk to you again.'

And so saying, he gave her hand a parting shake, and let it drop, and rising, he turned away, and strode stiffly from the garden. He was not often so voluble; and now the whole of this talk seemed to Alice Maybell a riddle. He could not be thinking of marrying; but was he thinking of leaving her the house and a provision for her life?

CHAPTER 6

THE OLD SQUIRE UNLIKE HIMSELF

He talked very little that night in the old-fashioned drawing-room, where Alice played his favourite old airs for him on the piano, which he still called the 'harpsichord.' He sat sometimes dozing, sometimes listening to her music, in the great chair by the fire, he ruminated, perhaps, but he did not open the subject, whatever it might be, which he had hinted at.

But before ten o'clock came, he got up and stood with his back to the fire. Is there any age at which folly has quite done with us, and we cease from building castles in the air?'

'My wife was a tartar,' said he rather abruptly, 'and she was always telling me I'd marry again before she was cold in her grave, and I made answer, "I've had enough of the market, I thank you; one wife in a life is one too many." But she wasn't like you – no more than chalk to cheese – a head devil she was. Play me the 'Week before Easter' again, lass.'

And the young lady thrice over played that pretty vulgar old air; and when she paused the gaunt old squire changed the refrain from the hearthrug, somewhat quaveringly and discordantly.

'You should have heard Tom Snedly sing that round a bowl of punch. My sons, a pair o' dull dogs – we were pleasanter fellows then – I don't care if they was at the bottom of the Lunnon canal. Gi'e us the 'Lincolnshire Poacher,' lass. Pippin-squeezing rascals – and never loved me. I sometimes think I don't know what the world's a-comin' to. I'd be a younger lad by a score o' years, if neighbours were as I remember 'em.'

At that moment entered old Tom Ward, who, like his master, had seen younger, if not better days, bearing something hot in a silver tankard on a little tray. Tom looked at the squire. The squire pointed to the little table by the hearthrug, and pulled out his great gold watch, and found it was time for his 'night-cap.'

Tom was skilled in the brew that pleased his master, and stood with his shrewd grey eyes on him, till he had swallowed his first glass, then the squire nodded gruffly, and he knew all was right, and was relieved, for everyone stood in awe of old Fairfield.

Tom was gone, and the squire drank a second glass, slowly, and then a third, and stood up again with his back to the fire and filled his glass with the last precious drops of his cordial, and placed it on the chimneypiece, and looked steadfastly on the girl, whose eyes looked sad on the notes, while her slender fingers played those hilarious airs which Squire Fairfield delighted to listen to.

'Down in the mouth, lass – hey?' said the squire with a suddeness that made the unconscious girl start.

When she looked up he was standing grinning upon her, from the hearthrug, with his glass in his fingers, and his face flushed.

'You girls, when you like a lad, you're always in the dumps – ain't ye? – mopin' and moultin' like a sick bird, till the fellow comes out wi' his mind, and then all's right, flutter and song and new feathers, and – come, what do you think o' me, lass?'

She looked at him dumbly, with a colourless and frightened face. She saw no object in the room but the tall figure of the old man, flushed with punch, and leering with a horrid jollity, straight before her like a vivid magic-lantern figure in the dark. He was grinning and wagging his head with exulting encouragement.

Had Squire Fairfield, as men have done, all on a sudden grown insane? and was that leering mask, the furrows and contortions of which, and its glittering eyes, were fixing themselves horribly on her brain, a familiar face transformed by madness?

'Come, lass, do ye like me?' demanded the phantom.

'Well, you're tongue-tied, ye little fool – shame-faced, and all that, I see,' he resumed after a little pause. 'But you *shall* answer – ye must; you do – you like old Wyvern, the old squire. You'd feel strange in another place – ye would, and a younger fellow would not be a tithe so kind as me – and I like ye well, chick-a-biddy, chick-a-biddy – ye'll be my little queen, and I'll keep ye brave satins and ribbons, and laces, and lawn; and I'll gi'e ye the jewellery – d'ye hear? – necklaces, and earrings, and bodkins, and all the rest, for your own, mind; for the Captain nor Jack shall never hang them on wife o' theirs, mind ye – and ye'll be the grandest lady as ever bin in Wyvern this hundred years – and ye'll have nothing to do but sit all day in the window, or ride in the coach, and order your maids about; and I'll leave you every acre and stick and stone, and silver spoon, that's in or round about Wyvern - for you're a good lass, and I'll make a woman of you; and I'd like to break them young rascals' necks – they never deserved a shilling o' mine; so gi'e's your hand, lass, and the bargain's made.'

So the squire strode a step or two nearer, extending his huge bony hand, and Alice, aghast, stared with wide open eyes fixed on him, and exclaimed faintly, 'Oh, sir! – oh, Mr Fairfield!'

'*Oh!* to be sure, and *oh*, Squire Fairfield!' chuckled he, mimicking the young lady, as he drew near; 'ye need not be shy, nor scared by me, little Alice; I like you too well to hurt the tip o' your little finger, look ye – and you'll sleep on't, and tell me all to-morrow morning.'

And he laid his mighty hands, that had lifted wrestlers from the earth, and hurled boxers headlong in his day, tremulously on her two little

shoulders. 'And ye'll say good-night, and gi'e me a buss; good-night to
ye, lass, and we'll talk again in the morning, and ye'll say naught, mind to
the boys, d——n 'em, till all's settled – ye smooth-cheeked, bright-eyed,
cherry-lipped little——'

And here the ancient squire boisterously 'bussed' the young lady, as he
had threatened, and two or three times again, till, scrubbed by the white
stubble of his chin, she broke away, with her cheeks flaming, and, still
more alarmed, reached the door.

'Say good-night, won't ye, hey?' bawled the squire, still in a chuckle
and shoving the chairs out of his way as he stumbled after her.

'Good-night, sir,' cried she, and made her escape through the door,
and under the arch that opened from the hall, and up the stairs toward
her room, calling as unconcernedly as she could, but with tremulous
eagerness to her old servant. 'Dulcibella, are you there?' and immensely
relieved when she heard her kindly old voice, and saw the light of her
candle.

'I say – hallo – why, wench, what the devil's come over ye?' halloed
the voice of the man from the foot of the stairs. 'That's the trick of you
rogues all – ye run away to draw us after; well, it won't do – another
time. I say, good-night, ye wild bird.'

'Thank you, sir – good-night, sir – good-night, sir.' repeated the voice
of Alice, higher and higher up the stairs, and he heard her door shut.

He stood with a flushed face, and a sardonic grin for a while, looking
up the stairs, with his big bony hand on the banister, and wondering how
young he was; and he laughed and muttered pleasantly, and resolved it
should all be settled between them next evening; and so again he looked
at his watch, and found that she had not gone, after all, earlier than usual,
and went back to his fire, and rang the bell, and got a second 'night-cap,'
as he called his flagon of punch.

Tom remarked how straight the squire stood that night, with his back
to the fire, eyeing him as he entered from the corners of his eyes, with a
grin, and a wicked way of his head.

'A dull dog, Tom. Who's a-goin' to hang ye? D——n ye, look
brighter, or I'll stir ye up with the poker. Never shake your head, man;
ye may brew yourself a tankard o' this, and ye'll find you're younger than
ye think for, and some of the wenches will be throwing a sheep's eye at
you – who knows?'

Tom did not quite know what to make of this fierce lighting up of
gaiety and benevolence. An inquisitive glance he fixed stealthily on his
master, and thanked him dubiously – for he was habitually afraid of him;
and as he walked away through the passages, he sometimes thought the
letter that came that afternoon might have told of the death of old lady
Drayton, or some relief of the estate; and sometimes his suspicions were

nearer the truth, for in drowsy houses like Wyvern, where events are few, all theses of conversation are valuable and speculation is active, and you may be sure that what was talked of in the town was no mystery in the servants' hall, though more gossiped over than believed.

Men who are kings in very small dominions are whimsical, as well as imperious – eccentricity is the companion of seclusion – and the squire had a jealous custom, in his house, which was among the oddities of his despotism; it was simply this: the staircase up which Alice Maybell flew, that night, to old Dulcibella and her room, is that which ascends the northern wing of the house. A strong door in the short passage leading to it from the hall shuts it off from the rest of the building on that level.

For this young lady, then, while she was still a child, Squire Fairchild had easily made an oriental seclusion in his household, by locking, with his own hand, that door every night, and securing more permanently the doors which, on other levels, afforded access to the same wing.

He had a slight opinion of the other sex, and an evil one of his own, and would have no Romeo and Juliet tragedies. As he locked this door after Miss Alice Maybell's 'good-night,' he would sometimes wag his head shrewdly and wink to himself in the lonely oak hall, as he dropped the key into his deep coat pocket – 'Safe bind, safe find,' 'Better sure than sorry,' and other wise saws seconding the precaution.

So this night he recollected the key, as usual, which in the early morning, when he drank his glass of beer at his room-door, he handed to old Mrs Durdin, who turned it in the lock, and restored access for the day.

This custom was too ancient – reaching back beyond her earliest memory – to suggest the idea of an affront, and so it was acquiesced in and never troubled Miss Maybell; the lock was not tampered with, the door was never passed, although the squire, versed in old saws, was simple to rely on that security against a power that laughs at locksmiths.

CHAPTER 7

THE SQUIRE'S ELDEST SON COMES HOME

Thus was old Squire Fairfield unexpectedly transformed, and, much to the horror of pretty Alice Maybell, appeared in the character of a lover, grim, ungainly, and without the least chance of that brighter transformation which ultimately more than reconciles 'beauty' to her conjugal relations with the 'beast.'

Grotesque and even ghastly it would have seemed at any time. But now it was positively dismaying, and poor troubled little Alice Maybell, on reaching her room, sat down on the side of her bed, and, to the horror and bewilderment of old Dulcibella, wept bitterly and long.

The harmless gabble of the old nurse, who placed herself by her side, patting her all the time upon the shoulder, was as the sound of a humming in the woods in summer time, or the crooning of a brook. Though her ear was hardly conscious of it, perhaps it soothed her.

Next day there was a little stir at Wyvern, for Charles – or, as he was oftener called, Captain Fairfield – arrived. This 'elderly young gentleman,' as Lady Wyndale called him, led a listless life there. He did not much affect rustic amusements; he fished now and then, but cared little for shooting, and less for hunting. His time hung heavy on his hands, and he did not well know what to do with himself. He smoked and strolled about a good deal, and rode into Wyvern and talked with the towns-people. But the country plainly bored him, and not the less that his sojourn had been in London, and the contrast made matters worse. Alice Maybell had a headache that morning, and, not caring to meet the squire earlier than was inevitable, chose to say so.

The captain, who, travelling by the mail, had arrived at eight o'clock, took his place at the breakfast-table at nine, and received for welcome a gruff nod from the squire, and the tacit permission to grasp the knuckles which he grudgingly extended to him to shake.

In that little drama in which the old squire chose now to figure, his son Charles was confoundedly in the way.

'Well, and what were you doin' in Lunnon all this time?' grumbled Squire Harry when he had finished his rasher and his cup of coffee, after a long, hard look at Charles, who, in happy unconsciousness, crunched his toast, and read the county paper.

'I beg your pardon, sir, I didn't hear – you were saying?' said Charles, looking up and lowering the paper.

'Hoo – yes – I was saying, I don't think you went all the way to Lunnon to say your prayers in St. Paul's; you've bin losing money in those hells and places; when your pocket's full away you go and leave it wi' them town blackguards, and back you come as empty as a broken sack to live on me, and so on. Come, now, how much rent do you take by the year from that place your fool of a mother left ye – the tartar! – hey?'

'I think, sir, about three hundred a year,' answered Charles.

'Three hundred *and eighty*,' said the old man, with a grin and a wag of his head. 'I'm not so old that I can't remember *that* – three hundred and eighty; and ye flung that away in Lunnon taverns and operas, on dancers and dicers, and ye come back here without a shillin' left to bless yourself, to ride my horses and drink wine; and ye call that fair play. Come along, here.'

And, followed by his mastiff, he marched stiffly out of the room.

Charles was surprised at his explosion, and sat looking after the grim old man, not knowing well what to make of it, for Squire Harry was open-hearted enough and never counted the cost of his hospitalities, and had never grudged him his home at Wyvern before.

'Much he knows about it,' thought Charles; 'time enough, though. If I am *de trop* here I can take my portmanteau and umbrella, and make my bow and go cheerfully.'

The tall captain, however, did not look cheerful, but pale and angry, as he stood up and kicked the newspaper, which fell across his foot, fiercely. He looked out of the window, with one hand in his pocket, in sour rumination. Then he took his rod and flies and cigar-case, and strolled down to the river, where, in that engrossing and monotonous delight, celebrated of old by Venables and Walton, he dreamed away the dull hours.

Blessed resource for those mysterious mortals to whom nature accords it – stealing away, as they wander solitary along the devious river bank, the memory, the remorse, and the miseries of life, like the flow and music of the shadowy Lethe.

This captain did not look like the man his father had described him – an anxious man, rather than a man of pleasure – a man who was no sooner alone than he seemed to brood over some intolerable care, and, except during the exercise of his 'gentle craft,' his looks were seldom happy or serene.

The hour of dinner came. A party of three, by no means well assorted. The old squire in no genial mood and awfully silent. Charles silent and abstracted too; his body sitting there eating its dinner, and his soul wandering with black care and other phantoms by far-off Styx. The young lady had her own thoughts to herself, uncomfortable thoughts.

At last the squire spoke to the intruder, with a look that might have laid him in the Red Sea.

'In my time young fellows were more alive, and had something to say for themselves. I don't want your talk myself over my victuals, but you should 'a spoke to *her* – 'tisn't civil – 'tweren't the way in my day. I don't think ye asked her 'How are ye?' since ye came back. Lunnon manners, maybe.'

'Oh, but I assure you I did. I could not have made such an omission. Alice will tell you I was not quite so stupid,' said Charles, raising his eyes, and looking at her.

'Not that it signifies, mind ye, the crack of a whip whether ye did nor no,' continued the squire; 'but ye may as well remember that ye're not brother and sister exactly, and ye'll call her Miss Maybell, and not Alice no longer.'

The captain stared. The old squire looked resolutely at the brandy flask from which he was pouring into his tumbler. Alice Maybell's eyes were lowered to the edge of her plate, and with the tip of her finger she fiddled with the crumbs on the tablecloth. She did not know what to say, or what might be coming.

So soon as the squire had quite compounded his brandy-and-water he lifted his surly eyes to his son with a flush on his aged cheek, and wagged his head with oracular grimness, and silence descended again for a time upon the three kinsfolk.

This uncomfortable party, I suppose, were off again, each on their own thoughts, in another minute. But no one said a word for some time.

'By the bye, Alice – Miss Maybell, I mean – I saw in London a little picture that would have interested you,' said the captain, 'an enamelled miniature of Marie Antoinette, a pretty little thing only the size of your watch; you can't think how spirited and beautiful it was.'

'And why the dickens didn't ye buy it, and make her a compliment of it? Much good tellin' her how pretty it was,' said the squire, sulkily; ''twasn't for want o' money. D—— it, in my day a young fellow'd be ashamed to talk of such a thing without he had it in his pocket to make an offer;' and the old squire muttered sardonically to his brandy-and-water, and neither Miss Alice nor Captain Fairfield knew well what to say. The old man seemed bent on extinguishing every little symptom of a lighting up of the gloom which his presence induced.

They came at last into the drawing-room. The squire took his accustomed place by the fire. In due time came his 'night-cap.' Miss Alice played his airs over and over on the piano. The captain yawned stealthily into his hand at intervals, and at last stole away.

'Well, Ally, here we are at last, girl. That moping rascal's gone to his bed; I thought he'd never 'a gone. And now come here, ye little fool, I want to talk to ye. Come, I say, what the devil be ye afeared on? I'd like to see the fellow 'd be uncivil to you. My wife, as soon as the lawyers can write out the parchments, the best settlements had ever bin made on a Fairfield's wife since my great uncle's time. Why, ye look as frightened, ye pretty little fool, as if I was a-going to rob ye, instead of making ye lady o' Wyvern, and giving ye every blessed thing I have on earth. That's right!'

He had taken her timid little hand in his bony tremulous grasp.

'I'll have ye grander than any that ever has been' – he was looking in her face with an exulting glare of admiration – 'and I'll give ye the diamonds for your own, mind, and I'll have your picture took by a painter. There was never a lady o' Wyvern fit to hold a candle to ye, and I'm a better man than half the young fellows that's going; and ye'll do as ye like – wi' servants, and house and horses and all – I'll deny ye in nothing. And why, sweetheart, didn't you come down this morning? Was you ailing, child – was pretty Ally sick in earnest?'

'A headache, sir, I – I have it still – if – if you would not mind, I'll be better, sir, in my room. I've had a very bad headache. It will be quite well, I dare say, by tomorrow. You are very kind sir; you have always been very kind, sir; I never can thank you – never, never, sir, as I feel.'

'Tut, folly, nonsense, child; wait till all's done, and thank me then, if ye will. I'll make ye as fine as the queen, and finer.' Every now and then he emphasised his harangue by kissing her cheeks and lips, which added to her perplexity and terror, and made her skin flame with the boisterous rasp of his stubbled chin. 'And ye'll be my little duchess, my beauty; ye will, my queen o' diamonds, you roguey-poguey-woguey, as cunning as a dog-fox,' and in the midst of these tumultuous endearments she managed to break away from the amorous ogre, and was out of the door and up the stairs to her room and old Dulcibella, before his tardy pursuit had reached the cross-door.

An hour has passed, and the young lady stood up, and placing her arms about her neck, kissed old Dulcibella.

'Will you take a candle, darling,' she said, 'and go down and see whether the cross-door is shut?'

Down went Dulcibella, the stairs creaking under her, and the young lady, drying her eyes, looked at her watch, drew the curtain at the window, placed the candle on the table near it, and then, shading her eyes with her hand, looked out earnestly.

The window did not command the avenue; it was placed in the side of the house. A moonlighted view she looked out upon; a soft declivity, from whose grassy slopes rose grand old trees, some in isolation, some in groups of twos and threes, all slumbering in the hazy light and still air, and beyond rose, softer in the distance, gentle undulating uplands, studded with trees, and near their summits more thickly clothed in forest.

She opened the window softly and, looking out, sighed in the fresh air of the night, and heard from the hollow the distant rush and moan of running waters, and her eye searched the foreground of this landscape. The trunk of one of the great trees near the house seemed to become animated, and projected a human figure, nothing awful or ghastly – a man in a short cloak, with a wide-awake hat on. Seeing the figure in the window, he lifted his hand, looking towards her, and approaching the side of the house with caution, glanced this way and that until he reached the house.

The old servant at the same time returned and told her that the door *was* locked as usual.

'You remain here, Dulcibella – no – I shan't take a candle,' and with a heavy sigh she left the room and treading lightly descended the stairs, and entered a wainscoted room, on the ground floor – with two windows, through which came a faint reflected light. Standing close to the nearer of these was the man with whom she had exchanged from the upper room the signals I have mentioned.

CHAPTER 8

NEVER DID RUN SMOOTH

Swiftly she went to the window and raised it without noise, and in a moment they were locked in each other's arms.

'Darling, darling,' was audible; and:–

'Oh, Ry! do you love me still?'

'Adore you, darling! adore you, my little violet, that grew in the shade – my only, only darling.'

'And I have been so miserable. Oh, Ry – that heart-breaking disappointment – that dreadful moment – you'll never know half I felt: as I knocked at that door, expecting to see my own darling's face – and then – I could have thrown myself from the rock over that glen. But you're here, and I have you after all – and now I must never lose you again – never, never.'

'Lose me, darling; you never did, and never shall; but I could not go – I dare not. Every fellow, you know, owes money, and I'm in that sorry plight like the rest, and just what I told you would have happened, and that you know would have been worse; but I think that's all settled, and lose me! not for one moment *ever* can you lose me, my beautiful idol.'

'Oh, yes – that's so delightful, and Ry and his poor violet will be so happy, and he'll never love any one but her.'

'Never, darling, never.'

And he never did.

'*Never* – of *course*, never.'

'And I'm sure it could not be helped your not being at Carwell.'

'Of course it couldn't – how could it! Don't you know everything? You're my own reasonable wise little girl, and you would not like to bore and worry your poor Ry. I wish to God I were my own master, and you'd soon see then who loves you best in all the world.'

'Oh yes, I'm sure of it.'

'Yes, darling, you are; if we are to be happy, you must be sure of it. If there's force in language, or proof in act, you can't doubt me – you must know I adore you – what motive on earth could I have in saying so, but one?'

'None, none, darling, darling Ry – it's only my folly, and you'll forgive your poor foolish little bird; and oh, Ry, is not this dreadful – but better, I suppose, that is, when a few miserable hours are over, and I gone – and we happy – your poor little violet and Ry happy together for the rest of our lives.'

'I think so, I do, all our days; and you understand everything I told you?'

'Everything – yes – about tomorrow morning – quite.'

'The walk isn't too much?'

'Oh, nothing.'

'And old Dulcibella shall follow you early in the day to Draunton – you remember the name of the house?'

'Yes, the Tanzy Well.'

'Quite right, wise little woman, and you know, darling, you must not stir out – quiet as it is, you might be seen; it is only a few hours' caution, and then we need not care; but I don't want pursuit, and a scene, and to agitate my poor little fluttered bird more than is avoidable. Even when you look out of the window keep your veil down; and – just reach the Tanzy House, and do as I say, and you may leave all the rest to me. Wait a moment – who's here? No – no – nothing. But I had better leave you now – yes, darling – it is wiser – some of the people may be peeping and I'll go.'

And so a tumultuous good-night, wild tears, and hopes, and panic, and blessings, and that brief interview was over.

The window was shut, and Alice Maybell in her room – the lovers not to meet again till forty miles away; and with a throbbing heart she lay down, to think and cry, and long for the morning she dreaded.

Morning came, and the breakfast hour, and the old squire over his cup of coffee and rasher, called for Mrs Durdin, the housekeeper, and said he:–

'Miss Alice, I hear, is ailing this morning; ye can see old Dulcibella, and make out would she like the doctor should look in, and would she like anything nice for breakfast – a slice of the goose pie, or *what?* and send down to the town for the doctor if she or old Dulcibella thinks well of it, and if it should be in church time, call him out of his pew, and find out what she'd like to eat or drink;' and with his usual gruff nod he dismissed her.

'I should be very happy to go to the town if you wish, sir,' said Charles Fairfield, desiring, it would seem, to re-establish his character for politeness, 'and I'm extremely sorry, I'm sure, that poor Ally – I mean, that Miss Maybell – is so ill.'

'You won't cry, though, I warrant; and there's people enough in Wyvern to send of her messages without troubling you,' said the squire.

The captain, however fiercely, had let this unpleasant speech pass unchallenged.

The old squire was two or three times at the foot of the stairs before church-time, bawling inquiries after Miss Alice's health, and messages for her private ear, to old Dulcibella.

The squire never missed church. He was as punctual as his ancestor, old Sir Thomas Fairfield, was there every Sunday and feast day, lying on his back praying, in tarnished red, blue, and gold habiliments of the reign of James I, in which he died, and took the form of painted stone, and has looked straight up, with his side to the wall, and his hands joined in supplication, ever since. If the old squire did not trouble himself with reading, nor much with prayer, and thought over such topics as suited him, during divine service – he at least went through the drill of the rubrics decorously, and stood erect, sat down, or kneeled, as if he were the ordained fugleman of his tenantry assembled in the old church.

Captain Fairfield, a handsome fellow, notwithstanding his years, with the keen blue eye of his race – a lazy man, and reserved, but with the hot blood of the Fairfields in his veins, which showed itself dangerously on occasion, occupied a corner of this great oak enclosure, at the remote end from his father. Like him he pursued his private ruminations with little interruption from the liturgy in which he ostensibly joined. These ruminations were, to judge from his countenance, of a saturnine and sulky sort. He was thinking over his father's inhospitable language, and making up his mind, for, though indolent, he was proud and fiery, to take steps upon it, and to turn his back, perhaps for many a day, on Wyvern.

The sweet old organ of Wyvern pealed, and young voices swelled the chorus of love and praise, and still father and son were confronted in dark antipathy. The vicar read his text from Holy Writ, and preached on the same awful themes; the transitoriness of our days; love, truth, purity, eternal life, death eternal; and still the same unnatural chill and darkness was between them. Moloch sat unseen by the old man's side, and in the diapason of the organ moaned his thirst for his sacrifices. Evil spirits amused the young man's brain with pictures of his slights and wrongs, and with their breath heated his vengeful heart. The dreams of both were interrupted by the vicar's sonorous blessing, and they shook their ears, and kneeled down, and their dreams came back again.

So it was Sunday – 'better day, better deed' – when a smouldering quarrel broke suddenly into fire and thunder in the manor house of Wyvern.

There is, we know, an estate of £6,000 a year, in a ring fence, round this old house. It owes something alarming, but the parish, village and manor of Wyvern have belonged, time out of mind, to the Fairfield family.

A very red sunset, ominous of storm, floods the western sky with its wild and sullen glory. The leaves of the great trees from whose recesses the small birds are singing their cheery serenade, flash and glimmer in it, as if a dew of fire had sprinkled them, and a blood-red flush lights up the brown feathers of the little birds.

These Fairfields are a handsome race – showing handsome, proud

English faces. Brown-haired, sometimes light, sometimes dark, with generally blue eyes, not mild, but fierce and keen.

They are a race of athletes; tall men, famous all that country round, generation after generation, for prowess in the wrestling ring, at cudgels, and other games of strength. Famous, too, for worse matters. Strong-willed, selfish, cruel, on occasion, but with a generosity and courage that make them in a manner popular. The character of the Fairfields has the vices, and some of the better traits of feudalism.

Charles Fairfield had been making up his mind to talk to his father. He had resolved to do so on his way home from church. With the cool air and clearer light, outside the porch, came a subsidence of his haste, and nodding here and there to friend or old acquaintance, as he strode through the churchyard, he went a solitary way home, instead of opening his wounds and purposes then to his father.

'Better at home; better at Wyvern; in an hour or so I'll make all ready, and see him then.'

So home, if home it was, by a lonely path, looking gloomily down on the daisies, strode Charles Fairfield.

CHAPTER 9

IN WHICH THE SQUIRE LOSES HIS GOLD-HEADED CANE

The sun, as I have said, was sinking among the western clouds with a melancholy glare; Captain Fairfield was pacing slowly to and fro upon the broad terrace that extends, with a carved balustrade, and many a stone flowerpot, along the rear of the old house. The crows were winging their way home, and the air was vocal with their faint cawings high above the grey roof, and the summits of the mighty trees, now glowing in that transitory light. His horse was ready saddled, and his portmanteau and other trifling effects had been despatched some hours before.

'Is there any good in bidding him good-bye?' hesitated the captain.

He was thinking of descending the terrace steps at the further end, and as he mounted his horse, leaving his valedictory message with the man who held it. But the spell of childhood is not easily broken when it has been respected for so many after-years. The captain had never got rid of the childish awe which began before he could remember. The virtues are respected; but such vices as pride, violence, and hard-heartedness in a father are more respected still.

Charles could approach a quarrel with that old despot; he could stand at the very brink, and with a resentful and defiant eye scan the abyss; but he could not quite make up his mind to the plunge. The old beast was so utterly violent and incalculable in his anger that no one could say to what weapons and extremities he might be driven in a combat with him, and where was the good in avowed hostilities? Must not a very few years, now, bring humiliation and oppression to an end?

Charles Fairfield was saved the trouble of deciding for himself, however, by the appearance of old Squire Harry, who walked forth from the handsome stone door-case upon the terrace, where his son stood ready for departure.

The old man was walking with a measured tread, holding his head very high, with an odd flush on his face, and a sardonic smile, and he was talking inaudibly to himself. Charles saw in all this the signs of storm. In the old man's hand was a letter firmly clutched. If he saw his son, who expected to be accosted by him, he passed him by with as little notice as he bestowed on the tall rose tree that grew in the stone pot by his side.

The squire walked down the terrace, southward, towards the steps, the wild sunset sky to his right, the flaming windows of the house to his left. When he had gone on a few steps, his tall son followed him. Perhaps he thought it better that Squire Harry should be informed of his intended departure from his lips than that he should learn it from the groom who held the bridle of his horse.

The squire did not descend the steps, however; he stopped short of them, and sat down in one of the seats that are placed at intervals under the windows. He leaned with both hands on his cane, the point of which he ground angrily into the gravel; in his fingers was still crumpled the letter. He was looking down with a very angry face, illuminated by the wild western sky, shaking his head and muttering.

The tall, brown captain stalked towards him, and touched his hat, according to his father's reverential rule.

'May I say a word, sir?' he asked.

The old man stared in his face and nodded fiercely, and with this ominous invitation he complied.

'You were pleased, sir,' said he, 'yesterday to express an opinion that, with the income I have, I ought to support myself, and no longer to trouble Wyvern. It was stupid of me not to think of that myself – very stupid – and all I can do is to lose no time about it; and so I have sent my traps away, and am going to follow now, sir; without saying farewell to you and——' He was on the point of adding – 'thanking you for all your kindness,' but recollected himself. *Thank* him, indeed! No, he could not bring himself to that. 'And I am leaving now, sir, and good-bye.'

'Ho, turning your back on Wyvern, like all the rest! Well, sir, the world's wide, you can choose your road. I don't ask none o' ye to stay and see me off – not I. I'll not be without someone when I die to shut down my eyes. I dare say. Get ye gone.'

'I thought, sir – in fact I was quite convinced,' said Charles Fairfield, a little disconcerted, 'that you had quite made up your mind, as I have mine, sir.'

'So I had, sir – so I had. Don't suppose I care a rush, sir, who goes – not a d——d rush – not I. Better an empty house than a bad tenant.'

Up rose the old man as he spoke, 'Away with them, say I; bundle 'em out – off wi' them, bag and baggage; there's more like ye – read *that*.' And he thrust the letter at him like a pistol, and leaving it in his hand, turned and stalked slowly up the terrace, while the captain read the following note:–

'Sir, – I hardly venture to hope that you will ever again think of me with that kindness which circumstances compel me so ungratefully to requite. I owe you more than I can ever tell. I began to experience your kindness in my infancy, and it has never failed me since. Oh, sir, do not, I entreat, deny me one last proof of your generosity – *your forgiveness*. I leave Wyvern, and before these lines are in your hand I shall have found another home. Soon, I trust, I shall be able to tell my benefactor *where*. In the meantime may God recompense you, as I never can, for all your goodness to me. I leave the place where all my life has passed amid continual and unmerited kindness with the keenest anguish, aggravated by my utter inability at present to repay your goodness by the poor acknowledgement of my confidence. Pray, sir, pardon me; pray restore me to your good opinion, or, at least if you cannot forgive and receive me again into your favour, spare me the dreadful affliction of your detestation, and in mercy try to forget

'Your unhappy, but ever grateful,

'Alice Maybell.'

When Charles Fairfield, having read this through, raised his eyes, they lighted on the old man, returning, and now within a few steps of him.

'Well, there's a lass for ye! I reared her like a child o' my own – better, kinder than ever child was reared, and she's hardly come to her full growth when she serves me like that. D——n ye, are ye tongue-tied? *what* do you think of her?'

'It would not be easy, sir, on that letter, to pronounce,' said Charles Fairfield, disconcerted. 'There's nothing there to show what her reasons are.'

'Ye'r no Fairfield – ye'r not, ye'r none. If ye were, ye'd know when ye'r house was insulted; but ye'r none; ye'r a cold-blooded sneak, and no Fairfield.'

'I don't see that anything I could say, sir, would mend the matter,' said the captain.

'Like enough; but I'll tell ye what I think of her,' thundered the old man, half beside himself. And his language became so opprobrious and frantic, that his son said, with a proud glare and swarthy flush on his face:—

'I take my leave sir, for language like that I'll not stay to hear.'

'But ye'll not take ye'r leave, sir, till I choose, and ye shall stay,' yelled the old squire, placing himself between the captain and the steps. 'And I'd like to know why ye shouldn't hear her called what she is – a —— and a ——.'

'Because she's *my* wife, sir,' retorted Charles Fairfield, whitening with fury.

'She is, is she?' said the old man, after a long gaping pause. 'Then ye'r a worse scoundrel, ye black-hearted swindler, than I took you for – and ye'll take that——'

And trembling with fury, he whirled his heavy cane in the air. But before it could descend, Charles Fairfield caught the hand that held it.

'None o' that – none o' that, sir,' he said, with grim menace, as the old man with both hands and furious purpose sought to wrest the cane free.

'Do you *want* me to do it?'

The grip of old Squire Harry was still powerful, and it required an exertion of the younger man's entire strength to wring the walking stick from his grasp.

Over the terrace balustrade it flew whirling, and old Squire Harry in the struggle lost his feet, and fell heavily on the flags.

There was blood already on his temple, and white furrowed cheeks, and he looked stunned. The young man's blood was up – the wicked blood of the Fairfields – but he hesitated, stopped, and turned.

The old squire had got to his feet again, and was holding giddily by the balustrade. His hat still lay on the ground, his cane was gone. The proud old squire was a tower dismantled. To be met and foiled so easily in a feat of strength – to have gone down at the first tussle with the 'youngster,' whom he despised as a 'milksop' and a 'Miss Molly,' was to the old Hercules, who still bragged of his early prowess, and was once the lord of the wrestling ring for five-and-twenty miles round, perhaps for the moment the maddest drop in the cup of his humiliation.

Squire Harry, with his trembling hand clutched on the stone balustrade, his tall figure swaying a little, had drawn himself up and held his head high and defiantly. There was a little quiver in his white old features, a wild smile in his eyes and on his thin, hard lips, showing the teeth that time had left him; and the blood that patched his white hair trickled down over his temple.

Charles Fairfield was agitated, and felt that he could have burst into tears – that it would have been a relief to fall on his knees before him for pardon. But the iron pride of the Fairfields repulsed this better emotion. He did, however, approach hurriedly, with an excited and troubled countenance, and he said hastily:–

'I'm awfully sorry, but it wasn't my fault; you know it wasn't. No Fairfield ever stood to be struck yet; I only took the stick, sir. D——n it, if it had been my mother I could not have done it more gently. I could not help your tripping. I couldn't; and I'm awfully sorry, by ——, and you won't remember it against me? Say you won't. It's the last time you'll ever see me in life, and there's no use in parting at worse odds than we need; and – and – won't you shake hands, sir?'

'I say, son Charlie, ye've spilled my blood,' said the old man. 'May God damn ye for it; and if ever ye come into Wyvern after this, while there's a breath in my body, I'll shoot ye like a poacher.'

And with this paternal speech Squire Harry turned his back and tottered stately and grimly into the house.

CHAPTER 10

THE DRIVE OVER CRESSLEY COMMON BY MOONLIGHT

The old squire of Wyvern wandered from room to room, and stood in this window and that. An hour after the scene on the terrace he was trembling still and flushed, with his teeth grimly set, sniffing, and with a stifling weight at his heart.

Night came, and the drawing-room was lighted up, and the squire rang the bell, and sent for old Mrs Durdin.

That dapper old woman, with a neat little cap on, stood prim in the doorway and curtseyed. She knew, of course, pretty well what the squire was going to tell her, and waited in some alarm to learn in what tone he would make his communication.

'Well,' said the squire, sternly, holding his head very high, 'Miss Alice is gone. I sent for you to tell ye, as y're housekeeper here. She's gone; she's left Wyvern.'

'She'll be coming again, sir, soon?' said the old woman after a pause.

'No, not she – no,' said the squire.

'Not returnin' to Wyvern, sir?'

'While there's breath in my body she'll never darken these doors.'

'Sorry she should 'a displeased you, sir,' said the good-natured little woman with a curtsey.

'*Displease* ye! Who said she displeased me? It ain't the turning of a pennypiece to me – *me*, by ——. Ha, ha! that's funny.'

'And – what do you wish done with the bed and the furniture, sir? Shall I leave it still in the room, please?'

'Out o' window wi' 't – pitch it after her; let the work'us people send up and cart it off for the poor-house, where she should 'a bin, if I hadn't 'a bin the biggest fool in the parish.'

'I'll have it took down and moved, sir,' said the old woman, interpreting more moderately; 'and the same with Mrs Crane's room; Dulcibella, she's gone too?'

'Ha, ha! well for her – plotting old witch. I'll have her ducked in the pond if she's found here; and never you name them, one or t'other more, unless you want to go yourself. I'm fifty pounds better. I didn't know how to manage or look after her – they're all alike. If I chose it I could send a warrant after her for the clothes on her back; but let her be. Away wi' her – a good riddance; and get her who may, I give him joy o' her.'

The squire was glad to see Tom Ward that night, and had a second tankard of punch.

'Old servant, Tom; I believe the old folk's the best after all,' said he. 'It's a d——d changed world, Tom. Things were otherwise in our time; no matter, I'll pay 'em off yet.'

And old Harry Fairfield fell asleep in his chair, and after an hour wakened up with a dream of little Ally's music still in his ears.

'Play it again, child, play it again,' he said, and listened – to silence and looked about the empty room, and the sudden pain came again, with a dreadful yearning mixed with his anger.

The squire cursed her for a devil, a wild-cat, a viper, and he walked round the room with his hands clenched in his coat pockets, and the proud old man was crying. With straining and squeezing the tears oozed and trickled from his wrinkled eyelids down his rugged cheeks.

'I don't care a d——n, I hate her; I don't know what it's for, I be such a fool; I'm *glad* she's gone, and I pray God the sneak's she gone wi' may break her heart, and break his own d——d neck after, over Carwell scaurs.'

The old man took his candle and from old habit, in the hall, was closing the door of the staircase that led up to her room.

'Ay, ay,' said he bitterly, recollecting himself, 'the stable door when the nag's stole. I don't care if the old house was blown down tonight – I wish it was. She was a kind little thing before that d——d fellow – what could she see in him – good for nothing – old as I am, I'd pitch him over my head like a stook o' barley. Here was a plot, she was a good little thing, but see how she was drew into it, d——n her, they're all so false. I'll find out who was in it, I will; I'll find it all out. There's Tom Sherwood, *he's* one. I'll pitch 'em all out, neck and crop, out o' Wyvern doors. I'd rather fill my house wi' rats than the two-legged vermin. Let 'em pack away to Carwell and starve with that big pippin-squeezing ninny. I hope in God's justice he'll never live to put his foot in Wyvern. I could shoot myself, I think, but for that. She might 'a waited till the old man died, at any rate; I was kind to her – a fool – a fool.'

And the tall figure of the old man, candle in hand, stalked slowly from the dim hall and vanished up the other staircase.

While this was going on at Wyvern, nearly forty miles away, under the bright moonlight, a chaise, in which were seated the young lady whose departure had excited so strange a sensation there, and her faithful old servant, Dulcibella Crane, was driving rapidly through a melancholy but not unpleasing country.

A wide undulating plain, with here and there patches of picturesque natural wood, oak, and whitethorn, and groups of silver-stemmed birch trees spread around them. Those were the sheep walks of Cressley Common. The soil is little better than peat, over which grows a short velvet verdure, altogether more prized by lovers of the picturesque than by graziers of Southdowns. Could any such scene look prettier than it did in the moonlight? The solitudes, so sad and solemn, the lonely clumps and straggling trees, the gentle hollows and hills, and the misty distance in that cold illusive light acquire the interest and melancholy of mystery.

The young lady's head was continually out of the window, sometimes looking forward, sometimes back, upon the road they had traversed. With an anxious look and a heavy sigh she threw herself back in her seat.

'You're not asleep, Dulcibella?' she said, a little peevishly.

'No, Miss; no dear.'

'You don't seem to have much to trouble you,' continued the young lady.

'*I?* Law bless, you, dear, nothing, thank God.'

'None of your own, and my troubles don't vex you, that's plain,' said her young mistress, reproachfully.

'I did not think, dear, you was troubled about anything – law! I hope nothing's gone wrong, darling,' said the old woman with more energy and a simple stare in her mistress's face.

'Well, you know he said he'd be with us as we crossed Cressley Common, and this is it, and he's not here, and I see no sign of him.'

And the young lady again popped her head out of the window, and, her survey ended, threw herself back once more with another melancholy moan.

'Why, Miss Alice, dear, you're not frettin' for that?' said Dulcibella. 'Don't you know, dear, if he isn't here, he's somewhere else? We're not to be troubling ourselves about every little thing like, and who knows, poor gentleman, what's happened to delay him?'

'That's just what I say, Dulcibella; you'll set me mad! Something has certainly happened. You know he owes money. Do you think they have arrested him? If they have, what's to become of us? Oh! Dulcibella, *do* tell me what you really think.'

'No, no, no – there now – there's a darling, don't you be worrying yourself about nothing; look out again, and who knows but he's coming?'

So said old Dulcibella, who was constitutionally hopeful and contented, and very easy about Master Charles, as she still called Charles Fairfield.

She was not remarkable for prescience, but here the worthy creature fluked prophetically; for Alice Maybell, taking her advice, did look out again, and she thought she saw the distant figure of a horseman in pursuit.

She rattled at the window, calling to the driver, and the man who sat beside him, and succeeded in making them hear her, and pull the horses up.

'Look back and see if that is not your master coming,' she cried eagerly.

He was still too distant for recognition, but the rider was approaching fast. The gentlemen of the road, once a substantial terror, were now but a picturesque tradition; the appearance of the pursuing horseman over the solitudes of Cressley Common would else have been anything but a source of pleasant anticipation. On he came, and now the clink of the horse-shoes sounded sharp on the clear night air. And now the rider passed the straggling trees they had just left behind them, and now his voice was raised and recognised, and in a few moments more, pale and sad in the white moonlight as Leonora's phantom trooper, her stalwart lover pulled up his powerful hunter at the chaise window.

A smile lighted up his gloomy face as he looked in.

'Well, darling, I *have* overtaken you at Cressley Common; and is my little woman quite well, and happy to see her Ry once more?'

His hand had grasped hers as he murmured these words through the window.

'Oh, Ry, darling – I'm so happy – you must let Tom ride the horse on, and do you come in and sit here, and Dulcibella can take my cloaks and sit by the driver. Come, darling, I want to hear everything.'

And so this little arrangement was completed, as she said, and Charles Fairfield sat himself beside his beautiful young wife, and as they drove on through the moonlit scene he pressed her hand and kissed her lovingly.

CHAPTER 11

HOME

'Oh, darling, I can scarcely believe it,' she murmured, smiling, and gazing up with her large soft eyes into his, 'it seems to me like heaven that I can look, and speak, and say everything without danger, or any more concealment, and always have my Ry with me – never to be separated again, you know, darling, while we live.'

'Poor little woman,' said he, fondly, looking down with an answering smile, 'she does love me a little bit, I think.'

'And Ry loves his poor little bird, doesn't he?'

'Adores her – idolatry – *idolatry*.'

'And we'll be so happy!'

'I hope so, darling.'

'*Hope?*' echoed she, chilled, and a little piteously.

'I'm *sure* of it, darling – quite certain,' he repeated, laughing tenderly; 'she's such a foolish little bird, one must watch their phrases; but I was only thinking – I'm afraid you hardly know what a place this Carwell is.'

'Oh, darling, you forget I've seen it – the most picturesque spot I ever saw – the very place I should have chosen – and any place you know, with you! But that's an old story.'

His answer was a kiss, and:–

'Darling, I can never deserve half your love.'

'All I desire on earth is to live alone with my Ry.'

'Yes, darling, we'll make out life very well here, I'm sure – my only fear is for you. I'll go out with my rod, and bring you home my basket full of trout, or sometimes take my gun, and kill a hare or a rabbit, and we'll live like the old baron and his daughters in the fairy tale – on the produce of the streams and solitudes about us – quite to ourselves; and I'll read to you in the evenings, or we'll play chess, or we'll chat while you work, and I'll tell you stories of my travels, and you'll sing me a song, won't you?'

'Too delighted – singing for joy,' said little Alice, in a rapture at his story of the life that was opening to them; 'oh, tell more.'

'Well, yes – and you'll have such pretty flowers.'

'Oh, yes – flowers – I love them – not expensive ones – for we are poor, you know; and you'll see how prudent I'll be – but annuals, they are so cheap – and I'll sow them myself, and I'll have the most beautiful you ever saw. Don't you love them, Ry?'

'Nothing so pretty, darling, on earth, except yourself.'

'What is my Ry looking out for?'

Charles Fairfield had more than once put his head out of the window, looking as well as he could along the road in advance of the horses.

'Oh, nothing of any consequence. I only wanted to see that our man had got on with the horse, he might as well knock up the old woman, and see that things were, I was going to say, comfortable, but less miserable than they might be.'

He laughed faintly as he said this, and he looked at his watch, as if he did not want her to see him consult it, and then he said:—

'Well, and you were saying – oh, about the flowers – annuals – yes.'

And so they resumed. But somehow it seemed to Alice that his ardour and his gaiety were subsiding, that his thoughts were away, and pale care stealing over him like the chill of death. Again she might have remembered the ghostly Wilhelm, who grew more ominous and spectral as he and his bride neared the goal of their nocturnal journey.

'I don't think you hear me, Ry, and something has gone wrong,' she said at last, in a tone of disappointment, that rose even to alarm.

'Oh! tell me, Charlie, if there is anything you have not told me yet? You're afraid of frightening me.'

'Nothing, nothing, I assure you, darling; what nonsense you do talk, you poor foolish little bird. No, I mean nothing, but I've had a sort of quarrel with the old man; you need not have written that letter, or at least it would have been better if you had told me about it.'

'But, darling, I couldn't, I had no opportunity, and I could not leave Wyvern, where he had been so good to me all my life, without a few words to thank him, and to entreat his pardon; you're not angry, darling, with your poor little bird?'

'Angry, my foolish little wife, you little know your Ry; he loves his bird too well to be ever angry with her for anything, but it was unlucky, at least his getting it just when he did, for, you may suppose, it did not improve his temper.'

'Very angry, I'm afraid, was he? But though he's so fiery, he's generous; I'm sure he'll forgive us, in a little time, and it will all be made up; don't you think so?'

'No, darling, I don't. Take this hill quietly, will you?' he called from the window to the driver; 'you may walk them a bit, there's near two miles to go still.'

Here was another anxious look out, and he drew his head in, muttering, and then he laid his hand on hers, and looked in her face and smiled, and he said:—

'They are such fools, aren't they? And – about the old man at Wyvern – oh, no, you mistake him, he's not a man to forgive; we can reckon on nothing but mischief from that quarter, and, in fact, he knows all about it, for he chose to talk about you as if he had a right to scold, and that I couldn't allow, and I told him so, and that you were my wife, and that no man living should say a word against you.'

'My own brave Ry; but oh! what a grief that I should have made this quarrel; but I love you a thousand times more; oh, my darling, we are everything now to one another.'

'Ho! never mind,' he exclaimed with a sudden alacrity, 'there he is. All right, Tom, is it?'

'All right, sir,' answered the man whom he had despatched before them on the horse, and who was now at the roadside still mounted.

'He has ridden back to tell us she'll have all ready for our arrival. Oh, no, darling,' he continued gaily, 'don't think for a moment I care a farthing whether he's pleased or angry. He never liked me, and he cannot do us any harm, none in the world, and soon or later Wyvern *must* be mine.' And he kissed her and smiled with the ardour of a man whose spirits are, on a sudden, quite at ease.

And as they sat, hand pressed in hand, she sidled closer to him, with the nestling instinct of the bird, as he called her, and dreamed that if there were a heaven on earth, it would be found in such a life as that on which she was entering, where she would have him 'all to herself.' And she felt now, as they diverged into the steeper road and more sinuous, that ascended for a mile the gentle wooded uplands to the grange of Carwell, that every step brought her nearer to Paradise.

Here is something paradoxical; is it? that this young creature should be so in love with a man double her own age. I have heard of cases like it, however, and I have read, in some old French writer – I have forgot who he is – the rule laid down with solemn audacity, that there is no such through-fire-and-water, desperate love as that of a girl for a man past forty. Till the hero has reached that period of autumnal glory, youth and beauty can but half love him. This encouraging truth is amplified and emphasised in the original. I extract its marrow for the comfort of all whom it may concern.

On the other hand, however, I can't forget that Charles Fairfield had many unusual aids to success. In the first place, by his looks, you would have honestly guessed him at from four or five years under his real age. He was handsome, dark, with white, even teeth, and fine dark blue eyes, that could glow ardently. He was the only person at Wyvern with whom she could converse. He had seen something of the world, something of foreign travel; had seen in pictures, and knew at least the names of some authors; and in the barbarous isolation of Wyvern, where squires talked of little but the last new plough, fat oxen, and kindred subjects, often with a very perceptible infusion of the country *patois* – he was to a young lady with any taste, either for books or art, a resource and a companion.

And now the chaise was drawing near to Carwell Grange. With a childish delight she watched the changing scene from the window. The clumps of wild trees drew nearer to the roadside. Winding always upward, and steeper and steeper, was the narrow road. The wood gathered closer around them. The trees were loftier and more solemn, and cast sharp shadows of foliage and branches on the white roadway. All the way her ear and heart were filled with the now gay music of her lover's talk. At last through the receding trees that crowned the platform of the rising grounds they had been ascending, gables, chimneys, and glimmering windows showed themselves in the broken moonlight; and now rose before them, under a great ash tree, a gatehouse that resembled a small square tower of stone, with a steep roof, and partly clothed in ivy. No light gleamed from its windows. Tom dismounted, and pushed open the old iron gate that swung over the grass-grown court with a long melancholy screak.

It was a square court, with a tolerably high wall, overtopped by the sombre trees, whose summits, like the old roofs and chimneys, were silvered by the moonlight.

This was the front of the building, which Alice had not seen before, the great entrance and hall door of Carwell Grange.

CHAPTER 12

THE OMEN OF CARWELL GRANGE

The high wall that surrounded the courtyard, and the towering foliage of the old trees, were gloomy. Still, if the quaint stone front of the house had shown through its many windows the glow of life and welcome, I dare say the effect of those sombre accessories would have been lost in pleasanter associations, and the house might have showed cheerily and cosily enough. As it was, with no relief but the cold moonlight that mottled the pavement and tipped the chimney tops, the silence and deep shadow were chilling, and it needed the deep enthusiasm of true love to see in that dismal frontage the delightful picture that Alice Maybell's eyes beheld.

'Welcome, darling, to our poor retreat, made bright and beautiful by your presence,' said he, with a gush of tenderness; 'but how unworthy to receive you none knows better than your poor Ry. Still for a short time – and it will be but short – you will endure it. Delightful your presence will make it to me; and to you, darling, my love will perhaps render it tolerable. Take my hand, and get down; and welcome to Carwell Grange.'

Lightly she touched the ground, with her hand on his strong arm, for love rather than for assistance.

'I know how I shall like this quaint, quiet place,' said she, 'love it, and grow perhaps fit for no other, if only my darling is always with me. You'll show it all to me in daylight to-morrow – won't you?'

Their little talk was murmured, and unheard by others, under friendly cover of the snorting horses, and the talk of the men about the luggage.

'But I must get our door opened,' said he with a little laugh; and with the heavy old knocker he hammered a long echoing summons at the door.

In a minute more lights flickered in the hall. The door was opened and the old woman smiling her best, though that was far from being very pleasant. Her eye was dark and lifeless and never smiled, and there were lines of ill-temper, or worse, near them which never relaxed. Still she was doing her best, dropping little curtseys all the time, and holding her flaring tallow candle in its brass candlestick, and thus illuminating the furrows and minuter wrinkles of her forbidding face with a yellow light that suited its box-wood complexion.

Behind her, with another mutton-fat, for this was a state occasion, stood a square-shouldered little girl, some twelve years old, with a brown, somewhat flat face, and no good feature but her dark eyes and white teeth. This was Lilly Dogger, who had been called in to help the crone who stood in the foreground. With a grave, observing stare, she was watching the young lady, who, smiling, stepped into the hall.

'Welcome, my lady – very welcome to Carwell,' said the old woman. 'Welcome, squire, very welcome to Carwell.'

'Thank you very much. I'm sure I shall like it,' said the young lady, smiling happily; 'it is such a fine old place; and it's so quiet – I like quiet.'

'Old enough and quiet enough, anyhow,' answered the old woman. 'You'll not see many new faces to trouble you here, Miss – Ma'am, my lady, I mean.'

'But we'll all try to make her as pleasant and comfortable as we can!' said Charles Fairfield, clapping the old woman on the shoulder a little impatiently.

'There don't lay much in *my* way to make her time pass pleasant, Master Charles; but I suppose we'll all do what we can.'

'And more we can't,' said Charles Fairfield. 'Come, darling. I suppose, there's a bit of fire somewhere; it's a little cold, isn't it?'

'A fire burning all day, sir, in the cedar-room; and the kettle's a-boiling on the hob, if the lady'd like a cup o' tea?'

'Yes, of course,' said Charles; 'and a fire in the room upstairs?'

'Yes, so there is, sir, a great fire all day long, and everything well aired.'

'Well, darling, shall we look first at the cedar-room?' he asked and smiling, hand in hand, they walked through the hall, and by a staircase, and through a second and smaller hall, with a back stair off it, and so into a comfortable panelled room, with a great cheery fire of mingled coal and wood, and old-fashioned furniture, which, though faded, was scrupulously neat.

Old and homely as was the room, it agreeably surprised Alice, who was prepared to be delighted with everything, and at sight of this, exclaimed quite in a rapture – so honest a rapture that Charles Fairfield could not forbear laughing, though he felt also very grateful.

'Well, I admit,' he said, looking round, 'it does look wonderfully comfortable, all things considered; but here, I am afraid, is the beginning and the end of our magnificence – for the present, of course, and by and bye, little by little, we may improve and extend; but I don't think in the whole house there's a habitable room – sitting-room, I mean – but this,' he laughed.

'It is the pleasantest room I ever was in, Charlie – a delightful room – I'm more than content,' said she.

'You are a good little creature,' said he; 'at all events, the best little wife in the world, determined to make the best of everything, and, as I said, we certainly shall be better very soon, and in the meantime good humour and cheerfulness will make our quarters, poor as they are, brighter and better than luxury and ill-temper could find in a palace. Here are tea-things, and a kettle boiling – very primitive, very cosy – we'll be more like civilised people tomorrow or next day, when we have had time to look about us, and in the meantime, suppose I make tea while you run upstairs and put off your things – what do you say?'

'Yes, certainly,' and she looked at the old woman, who stood with her ominous smile at the door.

'I ought to have told you her name, Mildred Tarnley – the *genius loci*. Mildred, you'll show your mistress to her room.'

And he and his young wife smiled a mutual farewell. A little curious she was to see something more of the old house, and she peeped about her as she went up, and asked a few questions as they went along. 'And this room,' she asked, peeping into the door that opened from the back stairs which they were ascending, 'it has such a large fireplace and little ovens, or what are they?'

'It was the still room once, my lady; my mother remembered the time, but it was always shut up in my day.'

'Oh, and can you tell me – I forget – where is my servant?'

'Upstairs, please, with your things, ma'am, when the man brought up your boxes.'

Still looking about her and delaying, she went on. There was nothing stately about this house; but there was that about it which, if Alice had been in less cheerful and happy spirits, would have quelled and awed her. Thick walls, windows deep sunk, double doors now and then, wainscoting, and oak floors, warped with age.

On the landing there was an archway admitting to a gallery. In this archway was no door, and on the landing, Alice Fairfield, as I may now call her, stood for a moment and looked round.

Happy as she was, I cannot tell what effect these faintly lighted glimpses of old and desolate rooms, aided by the repulsive companionship of her ancient guide, may have insensibly wrought upon her imagination, or what a trick that faculty may have just then played upon her senses, but turning round to enter the gallery under the open arch, the old woman standing by her, with the candle raised a little, Alice Fairfield stepped back startled, with a little exclamation of surprise.

The ugly face of old Mildred Tarnley peeped curiously over the young lady's shoulder. She stepped before her and peered, right and left, into the gallery; and then, with ominous inquiry into the young lady's eyes, 'I thought it might be a bat, my lady; there was one last night got in,' she said; 'but there's no such a thing now – was you afeard of anything, my lady?'

'I – didn't you see it?' said the young lady, both frightened and disconcerted.

'I saw'd nothing, ma'am.'

'It's very odd. I *did* see it; I *swear* I saw it, and felt the air all stirred about my face and dress by it.'

'On here, Miss – my lady; was it?'

'Yes; *here*, before us. I – weren't you looking?'

'Not that way, Miss – I don't know,' she said.

'Well something fell down before us – all the way – from the top to the bottom of this place.'

And with a slight movement of her hand and eyes she indicated the open archway before which they stood.

'Oh, lawk! Well, I dare to say it may 'a bin a fancy, just.'

'Yes; but it's very odd – a great heavy curtain of black fell down in folds from the top to the floor just as I was going to step through. It seemed to make a little cloud of dust about our feet; and I felt a wind from it quite distinctly.'

'Hey, then it was a *black* curtain, I suppose,' said the old woman, looking hard at her.

'Yes – but why do you suppose so?'

'Sich nonsense is always black, ye know. I see'd nothing – nothing – no more there was nothing. Didn't ye see me walk through?'

And she stepped back and forward, candle in hand, with an uncomfortable laugh.

'Oh, I know perfectly well there is nothing; but I saw it. I – I wish I hadn't,' said the young lady.

'I wish ye hadn't, too,' said Mildred Tarnley, pale and lowering. 'Them as says their prayers, they needn't be afeard o' sich things; and, for my part, I never see'd anything in the Grange, and I'm an old woman, and lived here, girl and woman, good sixty years and more.'

'Let us go on, please,' said Alice.

'At your service, my lady,' said the crone, with a curtsey, and conducted her to her room.

CHAPTER 13

AN INSPECTION OF CARWELL GRANGE

Through an open door, at the end of this short gallery, the pleasant firelight gleamed, sufficiently indicating the room that had been prepared for her reception. She felt a little oddly and frightened, and the sight of old Dulcibella Crane in the cheerful light, busily unpacking her boxes, reassured her.

The grim old woman, Mildred Tarnley, stopped at the door.

'It's very well aired, ma'am,' she said, making a little curtsey.

'It looks very comfortable; thank you – everything so neat; and such a bright nice fire,' said Alice, smiling on her as well as she could.

'There's the tapestry room, and the leather room; but they're not so dry as this, though it's wainscot.'

'Oak, I think – isn't it?' said the young lady, looking round.

'Yes, ma'am; and there's the pink paper chamber and dressing-room; but they're gone very poor – and the bed and all that being in here, I thought 'twas the best o' the lot; an' there's lots o' presses and cupboards in the wall, and the keys in them, and the locks all right; and I do think it's the most comfortablest room, my lady. That is the dressing-room, in there, please; and do you like some more wood or coal on the fire, ma'am?'

'Not any – it is very nice – thanks.'

And Alice sat down before the fire, and the smile seemed to evaporate in its glow, and she looked very grave – and even anxious. Mildred Tarnley made her curtsey, looked round the room, and withdrew.

'Well, Dulcibella, when are you going to have your tea?' asked Alice, kindly.

'I'll make a cup here, dear, if you think I may, after I've got your things in their places in a few minutes' time.'

'Would you like that better than taking it downstairs with the servant?'

'Yes, dear, I would.'

'I don't think you like her, Dulcibella?'

'I can't say I mislike her, dear; I han't spoke ten words wi' her – she may be very nice – I don't know.'

'There's something not very pleasant about her face, don't you think?' said Alice.

'Well, dear, but you *are* sharp; there's no hiding my thoughts from you; but there's many a face we gets used to that doesn't seem so agreeable-like at first. I think this rack 'll do very nice for hanging your cloak on,' she said, taking it from the young lady's hands. 'You're tired a bit, I'm afeard; ye look a bit tired – ye do.'

'No, nothing,' said her young mistress, 'only I can't help feeling sorry for poor old Wyvern and the squire, old Mr Fairfield – it seems so unkind; and there was a good deal to think about; and, I don't know how, I feel a little uncomfortable, in spite of so much that should cheer me; and now I must run down and take a cup of tea – come with me to the top of the stairs, and just hold the candle till I have got down.'

When she reached the head of the stairs she was cheered by the sound of Charles Fairfield's voice, singing, in his exuberant jollity, the appropriate ditty, 'Jenny, put the kettle on – Barney, blow the bellows strong,' etc.

And, hurrying downstairs, she found him ready to make tea, with his hand on the handle of the teapot, and the fire brighter than ever.

'Well, you didn't stay very long, good little woman. I was keeping up my spirits with a song; and, in spite of my music, beginning to miss you.'

And, meeting her as she entered the room, he led her, with his arm about her waist, to a chair, in which, with a kiss, he placed her.

'All this seems to me like a dream. I can't believe it; but, if it be, woe to the fool who wakes me! No, darling, it's no dream, is it?' he said, smiling, and kissed her again. 'The happiest day of *my* life,' he said, and through his eyes smiled upon her a flood of the tenderest love.

A little more such talk, and then they sat down to that memorable cup of tea – 'the first in our own house.'

The delightful independence – the excitement, the importance – *all* our own – cups, spoons, room, servants – and the treasure secured, and the haven of all our hopes no longer doubtful or distant. Glorious, beautiful dream! from which death, wrinkles, duns, are quite obliterated. Sip while you may, your pleasant cup of – madness, from that fragile, pretty china, and may the silver spoon wherewith you stir it prove to have come into the world at the moment of your birth, where fortune is said to place it sometimes. Next morning the sun shone clear over Carwell Grange, bringing into sharp relief the joints and wrinkles of the old grey masonry, the leaves and tendrils of the ivy, and the tufts of grass which here and there sprout fast in the chinks of the parapet, and casting, with angular distinctness upon the shingled roof, the shadows of the jackdaws that circled about the old chimney. A twittering of small birds fills the air, and the solemn cawing comes mellowed on the ear from the dark rookery at the other side of the ravine, that, crossing at the side of the Grange, debouches on the wider and deeper glen that is known as the Vale of Carwell.

Youth enjoys a change of abode, and with the instinct of change and adventure proper to its energies, delights in a new scene.

Charles Fairfield accompanied his young wife, who was full of curiosity and her head busy with a hundred plans, as in gay and eager spirits she surveyed her little empire.

'This is the garden – I tell you, lest you should mistake it for the forest where the enchanted princess slept, surrounded by great trees and thickets – it excels even the old garden at Wyvern. There are pear trees, and plum, and cherry, and apple. Upon my word, I forgot they were so huge, and the jungles are raspberries and gooseberries and currants. Did you ever see such thicket, and nettles between? I'm afraid you'll not make much of this. When I was a boy those great trees looked as big and mossgrown as they do now, and bore such odd crabbed little fruit, and not much even of that.'

'It will be quite beautiful when it is weeded, and flowers growing in the shade, and climbing plants trained up the stems of the trees, and it shan't cost us anything; but you'll see how wonderfully pretty it will be.'

'But what is to become of all your pretty plans, if flowers won't grow without sun. I defy any fairy – even my own bright little one – to make them grow here; but, if you won't be persuaded, by all means let us try. I think there's sunshine wherever you go, and I should not wonder, after all, if nature relented, and beautiful miracles were accomplished under your influence.'

'I know you are laughing at me,' she said.

'No, darling – I'll never laugh at you – you can make me believe whatever you choose; and now that we have looked over all the wild beauties of our neglected paradise, in which, you good little creature, you are resolved to see all kinds of capabilities and perfections – suppose we go now to the grand review of our goods and chattels, that you planned at breakfast – cups, saucers, plates, knives, forks, spoons, and all such varieties.'

'Oh, yes, let us come, Ry – it will be such fun, and so useful, and old Mrs Tarnley said she would have a list made out,' said Alice, to whom the new responsibilities and dignities of her married state were full of interest and importance.

So in they came together, and called for old Mildred, with a list of their worldly goods; and they read the catalogue together, with every now and then a peal of irrepressible laughter.

'I had not an idea how near we were to our last cup and saucer,' said Charles, 'and the dinner-service is limited to seven plates, two of which are cracked.'

The comic aspect of their poverty was heightened, perhaps, by Mrs Tarnley's peculiar spelling. The old woman stood in the doorway of the sitting room while the revision was proceeding, mightily displeased at the levity, looking more than usually wrinkled and bilious, and rolling her eyes upon them, from time to time, with a malignant ogle.

'I was never good at the pen – I know that – but your young lady desired me, and I did my best, and very de*spick*able it be, no doubt,' said Mildred, with grizzly scorn.

'Oh, my! I am so sorry – I assure you, Mrs Tarnley – pray tell her, Charlie – we were laughing only at there being so few things left.'

'Left! I don't know what ye mean by *left*, ma'am – there's not another woman as ever I saw would keep his bit of delf and chaney half as long as me; I never was counted a smasher o' things – no more I was.'

'But we didn't think you broke them – did we, Charlie?' appealed poor little Alice, who, being new to authority, was easily bullied.

'Nonsense, old Mildred – don't be a fool,' said Charles Fairfield, not in so conciliatory a tone as Alice would have wished.

'Well, fool's easily said, and there's no lack o' fools high or low, Master Charles, and I don't pretend to be no scholar; but I've read that o'er much laughing ends, ofttimes in o'er much crying – the Lord keeps us all from grief.'

'Hold your tongue – what a bore you are!' exclaimed he, sharply.

Mrs Tarnley raised her chin, and looked askance, but made no answer; she was bitter.

'Why the devil, old Mildred, can't you try to look pleasant for once?' he persisted. 'I believe there's not a laugh *in* you, nor even a smile, is there?'

'I'm not much given to laughin', thankee, sir, and there's people, mayhap, should be less so, if they'd only take warnin', and mind what they seed over night; and if the young lady don't want me no longer, I'd be better back in the kitchen before the chicken burns, for Lilly's out in the garden rootin' out the potatoes for dinner.'

And after a moment's silence she dropped a little curtsey and, assuming permission, took her departure.

CHAPTER 14

A LETTER

Alice looked a little paler, her husband a little discontented. Each had a different way of reading her unpleasant speech.

'Don't mind that old woman, darling – don't let her bore you. I do believe she has some as odious faults as are to be found on earth.'

'I don't know what she means by a warning,' said Alice.

'Nor I, darling, I am sure; perhaps she has had a winding-sheet on her candle, or a coffin flew out of the fire, or a death-watch ticked in the wainscot,' he answered.

'A warning – what could she mean?' repeated Alice, slowly, with an anxious gaze in her eyes.

'My darling, how can you? A stupid old woman!' said he, a little impatiently, 'and thoroughly ill-conditioned. She's in one of her tempers, just because we laughed, and fancied it was at her; and there's nothing she'd like better than to frighten you, if she could. I'll pack her off, if I find her playing any tricks.'

'Oh, the poor old thing, not for the world; she'll make it up with me, you'll find; I don't blame her the least, if she thought that, and I'll tell her we never thought of such a thing.'

'Don't mind her, she's not worth it – we'll just make out a list of the things that we want; I'm afraid we want a great deal more than we can get, for you have married a fellow, in all things but love, as poor as a church mouse.'

He laughed, and kissed her, and patted her smiling cheek.

'Yes, it will be such fun buying these things; such a funny little dinner service, and breakfast things, and how far away is Naunton?'

'I'm not sure we can get them at Naunton. Things come from London so easily now,' said he.

'Oh, but there is such a nice little shop, I remarked it, in Naunton,' said she, eagerly.

'Oh, is there?' said he. 'I forgot, I believe you drove through it.'

'I did,' she answered, 'and the whole pleasure of getting them would be buying them with you.'

'You kind little darling,' he said, with a faint smile, 'so it would to me, I know, choosing them with you; but are you sure there is a place there?'

'Such a nice little shop, with a great red and blue jug, hanging over the door for a sign,' she insisted cheerily, 'and there is something pleasant, isn't there, in the sort of queer rustic things one would meet in such an out-of-the-way place?'

'Yes, so there is, but, however, we'll think about it, and, in fact, it doesn't matter a farthing where we get them.'

Our friend Charles seemed put out a little, and his slight unaccountable embarrassment piqued her curiosity, and made her ever so little uncomfortable. She was, still, however, a very young wife, and in awe of her husband. It was, therefore, rather timidly that she said:—

'And why, darling Ry, can't we decide now, and go tomorrow, and choose our plates, and cups, and saucers? it would be such a pleasant little adventure to look forward to.'

'So it might, but we'll have to make up our minds to have many days go by, and weeks, too, here, with nothing pleasant to look forward to. You knew very well,' he continued, not so sharply, 'when you married me, that I owed money, and was a poor miserable devil, and not my own master, and you really must allow me to decide what is to be done, when a trifle might any day run us into mischief. There now, your eyes are full of tears – how can you be so foolish?'

'But, indeed, Ry, I'm not,' she pleaded, smiling through them. 'I was only sorry, I was afraid I had vexed you.'

'Vexed me! you darling; not the least. I am only teased to think I am obliged to deny you anything, much less to hesitate about gratifying so trifling a wish as this; but so it is, and such my hard fate; and though I seem to be vexed, it is not with you – you must not mistake – *never*, darling, with you; but in proportion as I love you, the sort of embarrassment into which you have ventured with your poor Ry grieves and even enrages him, and the thought, too, that so small a thing would set it all to rights. But we are not the only people, of course, there are others as badly off, and a great deal worse; there now, darling, you must not cry, you really mustn't; you must never fancy for a moment when anything happens to vex me, that I could be such a brute as to be angry with you. What's to become of me, if you ever suffer such a chimera to enter your pretty little head? I do assure you, darling, I'd rather blow my brains out, than inflict a single unhappy hour upon you; there now, won't you kiss me, and look quite happy again? And come, we'll go out again? did you not see the kennel, and the brewhouse, and fifty other interesting ruins? we must be twice as happy as ever for the rest of the day.'

And so this little cloud, light and swift, but still a cloud, blew over, and the sun shone out warm and brilliant again.

The buildings, which enclosed three sides of the quadrangle which they were now examining, were, with the exception of the stables, in such a state of dilapidation as very nearly to justify in sober earnest the term 'ruins,' which he had half jocularly applied to them.

'You may laugh as you will,' said Alice, 'but I think this might be easily made quite a beautiful place – prettier even than Wyvern.'

'Yes, very easily,' he laughed, 'if a fellow had two or three thousand pounds to throw away upon it. Whenever I have – and I may yet – you may restore, and transform, and do what you like; I'll give you *carte blanche*, and in better hands I believe neither house nor money could be placed. No one has such taste – though it is hardly for *me* to say that.'

Just at that moment the clank of a horseshoe was heard on the pavement, and, turning his head, Charles saw his man, Tom Sherwood, ride into the yard. Tom touched his hat and dismounted.

'A letter, sir.'

'Oh!' said Charles, letting go his wife's arm, and walking quickly towards him.

The man handed him a letter. Alice was standing, forgotten for the time, on the middle of the pavement, while her husband opened and read his letter.

When he had done he turned about and walked a few steps toward her, but still thinking anxiously and plainly not seeing her, and he stopped and read it through again.

'Oh, darling, I beg your pardon. I'm so stupid. What were we talking about? Oh! yes, the house, this old place. If I live to succeed to Wyvern you shall do what you like with this place, and we'll live here if you like it best.'

'Well, I don't think I should like to live here always,' she said, and paused.

She was thinking of the odd incident of the night before, and there lurked in one dark corner of her mind just the faintest image of horror, very faint, but still genuine, and which, the longer she looked at it, grew the darker; 'and I was going to ask you if we could change our room.'

'I think, darling,' said he, looking at her steadily, 'the one we have got is almost the only habitable bedroom in the house, and certainly the most comfortable, but if you like any other room better – have you been looking?'

'No, darling, only I'm such a coward, and so foolish; I fancied I saw something when I was going into it last night – old Mrs Tarnley was quite close to me.'

'If you saw *her* it was quite enough to frighten anyone. But what was it – robber, or only a ghost?' he asked.

'Neither, only a kind of surprise and a fright. I did not care to talk about it last night, and I thought it would have quite passed away by to-day; but I can't quite get rid of it – and, shall I tell it all to you now?' answered Alice.

You must tell me all by and bye,' he laughed; 'you shall have any room you like better, only remember they're all equally old; and now, *I* have a secret to tell you. Harry is coming to dine with us; he'll be here at six – and – look here, how oddly my letters come to me.'

And he held the envelope he had just opened by the corner before her eyes. It was thus:–

'Mr Thomas Sherwood,
 'Post Office,
 'Naunton.
 'To be called for.'

'There's evidence of the caution I'm obliged to practise in that part of the world. The world will never be without sin, poverty, and attorneys; and there is a cursed fellow there with eyes wide open and ears erect, and all sorts of poisoned arrows of the law to shoot at poor wayfarers like me; and that's the reason why I'd rather buy our modest teacups in London, and not be so much as heard of in Naunton. Don't look so frightened, little woman; every fellow has a dangerous dun or two, and I'm not half so much in peril as fifty I could name. Only my father's angry, you know, and when that quarrel gets to be known it mayn't help my credit, or make duns more patient. So I must keep well earthed here till the dogs are quiet again; and now, my wise little housekeeper will devise dinner enough for our hungry brother, who will arrive, in two hours' time, with the appetite that Cressley Common gives every fellow with as little to trouble him as Harry has.'

CHAPTER 15

HARRY ARRIVES

Six o'clock came, and seven, and not until half-past seven, when they had nearly given up, did Henry Fairfield arrive at the Grange.

'How does Madam Fairfield?' bawled Master Harry, as he strode across the floor, and kissed Alice's pretty cheek. 'Odds bobbins! – as the man says in the playhouse – I believe I bussed ye, did I? But don't let him be angry; I wasn't thinkin', Charlie, no more than the fellow that put Farmer Gleeson's fippun-note in his pocket last Trutbury fair. And how's all wi' ye, Charlie, hey? I'm glad to see the old house is standing still with a roof on since last gale. And how do ye like it, Alice? Rayther slow I used to think it; but you two wise heads are so in love wi' one another ye'd put up in the pound, or the cow-house, or the horse-pond, for sake o' each other's company. "I loved her sweet company better than meat," as the song says; and that reminds me – can the house afford a hungry man a cut o' beef or mutton and a mug of ale? I asked myself to dinner, ye know, and that's a bargain there's two words to, sometimes.'

Master Harry was a wag, after a clumsy rustic fashion – an habitual jester, and never joked more genially than when he was letting his companion in for what he called a 'soft thing,' in the shape of an unsound horse or a foolish wager.

His jocularity was supposed to cover a great deal of shrewdness, and some dangerous qualities also.

While their homely dinner was being got upon the table, honest Harry quizzed the lord and lady of Carwell Grange in the same vein of delicate banter, upon all their domestic arrangements, and when he found that there was but one sitting-room in a condition to receive them, his merriment knew no bounds.

'Upon my soul, you beat the cobbler in the song that "lived in a stall, that served him for parlour, and kitchen, and hall," for there's no mention of the cobbler's wife, and he, being a single man, you know, you and your lady double the wonder, don't ye, Alice – two faces under a hood, and a devilish pinched little hood, too, heh? Ha, ha, ha!'

'When did you get to Wyvern?' asked Charles Fairfield, after a considerable pause.

'Last night,' answered his brother.

'You saw the old man?'

'Not till morning,' answered Henry, with a waggish leer, and a sly glance at Alice.

It was lost, however, for the young lady was looking dreamily and sadly away, thinking, perhaps, of the old squire, not without self-upbraidings, and hearing nothing, I am sure, of all they said.

'Did you breakfast with him?'

'By Jove, I did, sir!'

'Well?'

'Well? Nothing particular, only let me see how long his stick is – his stick and his arm, together – say five feet six. Well, I counsel you, brother, not to go within five foot six inches of the old gentleman till he cools down a bit, anyhow.'

'No, we'll not try that,' said Charles, 'and he may cool down, as you say, or nurse his wrath, as he pleases, it doesn't much matter to me; he *was* very angry, but sometimes the thunder, and flame blow off, you know, and the storm hurts no one.'

'I hope so,' said Henry, with a sort of laugh. 'When I tell you to keep out of the way, mind, I'm advising you against myself. The more you and the old boy wool each other, the better for Hal.'

'He can't unsettle the place, Harry – not that I want to see him – I never owed him much love, and I think *now* he'd be glad to see me a beggar.'

Harry laughed again.

'Did you ever hear a bear with a sore head?' said Harry. 'Well, that's him, at present, and I give you fair notice, I think he'll leave all he can away from you.'

'So let him; if it's to you, Harry, I don't grudge it,' said the elder son.

'That's a handsome speech, bless the speaker. Can you give me a glass of brandy? This claret I never could abide,' said Harry, with another laugh; 'besides, it will break you.'

'I've put two bottles, and they have been three years here. Yes, you can have brandy, it's here.'

'I'll get it,' said Alice, brightening up in the sense of her housekeeping importance. 'It's — I *think* it's in this, ain't it?' she said, opening one of the presses inserted in the wainscot.

'Let me, darling; it's there, I ought to know, I put it there myself,' said Charles, getting up, and taking the keys from her and opening another cupboard.

'I'm so stupid,' said Alice, blushing, as she surrendered them, 'and so useless; but you're always right, Charlie.'

'He's a wonderful fellow, ain't he?' said Harry, winking agreeably at Charles; 'I never knew a brand new husband that wasn't. Wait a bit and the gold rubs off the gingerbread. — Didn't old Dulcibella — how's she? — never buy you a gingerbread husband down at Wyvern fair? and they all went, I warrant, the same road; the gilding rubs away, and then off with his head, and eat him up slops! That's not bad cognac — where do you get it? — don't know, of course; well, it *is* good.'

'Glad you like it, Harry,' said his brother. 'It was very kind of you coming over here so soon; you must come often — won't you?'

'Well, you know, I thought I might as well, just to tell you how things was — but, mind, is anyone here?'

He looked over his shoulder to be sure that the old servant was not near.

'Mind, you're not to tell the folk over at Wyvern that I came here, because you know it wouldn't serve me, no ways, with the old chap up there, and there's no use.'

'You may be very easy about that, Harry. I'm a banished man, you know. I shall never see the old man's face again; and rely on it, I shan't write.'

'I don't mean him alone,' said Harry, replenishing his glass; 'but don't tell any of them Wyvern people, nor you, Alice. Mind — I'm going back to-night, as far as Barnsley, and from there I'll go to Dawling, and round, d'ye mind, south, by Leigh Watton, up to Wyvern, and I'll tell him a thumpin' lie if he asks questions.'

'Don't fear for any such thing, Harry,' said Charles.

'Fear! I'm not afeard on him, nor never was.'

'Fancy, then,' said Charles.

'Only,' continued Harry, 'I'm not like you – I han't a house and a bit o' land to fall back on; d'ye see? He'd have me on the ropes if I vexed him. He'd slap Wyvern door in my face, and stop my allowance, and sell my horses, and leave me to the 'sizes and the lawyers for my rights; and I couldn't be comin' here spongin' on you, you know.'

'You'd always be welcome, Harry,' said Charles.

'Always,' echoed his wife, in whom everyone who belonged to Charlie had a welcome claim.

But Harry went right on with his speech without diverging to thank them.

'And you'll be snug enough here, you see, and I might go whistle, and dickens a chance I'll ha' left but to go 'list or break horses, or break stones, by jingo! and I ha' run risks enough in this thing o' yours – not but I'm willin' to run more, if need be; but there's no good in getting myself into pound, you know.'

'By me, Harry? You don't imagine I could be such a fool,' exclaimed Charles.

'Well, I think ye'll allow I stood to ye like a brick, and didn't funk nothin' that was needful – and I'd do it over again, I would.'

Charles took one hand of the generous fellow, and Alice took the other, and the modest benefactor smiled gruffly and flushed a little, and looked down as they poured forth in concert their acknowledgements.

'Why, see how you two thanks me. I always say to fellows, "Keep your thanks to yourselves, and do me a good turn when it lies in your ways." There's the sort o' thanks that butters a fellow's parsnips – and so – say no more.'

CHAPTER 16

A PARTY OF THREE

'I'd tip you a stave, only I've got a hoarseness since yesterday, and I'd ask Alice to play a bit, only there's no piano here to kick up a jingle with, and Charlie never sang a note in his life, and' – standing before the fire he yawned long and loud – 'by Jove, that wasn't civil of me, but old friends need not be stiff, I vote we yawn all round for company; and I'll forgive ye, for my hour's come, and I'll be taking the road.'

'I wish so much I had a bed to offer you, Harry; but you know all about it – there hasn't been time to arrange anything,' said Charles.

'Won't you stay and take some tea?' urged Alice.

'I never could abide it, child, thank ye all the same,' said he, 'I'd as soon drink a mug of whey.'

'And what about the grey hunter – you did not sell him yet?' asked Charles.

'I don't well know what to do about him,' answered his brother. 'I'd 'a sold him for fifty, only old Clinker wouldn't pass him for sound. Clinker and me, we had words about that.'

'I want fifty pounds very much, if I could get it,' said Charles.

'I never knew a fellow that didn't want fifty very bad, if he could get it,' laughed Harry; 'but you'll not be doin' that bad, I'm afeard, if ye get half the money.'

'The devil! – do you really – why, I thought, with luck, I might get seventy. I'm hard up, Harry, and I know you'll do your best for me,' said Charles, to whom this was really a serious question.

'And with luck, so you might; but chaps isn't easy done these times; and though I swear it's only his mouth, he steps short at the off side, and a fellow with an eye in his head won't mistake his action.'

'You will do the best you can for me, Harry, I know,' said Charles, who knew nothing about horses, and was lazy in discussion. 'But it's rather a blow just now, when a poor devil wants every shilling he can get together, to find himself fifty pounds nearly out of pocket.'

Was it fancy, or did Alice's pretty ear hear truly? It seemed to her that the tone in which Charlie spoke was a little more sour than need be, that it seemed to blame her as the cause of altered circumstances, and to hint, though very faintly, an unkind repentance. His eye met hers; full and sad it looked, and his heart smote him, for the intangible reproof was deserved.

'And here's the best little wife in the world,' he said, 'who would save a lazy man like me a little fortune in a year, and make that unlucky fifty pounds, if I could but get it, do as much as a hundred.'

And his hand was fondly placed on her shoulder, as he looked in her loving eyes.

'A good housewife, is she? that's something,' said Harry, who was inspecting his spur. 'Though, by Jove, it was hardly at Wyvern she learned thrift.'

'All the more merit,' said Charles, 'it's all her wise, good little self.'

'No, no; I can't take all that praise; it's your great kindness, Charlie. But I'll try. I'll learn all I can, and I'm sure the real secret is to be very anxious to do it well.'

'Ay, to be sure,' interrupted Harry, who, having completed his little arrangement, placed his foot again on the ground. 'The more you like it the better you'll do it – pare the cheeses, skin the flints, kill the fleas for the hide and tallow, pot the potato skins, sweat the shillin's and all that, and now I'll be going. Good-night, Alice. Will you let Charlie see me down to the end o' the lane, and I'll send him safe back to you? Come along, Charlie. God bless you, girl, and I'll look in again whenever I have a bit o' news to tell ye.'

And with that elegant farewell, he shook Alice by the hand and clapped her on the shoulder, and 'chucked' her under the chin.

'And don't ye be faint-hearted, mind – 'twill all come right, and I didn't think this place was so comfortable as it is. It is a snug old house; with a bit o' coal and a faggot o' wood, and a pair o' bright eyes, and a glass o' that, a man might make shift for a while. I'd do it myself. I didn't think it was so snug by half, and I'd rayther stay here to-night by a long chalk than ride to Barnsley, I can tell ye. Come, Charlie, it's time I should be on the road; and she says – don't you, Alice? – you may see me a bit o' the way.'

And so the leave-taking came to an end, and Charlie and Harry went out together; and Alice wondered what had induced Harry to come all that way for so short a visit, with so very little to tell. Perhaps, however, his own business, for he was always looking after horses, and thought nothing of five-and-thirty miles, had brought him to the verge of Cressley Common, and if so, he would have come on the few additional miles if only to bait his horse and get his dinner. Perhaps the old squire at Wyvern had broken out more angrily, and was threatening something in which there was real danger to Charlie, which the brothers did not choose to tell her. A kindly secrecy and considerate, but seldom unsuspected, and being so often fifty-fold more torturing than down-right ghastly frankness.

There had been a little chill and shadow over the party of three, she thought. Charlie thought his brother Harry the most thorough partisan that ever man had, and the most entirely sympathetic. If that were so – and should not he know best? – Harry had certainly laughed and joked after his fashion and enjoyed himself, and there could not be much wrong. But Charlie – was not there something more upon his mind than she quite knew? She stood too much in awe of her husband to follow them, as she would have wished, and implore of them if there was any new danger to let her hear it all. In her ear was the dismal iteration, as it were, of this little 'death-watch,' and, sighing, she got up and opened the window shutter and looked out upon the moonlighted scene.

A little platform of grass stood between the wall of the house and the precipitous edge of the vale of Marlow. Tall trees stood silent and lonely sentinels without the old grey walls, and a low ivied parapet guarded the sudden descent of the riven and wooded cliff. The broker screen of the solemn forest foreground showed in the distance the thicker masses of the wood that topped the summit of the further side of that sombre glen. Stiller, sadder scene fancy never painted.

She had opened the shutter, uncertain whether the window commanded the point from which her husband and his brother might be expected to emerge, for the geography of this complicated house was still new to her, and, disappointed, she lingered in contemplation of a view which so well accorded with the melancholy of her lonely misgivings.

How soon in the possession of our heart's desire comes the sense of disappointment, and the presence of the worm, and promise of the blight among the flowers of our vernal days. Pitch the tent or drop the anchor where we may, always a new campaign opening, always a new voyage beginning – quiet nowhere.

'I dare say it is only my folly – that nothing has gone wrong, and that they have no secrets to hide from me. I have no one else; he would not shut me out from his confidence, and leave me quite alone. No, Ry, you could not.'

With a full heart she turned again from the window.

'He'll come again in a minute; he'll not walk far with Harry.'

She went to the door and, opening it, listened. She heard a step enter the passage from the stable-yard, and called to ask who was there. It was only Tom, who had let out Master Harry's horse, and opened the gate for him. He led it out, and they walked together – Master Harry with the bridle in his hand, and Master Charles walking beside him. They took the narrow way along the little glen towards Cressley Common.

She knew that he would return probably in a few minutes; and more and more she wondered what those minutes might contain, she partly wondered at her own anxiety. So she returned to the room and waited there for him. But he remained longer away than she expected. The tea-things were on the table deserted. The fire flickered its genial invitation in vain, and she, growing more uncomfortable and lonely, and perhaps a little high at being thus forsaken, went upstairs to pay old Dulcibella Crane a visit.

CHAPTER 17

MILDRED TARNLEY'S WARNING STORY

As she reached the top of the stairs, she called to the old servant, not, I think, caring to traverse the haunted flooring that intervened alone. She heard Dulcibella talking, and a moment after her old nurse appeared, and standing by her shoulder Mildred Tarnley.

'Oh, Mrs Tarnley! I'm so glad to see you – you've been paying Dulcibella a visit. Pray, come back, and tell me some stories about this old house; you've been so long here, and know it so well, that you must have a great deal to tell.'

The old woman, with the unpleasant face, made a stiff curtsey.

'At your service, ma'am,' she said ungraciously.

'That is, if it don't inconvenience you,' pleaded Alice, who was still a little afraid of her.

'' Tis as you please, ma'am,' said the old servant, with another dry curtsey.

'Well, I'm so glad you can come. Dulcibella, have we a little bit of a fire? Oh, yes, I see – it looks so cheerful.'

So they entered the old-fashioned bedroom.

'I hope, Mrs Tarnley, I'm not keeping you from your tea?'

'No, I thank ye, ma'am. I've 'ad my tea an hour agone,' answered the old woman.

'And you must sit down, Mrs Tarnley,' urged Alice.

'I'll stand, if ye please, ma'am,' said the withered figure perversely.

'I should be so much happier if you would sit down, Mildred,' urged her young mistress; 'but, if you prefer it – I only mean that whatever is most comfortable to you you should do. I wanted so much to hear something about this old house. You remember what happend when I was coming upstairs with you – when I was so startled?'

'I didn't see it, Miss – ma'am. I only heard you say summat,' answered Mildred Tarnley.

'Oh, yes, I know; but you spoke to-day of a warning, and you looked when it happened as if you had heard of it before.'

The old woman raised her chin, and with her hands folded together made another curtsey, which mutually seemed to say:–

'If you have anything to ask, ask it.'

'Do you remember,' inquired Alice, 'having ever heard of anything strange being seen at that passage near the head of the stairs?'

'I ought, ma'am,' answered the old woman discreetly.

'And what was it?' inquired Alice.

'I don't know, ma'am, would the master be pleased if he was to hear I was talkin' o' such things to you,' suggested Mildred.

'He'd only laugh as I should, I assure you. I'm not the least a coward; so you need not be afraid of my making a fool of myself. Now, do tell me what it was!'

'Well, ma'am, you'll be pleased to remember 'tis you orders me, in case Master Charles should turn on me about it; but, as you say, ma'am there's many thinks 'tis all nothin' but old 'oman's tales and fribble-frabble; and 'tisn't for me to say——'

'I'll take all the blame to myself,' said Alice.

'There's no blame in't as I'm aware on; and if there was, I wouldn't ask no one to take it on themselves more than their right to share; and that I'd take leave to lay on them myself, without stoppin' to ask whether they likes it or no; but only I told you ma'am, that I should have your orders, and wi' them I'll comply.'

'Yes, certainly, Mrs Tarnley – and now do kindly go on,' said Alice.

'Well, please, ma'am, you'll tell me what you saw?'

'A heavy black drapery fell from the top of the arch through which we pass to the gallery outside the door, and for some seconds closed up the entire entrance,' answered the young lady.

'Ay, ay, no doubt that's it; but there was no drapery there, ma'am, such as this world's loom ever wove. Them as weaves that web is light o' hand and heavy o' heart, and the de'el himself speeds the shuttle,' and as she said this the old woman smiled sourly. 'I was talking o' that very thing to Mrs Crane here when you came up, ma'am.'

'Yes,' said old Dulcibella, quietly; 'it was very strange, surely.'

'And there came quite a cloud of dust from it rolling along the floor,' continued Alice.

'Yes, so there would – so there does: 'tis always so,' said Mrs Tarnley, with the same faint ugly smile; 'not that there's a grain o' dust in all the gallery, for the child Lilly Dogger and me washed it out and swept it clean. Dust ye saw; but that's not real dust, like what the minister means when he says, "Dust to dust." No, no, a finer dust by far – the dust o' death. No more clay in that than in yon smoke, or the mist in Carwell Glen below; no dust at all, but sich dust as a ghost might shake from its windin' sheet – an appearance, ye understand; that's all, ma'am – like the rest.'

Alice smiled, but old Mildred's answering smile chilled her, and she turned to Dulcibella; but good Mrs Crane looked in her face with round eyes of consternation and a very solemn countenance.

'I see, Dulcibella, if my courage fails I'm not to look to you for support. Well, Mrs Tarnley, don't mind – I shan't need her help; I'm not a bit afraid, so pray go on.'

'Well, ye see, ma'am, this place and the house came into the family, my grandmother used to say, more than a hundred years ago; and I was a little thing when I used to hear her say so, and there's many a year added to the tale since then; but it was in the days o' Sir Harry Fairfield. They called him Harry Boots in his day, for he was never seen except in his boots, for the matter o' that seldom out o' the saddle; for there was troubles in them days, and militia and yeomanry, and dear knows what all – and the Fairfields was ever a bold, dare-devil stock, and them dangerous times answered them well – and what with dragooning, and what with the hunting field, I do suppose his foot was seldom out o' the stirrup. So my grandmother told me some called him Booted Fairfield, and more called him Harry Boots – that was Sir Harry Fairfield o' them days.'

'I think I've seen his picture, haven't I? – at Wyvern. It's in the hall at the far end from the door, near the window, with a long wig and a lace cravat, and a great steel breast-plate?' inquired Alice.

'Like enough, Miss – ma'am, I mean – I don't know, I'm sure – but he was a great man in his time, and would have his picture took, no doubt. His wife was a Carwell – an heiress – there's not a Carwell in this country now, nor for many a day has been. 'Twas she brought Carwell Grange and the Vale o' Carwell to the Fairfields – poor thing – pretty she was. Her picture was never took to Wyvern, and much good her land, and houses, and good looks done her. The Fairfields was wild folk. I don't say there wasn't good among 'em, but whoever else they was good to, they was seldom kind to their wives. Hard, bad husbands they was – that's sure.'

Alice smiled, and stirred the fire quietly, but did not interrupt, and as the story went on, she sighed.

'They said she was very lonesome here. Well, it is a lonesome place, you know – awful lonesome, and always the same. For old folk like me it doesn't matter, but young blood's different, you know, and they likes to see the world a bit, and talk and hear what's a-foot, be it fun or change, or what not; and she was very lonesome, mopin' about the old garden, plantin' flowers, or pluckin' roses – all to herself – or cryin' in the window – while Harry Boots was away wi' his excuses – now wi' his sogerin', and now wi' his hounds, and truly wi' worse matters, if all were out. So, not twice in a year was his face – handsome Harry Boots they ca'd him – seen down here, and his pretty lady was sick and sore and forsaken, down in her own lonesome house, by the Vale of Carwell, where I'm telling you this.'

Alice smiled, and nodded in sign of attention, and the old woman went on.

'I often wonder they try to hide things – 'twould be better sometimes they were more outspoken, for sooner or later all will out, and then there's wild work, and mayhap it's past ever makin' up between them. So stories travel a'most without legs to carry 'em, and there's no gainsaying the word o' God that said. "Let there be light," for, sooner or later, light 'twill be, and all will be cleared up, and the wicked doin's of Harry Boots, far away, and cunning, as all was done, come clear to light, so as she could no longer have hope or doubt in the matter. Poor thing – she loved him better than life – better than her soul, mayhap, and that's all she got by't – a bad villain that was.'

'He was untrue to her?' said Alice.

'Lawk! to be sure he was,' replied Mrs Tarnley, with a cynical scorn.

'And so she had that to think of all alone, along with the rest – for she might have had a greater match than Sir Harry – a lord he was. I forget his name, but he'd given his eyes a'most to 'a got her. But a' wouldn't do, for she loved Booted Harry Fairfield, and him she'd have, and wouldn't hear o' no other, and so she had enough to think on here, in Carwell Grange. The house she had brought the Fairfields − poor bird alone, as we used to say − but the rest of her time wasn't very long − it wasn't to be − she used to walk out sometimes, but she talked to no one, and she cared for nothin' after that; and there's the long sheet o' water, in the thick o' the trees, with the black yew hedge round it.'

'I know,' said Alice, 'a very high hedge, and trees behind it − it is the darkest place I ever saw − beyond the garden. Isn't that the place?'

'Yes, that's it; she used to walk round it − sometimes cryin' − sometimes not; and there she was found drowned, poor thing. Some said 'twas by mischance, for the bank was very steep and slippery − it had been rainy weather − where she was found, and more said she made away wi' herself, and that's what was thought among the Carwell folk, as my grandmother heared; for what's a young creature to do wi' nothing more to look to, and all alone, wi' no one ever to talk to, and the heart quite broke?'

'You said, I think, that there was a picture here?' inquired Alice.

'I said 'twasn't took to Wyvern, ma'am; there was a picture here they said 'twas hers − my grandmother said so, and she should know. 'Twas the only picture I remember in the Grange.'

'And where is it?' inquired Alice.

'Dropped to pieces long ago. 'Twas in the room they called the gun-room, in my day. The wall was damp; 'twas gone very poor and rotten in my time, and so black you could scarce make it out. Many a time when I was a bit of a girl, some thirteen or fourteen years old, I stood on the table for a long time together a-looking at it. But it was dropping away that time in flakes, and the canvas as rotten as tinder, and every time it got a stir it lost something, till ye couldn't make nothing of it. It's all gone long ago, and the frame broke up I do suppose.'

'What a pity!' said Alice. 'Oh, what a pity! Can you, do you think, remember anything of it?'

'She was standin' − you could see the point o' the shoe − white satin it looked like, wi' a buckle that might be diamonds; there was a nosegay, I mind, in her fingers, wi' small blue flowers, and a rose, but the face was all faded and dark, except just a bit o' the mouth, red, and smilin' at the corner − very pretty. But 'twas all gone very dark, you know, and a deal o' the paintin' gone; and that's all I ever seen o' the picture.'

'Well, and did anything more happen?' asked Alice.

'Hoo, yes, lots! Down comes Booted Fairfield, now there was no one left to care whether he came or went. The Carwell people didn't love him, but 'twas best to keep a civil tongue, for the Fairfields were dangerous folk always, 'twas a word and a blow wi' them, and no one cared to cross them, and he made a bother about it to be sure, and had the rooms hung wi' black, and the staircase and the drapery hung over the arch in the gallery, outside, down to the floor, for she, poor thing, lay up there.'

'Not in this room!' said Alice, who even at that distance of time did not care to invade the sinister sancitity of the lady's room.

'No, not this, the room at t' other end o' the gallery; 't would require a deal o' doing up, and plaster, and paper, before you could lie in't. But Harry Boots made a woundy fuss about his dead wife. They was cunning after a sort, them Fairfields, and I suppose he thought 'twas best to make folk think he loved his wife, at least to give 'em something good to say o' him if they liked, and he gave alms to the poor, and left a good lump o' money they say for the parish, both at Cressley church and at Carwell Priory – they call the vicarage so – and he had a grand funeral as ever was seen from the Grange, and she was buried down at the priory, which the Carwells used to be, in a new vault, where she was laid the first, and has been the last, for Booted Fairfield married again, and was buried with his second wife away at Wyvern. So the poor thing, living and dying, has been left to herself.'

'But is there any story to account for what I saw as I came into the gallery with you?' asked Alice.

'I told you, Miss, it was hung with black, as I heard my grandmother say, and thereupon the story came, for there was three ladies of the Fairfield family at different times before you, ma'am, as saw the same thing. Well, ma'am, at the funeral, as I've heard say, the young lord that liked her well, if she'd 'a had him – and liked her still in spite of all – gave Sir Harry a lick or two wi' the rough side o' his tongue, and a duel came out o' them words more than a year afterwards, and Harry Boots was killed, and he's buried down at Wyvern.'

'Well, see there! Ain't it a wonder how gentleman that has all this world can give will throw away their lives at a word, like that,' moralised Dulcibella Crane – 'and not knowing what's to become o' them, when they've lost all here – all in the snap of a pistol. If it was a poor body, 'twould be another matter, but – well, it does make a body stare.'

'You mentioned, Mrs Tarnley, that something had occurred about some ladies of the Fairfield family; what was it?' inquired Alice.

'Well, they say Sir Harry – that's Booted Fairfield, you know – brought his second wife down here, only twelve months after the first one died, and she saw, at the very same place, when she was setting her first step on the gallery, the same thing ye seen yourself; and two months after he was in his grave, and she in a madhouse.'

'Well, I think, Mrs Tarnley, ye needn't be tellin' all that to fright the young lady.'

'Frighten the young lady? And why not, if she's frightened wi' truth? She has asked for the truth, and she's got it. Better to fright the young lady than fool her,' answered Mildred Tarnley, coldly and sternly.

'I don't say you should fool her, by no chance.' answered honest Dulcibella; 'but there's no need to be filling her head wi' them frightful fancies. Ye ha' scared her, and ye saw her turn pale.'

'Ay, and so well she ought. There was three other women o' the Fairfields seen the same thing, in the self-same place, and every one to her sorrow. One fell over the pixie's cliff; another died in fits poor thing, wi' her first baby; and the last was flung beside the quarry in Cressley Common, ridin' out to see the hunt, and was never the better o't in brain or bone after. Don't tell me, woman. I know rightly what I'm doin'.'

'Pray, Dulcibella, don't. I assure you, Mrs Tarnley, I'm very much obliged,' interposed Alice Fairfield, frighted at the malignant vehemence of the old woman.

'Obliged! Not you; why should you?' retorted Mildred Tarnley. 'Ye're not obliged; ye're frightened, I dare say. But 'tis all true; and no Fairfield has any business bringing his wife to Carwell Grange; and Master Charles knows that as well as me; and, now, the long and the short o't 's this, ma'am – ye've got your warning, and ye had better quit this without letting grass grow under your feet. You've seen your warnin', ma'am, and I 'a told you, stark enough, the meanin' o't. My conscience is clear, and ye'll do as ye like; and if, after this, ye expect me to spy for you and fetch and carry stories, and run myself into trouble with other people, to keep you out of it, ye're clean out o' your reckoning. Ye'll have no more warnings, mayhap – none from me – and so ye may take it, ma'am, or leave it, as ye see fit; and now Mildred Tarnley's said her say. Ye have my story, and ye have my counsel; and if ye despise both one and t'other, and your own eyesight beside, ye'll even take what's coming.'

'Ye *shouldn't* be frightening Miss Alice like that, I tell you – you should not. Don't grow frightened at any such story, dear. I say it's a shame. Don't you see how ye have her as white as a handkercher – in a reg'lar state?'

'No, Dulcibella, indeed,' said Alice, smiling, very pale, and her eyes filled up with tears.

'I'll frighten her no more; and that you may be sure on; and if what I told her be frightful, 'tisn't me as made it so. Thankless work it be; but 'tisn't her nor you I sought to please, but just to take it off my shoulders, and leave her none to blame but herself if she turns a deaf ear. It's ill offering counsel to a wilful lass. Ye'll excuse me, ma'am, for speaking so plain, but better now than too late,' she added, recollecting herself a little.

'And can I do anything, please, ma'am, below stairs? I should be going, for who knows what that child may be a-doing all this time?'

'Thanks, very much; no, not anything,' said Alice.

And Mildred Tarnley, with a hard dark glance at her, dropped another stiff little curtsey, and withdrew.

'Well, I never see such a one as that,' said old Dulcibella, gazing after her, as it were through the panel of the door. 'You must not let her talk that way to you, my darling. She's no business to talk up to her mistress that way. I don't know what sort o' manners people has in these here out-o'-the-way places, I'm sure; but I think ye'll do well, my dear, to keep that one at arm's length, and make her know her place. Nothing else but encroaching and impudence and domineering from such as her, and no thanks for any condescension, only the more affable you'll be, the more saucy and conceited she'll grow, and I don't think she likes you, Miss Alice, no more I do.'

It pains young people, and some persons always, to hear from an impartial observer such a conclusion. There is much mortification, and often some alarm.

'Well, it doesn't matter,' said Alice. 'I don't think she can harm me much. I don't suppose she would if she could, and I don't mind such stories.'

'Why should you, my dear? No one minds the like nowadays.'

'But I wished she liked me; there are so few of us here. It is such a little world, and I have never done anything to vex her. I can't think what good it can do her hating me.'

'No good, dear; but she's bin here so long – the only hen in the house, and she doesn't like to be drove off the roost, I suppose; and I don't know why she told you all that, if it wasn't to make your mind uneasy; and, dear knows, there's enough to trouble it in this moping place without her riggamarolin' sich a yarn.'

'Hush, Dulcibella; isn't that a horse? Perhaps Charles is coming home.'

She opened the window, which commanded a view of the stable-yard.

'And is he gone a-riding?' asked old Dulcibella.

'No, there's nothing,' said Alice, gently. 'Besides, you remind me he did not take a horse; he only walked a little way with Mr Henry; and he'll soon be back. Nothing is going wrong, I hope.'

And, with a weary sigh, she threw herself into a great chair by the fire, and thought, and listened, and dreamed away a long time, before Charlie's step and voice were heard again in the old house.

CHAPTER 18

THE BROTHERS' WALK

When the host and his guest had gone out together, to the paved yard, it was already night, and the moon was shining brilliantly.

Tom had saddled the horse, and at the first summons led him out; and Harry, with a nod and a grin, for he was more prodigal of his smiles than of his shillings, took the bridle from his fingers, and with Charlie by his side, walked forth silently from the yard gate, upon that dark and rude track which followed for some distance the precipitous edge of the ravine which opens upon the deeper glen of Carwell.

Very dark was this narrow road, overhung and crossed by towering trees, through whose boughs only here and there an angular gleam or minute mottling of moonlight hovered and floated on the white and stony road, with the uneasy motion of the branches, like little flights of quivering wings.

There was a silence corresponding with this darkness. The clank of the horse's hoofs and their own more muffled tread were the only sounds that mingled with the sigh and rustle of the boughs above them. The one was expecting, the other meditating, no very pleasant topic, and it was not the business of either to begin, for a little while.

They were not walking fast. The horse seemed to feel that the human wayfarers were in a sauntering mood, and fell accommodatingly into a lounging gait like theirs.

If there were eyes there constructed to see in the dark, they would have seen two countenances – one sincere, the other adjusted to that sort of sham sympathy and regret which Hogarth, with all his delicacy and power, portrays in the paternal alderman who figures in the last picture of 'Marriage à la Mode.'

There was much anxiety in Charles' face, and a certain brooding shame and constraint which would have accounted for his silence. In that jolly dog Harry was discoverable, as I have said, quite another light and form of countenance. There was a face that seemed to have discharged a smile, that still would not quite go. The eyelids drooped, the eyebrows raised, a simulated condolence, such as we all have seen.

In our moral reviews of ourselves we practise optical delusions even upon our own self-scrutiny, and paint and mask our motives, and fill our ears with excuses and with downright lies. So inveterate is the habit of deceiving, and even in the dark we form our features by hypocrisy, and scarcely know all this.

'Here's the turn at last to Cressley Common; there's no talking comfortably among these trees; it's so dark, anyone might be at your elbow and you know nothing about it – and so the old man is very angry.'

'Never saw a fellow so riled,' answered Harry; 'you know what he is when he is riled, and I never saw him so angry before. If he knew I was here – but you'll take care of me?'

'It's very kind of you, old fellow; I won't forget it – indeed I won't, but I ought to have thought twice; I ought not to have brought poor Alice into this fix; for d——n me if I know how we are to get on.'

'Well, you know, it's only just a pinch, an ugly corner, and you are all right – it can't last.'

'It may last ten years, or twenty for that matter,' said Charlie. 'I was a fool to sell out. I don't know what we are to do; do you?'

'You're too down in the mouth; can't ye wait and see? There's nothing yet, and it won't cost ye much carrying on down here.'

'Do you think, Harry, it would be well to take up John Wauling's farm, and try whether I could not make something of it in my own hands?' asked Charles.

Harry shook his head.

'You don't?' said Charlie.

'Well, no, I don't; you'd never make the rent of it,' answered Harry; 'besides, if you begin upsetting things here, the people will begin to talk, and that would not answer; you'll need to be d——d quiet.'

There was here a pause, and they walked on in silence until the thick shadows of the trees begun to break a little before them, and the woods grew more scattered; whole trees were shadowed in distinct outline, and the wide common of Cressley, with its furze and fern, and broad undulations, stretched mistily before them.

'About money – you know, Charlie, there's money enough at present, and no debts to signify; I mean, if you don't make them you needn't. You and Alice, with the house and garden, can get along on a trifle. The tenants give you three hundred a year, and you can manage with two.'

'Two hundred a year!' exclaimed Charlie, opening his eyes.

'Ay, two hundred a year! – that girl don't eat sixpenn'orth in a day,' said Harry.

'Alice is the best little thing in the world, and will look after everything, I know; but there are other things beside dinner and breakfast,' said Charles, who did not care to hear his wife called 'that girl.'

'Needs must when the devil drives, my boy; you'll want a hundred every year for contingencies,' said Harry.

'Well, I suppose so,' Charles winced, 'and all the more need for a few more hundreds; for I don't see how anyone could manage to exist on such a pittance.'

'You'll have to contrive, though, my lad, unless, they'll manage a *post obit* for you,' said Harry.

'There is some trouble about that, and people are such d——d screws,' said Charles, with a darkening face.

'Al'ays was and ever will be,' said Harry, with a laugh.

'And it's all very fine talking of a "hundred a year," but *you* know *I* know that won't do, and never did,' exclaimed Charles, breaking forth bitterly, and then looking hurriedly over his shoulder.

'Upon my soul, Charlie, I don't know a curse about it,' answered Harry, good-humouredly; 'but if it won't do, it won't, that's certain.'

'Quite certain,' said Charles, and sighed very heavily; and again there was a little silence.

'I wish I was as sharp a fellow as you are, Harry,' said Charles, regretfully.

'Do you really think I'm a sharp chap – do you, though? I al'ays took myself for a bit of a muff, except about cattle – I did, upon my soul,' said Harry, with an innocent laugh.

'You are a long way a cleverer fellow than I am, and you are not half so lazy; and tell me what you'd do if you were in my situation?'

'What would I do if I was in your place?' said Harry, looking up at the stars, and whistling low for a minute. 'Well, I couldn't tell you off hand; 'twould puzzle a better man's head for a bit to answer that question – only I can tell you one thing, I'd never agone into that situation, as ye call it, at no price; 'twouldn't 'av answered me by no chance. But don't you be putting your finger in your eye yet a bit; there's nothing to cry about now that I knows of; time enough to hang your mouth yet, only I thought I might as well come over and tell you.'

'I knew, Harry, there was something to tell,' said Charles.

'Not over much – only a trifle when all's told,' answered Harry; 'but you are right, for it was that brought me over here. I was in Lon'on last week, and I looked in at the place at Hoxton, and found just the usual thing, and came away pretty much as wise as I went in.'

'Not more reasonable?' asked Charles.

'Not a bit,' said Harry.

'Tell me what you said?' asked Charles.

'Just what we agreed,' he answered.

'Well, there was nothing in that that was not kind and conciliatory, and common sense – was there?' pleaded Charles.

'It did not seem to strike the plenipotentiary,' said Harry.

'You seem to think it very pleasant,' said Charles.

'I wish it was pleasanter,' said Harry; 'but, pleasant or no, I must tell my story straight. I ran in in a hurry, you know, as if I only wanted to pay over the twenty pounds – you mind?'

'Ay,' said Charles. 'I wish to heaven I had it back again.'

'Well, I don't think it made much difference in the matter of love and liking, I'll not deny: but I looked round, and I swore I wondered anyone would live in such a place when there were so many nice places where money would go three times as far in foreign countries; and I wondered you did not think of it, and take more interest yourself, and upon that I could see the old soger was thinking of fifty things, suspecting poor me of foul play among the number; and I was afraid for a minute I was going to have half a dozen claws in my smeller; but I turned it off, and I coaxed and wheedled a bit. You'd a laughed yourself black, till I had us both a-purring like a pair of old maid's cats.'

'I tell you what, Harry, there's madness there − literal madness,' said Charles, grasping his arm as he stopped and turned towards him, so that Harry had to come also to a standstill. 'Don't you know it − as mad as Bedlam? Just think!'

Harry laughed.

'Mad enough, by jingo!' said he.

'But don't you think so − actually mad?' repeated Charles.

'Well, it is near the wood, maybe, but I would not say quite mad − worse than mad, I dare say, by chalks, but I wouldn't place the old soger there,' said Harry.

'Where?' said Charles.

'I mean exactly among the mad 'uns. No, I wouldn't say mad, but as vicious − and worse, mayhap.'

'It does not matter much what we think, either of us; but I know what another fellow would have done long ago, but I could not bring myself to do that. I have thought it over often, but I couldn't − I *couldn't*.'

'Well, then, it ain't no great consequence,' said Harry, and he tightened his saddle girth a hole or two − 'no great consequence; but I couldn't 'a put a finger to that − mind; for I think the upper works is as sound as any, only there's many a devil beside mad 'uns. I give it in to you there.'

'And what do you advise me to do? − this sort of thing is dreadful,' said Charles.

'I was going to say, I think the best thing to be done is just to leave all that business, d'ye mind, to me.'

Harry mounted, and, leaning on his knee, he said:−

'I think I have a knack, if you leave it to me. Old Pipeclay doesn't think I have any reason to play false.'

'Rather the contrary,' said Charles, who was attentively listening.

'No interest at all,' pursued Harry, turning his eyes towards the distant knoll of Torston, and going on without minding Charles' suggestion:−

'Look, now, that beast'll follow my hand as sweet as sugar-candy, when you'd have nothing but bolting and baulking, and rearin' or worse.

There's plenty o' them little French towns or German – and don't you be botherin' your head about it; only do just as I tell ye, and I'll take all in hand.'

'You're an awfully good fellow, Harry; for, upon my soul, I was at my wits' end almost; having no one to talk to, and not knowing what anyone might be thinking of; and I feel safe in your hands, Harry, for I think you understand that sort of work so much better than I do – you understand people so much better – and I never was good at managing anyone, or anything for that matter; and – and when will business bring you to town again?'

'Three weeks or so, I wouldn't wonder,' said Harry.

'And I know, Harry, you won't forget me. I'm afraid to write to you almost; but if you'd think of any place we could meet and have a talk, I'd be ever so glad. You have no idea how fidgety and miserable a fellow grows that doesn't know what's going on.'

'Ay, to be sure; well, I've no objection. My book's made for ten days or so – a lot of places to go to – but I'll tip you a stave.'

'That's a good fellow; I know you won't forget me,' said Charles, placing his hand on his brother's arm.

'No – of course. Good-night, and take care of yourself, and give my love to Ally.'

'And – and, Harry?'

'Well?' answered Harry, backing his restless horse a little bit.

'I believe that's all.'

'Good-night, then.'

'Good-night,' echoed Charles.

Harry touched his hat with a smile, and was away the next moment, flying at a ringing trot over the narrow unfenced road that traverses the common, and dwindling in the distant moonlight.

'There he goes – light of heart; nothing to trouble him – life a holiday – the world a toy.'

He walked a little bit slowly in the direction of the disappearing horseman, and paused again, and watched him moodily till he was fairly out of sight.

'I hope he won't forget; he's always so busy about those stupid horses – a lot of money he makes, I dare say. I wish I knew something about them. I must beat about for some way of turning a penny. Poor little Alice! I hope I have not made a mull of it! I'll save every way I can – of course that's due to her; but when you come to think of it, and go over it all, there's very little you *can* give up. You can lay down your horses, if you have them, except one. You must have *one* in a place like this – you'd run a risk of starving, or never getting your letters, or dying for want of the doctor. And – I won't drink wine; brandy or Old Tom does just as well, and I'll give up smoking *totally*. A fellow must make sacrifices. I'll just work through this one box slowly, and order no more: it's all a bad habit, and I'll give it up.'

So he took a cigar from his case and lighted it.

'I'll not spend another pound on them, and the sooner these are out the better.'

He sauntered slowly away with his hands in his pockets to a little eminence about a hundred yards to the right, and mounted it, and looked all around, smoking. I don't think he saw much of that extensive view; but you would have fancied him an artist in search of the picturesque.

His head was full of ideas of selling Carwell Grange; but he was not quite sure that he had power, and did not half like asking his attorney, to whom he already owed something. He thought how snug and pleasant they might be comparatively in one of those quaint little toy towns in Germany, where dull human nature bursts its cerements, and floats and flutters away into a butterfly life of gold and colour – where the punter and the croupier assist at the worship of the brilliant and fickle goddess, and bands play sweetly, and people ain't buried alive in deserts and forests among dogs and 'chaw-bacons' – where little Alice would be all wonder and delight. Was it quite fair to bring her down here to immure her in the mouldering cloister of Carwell Grange?

He had begun now to re-enter the wooded ascent towards that melancholy mansion; his cigar was burnt out, and he said, looking towards his home through the darkness:–

'Poor little Alice! She does love me, I think – and that's something.'

CHAPTER 19

COMING IN

When at last her husband entered the room where she awaited him that night:–

'Oh! Charlie, it is very late,' said Alice, a little reproachfully.

'Not very, is it, darling?' said he, glancing at his watch. 'By Jove! it is. My poor little woman, I had not an idea.'

'I suppose I am very foolish, but I love you so much, Charlie, that I grow quite miserable when I am out of your sight.'

'I'm sorry, my darling, but I fancied he had a great deal more to tell me than he really had. I don't think I'm likely, at least for a little time, to be pressed by my duns – and – I wanted to make out exactly what money he's likely to get me for a horse he is going to sell, and I'm afraid, from what he says, it won't be very much; really, twenty pounds, one way or other, seems ridiculous, but it does make a very serious difference just now, and if I hadn't such a clever, careful little woman as you, I don't really know what I should do.'

He added this little complimentary qualification with an instinctive commiseration for the pain he thought he saw in her pretty face.

'These troubles won't last very long, Charlie, *perhaps*. Something, I'm sure, will turn up, and you'll see how careful I will be. I'll learn everything old Mildred can teach me, ever so much, and you'll see what a manager I will be.'

'You are my own little treasure. You always talk as if you were in the way, somehow, I don't know how. A wife like you is a greater help to me than one with two thousand a year and the reckless habits of a fine lady. Your wise little head and loving heart, my darling, are worth whole fortunes to me without them, and I do believe you are the first really good wife that ever a Fairfield married. You are the only creature I have on earth, that I'm quite sure of – the only creature.'

And so saying he kissed her, folding her in his arms, and, with a big tear filling each eye, she looked up, smiling unutterable affection, in his face. As they stood together in that embrace his eyes also filled with tears and his smile met hers, and they seemed wrapt for a moment in one angelic glory, and she felt the strain of his arm draw her closer.

Such moments come suddenly and are gone; but, remaining in memory, they are the lights that illuminate a dark and troublous retrospect for ever.

'We'll make ourselves happy here, little Ally, and I – in spite of everything, my darling! – and I don't know how it happened that I stayed away so long; but I walked with Harry farther than I intended, and when he left me I loitered on Cressley Common for a time with my head full of business; and so, without knowing it, I was filling my poor little wife's head with alarms and condemning her to solitude. Well, all I can do is to promise to be a good boy and to keep better hours for the future.'

'That's so like you – you are so good to your poor, foolish little wife,' said Alice.

'I wish I could be, darling,' said he; 'I wish I could prove one-half my love; but the time will come yet. I shan't be so poor or powerless always.'

'But you're not to speak so – you're not to think that. It is while we are poor that I can be of any use,' she said eagerly; 'very little, very miserable my poor attempts, but nothing makes me so happy as trying to deserve ever so little of all the kind things my Ry says of me; and I'm sure, Charlie, although there may be cares and troubles, we will make our time pass here very happily, and perhaps we shall always look back on our days at Carwell as the happiest of our lives.'

'Yes, darling, I am determined we shall be very happy,' said he.

'And Ry will tell me everything that troubles him?'

Her full eyes were gazing sadly up in his face. He adverted his eyes, and said: 'Of course I will, darling.'

'Oh! Ry, if you knew how happy that makes me!' she exclaimed. But there was that in the exclamation which seemed to say, 'If only I could be sure that you meant it.'

'Of course I will – that is, everything that could possibly interest you, for there are very small worries as well as great ones; and you know I really can't undertake to remember everything.'

'Of course, darling,' she answered; 'I only meant that if anything were really – any great anxiety – upon your mind, you would not be afraid to tell me. I'm not such a coward as I seem. You must not think me so foolish; and really, Ry, it pains me more to think that there is any anxiety weighing upon you, and concealed from me, than any disclosure could; and so I *know* – won't you?'

'Haven't I told you, darling, I really will,' he said, a little pettishly. 'What an odd way you women have of making a fellow say the same thing over and over again! I wonder it does not tire you – I know it does *us* awfully. Now, there, see, I really do believe you are going to cry.'

'Oh no, indeed!' she said, brightening up, and smiling with a sad little effort.

'And now, kiss me, my poor good little woman – you're not vexed with me? – no, I'm sure you're not,' said he.

She smiled a very affectionate assurance.

'And really, you poor little thing, it is awfully late, and you must be tired, and I've been – no, *not* lecturing, I'll never lecture, I hate it – but boring or teasing; I'm an odious dog, and I hate myself.'

So this little dialogue ended happily, and for a time Charles Fairfield forgot his anxieties, and a hundred pleasanter cares filled his young wife's head.

In such monastic solitudes as Carwell Grange the days pass slowly, but the retrospect of a month or a year is marvellously short. Twelve hours without an event is very slow to get over. But that very monotony, which is the soul of tediousness, robs the background of all the irregularities and objects which arrest the eye and measure distance in review, and thus it cheats the eye.

An active woman may be well content with an existence of monotony which would all but stifle even an indolent man. So long as there is a household – ever so frugal – to be managed, and the more frugal the more difficult and harassing – the female energies are tasked, and healthily because usefully exercised. But in this indoor administration the man is incompetent and in the way. His ordained activities are out of doors; and if these are denied him, he mopes away his days and feels that he cumbers the ground.

With little resource but his fishing-rod, and sometimes, when a fit of unwonted energy inspired him, his walking-stick, and a lonely march over the breezy expanse of Cressley Common, days, weeks, and months loitered their drowsy way into the past.

There were reasons why he did not care to court observation. Under other circumstances he would have ridden into the neighbouring towns and heard the news, and lunched with a friend here or there. But he did not want anyone to know that he was at the Grange; and if it should come out that he had been seen there, he would have had it thought that it was but a desultory visit.

A man less indolent, and perhaps not much more unscrupulous, would have depended upon a few offhand lies to account for his appearance, and would not have denied himself an occasional excursion into human society in those rustic haunts within his reach. But Charles Fairfield had not decision to try it, nor resource for a system of fibbing, and the easiest and dullest course he took.

In Paradise the man had his business – 'to dress and to keep' the garden, and, no doubt, the woman hers, suitable to her sex. It is a mistake to fancy that it is either a sign of love or conducive to its longevity that the happy pair should always pass the entire four-and-twenty hours in each other's company, or get over them in anywise without variety or usefulness.

Charles Fairfield loved his pretty wife. She made his inactive solitude more endurable than any man could have imagined. Still it was a dull existence, and, being also darkened with an ever-present anxiety, was a morbid one.

Small matters harassed him now. He brooded over trifles, and the one care which was really serious grew and grew in his perpetual contemplation until it became tremendous, and darkened his entire sky.

I can't say that Charles grew morose. It was not his temper but his spirits that failed – careworn and gloomy – his habitual melancholy depressed and even alarmed his poor little wife, who yet concealed her anxieties, and exerted her music and her invention – sang songs – told him old stories of the Wyvern folk, touched him with such tragedy and comedy as may be found in such miniature centres of rural life, and played backgammon with him, and sometimes écarté, and, in fact, nursed his sick spirits, as such angelic natures will.

Now and then came Harry Fairfield, but his visits were short and seldom, and, what was worse, Charles always seemed more harassed or

gloomy after one of his calls. There was something going on, and by no
means prosperously, she was sure, from all knowledge of which, however
it might ultimately concern her, and did immediately concern her
husband, she was jealously excluded.

Sometimes she felt angry – often pained – always troubled with untold
fears and surmises. Poor little Alice! It was in the midst of these secret
misgivings that a new care and hope visited her – a trembling, delightful
hope, that hovers between life and death sometimes in sad and mortal
fear – sometimes in delightful anticipation of a new and already beloved
life, coming so helplessly into this great world – unknown, to be her little
comrade, all dependent on that beautiful love with which her young
heart was already overflowing.

So almost trembling – hesitating – she told her little story with smiles
and tears, in a pleading, beseeching, almost apologetic way, that melted
the better nature of Charles, who told her how welcome to him, and
how beloved for her dear sake, the coming treasure should be, and held
her beating heart to his, in a long loving embrace, and, more than all, the
old love revived, and he felt how lonely he would be if his adoring little
wife were gone, and how gladly he would have given his life for hers.

And now came all the little cares and preparations that so mercifully
and delightfully beguile the period of suspense.

What is there so helpless as a new-born babe entering this great, rude,
cruel world? Yet we see how the beautiful and tender instincts which are
radiated from the sublime love of God provide everything for the
unconscious comer. Let us, then, take heart of grace when, the sad journey
ended, we, children of dust, who have entered so, are about to make the
dread exit, and, remembering what we have seen, and knowing that we go
in the keeping of the same 'faithful Creator', be sure that His love and tender
forecast have provided with equal care for our entrance into another life.

CHAPTER 20

HARRY APPEARS AT THE GRANGE

It was about four o'clock one afternoon, while Charles was smoking a
cigar – for, notwithstanding his self-denying resolutions, his case was
always replenished still – that his brother Harry rode into the yard, where
he was puffing away contemplatively at an open stable door.

'Delighted to see you, Harry. I was thinking of you this moment, by
Jove! and I can't tell you how glad I am,' said Charles, smiling as he
advanced, yet with an anxious inquiry in his eyes.

Harry took his extended hand, having dismounted, but he was looking at his horse, and not at Charles, as he said:–

'The last mile or so I noticed something in the off forefoot; do you? Look now – 'tain't brushing, nor he's not gone lame, but tender like; do you notice?' and he led him round a little bit.

'No,' said Charles, 'I don't see anything; but I am an ignoramus, you know – no – I think, nothing.'

''Tain't a great deal, anyhow,' said Harry, leading him towards the open stable door. 'I got your note, you know – and how are you all, and how is Ally?'

'Very well, poor little thing – we are all very well. Did you come from Wyvern?' said Charles.

'Yes.'

'And the old man just as usual, I suppose?'

'Just the same, only not growing no younger, you'll suppose.'

Charles nodded.

'And a d——d deal crosser, too. There's times, I can tell you, he won't stand no one nigh him – not even old Drake – d——d vicious.'

Harry laughed.

'They say he liked Ally – they do, upon my soul, and I wouldn't wonder – 'tis an old rat won't eat cheese – only you took the bit out o' his mouth, when you did, and that's enough to rile a fellow, you know.'

'Who says so?' asked Charles, with a flush on his face.

'The servants – yes – and the townspeople – it's pretty well about, and I think if it came to the old boy's ears there would be black eyes and bloody noses about it, I do.'

'Well, it's a lie,' said Charles; 'and don't, like a good fellow, tell poor little Alice there's any such nonsense talked about her at home – it would only vex her.'

'Well, I won't, if I think of it. Where's Tom? But 'twouldn't vex her – not a bit – quite 'tother way – there's never a girl in England wouldn't be pleased if old Parr himself wor in love wi' her, so she hadn't to marry him. But the governor, by Jove! I don't know a girl twelve miles round Wyvern, as big an old brute as he is, would turn up her nose at him, wi' all he has to grease her hand. But where's Tom? – the nag must have a feed.'

So they bawled for Tom, and Tom appeared, and took charge of the horse, receiving a few directions about his treatment from Master Harry, and then Charles led his brother in.

'I'm always glad to see you, Harry, but always, at the same time, a little anxious when you come,' said Charles, in a low tone, as they traversed the passage towards the kitchen.

''Tain't much – I have to tell you something, but first gi' me a mouthful, for I'm as hungry as a hawk, and a mug o' beer wouldn't hurt me while I'm waitin'. It's good hungry air this; you eat a lot, I dessay; the air alone stands you in fifty pounds a year, I reckon; that's paying pretty smart for what we're supposed to have for the takin'.'

And Harry laughed at his joke as they entered the dark old dining-room.

'Ally not here?' said Harry, looking round.

'She can't be very far off, but I'll manage something if she's not to be found.'

So Charles left Harry smiling out of the window at the tops of the trees, and drumming a devil's tattoo on the pane.

'Ho! Dulcibella. Is your mistress upstairs?'

'I think she is gone out to the garden, sir; she took her trowel and garden gloves, and the little basket wi' her,' answered the old woman.

'Well, don't disturb her – we'll not mind. I'll see old Mildred.'

So to old Mildred he betook himself.

'Here's Master Harry come very hungry, so send him anything you can make out, and in the meantime some beer, for he's thirsty too, and, like a good old soul, make all the haste you can.'

And with this conciliatory exhortation he returned to the room where he had left his brother.

'Ally has gone out to visit her flowers, but Mildred is doing the best she can for you, and we can go out and join Alice by-and-bye; but we are as well to ourselves for a little. I – I want to talk to you.'

'Well, fire away, my boy, with your big oak stick, as the Irishman says, though I'd rather have a mouthful first. Oh, here's the beer – thank ye, Chick-a-biddy. Where the devil did you get that queer-looking fair one?' he asked, when the Hebe, Lilly Dogger, disappeared. 'I'll lay you fifty it was Ally chose that one.'

And he laughed obstreperously.

And he poured out a tumbler of beer and drank it, and then another and drank it, and poured out a third to keep at hand while he conversed.

'There used to be some old pewter goblets here in the kitchen – I wonder what's gone wi' them – they were grand things for drinking beer out of – the pewter, while ye live – there's nothing like it for beer – or porter, by Jove! Have you got any porter?'

'No, not any; but do, like a good old fellow, tell me anything you have picked up that concerns me – there's nothing pleasant, I know – there can be nothing pleasant, but if there's anything, I should rather have it now, than wait, be it ever so bad.'

'I wish you'd put some other fellow on this business, I know – for you'll come to hate the sight of me if I'm always bringing you bad news; but it is *not* good, that's a fact; that beast is getting unmanageable. By the law, here comes something for a hungry fellow; thank ye, my lass, God bless ye, feeding the hungry. How can I pay ye back, my dear? I don't know, unless by takin' ye in – ha, ha, ha! – whenever ye want shelter, mind; but you're too sharp, I warrant, to let any fellow take you in, with them roguish eyes you've got. See how she blushes, the brown little rogue!' he giggled after her with a leer, as Lilly Dogger, having placed his extemporised luncheon on the table, edged hurriedly out of the room.

'Devilish fine eyes she's got, and a nice little set of ivories, sir. By Jove! I didn't half see her; pity she's not a bit taller; and them square shoulders. But hair – she has nice hair, and teeth and eyes goes a long way.'

He had stuck his fork in a rasher while making his pretty speech, and was champing away greedily by the time he had come to the end of his sentence.

'But what has turned up in that quarter? You were going to tell me something when this came in,' asked Charles.

'About the old soger? Well, if you don't mind a fellow's talkin' with his mouth full, I'll try when I can think of it; but the noise of eating clears a fellow's head of everything, I think.'

'Do, like a dear fellow. I can hear you perfectly,' urged Charles.

'I'm afraid,' said Harry, with his mouth full, as he had promised, 'she'll make herself devilish troublesome.'

'Tell us all about it,' said Charles, uneasily.

'I told you I was running up to London – we haven't potatoes like these up at Wyvern – and so I did go, and, as I promised, I saw the old beast at Hoxton; and hang me, but I think someone has been putting her up to mischief.'

'How do you mean? – what sort of mischief?' asked Charles.

'I think she's got uneasy about you. She was asking all sorts of questions.'

'Yes – well?'

'And I wouldn't wonder if some one was telling her – I was going to say lies – but I mean something like the truth – ha, ha, ha! By the law, I've been telling such a hatful of lies about myself, that I hardly know which is which, or one end from t'other.'

'Do you mean to say she was abusing me, or *what*?' urged Charles, very uncomfortably.

'I don't suppose you care very much what the old soger says of you. It ain't pretty, you may be sure, and it don't much signify. But it ain't all talk, you know. She's always grumblin', and I don't mind *that* – her ticdooleroo, and her nerves, and her nonsense. She wants carriage exercise, she says, and the court doctor – I forget his name – ha, ha, ha! and she says you allow her next to nothing, and keeps her always on the starving line, and she won't stand it no longer, she swears; and you'll have to come down with the dust, my boy.'

And florid, stalwart Harry laughed again as if the affair was a good joke.

'I can't help it, Harry; she has always had more than her share. I've been too generous, I've been a d———d fool always.'

Charles spoke with extreme bitterness, but quietly, and there was a silence of two or three minutes, during which Harry's eyes were on his plate, and the noise of his knife and fork and the crunching of his repast under his fine teeth were the only sounds heard.

Seeing that Harry seemed disposed to confine his attention for the present to his luncheon, Charles Fairfield, who apprehended something worse, said:—

'If that's all, it is nothing very new. I've been hearing that sort of thing for fully ten years. She's ungrateful, and artful, and violent. There's no use in wishing or regretting now; but God knows, it was an evil day for me when first I saw that woman's face.'

Charles was looking down on the table as he spoke, and tapping on it feverishly with the tips of his fingers. Harry's countenance showed that unpleasant expression which sometimes overcame its rustic freshness. The attempt to discharge an unsuitable smile or a dubious expression from the face – the attempt, shall we bluntly say, of a rogue to look simple.

It is a loose way of talking and thinking which limits the vice of hypocrisy to the matter of religion. It counterfeits all good, and dissimulates all evil, every day and hour; and among the men who frankly admit themselves to be publicans and sinners, whose ways are notoriously worldly, and who never affected religion, are some of the worst and meanest hypocrites on earth.

Harry Fairfield having finished his luncheon, had laid his knife and fork on his plate, and, leaning back in his chair, was ogling them with an unmeaning stare, and a mouth a little open, affecting a brown study; but no effort can quite hide the meaning and twinkle of cunning, and nothing is more repulsive than this semi-transparent mask of simplicity.

Thus the two brothers sat, neither observing the other much, with an outward seeming of sympathy, but with very divergent thoughts.

Charles, as we know, was a lazy man, with little suspicion, and rather an admiration of his brother's worldly wisdom and activity – with a wavering belief in Harry's devotion to his cause, sometimes a little disturbed when Harry seemed for a short time hard and selfish, or careless, but generally returning with a quiet self-assertion, like the tide on a summer day.

For my part I don't exactly know how much or how little Harry cared for Charles. The Fairfields were not always what is termed a 'united' family, and its individual members, in prosecuting their several objects, sometimes knocked together, and occasionally, in the family history, more violently and literally than was altogether seemly.

CHAPTER 21

HARRY'S BEER AND CONVERSATION

At last, Harry, looking out of the window, as he leaned back in his chair, said, in a careless sort of way, but in a low tone:

'Did you ever tell Alice anything about it before you came here?'

'Alice?' said Charles, wincing and looking very pale. 'Well, you know, why should I?'

'You know best, of course, but I thought you might, maybe,' answered Harry, stretching himself with an imperfect yawn.

'No,' said Charles, looking down with a flush.

'She never heard anything about it at any time, then? – and mind, my dear fellow, I'm only asking. You know much better than me what's best to be done; but the old brute will give you trouble, I'm afeard. She'll be writing letters, and maybe printing things; but you don't take in the papers here, so it won't come so much by surprise, like.'

'Alice knows nothing of it. She never heard of her,' said Charles.

'I wish she may have heard as little of Alice,' said Harry.

'Why, you don't mean to say——' began Charles, and stopped.

'I think the woman has got some sort of a maggot in her head. I think she has, more than common, and you'll find I'm right.'

Charles got up and stood at the window for a little.

'I can't guess what you mean, Harry. I don't know what you think. Do tell me, if you have any clear idea, what is she thinking of?'

'I don't know what to think, and upon my soul that one's so deep!' said Harry. 'But I'd bet something she's heard more than we'd just like about this, and, if so, there'll be wigs on the green.'

'There has been nothing – I mean no letter; I have not heard from her for months – not since you saw her before. I think if there had been anything unusual in her mind she would have written. Don't you? I dare say what you saw was only one of those ungoverned outbreaks of temper that mean nothing.'

'I hope so,' said Harry.

'I blame myself – I'm no villain, I didn't mean badly, but I'm a cursed fool. It's all quite straight, though, and it doesn't matter a farthing what she does – not a farthing,' broke out Charles Fairfield. 'But I would not have poor little Alice frightened and made miserable; and what had I best do, and where do you think we had best go?' He lowered his voice, and glanced towards the door as he said this, suddenly remembering that Alice might come in the midst of their consultation.

'Go? For the present aren't you well enough where you are? Wait a bit, anyhow. But I wonder you didn't tell Alice; she ought to 'a known something about it – oughtn't she, before you married her, or whatever you call it.'

'Before I married her? of course,' said Charles, sternly; 'married her! – you don't mean, I fancy, to question my marriage?'

Charles was looking at him with a very grim, steady gaze.

'Why, what the devil should I know, or care about lawyers' nonsense and pleadings, my dear fellow? I never could make head or tail of them, only as we are talking here so confidential, you and me, whatever came uppermost – I forget what – I just rapped out. Has that Hoxton lady any family?'

'Don't you know she has not?' replied Charles.

'I know it now, but she might have a sieve full for anything I knew,' answered Harry.

'I think, Harry, if you really thought she and I were married, that was too important a question for you, wasn't it, to be forgotten so easily?' said Charles.

'Important – how so?' asked Harry.

'How so, my dear Harry? Why, you can't be serious – you haven't forgot that the succession to Wyvern depends on it,' exclaimed Charles Fairfield.

'Bah! Wyvern indeed! Why, man, the thought never came near me – me Wyvern! Sich pure rot! We Fairfields lives good long lives mostly, and marries late sometimes; there's forty good years before ye. Gad, Charlie, you must think o' summat more likely if you want folk to believe ye. Ye'll not hang me on that count – no, no.'

And he laughed.

'Well, I think so; I'm glad of it, for you know I wrote to tell you about what is, I hope, likely to be. It has made poor little Alice so happy; and if there should come an heir, you know he'd be another squire of Wyvern in a long line of Fairfields, and it wouldn't do, Harry, to have a doubt thrown on him, and I'm glad to hear you say the pretence of that d——d woman's marriage is a lie.'

'Well, you know best,' said Harry. 'I'm very sorry for Alice, poor little thing, if there's ever any trouble at all about it.'

And he looked through the windows along the tops of the tufted trees that caught the sunlight softly, with his last expression of condolence.

'You *have* said more than once – I don't say to-day – that you were sure – that you knew as well as I did there was nothing in that woman's story.'

'Isn't that someone coming?' said Harry, turning his head towards the door.

'No – no one,' said Charles, after a moment's silence. 'But you *did* say so, Harry – you *know* you did.'

'Well, if I did I did, that's all, but I don't remember,' said Harry, 'and I am sure you make a mistake.'

'A mistake? What do you mean?' asked Charles.

'I mean, marriage or no marriage, I never meant to say as you suppose – I know nothing about it, whatever I may think,' said Harry, sturdily.

'You know everything that I know – I've told you everything,' answered Charles Fairfield.

'And what o' that? How can you or me tell whether it makes a marriage or not; and I won't be quoted by you or anyone else, as having made such a mouth of myself as to lay down the law in a case that might puzzle a judge,' said Harry, darkening.

'You believe the facts I've told you, I fancy?' said Charles, sternly.

'You meant truth, I'm sure o' that, and beyond that I believe nothing but what I have said myself, and more I won't say for the king,' said Harry, putting his hands in his pockets, and looking sulkily at Charles, with his mouth a little open.

Charles looked awfully angry.

'You know very well, Harry, you have fifty times told me there was nothing in it, and you have even said that the person herself thinks so too,' he said at last, restraining himself.

'That I never said, by –,' said Harry, coolly, who was now standing with his back against the window shutters, and his hands in his pockets. As he so spoke he crossed one sinewy leg over the other, and continued to direct from the corner of his eye a sullen gaze upon his brother.

With the same oath that brother told him he lied.

Here followed a pause, as when a train is fired and men are doubtful whether the mine will spring. The leaves rustled and the flies hummed happily outside as if those seconds were charged with nothing, and the big feeble bee, who had spent the morning in walking up a pane of glass and slipping down again, continued his stumbling exercise as if there was nothing else worth attending to for a mile round Carwell Grange.

Harry had set both heels on the ground at this talismanic word; one hand clenched had come from his pocket to his thigh, and from his eyes 'leaped' the old Fairfield fury.

It was merely, as Harry would have said, the turn of a shilling whether a Fairfield battle, short, sharp, and decisive, had not tried the issue at that instant.

'I don't vally a hot word spoke in haste; it's ill raising hands between brothers – let it pass. I'm about the last friend ye've left just now, and I don't see why ye should seek to put a quarrel on me. It's little to me, you know – no thanks, loss o' time, and like to be more kicks than ha'pence.'

Harry spoke these words after a considerable pause.

'I was wrong, Harry, I mean, to use such a word, and I beg your pardon,' said Charles, extending his hand to his brother, who took his fingers and dropped them with a rather short and cold shake.

'Ye shouldn't talk that way to a fellow that's taken some trouble about ye, and ye know I'm short tempered – we all are, and 'tisn't the way to handle me,' said Harry.

'I was wrong, I know I was, and I'm sorry – I can't say more,' answered Charles. 'But there it is! If there's trouble about this little child that's coming, what am I to do? Wouldn't it be better for me to be in Wyvern churchyard?'

Harry lowered his eyes, with his mouth still open, to the threadbare carpet. His hands were again both reposing quietly in his pockets.

After a silence he said:–

'If you had told me anything about what was in your head concerning Alice Maybell, I'd 'a told you my mind quite straight; and if you ask it now, I can only tell you one thing, and that is, I think you're married to t'other woman – I hate her like poison, but that's nothing to do wi't, and I'd a been for making a clear breast of it, and telling Ally everything, and let her judge for herself. But you wouldn't look before you, and you've got into a nice pound, I'm afraid.'

'I'm not a bit afraid about it,' said Charles, very pale. 'Only for the world I would not have her frightened and vexed just now – and, Harry, there's nothing like speaking out, as you say, and I can't help thinking that your opinion [and at another time, perhaps, he would have added, your memory] is biased by the estate.'

Charles spoke bitterly or petulantly, which you will. But Harry seemed to have made up his mind to take this matter coolly, and so he did.

'Upon my soul, I wouldn't wonder,' he said, with a kind of laugh. 'Though if it does I give you my oath I am not aware of it. But take it so if you like; it's only saying a fellow loves his shirt very well, but his skin better, and I suppose so we do, you and me, both of us; only this I'll say, 'twill be all straight and above board 'twixt you and me, and I'll do the best I can for ye – you don't doubt that?'

'No, Harry, you'll not deceive me.'

'No, of course; and, as I say, I think that brute – the Hoxton one – she's took a notion in her head——'

'To give me trouble?'

'A notion,' continued Harry, 'that there's another woman in the case; and, if you ask me, I think she'll not rest quiet for long. She says she's your wife; and one way or another she'll pitch into any girl that says the same for herself. She's like a mad horse, you know, when she's riled; and she'd kick through a wall and knock herself to pieces to get at you, I wish she was sunk in the sea.'

'Tell me, what do you think she is going to do?' asked Charles, uneasily.

'Upon my soul, I can't guess; but 'twouldn't hurt you, I think, if you kept fifty pounds or so in your pocket to give her the slip, if she should begin manoeuvring with any sort o' dodges that looked serious; and if I hear any more I'll let you know; and I've stayed here longer than I meant; and I ha'n't seen Ally; but you'll make my compliments, and tell her I was too hurried; and my nag's had his feed by this time; and I've stayed too long.'

'Well, Harry, thank you very much. It's a mere form asking you to remain longer; there's nothing to offer you worth staying for; and this is such a place, and I so heart-broken – and – we part good friends – don't we?'

'The best,' said Harry carelessly. 'Have you a cigar or two? Thanks; you may as well make it three – thank ye – jolly good 'uns. I've a smart ride before me; but I think I'll make something of it, *rayther*. My hands are pretty full always. I'd give ye more time if they wasn't; but keep your powder dry, and a sharp look-out, and so will I, and gi' my love to Ally, and tell her to keep up her heart, and all will go right, I dare say.'

By this time they had threaded the passage and were in the stable-yard again; and, mounting his horse, Harry turned, and, with a wag of his head and a farewell grin, rode slowly over the pavement, and disappeared through the gate.

Charles was glad that he had gone without seeing Alice. She would certainly have perceived that something was wrong. He thought for a moment of going to the garden to look for her, but the same consideration prevented him doing so, and he took his fishing-rod instead, and went off the other way, to look for a trout in the brook that flows through Carwell Glen.

CHAPTER 22

THE TROUT

Down the glen, all the way to the ruined windmill, sauntered Charles Fairfield, before he put his rod together and adjusted his casting line. Very nervous he was, almost miserable. But he was not a man instinctively to strike out a course on an emergency, or to reduce his resolves promptly to action; neither was he able yet to think very clearly on his situation. Somehow his brother Harry was constantly before him in a new and dismal light. Had there not peeped out to-day, instead of the boot of that horsey, jolly fellow, the tip of a cloven hoof that cannot be mistaken? Oh, Harry, brother! Was he meditating treason, and going to take arms in the cause of the murderer of his peace? He was so cunning and so energetic that Charles stood in awe of him, and thought if his sword were pointed at his breast that he might as well surrender and think no more of safety. Harry had been too much in his confidence, and had been too often in conference with that evil person whom he called 'the old soger,' to be otherwise than formidable as an enemy. An enemy he trusted he never would see him. An unscrupulous one in his position could work fearful mischief to him by a little colouring and perversion of things that had occurred. He would not assume such a transformation possible.

But always stood before him Harry in his altered mien and estranged looks, as he had seen him, sullen and threatening, that day.

What would he not have given to be sure that the wicked person whom he now dreaded more than he feared all other powers had formed no actual design against him? If she had, what was the agency that had kindled her evil passions and excited her activity? He could not fancy Harry such a monster.

What were her plans? Did she mean legal proceedings? He would have given a good deal for light, no matter what it may disclose; anything but suspense, and the phantasmal horrors with which imagination peoples darkness.

Never did harassed brain so need the febrifuge of the angler's solace, and quickly his cares and agitations subsided in that serene absorption. One thing only occurred for a moment to divert his attention from his tranquillising occupation. Standing on a flat stone near midway in the stream, he was throwing his flies over a nook where he had seen a trout rise, when he heard the ring of carriage wheels on the road that passes round the base of the old windmill, and pierces the dense wood that darkened the glen of Carwell.

Raising his eyes, he did see a carriage following that unfrequented track. A thin screen of scattered trees prevented his seeing this carriage very distinctly. But the road is so little a thoroughfare that, except an occasional cart, few wheeled vehicles ever traversed it. A little anxiously he watched this carriage till it disappeared totally in the wood. He felt uncomfortably that its destination was Carwell Grange, and at that point conjecture failed him.

This little incident was, I think, the only one that for a moment disturbed the serene abstraction of his trout-fishing.

And now the sun beginning to approach the distant hills warned him that it was time to return. So listlessly he walked homeward, and as he ascended the narrow and melancholy track that threads the Glen of Carwell his evil companions, the fears and cares that tortured him, returned.

Near Carwell Grange the road makes a short but steep ascent, and a slight opening in the trees displays on the eminence a little platform on the verge of the declivity, from which a romantic view down the glen and over a portion of the lower side unfolds itself.

Here for a time he paused, looking westward on the sky already glowing in the saddened splendours of sunset. From this miserable rumination he carried away one resolution, hard and clear. It was painful to come to it – but the torture of concealment was more dreadful. He had made up his mind to tell Alice exactly how the facts were. One ingredient – and he fancied, just then, the worst in his cup of madness – was the torture of secrecy, and the vigilance and the uncertainties of concealment. Poor little Alice, he felt, ought to know. It was her right. And the attempt longer to conceal it would make her much more miserable, for he could not disguise his sufferings, and she would observe them, and be abandoned to the solitary anguish of suspense.

As he entered the Grange he was reminded of the carriage which he had observed turning up the narrow Carwell road by actually seeing it standing at the summit of the short and steep ascent to the Grange.

Coming suddenly upon this object, with its natty well-appointed air, contrasting with the old-world neglect and homeliness of all that surrounded, he stopped short with an odd Robinson Crusoe shyness and surveyed the intruding vehicle.

This survey told him nothing. He turned sharply into the back entrance of the Grange, disturbed, and a good deal vexed.

It could not be an invasion of the enemy. Carriage, harness, and servants were much too smart for that. But if the neighbours had found them out, and that this was the beginning of a series of visits, could anything in a small way be more annoying, and even dangerous? Here was a very necessary privacy violated, with what ulterior consequences who could calculate.

This was certainly Alice's doing. Women *are* such headstrong, silly creatures!

CHAPTER 23

THE VISITOR

The carriage which Charles Fairfield had seen rounding the picturesque ruin of Gryce's Mill was that of Lady Wyndale. Mrs Tarnley opened the door to her summons, and, acting on her general instructions, said, 'Not at home.'

But good Lady Wyndale was not so to be put off. She had old Mildred to the side of the carriage.

'I know my niece will be glad to see me,' she said. 'I'm Lady Wyndale, and you are to take this card in, and tell my niece, Mrs Fairfield, I have come to see her.'

Mrs Tarnley looked with a dubious scrutiny at Lady Wyndale, for she had no idea that Alice could have an aunt with a title and a carriage. On the whole, however, she thought it best to take the card in, and almost immediately it was answered by Alice, who ran out to meet her aunt and throw her arms about her neck, and led her into Carwell Grange.

'Oh! darling, darling! I'm so delighted to see you! It was so good of you to come. But how did you find me out?' said Alice, kissing her again and again.

'There's no use, you see, in being secret with me. I made out where you were, though you meant to keep me quite in the dark, and I really don't think I ought to have come near you, and I am very much affronted,' said kind old Lady Wyndale, a little high.

'But, auntie, darling, didn't you get my letter telling you that we were married?' pleaded Alice.

'Yes, and that you had left Wyvern; but you took good care not to tell me where you were going, and in fact if it had not been for the good housekeeper at Wyvern, to whom I wrote, I suppose I should have lived and died within fifteen miles of you, thinking all the time that you had gone to France.'

'We were thinking of that, I told you,' pleaded Alice, eagerly.

'Well, here you have been for three months, and I've been living within a two hours' drive of you, and dreading all the time that you were four hundred miles away. I have never once seen your face. I don't think that was good-natured.'

'Oh, dear aunt, forgive me,' entreated Alice. 'You will when you know all. If you knew how miserable I have often been, thinking how ungrateful and odious I must have appeared, how meanly reserved and basely suspicious, all the time longing for nothing on earth so much as a sight of your beloved face, and a good talk over everything with you, my best and truest friend.'

'There, kiss me, child; I'm not angry, only sorry, darling, that I should have lost so much of your society, which I might have enjoyed often very much,' said the placable old lady.

'But, darling aunt, I *must* tell you how it was – you must hear me. You know how I idolise you, and you can't know, but you may imagine, what, in this solitary place, and with cares and fears so often troubling me, your kind and delightful society would have been to me; but my husband made it a point, that just for the present I should divulge our retreat to no one on earth. I pleaded for you, and in fact there is not another person living to whom I should have dreamed of disclosing it;

but the idea made him so miserable, and he urged it with so much entreaty and earnestness, that I could not without a quarrel have told you, and he promised that my silence should be enforced only for a very short time.'

'Dear me! I'm so sorry,', said Lady Wyndale, very much concerned. 'It must be that the poor man is very much dipped and is literally hiding himself here. You poor little thing! Is he in debt?'

'I am afraid he is. I can't tell you how miserable it sometimes makes me; not that he allows me ever to feel it, except in these precautions, for we are, though in a very homely way, perfectly comfortable – you would not believe how comfortable – but we really are,' said poor, loyal little Alice, making the best of their frugal and self-denying life.

'Your room is very snug. I like an old-fashioned room,' said the good-natured old lady, looking round; 'and you make it so pretty with your flowers. Is there any ornament like them? And you have such an exquisite way of arranging them. It is an art; no one can do it like you. You know I always got you to undertake ours at Oulton, and you remember Tremaine standing beside you, trying, as he said, to learn the art, though I fancy he was studying something prettier.'

Alice laughed. Lord Tremaine was a distant figure now, and this little triumph a dream of the past. But is not the spirit of woman conquest? Is not homage the air in which she lives and blooms? So Alice's dark, soft eyes dropped for a moment sidelong with something like the faintest blush, and a little dimpling smile.

'But all that's over, you know,' said Lady Wyndale; 'you would insist on putting a very effectual extinguisher upon it, so there's an end of my match-making, and I hope you may be very happy your own way, and I'm sure you will, and you know any little money trouble can't last long, and then I'm told Wyvern *must* be his; and the Fairfields were always thought to have some four or five thousand a year, and although the estate, they say, owes something, yet a prudent little woman like you will get all that right in time.'

'You are always so kind and cheery, you darling,' said Alice, looking fondly and smiling in her face as she placed a hand on each shoulder. 'It is delightful seeing you at last. But you are tired, ain't you? You must take something.'

'Thanks, dear. I'll have a little tea – nothing else. I lunched before we set out.'

So Alice touched the bell, and the order was taken by Mildred Tarnley.

'And how is that nice, good-natured old creature, Dulcibella Crane? I like her so much. She seems so attached. I hope you have her still with you?'

'Oh yes. I could not exist without her – dear old Dulcibella, of course.'

There was here a short silence.

'I was thinking of asking you if you could all come over to Oulton for a month or so. I'm told your husband is such an agreeable man, and very unlike Mr Harry Fairfield, his brother – a mere bear, they tell me; and do you think your husband would venture? We should be quite to ourselves if you preferred it, and we could make it almost as quiet as here.'

'It is so like you, you darling, and to me would be so delightful; but no, no, it is quite out of the question; he is really – this is a great secret, and you won't say a word to anyone – I am afraid very much harassed. He is very miserable about his affairs. There has been a quarrel with old Mr Fairfield which makes the matter worse. His brother Harry has been trying to arrange with his creditors, but I don't know how that will be; and Charlie has told me that we must be ready on very short notice to go to France or somewhere else abroad; and I'm afraid he owes a great deal – he's so reserved and nervous about it; and you may suppose how I must feel, how miserable sometimes, knowing that I am, in great measure, the cause of his being so miserably harassed. Poor Charlie! I often think how much happier it would have been for him never to have seen me.'

'Did I ever hear such stuff! But I won't say half what I was going to say, for I can't think you such a fool, and I must only suppose you want me to say ever so many pretty things to you, which, in this case, I am bound to say would be, unlike common flatteries, quite true. But if there really is any trouble of that kind – of the least consequence, I mean – I think it quite a scandal, not only shabby but wicked, that old Mr Fairfield, with one foot in the grave, should do nothing. I always knew he was a mere bruin; but people said he was generous in the matter of money, and he ought to think that, in the course of nature, Wyvern should have been his son's years ago, and it is really quite abominable his not coming forward.'

'There's no chance of that; there has been a quarrel,' said Alice, looking down on the threadbare carpet.

'Well, darling, remember, if it should come to that – I mean if he should be advised to go away for a little, remember that your home is at Oulton. He'll not stay away very long, but, if you accept my offer, the longer the happier for me. You are to come over to Oulton, you understand, and to bring old Dulcibella; and I only wish that you had been a few years married that we might set up a little nursery in that dull house. I think I should live ten years longer if I had the prattle and laughing and pleasant noise of children in the old nursery – the same nursery where my poor dear George ran about, sixty years ago nearly, when he was a child. We should have delightful times, you and I, and I'd be your head nurse.'

'My darling, I think you are an angel,' said Alice, with a little laugh, and throwing her arms about her she wept on her thin old neck; and the old lady, weeping also happy and tender tears, patted her shoulder gently in that little silence.

'Well, Alice, you'll remember, and I'll write to your husband as well as to you, for this kind of invitation is never attended to, and you would think nothing of going away and leaving your old auntie to shift for herself; and if you will come it will be the kindest thing you ever did, for I'm growing old, and strangers don't amuse me quite as much as they did, and I really want a little home society to exercise my affections and prevent my turning into a selfish old cat.'

So the tea came in, and they sipped it to the accompaniment of their little dialogue, and time glided away unperceived, and the door opened, and Charles Fairfield, in his careless fishing costume, entered the room.

He glanced at Alice a look which she understood; her visitor also perceived it; but Charles had not become a mere Orson in this wilderness, so he assumed an air of welcome.

'We are so glad to see you here, Lady Wyndale, though, indeed, it ain't easy to see anyone, the room is so dark. It was so very good of you to come this long drive to see Alice.'

'I hardly hoped to have seen you,' replied the old lady, 'for I must go in a minute or two more, and – I'm very frank, and you won't think me rude, but I have learned everything, and I know that I ought not to have come without a little more circumspection.'

He laughed a little, and Alice thought, as well as the failing light enabled her to see, that he looked very pale, as, laughing, he fixed for a moment a hard look on her.

'All is not a great deal,' he said, not knowing very well what to say.

'No, no,' said the old lady: 'there's no one on earth, almost, who has not suffered at one time or other that kind of passing annoyance. You know that Alice and I are such friends, so very intimate that I feel as if I knew her husband almost as intimately, although you were little more than a boy when I last saw you, and I'm afraid it must seem very impertinent my mentioning Alice's little anxieties, but I could not well avoid doing so without omitting an explanation which I ought to make, because this secret little creature, your wife, with whom I was very near being offended, was perfectly guiltless of my visit, and I learned where she was from your old housekeeper at Wyvern, and from no one else on earth did I receive the slightest hint, and I thought it very ill-natured, being so near a relation and friend, and when you know me a little better, Mr Fairfield, you'll not teach Alice to distrust me.'

Then the kind old lady diverged into her plans about Alice and Oulton, and promised a diplomatic correspondence, and at length she took her leave for the last time, and Charles saw her in her carriage, and bade her a polite farewell.

Away drove the carriage, and Charles stood listlessly at the summit of the embowered and gloomy road that descends in one direction into the Vale of Carwell, and passes in the other, with some windings, to the wide heath of Cressley Common.

The visit, untoward as it was, was, nevertheless, a little stimulus. He felt his spirits brightening, his pulse less sluggish, and something more of confidence in his future.

'There's time enough in which to tell her my trouble,' thought he, as he turned towards the house; 'and, by Jove! we haven't had our dinner. I must choose the time. To-night it shall be. We will both be, I think, less miserable when it is told,' and he sighed heavily.

He entered the house through the back gate, and as he passed the kitchen door called to Mildred Tarnley, the emphatic word 'Dinner!'

CHAPTER 24

THE SUMMONS

When Charles Fairfield came into the wainscoted dining-room a few minutes later it looked very cosy. The sun had broken the pile of western clouds, and sent low and level a red light flecked with trembling leaves on the dark panels that faced the windows.

Outside in that farewell glory of the day the cawing crows were heard returning to the sombre woods of Carwell, and the small birds whistled and warbled pleasantly in the clear air, and chatty sparrows in the ivy round gossiped and fluttered merrily before the little community betook themselves to their leafy nooks and couched their busy little heads for the night under their brown wings.

He looked through the window towards the gloriously stained sky and darkening trees, and he thought:—

'A fellow like me, who has seen out his foolish days and got to value better things, who likes a pretty view, and a cigar, and a stroll by a trout brook, and a friendly guest, and a quiet glass of wine, and who has a creature like Alice to love and be loved by, might be devilish happy in this queer, lonely corner, if only the load were off his heart.'

He sighed; but something of that load was for the moment removed; and as pretty Alice came in at the open door he went to meet her, and drew her fondly to his heart.

'We must be very happy this evening, Alice. Somehow I feel that everything will go well with us yet. If just a few little hitches and annoyances were got over, I should be the happiest fellow, I think, that ever bore the name of Fairfield; and you, darling creature, are the light of that happiness. My crown and my life – my beautiful Alice, my joy and my glory – I wish you knew half how I love you, and how proud I am of you.'

'Oh, Charlie, Charlie, this is delightful. Oh, Ry, my darling! I'm too happy.'

And with these words, in the strain of her slender embrace, she clung to him as he held her locked to his heart.

The affection was there; the love was true. In the indolent nature of Charles Fairfield capabilities of good were not wanting. That dreadful interval in the soul's history, between the weak and comparatively noble state of childhood and that later period when experience saddens and illuminates and begins to turn our looks regretfully backward, was long past with him. The period when women 'come out' and see the world, and men in the old-fashioned phrase 'sow their wild oats' – that glorious summer time of self-love, sin, and folly – that bleak and bitter winter of the soul, through which the mercy of God alone preserves for us alive the dormant germs of good, was past for him, without killing, as it sometimes does, all the tenderness and truth of the nursery. In this man, Charles Fairfield, were the trodden-down but still living affections which now, in this season, unfolded themselves anew – simplicity unkilled, and the purity not of Eden, not of childhood, but of *recoil*. Altogether a man who had not lost himself – capable of being happy – capable of being regenerated.

I know not exactly what had evoked this sudden glow and effervescence. Perhaps it needs some manifold confluence of internal and external conditions, trifling and unnoticed, except for such unexplained results, to evolve these tremblings and lightings up that surprise us like the fiercer analogies of volcanic chemistry.

It is sad to see what appear capabilities and opportunities of a great happiness so nearly secured, and yet by reason of some inflexible caprice of circumstance quite unattainable.

It was not for some hours, and until after his wife had gone to her room, that the darkness and chill that portended the return of his worst care crept over him as he sat and turned over the leaves of his book.

He got up and loitered discontentedly about the room. Stopping now before the little bookshelves between the windows and adjusting unconsciously their contents; now at the little oak table, and fiddling with the flowers which Alice had arranged in a tall old glass, one of the relics of other days of Carwell; and so on, listless, irresolute.

'So here I am once more – back again among my enemies! Happiness for me, a momentary illusion – hope a cheat. My *reality* is the blackness of the abyss. God help me!'

He turned up his eyes, and he groaned this prayer, unconscious that it was a prayer.

'I will,' he thought, 'extract the sting from this miserable mystery. Between me and Alice it shall be a secret no longer. I'll tell her to-morrow. I'll look out an opportunity; I will, by——'.

And to nail himself to his promise this irresolute man repeated the same passionate oath, and he struck his hand on the table.

Next day, therefore, when Alice was again among the flowers in the garden, he entered that antique and solemn shade with a strange sensation at his heart of fear and grief. How would Alice look on him after it was over? How would she bear it?

Pale as the man who walks after the coffin of his darling, between the tall grey piers he entered that wild and umbrageous enclosure.

His heart seemed to stop still as he saw little Alice, all unsuspicious of his dreadful message, working with her tiny trowel at the one sunny spot of the garden.

She stood up – how pretty she was! – looking on her work; and as she stood with one tiny foot advanced, and her arms folded, with her garden gloves on, and the little diamond-shaped trowel glittering in her hand, she sang low to herself an air which he remembered her singing when she was quite a little thing long ago at Wyvern – when he never dreamed she could be anything to him – just a picture of a little brown-haired girl and nothing dearer.

Then she saw him, and:—

'Oh, Ry, darling!' she cried, as, making a diagonal from the distant point, she ran towards him through tall trees and old raspberries, and under the boughs of over-grown fruit trees, which nowadays bore more moss and lichen than pears or cherries upon them.

'Ry, how delightful! You so seldom come here, and, now I have you, you shall see all I'm doing, and how industrious I have been; and we are going to have such a happy little ramble. Has anything happened, darling?' she said, suddenly stopping and looking in his face.

Here was an opportunity; but if his resolution was still there, presence of mind failed him, and, forcing a smile, he instantly answered:—

'Nothing, darling – nothing whatever. Come, let us look at your work; you are so industrious, and you have such wonderful taste.'

And as, reassured, and holding his hand, she prattled and laughed, leading him round by the grass-grown walks to her garden, as she called that favoured bit of ground on which the sun shone, he hardly saw the old currant bushes or grey trunks of the rugged trees; his sight seemed dazzled; his hearing seemed confused; and he thought to himself:—

'Where am I – what is this – and can it be true that I am so weak or so mad as to be turned from the purpose over which I have been brooding for a day and a night, and to which I had screwed my courage so resolutely, by a smile and a question. – What is this? Black currant; and this is groundsel; and little Alice, your glove wants a stitch or two,' he added aloud; 'and, oh! here we are. Now you must enlighten me; and what a grove of little sticks, and little inscriptions. These are your annuals, I suppose?'

And so they talked, and she laughed and chatted very merrily, and he had not the heart – perhaps the courage – to deliver his detested message; and again it was postponed.

The next day Charles Fairfield fell into his old gloom and anxieties; the temporary relief was felt no more, and the usual reaction followed.

It is something to have adopted a resolution. The anguish of suspense, at least, is ended, and even if it be to undergo an operation, and to blow one's own brains out, men will become composed, and sometimes even cheerful, as the coroner's inquest discovers, when once the way and the end are known.

But this melancholy serenity now failed Charles Fairfield, for, without acknowledging it, he began a little to recede from his resolution. Then was the dreadful question, How will she bear it, and, even worse, how will she view the position? Is she not just the person to leave forthwith a husband thus ambiguously placed, and to insist that this frightful claim, however shadowy, should be met and determined in the light of day?

'I know very well what an idol she makes of me, poor little thing; but she would not stay here an hour after she heard it; she would go straight to Lady Wyndale. It would break her heart, but she would do it.'

It was this fear that restrained him. Impelling him, however, was the thought that, sooner or later, if Harry's story were true, his enemy would find him out, and his last state be worse than his first.

Again and again he cursed his own folly for not having consulted his shrewd brother before his marriage. How horribly were his words justified! How easy it would have been comparatively to disclose all to Alice before leading her into such a position! He did not believe that there was actual danger in this claim. He could swear that he meant no villainy. Weak and irresolute in a trying situation, he had been – that was all. But could he be sure that the world would not stigmatise him as a villain?

Another day passed, and he could not tell what a day might bring – a day of feverish melancholy, of abstraction, of agitation.

She had gone to her room. It was twelve o'clock at night, when, having made up his mind to make his agitating shrift, he mounted the old oak stairs, with his candle in his hand.

'Who's there?' said his wife from the room.

'I, darling.'

And at the door she met him in her dressing-gown. Her face was pale and miserable, and her eyes swollen with crying.

'Oh, Ry, darling, I'm so miserable; I think I shall go mad.'

And she hugged him fast in trembling arms, and sobbed convulsively on his breast.

Charles Fairfield froze with a kind of terror. He thought, 'She has found out the whole story.' She looked up in his face, and that was the face of a ghost.

'Oh, Ry, darling, for God's sake tell me – is there anything very bad – is it debt only that makes you so wretched? I am in such dreadful uncertainty. Have mercy on your poor little miserable wife, and tell me whatever it is – tell me all!'

Here you would have said was something more urgent than the opportunity which he coveted; but the sight of that gaze of wildest misery smote and terrified him, it looked in reality so near despair, so near insanity.

'To tell her will be to kill her,' something seemed to whisper, and he drew her closer to him, and kissed her and laughed.

'Nothing on earth but money – the want of money – debt. Upon my soul, you frightened me, Alice, you looked so – so piteous. I thought you had something dreadful to tell me; but, thank God, you are quite well, and haven't even seen a ghost. You must not always be such a foolish little creature. I'm afraid this place will turn our heads. Here we are safe and sound, and nothing wrong but my abominable debts. You would not wonder at my moping if you knew what debt is; but I won't look, if I can help it, quite so miserable for the future; for, after all, we must have money soon, and you know they can't hang me for owing them a few hundreds; and I'm quite angry with myself for having annoyed you so, you poor little thing.'

'My noble Ry, it is so good of you – you make me so happy. I did not know what to think, but you have made me quite cheerful again, and I really do think it is being so much alone. I watch your looks so much, and everything preys on me so, and that seems so odious when I have my darling along with me; but Ry will forgive his foolish little wife, I know he will – he's always so good and kind.'

Then followed more reassuring speeches from Charles, and more raptures from poor Alice. And the end was that for a time Charles was quite turned away from his purpose. I don't know, however, that he was able to keep his promise about more cheerful looks, certainly not beyond a day or two.

A few days later he heard a tragic bit of news. Tom related to him that the miller's young wife, down at Raxleigh, hearing on a sudden that her husband was drowned in the mill-stream, though 'twas nothing after all but a ducking, was 'took wi' fits, and died in three days' time.'

So much for surprising young wives with alarming stories! Charles Fairfield listened, and made the application for himself.

A few days later a letter was brought into the room where, rather silently, Charles and his wife were at breakfast. It came when he had almost given up the idea of receiving one for some days, perhaps weeks, and he had begun to please himself with the idea that the delay augured well, and Harry's silence was a sign that the alarm was subsiding.

Here, however, was a letter addressed to him in Harry's bold hand. His poor little wife, sitting next the tea-things, eyed her husband, as he opened it, with breathless alarm; she saw him grow pale as he glanced at it; he lowered it to the tablecloth, and bit his lip, his eye still fixed on it.

As he did not turn over the leaf, she saw it could not be a long one, and must all be comprised within one page.

'Ry, darling,' she asked, also very pale, in a timid voice, 'it's nothing very bad. Oh, darling, what is it?'

He got up and walked to the window silently.

'What do you say, darling?' he asked, suddenly, after a little pause.

She repeated her question.

'No, darling, nothing, but – but possibly we may have to leave this. You can read it, darling.'

He laid the letter gently on the tablecloth beside her, and she picked it up and read:–

'MY DEAR CHARLIE, – The old soldier means business. I think you must go up to London, but be sure to meet me to-morrow at Hatherton, say the "Commercial Hotel", at four o'clock, P.M.

'Your affectionate brother,
'HARRY FAIRFIELD.'

'Who does he mean by the old soldier?' asked Alice, very much frightened, after a silence.

'One of those d——d people who are plaguing me,' said Charles, who had returned to the window, and answered, still looking out.

'And what is his real name, darling?'

'I'm ashamed to say that Harry knows ten times as well as I all about my affairs. I pay interest through his hands, and he watches those people's movements; he's a rough diamond, but he has been very kind, and you see his note – where is it? Oh, thanks. I must be off in half an hour, to meet the coach at the "Pied Horse".'

'Let me go up, darling, and help you to pack – I know where all your things are,' said poor little Alice, who looked as if she was going to faint.

'Thank you, darling; you are such a good little creature, and never think of yourself – never, never – *half enough*.'

His hands were on her shoulders, and he was looking in her face, with sad, strange eyes, as he said this, slowly, like a man spelling out an inscription.

'I wish – I wish a thousand things. God knows how heavy my heart is. If you cared for yourself, Alice, like other women, or that I weren't a fool – but – but you, poor little thing, it was such a venture, such a sea, such a crazy boat to sail in.'

'I would not give up my Ry, my darling, my husband, my handsome, clever, noble Ry – I'd lose a thousand lives if I had them, one by one, for you, Charlie; and oh, if you left me, I should die.'

'Poor little thing!' he said, drawing her to him with a trembling strain, and in his eyes, unseen by her, tears were standing.

'If you leave this, won't you take me, Charlie? Won't you let me go wherever you go? And oh, if they take my man – I'm to go with you, Charlie, promise that, and oh, my darling, you're not sorry you married your poor little Ally?'

'Come, darling, come up; you shall hear from me in a day or two, or see me. This will blow over, as so many other troubles have done,' he said, kissing her fondly.

And now began the short fuss and confusion of a packing on brief notice, while Tom harnessed the horse and put him to the dogcart.

And, the moment having arrived, down came Charles Fairfield, and Tom swung his portmanteau into its place, and poor little Alice was there with, as old Dulcibella said, 'her poor little face all cried,', to have a last look, and a last word, her tiny feet on the big unequal paving stones, and her eyes following Charlie's face, as he stepped up and arranged his rug and coat on the seat, and then jumped down for the last hug; and the wild, close, hurried whisperings, last words of love and cheer from laden hearts, and pale smiles, and the last, *really* the last look, and the dogcart and Tom, and the portmanteau and Charlie, and the sun's blessed light, disappear together through the old gateway under the wide stone arch, with tufted ivy and careless sparrows, and little Alice stands alone on the pavement for a moment, and runs out to have one last wild look at the disappearing 'trap', under the old trees, as it rattled swiftly down to the narrow road of Carwell Valley.

It vanished – it was gone – the tinkling of the wheels was heard no more. The parting, for the present, was quite over, and poor little Alice turned at last, and threw her arms about the neck of kind old Dulcibella, who had held her when a baby in her arms in the little room at Wyvern Vicarage, and saw her now a young wife, 'wooed and married, and a',' in the beauty and sorrows of life; and the light air of autumn rustled in the foliage above her, and a withered leaf or two fell from the sunlit summits to the shadow at her feet; and the old woman's kind eyes filled with tears, and she whispered homely comfort, and told her she would have him back again in a day or two, and not to take on so; and with her gentle hand, as she embraced her, patted her on the shoulder, as she used in other years – that seemed like yesterday – to comfort her in nursery troubles. But our sorrows outgrow their simple consolations, and turn us in their gigantic maturity to the sympathy and wisdom that is sublime and eternal.

Days passed away, and a precious note from Charlie came. It told her where to write to him in London, and very little more.

The hasty scrawl added, indeed emphatically, that she was to tell his address to no one. So she shut it up in the drawer of the old-fashioned dressing-table, the key of which she always kept with her.

Other days passed. The hour was dull at Carwell Grange for Alice. But things moved on in their dull routine without event or alarm.

Old Mildred Tarnley was sour and hard as of old, and up to a certain time neither darker nor brighter than customary. Upon a day, however, there came a shadow and a fear upon her.

Two or three times on that day and the next was Mrs Tarnley gliding, when old Dulcibella with her mistress was in the garden, about Alice's bedroom, noiselessly as a shadow. The little girl downstairs did not know where she was. It was known but to herself – and what she was about. Coming down those dark stairs, and going up, she went on tiptoe, and looked black and stern as if she was 'laying out' a corpse upstairs.

Accidentally old Dulcibella, coming into the room on a message from the garden, surprised lean, straight Mrs Tarnley feloniously trying to turn a key, from a bunch in her hand, in the lock of the dressing-table drawer.

'Oh, la! Mrs Tarnley,' cried old Dulcibella, very much startled.

The two women stood perfectly still, staring at each other. Each looked scared. Stiff Mildred Tarnley, without, I think, being the least aware of it, dropped a stiff short curtsey, and for some seconds more the silence continued.

"What *be* you a-doing here, Mrs Tarnley?' at length demanded Dulcibella Crane.

'No occasion to tell *you*,' replied Mildred, intrepidly. 'Another one, that owed her as little as I'm like ever to do, would tell your young mistress. But I don't want to break her heart – what for should I? There's dark stories enough about the Grange without no one hangin' theirself in their garters. What I want is where to direct a letter to Master Charles – that's all.'

'I can't say, I'm sure,' said old Dulcibella.

'She got a letter from him o' Thursday last; 'twill be in it no doubt, and that I take it, ma'am, is in this drawer, for she used not to lock it; and I expect you, if ye love your young mistress, to help me to get at it,' said Mrs Tarnley, firmly.

'Lor, Mrs Tarnley, ma'am! *me* to pick a lock, ma'am! I'd die first. Ye can't mean it?'

'I know'd ye was a fool. I shouldn't 'a said nothing to ye about it,' said Mildred, with sharp disdain.

'Lawk! I never was so frightened in my life!' responded Dulcibella.

'Ye'll be more so, mayhap. I wash my hands o' ye,' said Mrs Tarnley with a furious look, and a sharp little stamp on the floor. 'I thought o' nothing but your mistress's good, and if ye tell her I was here I'll explain all, for I won't lie under no surmises, and I think 'twill be the death of her.'

'Oh, this place, this hawful place! I never was so frightened in my days,' said Dulcibella, looking very white.

'She's in the garden now, I do suppose,' said Mildred, 'and if ye mean to tell her what I was about, 'tain't a pin's head to me, but I'll go out and tell her myself, and even if she lives through it she'll never hold up her head more, and that's all *you'll* hear from Mildred Tarnley.'

'Oh, dear! dear! dear! My heart, how it goes!'

'Come, come, woman, you're nothin' so squeamish, I dare say.'

'Well,' said Dulcibella, 'it may be all as you say, ma'am, and I'll say ye this justice, I ha'n't missed to the value of a pennypiece since we come here, but if ye promise me, only ye won't come up here no more while we're out, Mrs Tarnley, I won't say nothing about it.'

'That settles it – keep your word, Mrs Crane, and I'll keep mine; I'll burn my fingers no more in other people's messes;' and she shook the key with a considerable jingle of the whole bunch from the keyhole, and popped it grimly into her pocket.

'Your sarvant, Mrs Crane.'

'Yours, Mrs Tarnley, ma'am,' replied Dulcibella.

And the interview, which had commenced so brusquely, ended with ceremony, as Mildred Tarnley withdrew.

That old woman was in a sort of fever that afternoon and the next day, and her temper, Lilly Dogger thought, grew more and more savage as night approached. She had in her pocket a friendly fulsome little letter, which had reached her through the post, announcing an arrival for the night that was now approaching. The coach that changed horses at the 'Pied Horse' was due there at half-past eleven, P.M., but might not be there till twelve, and then there was a long drive to Carwell Grange.

'I'm wore out wi' them; I'm tired to death; I'm wore off my feet wi' them; I'm worked like a hoss. 'Twould be well for Mildred Tarnley, I'm thinkin', she was under the mould wi' a stone at her head, and shut o' them all.'

CHAPTER 25

LILLY DOGGER IS SENT TO BED

That night the broad-shouldered child, Lilly Dogger, was up later than usual. An arrear of pots and saucepans to scour, along with customary knives and forks to clean, detained her.

'Bustle, you hussy, will ye?' cried the harsh voice of old Mildred, who was adjusting the kettle on the kitchen fire, while in the scullery the brown-eyed little girl worked away at the knife-board. A mutton-fat, fixed in a tin sconce in the wall, so as to command both the kitchen and the scullery, economically lighted each, the old woman and her drudge, at her work.

'Yes'm, please?' she said interrogatively, for the noise of her task prevented her hearing distinctly.

'Be alive, I say. It's gone eleven, you slut; ye should 'a bin in your bed an hour,' screeched Mildred, and then relapsed into her customary grumble.

'Yes, Mrs Tarnley, please'm,' answered the little girl, resuming with improved energy.

Drowsy enough was the girl. If there had been a minute's respite from her task, I think she would have nodded.

'Be them things rubbed up or no, or do you mean to 'a done to-night, hussy?' cried Mrs Tarnley, this time so near as to startle her, for she had unawares put her wrinkled head into the scullery. 'Stop that for to-night, I say. Leave 'em lay – ye'll finish in the morning.'

'Shall I take down the fire, Mrs Tarnley, ma'am, please?' asked Lilly Dogger, after a little pause.

'No, ye shan't. What's that ye see on the fire! Have ye eyes in your head? Don't you see the kettle there? How do I know but your master'll be home to-night, and want a cup o' tea, or – law knows what?'

Mrs Tarnley looked put about, as she phrased it, and in one of those special tempers which accompanied that state. So Lilly Dogger, eyeing her with wide-open eyes, made her a frightened little curtsey.

'Why don't ye get up betimes in the morning, hussy, and then ye needn't be mopin' about half the night? All the colour's washed out o' your big, ugly, platter face, wi' your laziness – as white as a turnip. When I was a girl, if I left my work over so, I'd 'a the broomstick across my back, I promise ye, and bread and water next day too good for my victuals; but now ye thinks ye can do as ye likes, and all's changed! An' every upstart brat is as good as her betters. But don't ye think ye'll come it over me, lass, don't ye. Look up there at the clock, will ye, or do you want me to pull ye up by the ear – ten minutes past eleven – wi' your dawdling, ye limb!'

The old woman whisked about, and, putting her hand on a cupboard door, she turned round again before opening it, and said:—

'Come on, will ye, and take your bread if you want it, and don't ye stand gaping there, ye slut, as if I had nothing to do but attend upon you, with your impittence. I shouldn't give ye *that*.'

She thumped a great lump of bread down on the kitchen table by which the girl was now standing.

'Not a bit, if I did right, and ye'll not be sittin' up to eat that, mind ye; ye'll take it wi' ye to yer bed, young lady, and tumble in without delay, d'ye mind? For if I find ye out o' bed when I go in to see all's right, I'll just gi'e ye that bowl o' cold water over yer head. In wi' ye, an' get ye twixt the blankets before two minutes — get along.'

The girl knew that Mrs Tarnley could strike as well as 'jaw', and seldom threatened in vain, so, with eyes still fixed upon her, she took up her fragment of loaf, with a hasty curtsey, of which the old woman took no notice, and vanished frightened through a door that opened off the kitchen.

The old woman, holding the candle over her head, soon peeped in as she had threatened.

Lilly Dogger lay close, affecting to be asleep, though that feat in the time was impossible, and was afraid that the thump, thump of her heart — for she greatly feared Mrs Tarnley — might be audible to that severe listener.

Out she went, however, without anything more, to the great relief of the girl.

Lilly Dogger lay awake; for fear is vigilant, and Mrs Tarnley's temper, she knew, was capricious as well as violent.

Through the door she heard the incessant croak of the old woman's voice, as she grumbled and scolded in soliloquy, poking here and there about the kitchen. The girl lay awake, listening vaguely in the dark, and watching the one bright spot on the whitewashed wall at the foot of her bed, which Mrs Tarnley's candle in the kitchen transmitted through the keyhole. It flitted and glided, now hither, now thither, now up, now down, like a white butterfly in a garden, silently indicating the movements of the old woman, and illustrating the clatter of her clumsy old shoes.

In a little while the door opened again, and the old woman entered, having left her candle on the dresser outside.

Mrs Tarnley listened for a while, and you may be sure Lilly Dogger lay still. Then the old woman, in a hard whisper, asked, 'Are you awake?' and listened.

'Are ye awake, lass?' she repeated, and, receiving no answer, she came close to the bed, by way of tucking in the coverlet, in reality to listen.

So she stood in silence by the bed for a minute, and then very quickly withdrew and closed the door.

Then Lilly Dogger heard her make some arrangements in the kitchen, and move, as she rightly concluded, a table which she placed against her door.

Then the white butterfly, having made a sudden sweep round the side wall, hovered no longer on Lilly Dogger's darkened walls, and old Mildred Tarnley and her candle glided out of the kitchen.

The girl had grown curious, and she got up and peeped, and found that a clumsy little kitchen table had been placed against her door, which opened outward.

Through the keyhole she also saw that Mildred had not taken down the fire. On the contrary, she had trimmed and poked it, and a kettle was simmering on the bar.

She did not believe that Mrs Tarnley expected the arrival of her master, for she had said early in the day that she thought he would come next evening. Lilly Dogger was persuaded that Mrs Tarnley was on the look out for someone else, and guarding that fact with a very jealous secrecy.

She went again to her bed; wondering, she listened for the sounds of her return, and looked for the little patch of light on the white-washed wall; but that fluttering evidence of Mrs Tarnley's candle did not reappear before the tired little girl fell asleep.

She was wakened in a little time by Mrs Tarnley's somewhat noisy return. She was grumbling bitterly to herself, poking the fire, and pitching the fire-irons and other hardware about with angry recklessness.

The girl turned over, and, notwithstanding all Mildred's noisy soliloquy, was soon asleep again.

Again she woke – I suppose recalled to consciousness by some noise in the kitchen. The little white light was in full play on the wall at the foot of her bed, and Mrs Tarnley was talking fluently in an undertone. Then came a silence, during which the old Dutch clock struck one.

Lilly Dogger's eyes were wide open now, and her ears erect. She heard no one answer the old woman, who resumed her talk in a minute; and now she seemed careful to make no avoidable noise – speaking low, and when she moved about the kitchen treading softly, and moving anything she had to stir gently. Altogether she was now taking as much care not to disturb as she had shown carelessness upon the subject before.

Lilly Dogger again slipped out of bed and peeped through the keyhole. But she could not see Mrs Tarnley nor her companion, if she had one.

Old Mildred was talking on, not in her grumbling interrupted soliloquy, but in the equable style of one spinning a long narrative. This hum was relieved now and then by the gentle click of a teacup, or the jingle of a spoon.

If Mrs Tarnley was drinking her tea alone at this hour of night and talking so to herself, she was doing that she had never done before, thought the curious little girl; and she must be a-going mad. From this latter apprehension, however, she was relieved by hearing someone cough. It was not Mrs Tarnley, who suspended her story, however. But there was an unmistakable difference of tone in this cough, and old Mildred said more distinctly something about a cure for a cough which she recommended.

Then came an answer in an odd, drawling voice. The words she could not hear, but there could no longer be any doubt as to the presence of a stranger in the kitchen.

Lilly Dogger was rather frightened, she did not quite know why, and listened without power to form a conjecture. It was plain that the person who enjoyed old Mildred's hospitality was not her master, nor her mistress, nor old Dulcibella Crane.

As she listened, and wondered, and speculated, sleep overtook her once more, and she quite forgot the dialogue, and the kitchen, and Mildred Tarnley's tea, and went off upon her own adventures in the wild land of dreams.

CHAPTER 26

THE LADY HAS HER TEA

'You suffers dreadful, ma'am,' said Mildred Tarnley. 'Do you have them toothaches still?'

''Twas not toothache – a worse thing,' said the stranger, demurely, who, with closed eyes, and her hand propping her head, seemed to have composed herself for a doze in the great chair.

'Wuss than toothache! That's bad. Earache, mayhap?' inquired Mrs Tarnley, with pathetic concern, though I don't think it would have troubled her much if her guest had tumbled over the precipice of Carwell Valley and broken her neck among the stones in the brook.

'Pain in my face – it is called tic,' said the lady, with closed eyes, in a languid drawl.

'Tic? lawk! Well, I never heard o' the like, unless it be the field-bug as sticks in the cattle – that's a bad ailment, I do suppose,' conjectured Mrs Tarnley.

'You may have it yourself some day,' said this lady, who spoke quietly and deliberately, but with fluency, although her accent was foreign. 'When we are growing a little old our bones and nerves they will not be young still. You have your rheumatism, I have my tic – the pain in my cheek and mouth – a great deal worse, as you will find, whenever you taste of it, as it may happen. Your tea is good – after a journey tea is so refreshing. I cannot live without my cup of tea, though it is not good for my tic. So, ha, ha, he-ha! There is the tea already in my cheek – oh! Well, you will be so good to give me my bag.'

Mildred looked about, and found a small baize bag with an umbrella and a bandbox.

'There's a green bag I have here, ma'am.'

'A baize bag?'

'Yes'm.'

'Give it me. Ha, yes, my bibe – my bibe – and my box.'

So this lady rummaged and extricated a pipe very like a meerschaum, and a small square box.

'Tibbacca!' exclaimed Mrs Tarnley. The stranger interrupted the exclamation, without interrupting her preparations.

'Dobacco? no, better thing – some opium. You are afraid Mrs Harry Fairfield, she would smell id. No – I did not wish to disturb her sleeb. I am quite private here, and do not wish to discover myself. Ya, ya, ya, hoo!'

It was another twinge.

'Sad thing, ma'am,' said Mildred. 'Better now, perhaps?'

'Put a stool under my feed. Zere, zere, sat will do. Now you light that match and hold to the end of ze bibe, and I will zen be bedder.'

Accordingly Mildred Tarnley, strongly tempted to mutter a criticism, but possibly secretly in awe of the tall and 'big-made' woman who issued these orders, proceeded to obey them.

'No great odds of a smell, arter all,' said Mrs Tarnley, approvingly, after a little pause.

'And how long since Harry married?' inquired the smoker after another silence.

'I can't know that nohow; but 'tis since Master Charles gave 'em the lend o' the house.'

'Deeb people these Vairvields are,' laughed the big woman, drowsily.

'When will he come here?'

'To-morrow or next day, I wouldn't wonder; but he never stays long, and he comes and goes as secret-like as a man about a murder a'most.'

'Ha, I dare say. Old Vairvield would cut him over the shoulders with his horsewhip, I think. And when will your master come?'

'Master comes very seldom. Oh! ve-ry. Just when he thinks to find Master Henry here, maybe once in a season.'

'And where does he live – at home or where?' asked the tall visitor.

'Well, I can't say, I'm sure, if it bain't at Wyvern. At Wyvern, I do suppose, mostly. But I dare say he travels a bit now and again. I don't know, I'm sure.'

'Because I wrote to him to Wyvern to meet me here. Is he at Wyvern?'

'Well, faith, I can't tell. I know no more than you, ma'am, where Master Charles is,' said Mildred, with energy, relieved in the midst of her rosary of lies to find herself free to utter one undoubted truth.

'You have been a long time in the family, Mrs Tarnley?' drawled the visitor, listlessly.

'Since I was the height o' that – before I can remember. I was born in Carwell gate-house here. My mother was here in old squire's time, meanin' the father o' the present Harry Fairfield o' Wyvern that is, and grandfather o' the two young gentlemen, Master Charles and Master Harry. Why, bless you, my grandfather, that is my mother's father, was in charge o' the house and farm, and the woods, and the tenants, and all; there wasn't a tree felled, nor a cow sold, nor an acre o' ground took up, but jest as he said. They called him honest Tom Pennecuick; he was thought a great deal of, my grandfather was, and Carwell never turned in as good a penny to the Fairfields as in his time; not since, and not before – never, and never will, that's sure.'

'And which do you like best, Squire Charles or Squire Harry?' inquired the languid lady.

'I like Charles,' said Mrs Tarnley, with decision.

'And why so?'

'Well, Harry's a screw; ye se he'd as lief gi'e a joint o' his thumb as a sixpence. He'll take his turn out of everyone good-humoured enough, and pay for trouble wi' a joke and a laugh; a very pleasant gentleman for such as has nothing to do but exchange work for his banter and live without wages; all very fine. I never seed a shillin' of hisn since he had one to spend.'

'Mr Charles can be close-fisted too, when he likes it?' suggested the old lady.

'No, no, no, he's not that sort if he had it. Open-handed enough, and more the gentleman every way than Master Harry – more the gentleman,' answered Mildred.

'Yes, Harry Fairfield is a shrewd, hard man, I believe; he ought to have helped his brother a bit; he has saved a nice bit o' money, I dare say,' said the visitor.

'If he hasn't a good handful in his kist corner, 'tain't that he wastes what he gets.'

'I do suppose he'll pay for no more than he can help,' observed Mildred.

'It's a comfortable house,' pursued the stranger; ''twas so when I was here.'

'Warm and roomy,' acquiesced Mrs Tarnley – 'chimbley, roof, and wall – staunch and stout; 'twill stand a hundred year to come, wi' a new shingle and a daub o' mortar now and again. There's a few jackdaws up in the chimbleys that ought to be drew out o' that wi' their sticks and dirt,' she reflected respectfully.

'And do you mean to tell me he pays no rent for the Grange, and keeps his wife here?' demanded the lady, peremptorily.

'I know nothing about their dealings,' answered Mrs Tarnley, as tartly. 'And 'tain't clear to me I should care much neither; they'll settle that, like other matters, without stoppin' to ask Mildred what she thinks o't; and I dare say Master Harry will be glad enough to take it for nothing, if Master Charles will be fool enough to let him.'

'Well, he sha'n't do that, I'll take care,' said the lady, maintaining her immovable pose, which, with a certain peculiarity in the tone of her voice, gave to her an indescribable and unpleasant languor. 'I never have two pounds to lay on top o' one another. Jarity begins at home. I'll not starve for Master Harry,' and she laughed softly and unpleasantly. 'His wife, you say, is a starved gurate's daughter!'

'Parson Maybell – poor he was, down at Wyvern Vicarage – meat only twice or thrice a week, as I have heard say, and treated old Squire Harry bad, I hear, about his rent; and old Squire Fairfield was kind – to *her*, anyhow, and took her up to the hall, and so when she grew up she took her opportunity and married Master Harry.'

'She was clever to catch such a shrewd chap – clever. Light again; I shall have three four other puff before I go to my bed – very clever. How did she take so well, and hold so fast, that wise fellow, Harry Fairfield?'

'Hoo! fancy, I do suppose, and likin'. She's a pretty lass. All them Fairfields married for beauty mostly. Some o' them got land and money, and the like, but a pretty face allays along with the fortune.'

The blind stranger – for blind she was – smiled downward, faintly and slily, while she was again preparing the pipe.

'When will Harry come again?' she asked.

'I never knows; he's so wary; do you want to talk to him, ma'am?' asked Mildred.

'Yes, I do,' said she. 'Hold the match now, Mrs Tarnley, please.'

So she did, and – puff, puff, puff – about a dozen times when the smoke, and the smoker was satisfied.

'Well, I never knows the minute, but it mightn't be for a fortnight,' said Mrs Tarnley.

'And when Mr Charles Fairfield come?' asked the visitor.

'If he's got your letter he'll be here quick enough. If it's missed him he mayn't set foot in it for three months' time. That's how it is wi' him,' answered Mildred.

'What news of old Harry at Wyvern?' asked the stranger.

'No news in partic'lar,' answered Mildred, 'only he's well and hearty – but that's no news; the Fairfields is a long-lived stock, as everyone knows; he'll not lie in oak and wool for many a day yet, I'm thinkin'.'

Perhaps she had rightly guessed the object of the lady's solicitude, for a silence followed.

'There's a saying in my country – "God's children die young,"' said the tall lady.

'And hereabout they do say the devil takes care of his own,' said Mildred Tarnley. 'But see how my score o' years be runnin' up; I take it sinners' lives be lengthened out a bit by the Judge of all, to gi'e us time to say our thoughts a little, and repeat our misdeeds, while yet we may.'

'You have made a little fire in my room, Mrs Tarnley?' inquired the stranger, who had probably no liking for theology.

'Yes'm; everything snug.'

'Would you mind running up and looking? I detest a chill,' said this selfish person.

At that hour no doubt Mrs Tarnley resented this tax on her rheumatics; but though she was not a woman to curb her resentments, she made shift on this occasion; that did not prevent her, however, from giving the stranger a furious look, while she muttered inaudibly a few words.

'I'll go with pleasure, ma'am; but I'm sure it's all right,' she said aloud, very civilly, and paused, thinking perhaps that the lady would let her off the long walk upstairs to the front of the house.

'Very good; I'll wait here,' said the guest, unfeelingly.

'As you please 'm,' said Mildred, and, with a parting look round the kitchen, she took the candle, and left the lady to the light of the fire.

The lady was almost reclining in her chair, as if she were dozing; but in a few moments up she stood, and, placing her hand by her ear, listened; then, with her hands advanced, she crept slowly, and as noiselessly as a cat, across the floor. She jostled a little against the table at Lilly Dogger's door; then she stopped perfectly still, withdrew the table without a sound; the door swung a little open, and the gaunt figure in grey stood at it, listening. A very faint flicker from the fire lighted this dim woman, who seemed for the moment to have no more life in her than the tall grey stone of the Druid's hoe on Cressley Common.

Lilly Dogger was fast asleep; but broken were her slumbers destined to be that night. She felt a hand on her neck, and looking up, could not for a while see anything, so dark was the room.

She jumped up in a sitting posture, with a short cry of fear, thinking that she was in the hands of a robber.

'*Be* quiet, fool,' said the tall woman, slipping her hand over the girl's mouth. 'I'm a lady, a friend of Mrs Mildred Tarnley, and I'm come to stay in the house. Who is the lady that sleeps upstairs in the room that used to be Mr Harry's? You must answer true, or I'll pull your ear very hard.'

'It is the mistress, please 'm,' answered the frightened girl.

'Married lady?'

'Yes 'm.'

'Who is her husband?'

With this question the big fingers of her visitor closed upon Lilly Dogger's ear with a monitory pinch.

'The master, ma'am.'

'And what's the master's name, you dirdy liddle brevarigator?'

And with these words her ear was wrung sharply.

She would have cried, very likely, if she had been less frightened, but she only winched, with her shoulders up to her ears, and answered in tremulous haste:–

'Mr Fairfield, sure.'

'There's three Mr Vairvields: there's old Mr Vairvield, there's Mr Charles Vairvield, and there's Mr Harry Vairvield – you *shall* speak plain.'

And at each name in her catalogue she twisted the child's ear with a sharp separate wring.

'Oh, law, ma'am. Please 'm, I mean Mr Charles Fairfield. I didn't mean to tell you no story, indeed, my lady.'

'Ho, ho – yes – Charles, Charles – very goot. Now, you tell me how you know Mr Harry from Mr Charles?'

'Oh, law, ma'am! oh, law! oh, ma'am, dear! sure, you won't pull it no more, good lady, please – my ear's most broke,' gasped the girl, who felt the torture beginning again.

'You tell truth. How do you know Mr Charles from Mr Harry?'

'Mr Charles has bigger eyes, ma'am, and Mr Harry has lighter hair, and a red face, please 'm, and Mr Charles's face is brown, and he talks very quiet-like, and Mr Harry talks very loud, and he's always travellin' about a-horseback, and Mr Charles is the eldest son, and the little child they're lookin' for is to be the Squire o' Wyvern.'

The interrogator gave her a hard pinch by the ear, perhaps without thinking of it, for she said nothing for a minute nearly, and the girl remained with her head buried between her shoulders, and her eyes wide open, staring straight up where she conjectured her examiner's face might be.

'Is the man that talks loud – Mr Harry – here often?' asked the voice at her bedside.

'But seldom, ma'am – too busy at fairs and races, I hear them say.'

'And Mr Charles – is he often here?'

'Yes 'm; master be always here, exceptin' this time only he's gone about a week.'

'About a week, Mr Charles?'

'Oh, la, ma'am – yes, indeed, ma'am, dear, it's just a week to-day since master went.'

Here was a silence.

'That will do. If I find you've been telling me lies I'll take ye by the back of the neck and squeeze your face against the kitchen bars till it's burnt through and through – do you see; and I give you this one chance, if you have been telling lies to say so, and I'll forgive you.'

'Nothing but truth, indeed and indeed, ma'am.'

'Old Tarnley will beat you if she hears you have told me anything. So keep your own secret, and I'll not tell of you.'

The child saw the brawny outline of the woman faintly like a black shadow as she made her way through the door into the kitchen, and she heard the door close, and the table shoved cautiously back into its place, and then, with a beating heart, she lay still and awfully wide awake in the dark.

CHAPTER 27

THROUGH THE HOUSE

This stalwart lady stumbled and groped her way back to her chair, and sat down again in the kitchen. The chair in which she sat was an old-fashioned armchair of plain wood, uncoloured and clumsy.

When Mildred Tarnley returned, the changed appearance of her guest struck her.

'Be ye sick, ma'am?' she asked, standing, candle in hand, by the chair.

The visitor was sitting bolt upright, with a large hand clutched on each arm of the chair, with a face deadly pale and distorted by a frown or a spasm that frightened old Mildred, who fancied, as she made no sign, not the slightest stir, that she was in a fit, or possibly dead.

'For God's sake, ma'am,' conjured old Mildred, fiercely, '*will* ye speak?'

The lady in the chair started, shrugged, and gasped. It was like shaking off a fit.

'Ho! oh, Mildred Tarnley, I was thinking – I was thinking – did you speak?'

Mildred looked at her, not knowing what to make of it. Too much laudanum – was it? or that nervous pain in her head?

'I only asked you how you were, ma'am – you looked so bad. I thought you was just going to work in a fit.'

'What an old fool! I never was better in my life. *Fit!* I never had a fit –
not I.'

'You used to have 'em sometimes, long ago, ma'am, and they came in
the snap of a finger, like,' said Mildred, sturdily.

'Clear your head of those fits, for they have left me long ago. I'm well,
I tell you – never was better. You're old – you're old, woman, and that
which has made you so pious is also making you blind.'

'Well, you look a deal better now – you *do*,' said Mildred, who did not
want to have a corpse or an epileptic suddenly on her hands, and was
much relieved by the signs of returning vivacity and colour.

'Tarnley, you've been a faithful creature and true to me; I hope I may
live to reward you,' said the lady, extending her hand vaguely towards the
old servant.

'I'm true to them as gives me bread, and ever was, and that's old
Mildred Tarnley's truth. If she eats their bread, she'll maintain their right,
and that's only honest – that's reason, ma'am.'

'I have no right to cry no; I cry excellent, good, good, very good, for,
as you are my husband's servant, I have all the benefit of your admirable
fidelity. Boo! I am so grateful, and one day or other, old girl, I'll reward
you – and very good tea, and every care of me. I will tell Mr Vairvield
when he comes how good you have been – and, tell me, how is the fire,
and the bed, and the bedroom – all quite comfortable?'

'Comfortable, quite, I hope, ma'am.'

'Do I look quite well now?'

'Yes 'm, pure and hearty. It was only just a turn.'

'Yes, just so, perhaps, although I never felt it, and I could dance now
only for – fifty things, so I won't mind.' She laughed. 'I'm sleepy, and
I'm *not* sleepy; and I love you, old Mildred Tarnley, and you'll tell me
some more about Master Harry and his wife when we get upstairs.
Who'd have thought that wild fellow would ever tie himself to a wife?
Who'd have fancied that clever young man that loves making money
so well would have chosen out a wife without a florin to her fortune?
Everything is so surprising. Come, let's have a laugh, you and me
together.'

'My laughing days is over, ma'am – not that I see much to laugh at for
anyone, and many a thing I thought a laughing matter when I was young
seems o'er like a crying matter now I'm grown old,' said old Mildred,
and snuffed the kitchen candle with her fingers.

'Well, give me your arm, Mildred; there's a good old thing – yes.'

And up she got her long length. Mildred took the candle, and took the
tall lady gently by the wrist. The guest, however, placed her great hand
upon Mildred's shoulder, and thus they proceeded through the passages.

Leaving the back stair that led to Alice's room, at the right, they mounted the great staircase and reached a comfortably warm room with a fire flickering on the hearth, for the air was sharp. In other respects the apartment had not very much to boast.

'There's fire here, I feel it; place my chair near it. The bed in the old place?' said the tall woman, coming to a halt.

'Yes 'm. Little change here, ever, I warrant ye, only the room's bin new papered,' answered Mildred.

'New papered, has it? Well, I'll sit down – thanks – and I'll get to my bed, just now.'

'Shall I assist ye, ma'am?'

'By-and-bye, thanks; but not till I have eaten a bit. I have grown hungry – what your master calls peckish. What do you advise?'

'I would advise your eating something,' replied Mildred.

'But what?'

'There's very little; there's eggs quite new, there's a bit o' bacon, and there's about half a cold chicken – roast, and there's a corner o' Cheddar cheese, and there's butter, and there's bread – 'tain't much,' answered Mrs Tarnley, glibly.

'The chicken will do very nicely, and don't forget bread and salt, Mrs Tarnley, and a glass of beer.'

'Yes 'm.'

Mrs Tarnley poked the fire and looked about her, and then took the only candle, marched boldly off with it, shutting the door.

Toward the door the lady turned her face and listened. She heard old Mildred's step receding.

This tall woman was not pleasant to look at. Her large features were pitted with the small-pox, and deadly pale with the pallor of anger, and an unpleasant smile lighted up the whiteness of her face.

'Patience, patience!' she repeated. 'What a d——d trick! No matter – wait a little.'

She did wait a little in silence, screwing her lips and knitting her brows, and then a new resource struck her, and she groped in her bag and drew forth a bottle, which she applied to her lips more than once, and seemed better. It was no febrifuge nor opiate; but though the flicker of the fire showed no flush on her pallid features, the odour declared it brandy.

CHAPTER 28

THE BELL RINGS

'Will that beast never go to bed – even there, I mind, she used to sleep with an eye open and an ear cocked – and nowhere safe from her never – here and there, up and down, without a stir of a breath, like a ghost or a devil?' – thought Mrs Tarnley. 'Thank God, she's blind now, that will quiet her.'

Mildred was afraid of that woman. It was not only that she was cold and hard, but she was so awfully violent and wicked.

'Satan's her name. Lord help us, in what hell did he pick her up?' Mildred would say to herself in old times, as with the important fury of fear she used to knock about the kitchen utensils, and deal violently with every chair, table, spoon, or 'cannikin' that came in her way.

The woman had fits, and bad fits too, in old times, when she knew her well.

And she drank like a fish cognac neat – and she was alive still, and millions of people, younger and better, that never had a fit, and kept their bodies in soberness and temperance, was gone dead and buried since; and that drunken, shattered, battered creature, wi' her fallin' sickness and her sins and her years, was here alive and strong to plague and frighten better folk. Well, she's 'ad small-pox, thank God, and well mauled she is, and them spyin', glarin' eyes o' hers, the wild beast.'

By this time Mrs Tarnley was again in the kitchen. She did not take down the fire yet. She did not know, for certain, whether Charles Fairfield might not arrive. The London mail that passed by the town of Darwynd, beyond Cressley Common, came later than that divergent stage coach, that changed on the line of road that passes the 'Pied Horse'.

What a situation it would have been if Charles Fairfield and the Vrau had found themselves *vis-a-vis* as inside passengers in the coach that night! Would the matter have been much mended if the Dutch woman had loitered long enough in the kitchen for Charles to step in and surprise her? It was a thought that occurred more than once to Mildred with a qualm of panic. But she was afraid to hasten the stranger's departure to her room, for that lady's mind swarmed with suspicion which a stir would set in motion.

'The Lord give us dominion over the beast o' the field, Parson Winyard said in his sermon last Sunday; but we ain't allowed to kill nor hurt, but for food or for defence; and good old Parson Buckles, that was as good as two of he, said, I mind, the very same words. I often thought o' them of late – merciful to them brutes, for they was made by the one

Creator as made ourselves. So the merciful man is merciful to his beast – will ye?'

Mrs Tarnley interrupted herself sharply, dealing on the lean ribs of the cat, who had got its head into a saucepan, a thump with a wooden spoon, which emitted a hollow sound and doubled the thief into a curve.

'Merciful, of course, except when they're arter mischief; but them that's noxious, and hurtful, and dangerous, we're free to kill; and where's the beast so dangerous as a real bad man or woman? God forbid I should do wrong. I'm an old woman, nigh-hand the grave, and murder's murder! – I do suppose and allow that's it. Thou shalt do no murder. No more I would – no, not if an angel said do it; no, I wouldn't for untold goold. But I often wondered why if ye may, wi' a good conscience, knock a snake on the head wi' a stone, and chop a shovel down smack on a toad, ye should stay your hand, and let a devil incarnate go her murdering way through the world, blastin' that one wi' lies, robbin' this one wi' craft, and murderin' t'other, if it make for her interest, wi' poison or perjury. Lord help my poor head, and forgive me if it be sin, but I can find neither right nor reason in that, nor see, nohow, why she shouldn't be killed offhand like a rat or a sarpent.'

At this point the bell rang loud and sudden, and Mrs Tarnley bounced and blessed herself. There was no great difficulty in settling from what quarter the summons came, for, except the hall door bell, which was a deep-toned, sonorous one, there was but one in the house in ringing order, and that was of the bedroom where her young mistress lay.

'Well, here's a go! Who'd a' thought o' her awake at these hours, and out o' her bed, and a-pluckin' at her bell. I doubt it *is* her. The like was never before. 'Tis enough to frighten a body. The Lord help us.'

Mrs Tarnley stood straight as a grenadier on drill with her back to the fire, the poker with which, during her homily, she had been raking the bars, still in her hand.

'This night'll be the death o' me. Everything's gone cross and contrary. Here's that young silly lass awake and out o' her bed, that never had an eye open at these hours, since she came to the Grange, before; and there's that other one in the state-room, not that far from her, as wide awake as she; and here's Master Charles a comin', mayhap, this minute wi' his drummin' and bellin' at the hall door. 'Tis enough to make a body swear; 't has given me the narves and the tremblin's, and I don't know how it's to end.'

And Mrs Tarnley unconsciously shouldered her poker as if awaiting the assault of burglars, and vaguely thought, if Charles arrived as she had described, what power on earth could keep the peace?

Again the bell rang.

'Well, *there's* patience for ye!'

She halted at the kitchen door, with the candle in her hand, listening with a stern, frightened face. She was thinking whether Alice might not have been frightened by some fantastic terror in her room.

'She has that old fat fool, Dulcibella Crane, only a room off – why don't she call up her?'

But Mrs Tarnley at length did go on, and up the stairs, and heard Alice's voice call along the passage, in a loud tone:–

'Mrs Tarnley! Is that *you*, Mrs Tarnley?'

'Me, ma'am? Yes 'm. I thought I heard your bell ring, and I had scant time to hustle my clothes on. Is there anything uncommon a-happenin', ma'am, or what's expected just now from an old woman like me?'

'Oh, Mrs Tarnley, I beg your pardon – I'm so sorry, and I would not disturb you, only that I heard a noise, and I thought Mr Charles might have arrived.'

'No, ma'am, he's not come, nor no sign o' him. You told me, ma'am, his letter said there was but small chance o't.'

'So I did, Mildred – so it did. Still a chance – just a chance – and I thought, perhaps——'

'There's no perhaps in it, ma'am; he bain't come.'

'Dulcibella tells me she thought some time ago she heard someone arrive.'

'So she did, mayhap, for there did come a message for Master Harry from the farmer beyond Gryce's Mill; but he went his way again.'

Mildred was fibbing with a fluency that almost surprised herself.

'I dessay you've done wi' me now, ma'am?' said Mildred. 'Lugged out o' my bed, ma'am, at these hours – my achin' old bones – 'tain't what I'm used to, asking your pardon for making so free.'

'I'm really very sorry – you won't be vexed with me. Good night, Mildred.'

'Your servant, ma'am.'

And Mrs Tarnley withdrew from the door where Alice stood before her with her dressing-gown about her shoulders, looking so pale and deprecatory and anxious, that I wonder even Mildred Tarnley did not pity her.

'I'm tellin' lies enough to break a bridge, and me that's vowed against lying so stiff and strong over again only Monday last.'

She shook her head slowly, and with a sudden qualm of conscience.

'Well, in for a penny in for a pound. It's only for to-night; mayhap, and I can't help it, and if that old witch was once over the door-stone I'd speak truth the rest o' my days, as I ha' done, by the grace o' God, for more than a month and here's a nice merry-go-round for my poor old head. Who's to keep all straight and smooth wi' them that's in the house, and, mayhap, comin'? And that ghost upstairs – she'll be gropin' and screechin' through the house, and then there'll be the devil to pay wi' her and the poor lass up there – if I don't gi'e her her supper quick. Come, bustle, bustle, be alive,' she muttered, as this thought struck her with new force; and so to the little 'safe' which served that miniature household for larder she repaired. Plates clattered, and knives and forks, and the dishes in the safe slid forth, and how near she was forgetting the salt! and 'the bread, all right,' so here was a tray very comfortably furnished, and setting the candlestick upon it also, she contemplated the supper, with a fierce sneer, and a wag of her head.

'How sick and weak we be! Tea and toast and eggs down here, and this little bit in her bedroom – heaven bless her – la' love it, poor little darling, don't I hope it may do her good? – I wish the first mouthful may choke her – keeping me on the trot to these hours, old beast.'

Passing the stairs Mrs Tarnley crept softly, and took pains to prevent her burden from rattling on the tray, while there rose in her brain the furious reflection:–

'Pretty rubbish that I should be this way among 'em!'

And she would have liked to dash the tray on the floor at the foot of the stairs, and to leave the startled inhabitants to their own courses.

This, of course, was but an emotion. The old woman completed her long march cautiously, and knocked at the Vrau's door.

'Come in, dear,' said the inmate, and Mildred Tarnley, with her tray in her hands, marched into the room, and looked round peevishly for a table to set it down on.

'You'll find all you said, 'm,' said old Tarnley. 'Shall I set it before you, or will you move this way, please 'm?'

'Before me, dear.'

So Mildred carried the table and supper over, and placed it before the lady, who sat up and said:–

'Good Mildred, how good you are! Give me now the knife and fork, in my fingers, and put some salt just there. Very good. How good of you to take so much trouble for poor me, you kind old Mildred!'

How wondrous sweet she had grown in a minute. The old servant, who knew her, was not conciliated, but disgusted, and looked hard at the benevolent lady, wondering what could be in her mind.

'If everything's right, I'll wish you good-night, 'm, and I'll go down to my bed, ma'am, please.'

'Wait a while with me. Do, there's a good soul! I'll not detain you long, you dear old lass.'

'Well, ma'am, I must go down and take down the fire, and shut-to the door, or the rats will be in from the scullery; and I'll come up again, ma'am, in a few minutes.'

And, not waiting for permission, Mildred Tarnley, who had an anxiety of another sort in her head, took the candle in her hand and left the guest at her supper by the light of the fire.

She shut the door quickly, lest her departure should be countermanded, and trotted away downstairs, but not to the kitchen.

CHAPTER 29

TOM IS ORDERED UP

When she reached the foot of the stairs that lead to the gallery on which the room occupied by Alice opens, instead of pursuing her way to the kitchen she turned into a narrow and dark passage that is hemmed in on the side opposite to the wall by the ascending staircase.

The shadows of the banisters on the panelled oak flew after one another in sudden chase as the old woman glided by, and looking up and back she stopped at the door of a small room, constructed as we see in similar old houses, under the stairs. On the panel of this she struck a muffled summons with her fist, and on the third or fourth the startled voice of Tom demanded roughly from within:—

'*What's* that?'

'Hish!' said the old woman, through a bit of the open door.

''Tis Mrs Tarnley – only me.'

'Lauk, woman, ye did take a rise out o' me! I thought ye was – I don't know what – I was a-dreaming, I think.'

'Never mind, you must be awake for an hour or so,' said Mrs Tarnley, entering the den without more ceremony.

Tom didn't mind Mrs Tarnley, nor Mrs Tarnley Tom, a rush. She set the candle on the tiled floor. Tom was sitting in his shirt on the side of his 'settlebed,' with his hands on his knees.

'Ye must get on your things, Tom, and, if ever you stirred yourself, be alive now. The master's a-comin', and may be here, across Cressley Common, in half an hour, or might be in five minutes, and ye must go out a bit and meet him, and – are ye awake?'

'Starin'. Go on.'

'Ye'll tell him just this – the big woman as lives at Hoxton——'

'Hoxton! *Well?*'

'That Master Harry has all the trouble wi', has come here, angry, in search of Master Harry, mind, and is in the bedroom over the hall door. Will ye mind all that, now?'

'Ay,' said Tom, and repeated it.

'Well, he'll know better whether it's best for him to come on or turn back. But if come on he will, let him come in at the kitchen door, mind, and you go that way too, and he'll find neither bolt nor bar, but open doors, and nothing but the latch between him and the kitchen, and me sitting by the fire; but don't you clap a door, nor tread heavy, but remember there's a sharp pair of ears that'd hear a cricket through the three walls of Carwell Grange.'

She took up the candle, and herself listened for a moment at the door, and again turned her earnest and sinister face on Tom.

'And again, I say, Tom, if ever ye was quick, be quick now,' and she clapped her lean hand down on his shoulder with a sort of fierce shake; 'and if ever ye trod soft, go softly now, *mind*.'

Tom, who was scratching his head and staring in her face, nodded.

'And mind you, the kitchen way, and afraid o' slips – say ye the message over again to me!'

This he did, glibly enough.

'Here, light your candle from this, and if ye fail your master now, never call yourself man again.'

Having thus charged him, she went softly from this nook, with its slanting roof, and thinking of the thankless world, and all the trouble her old bones and brain were put to, she lost her temper, at the foot of the great staircase, and was near turning back again to the kitchen, or perhaps whisking out of the door herself, and marching off to Cressley Common to meet her master, and shock and scare him all she could, and place her resignation, as more distinguished functionaries sometimes do theirs, in the hands of her employer, to prove his helplessness and her own importance, and so assert herself for time past and to come.

Her interview with Tom had not occupied much time. She knocked at the Vrau's door, and, entering, found that person at the close of a greedy repast.

Emotions of fear, I suppose, disturb the appetite, much more than others. Not caring one farthing about Charles, she did not grieve at his infidelity; taking profligacy for granted as the rule of life, it did not even shock her. But she was stung with a furious pang of jealousy, for that needs no love, being in its essence the sense of property invaded, supremacy insulted, and self despised. In this sort of jealousy there is neither the sublimity of despair nor the pathos of sorrow, but simply the malice, fury, and revenge of outraged egotism.

There she sat, unconscious of the glimmer of the firelight, feeding as a beast will bleeding after a blow. Beast she was, with the bestial faculty of cherishing a long revenge, with bestial treachery and seeming unconcern.

'Ho oh! you've come back,' she cried, with playful reproach, 'cruel old girl! You leave your poor Vrau alone, alone among the ghosts – now, sit down – are you sitting? – and tell me everything, and all the news – did you bring a little brandy, or what?'

Her open hand was extended, and gently moving over the tray at about the level of the top of a bottle.

'No, ma'am, I haven't none in my charge, but there's a smell o' brandy about,' said Mildred, who liked saying a disagreeable thing.

'So there ought,' said the gaunt woman placidly, and lifted a big black bottle that lay in her lap, like a baby, folded in a grey shawl. 'But I'll want this, don't you see, when I'm on my rambles again – get a little, there's a good girl, or if you can't get that, there's rum or gin; there never was a country house without something in it; you know very well where Harry Vairvield is there will be liquor – I know him well.'

'But he bain't here now, as is well known to you, ma'am,' said Mildred, drily.

'I'm not going to waste my drink, while I think there's drink in the house. Who has a right before me, old girl?' said the stranger, grimly.

'Tut, ma'am, 'tis childish talkin' so; there's none in my charge, never a drop. Master Harry, I dare say, has summat under lock and key, but not me, and why should I tell you a lie about the like?'

'You never tell lies, old Mildred, I forgot that – but young as she is, I lay my life the woman, Mrs Harry Vairvield, upstairs, likes a nip now and then, hey? and she has a boddle, I'll be bound, in her wardrobe, or if she's shy, 'twixt her bed and her mattress, ole rogue! You know very well, I think, does she? and if she likes it she sleeps sound, and go you, and while she snores, borrow you the bottle.'

'She's nothing of the sort; she drinks nothing nowhere, much less in her bedroom – she's a perfect lady,' said Mrs Tarnley, in no mood to flatter her companion.

'Oh, ho! that's so like old Mildred Tarnley! Dear old cat, I'm so amused, I could stroke her thin ribs, and pet her for making me laugh so by her frisks and capers instead of throwing you by the neck out of the window for scratching and spitting – I'm so good-natured. Do you tell lies, Mildred?'

'I ha' told a shameful lot in my day, ma'am, but not more mayhap than many a one that hasn't grace to say so.'

'You read your Bible, Mildred,' said the lady, who with a knife and fork was securing on her plate the morsels to which old Mildred helped her.

'Ay, ma'am, a bit now, and a bit again – never too late to repent, ma'am.'

'Repentance and grace – you'll do, Mrs Tarnley. It's a pleasure to hear you,' said the lady, with her mouth rather full; 'and you never see my husband?'

'Now and again, now and again, once and away he looks in.'

'Never stays a week or a month at a time?'

'Week or a month!' echoed Mrs Tarnley, looking quickly in the serene face of the lady, and then laughing off the suggestion scornfully. 'You're thinking of old times, ma'am.'

'Thinking – thinking. I don't think I was thinking at all,' said the lady, answering Mildred's laugh with one more careless. 'Old times when he had a wife here – eh? Old times! How old are they? Eh – that's eighteen years ago – you hardly knew me when I called here?'

'There was a change, surely. I'd like to know who wouldn't in eighteen years – there's a change in me since then.'

'I shouldn't wonder,' said the lady quietly. 'Did he ever tell you how we quarrelled?'

'Not he,' answered Mildred.

'He's very close,' said the stranger.

'A deal closer than Mr Harry,' acquiesced Mildred.

'Not like you and me, Mrs Tarnley, that can't keep a secret – *never*. That tell truth, and shame the devil. I, because I don't care a snap of my fingers for you, or him, or the Archbishop of Canterbury; and you, because you're all for grace and repentance. How am I looking to-night – tired?'

'Tired, to be sure; you ought to be in your bed, ma'am, an hour ago; you're as white as that plate, ma'am.'

'White are they? – so they used to be long ago,' said the visitor.

'The same set, ma'am. 'Twas a long set in my mother's time, though 'tis little better than a short set now; but I don't think there's more than three plates, and the cracked butter-boat, that had a stitch in it – you'll mind, although ye may ha' forgot, for I usen't to send it up to table – only them three, and the butter-boat broke since; and that butter-boat, 'twouldn't a brought three ha'pence by auction, and 'twas that little slut downstairs, that doesn't never do nothing right, that knocked it off the shelf, with her smashing.'

'And I'm not looking well to-night,' said this pallid woman.

'You'd be the better of a little blood to your cheeks; you're as white as paper, ma'am,' answered Mildred.

'I never *have* any colour now, they tell me – always pale, pale, pale; but it isn't muddy; 'tain't what you call *putty*?'

'Well, no.'

'Ha! no; I knew that – *no*, and I'd rather be a little pale. I don't like your great, coarse, peony-faced women; it's seven years in May last since I lost my sight. Some people are persecuted; one curse after another – rank injustice! Why should *I* lose my sight, that never did anything to signify – not half what others have, who enjoy health, wealth, rank – everything. Things are topsy-turvey a bit just now, but we'll see them righted yet.'

CHAPTER 30

THE OLD SOLDIER GROWS MORE FRIENDLY, AND FRIGHTENS MRS TARNLEY

The 'Dutchwoman' resumed in a minute, and observed:–

'Well, old Tarnley, there's no good in talking where you can't right yourself, and where you can revenge, there's no good in talk either; but gone it is, and the doctors say no cutting, nothing safe in my case; no cure, so let it be. I liked dress once; I dressed pretty well.'

'Beautiful!' exclaimed old Mildred, kindling for a moment into her earlier admiration of the French and London finery, with which once this tall and faded beauty had amazed the solitudes of Carwell.

The bleached, big woman smiled – almost laughed with gratified vanity.

'Yes, I was well dressed – something better than the young dowdies and old fromps in this part of the world. How I used to laugh at them! I went to church, and to the races, to see them. Well, we'll have better times yet at Wyvern; the old man there can't live for ever; he's not the Wandering Jew, and he can't be far from a hundred; and so sure as Charles is my husband, I'll have you there, if you like it, or give you a snug house, and a bit of ground, and a garden, and a snug allowance monthly, if you like this place best. I love my own, and you've been true to me, and I never failed a friend.'

'I'm growing old and silly, ma'am – never so strong as I was took for. The will was ever stronger with Mildred than the body, bless ye – no, no; two or three quiet years to live as I should ha' lived always, wi' an eye on my Bible and an eye on my ways – not that I ever did aught I need be one bit ashamed on – no, not I; honest and sober, and most respectable, thank God, as the family will testify, and the neighbours; but I'll not deny, 'twould be something not that bad if my old bones could rest a bit,' said old Mildred.

'Ha, girl, they *shall* – your old bones shall rest, my child,' said the lady.

'They'll rest some day in the old churchyard o' Carwell, but not much sooner, I'm thinking,' said Mrs Tarnley.

'Folly, folly! ole girl! you've many a year to go before that journey; you'll live to see me Mrs Vairvield, of Wyvern, and it won't be a bad day for you, old Mildred.'

The 'Dutchwoman', or the old soldier, as they used to call her long ago in this sequestered nook, drawled this languidly, and yawned a long, listless yawn.

'Well, ma'am, if you're tired, so am I,' said Mildred, a little tartly; 'and as for dreamin' o' quiet in this world, I ha' cleared my head o' that nonsense many a year ago. There's little good can happen old Mildred now, and less I look for, and none I'll seek, ma'am; and as for a roof over my head for nothing, and that bit o' ground ye spoke of, and wages to live on without no work, I don't believe there's no such luck going for no one.'

'Listen to me, Mildred,' said the stranger, more sternly than before; 'is it because I don't swear you won't believe? Here, now, once for all, and understand: I'll make that a good day for you that makes me the lady of Wyvern. Sharp and hard I've been with those I owed a knock to, but I never yet forgot a friend; you may do me a service to-morrow or next day, *mind*, and if you stand by me, I'll stand by you; you need but ask and have, ask what you *will*.'

'Well, now, ma'am – bah! what talk it is! Lawk, ma'am; don't I know the world, ma'am, and what sort o' place it is? I 'a bin promised many a fine thing in my day, and here I am still – old and weary – among the pots and pans every night and mornin', and up to my elbows in suds every Saturday; that's all that ever came o' fine promises to Mildred Tarnley.'

'Well, you used to say it's a long lane that has no turn. You'll have a glass of this?' and she popped the brandy bottle on the table beside her, with her hand fast on its neck.

'No brandy – no nothing, ma'am, I thank ye.'

'What! no brandy? Pish, girl, nonsense.'

'No, ma'am, I thank ye; I never drinks nothing o' the sort – a mug o' beer after washing or the like – but my headache never would abear brandy.'

'Once and away – come,' solicited the old soldier.

'No, I thank ye, ma'am; I'll swallow nothing o' the kind, please.'

'What a mule! You won't have a nip with an old friend, after so long an absence – come, Mildred, come; where's the glass?'

'Here's the glass, 'm, but not a drop for me, ma'am; I won't drink nothing o' the sort, please.'

'Not from me, I suppose; but if you mean to say you never do, I don't believe you,' said the Dutchwoman, more nettled, it seemed, than such a failure of good fellowship in Mrs Tarnley would naturally have warranted. Perhaps she had particularly strong reasons for making old Mildred frank, genial, and intimate that night.

'I don't tell lies,' said Mildred.

'Don't you?' said the old soldier, and elevated the brows of her sightless eyes, and screwed her lips with ugly ridicule.

Mrs Tarnley looked with a dark shrewdness upon this meaning mask, trying to discover the exact force of its significance. She felt very uncomfortable.

The blind woman's face expanded into a broad smile. She shrugged, shook her head, and laughed. How odiously wide her face looked as she laughed. Mildred did not know exactly what to make of her.

'But if you did tell lies,' drawled the lady, 'even to me, what does it matter, if you promised to tell no more? So let us shake hands – where's your hand?'

And she kept shuffling her big hand upon the table, palm upward, with its fingers groping in the air like the claws of a crab upon its back.

'Give me – give me – give me your hand, I say,' said she.

''Tain't for the like o' me,' replied Mildred, with grim formality.

'You'd better be friendly. Come, give me your hand.'

'Well, ma'am, 'tain't for me to dispute your pleasure,' answered the old servant, and she slipped her hard fingers upon the upturned palm of the Dutchwoman, who clutched them with a strenuous friendship, and held them fast.

'I like you, Tarnley; we've had rough words, sometimes, but no ill blood, and I'll do what I said. I never failed a friend, as you will see, if only you *be* my friend; and why or for whom should you *not*? Tut, we're not fools!'

'The time is past for me to quarrel, being to the wrong side o' sixty more than you'd suppose, and quiet all I wants – quiet, ma'am.'

'Yes, quiet and comfort, too, and both you shall have, Mildred Tarnley, if you don't choose to quarrel with those who *would* be kind to you, if you'd let them. Yes, indeed, who *would* be kind, and *very* kind, if you'd only let them. No, leave your hand where it is; I can't see you, and it's sometimes dull work talking only to a voice. If I can't see you I'll feel you, and hold you, old girl – hold you fast till I know what terms we're on.'

All this time she had Mildred Tarnley's hand between hers, and was fondling and kneading it as a rustic lover in the agonies of the momentous question might have done fifty years ago.

'I don't know what you want me to say, ma'am, no more than the plate there. Little good left in Mildred Tarnley now, and small power to help or hurt anyone, great or small, at these years.'

'I want you to be friendly with me, that's all; I ask no more, and it ain't a great deal, all things considered. Friendly talk, of course, ain't all I mean; that's civility, and civility's very well, very pleasant, like a lady's fan, or her lap-dog, but nothing at a real pinch, nothing to fight a wolf with. Come, old Mildred, Mildred Tarnley, good Mildred, can I be sure of you, *quite* sure?'

'Sure and certain, ma'am, in all honest service.'

'Honest service! Yes, of course; what else could we think of? You used to like, I remember, Mildred, a nice ribbon in your bonnet. I have two pieces quite new. I brought them from London. Satin ribbon – purple one is – I know you'll like it, and you'll drink a glass of this to please me.'

'Thanks for the ribbons, ma'am – I'll not refuse 'em; but I won't drink nothing, ma'am, I thank you.'

'Well, please yourself in that. Pour out a little for me – there's a glass, ain't there?'

'Yes 'm. How much will you have, ma'am?'

'Half a glass. There's a dear. Stingy half a glass,' she continued, putting her finger in to gauge the quantity. 'Go on, go on – remember my long journey to-day. Do you smoke, Mildred?'

'Smoke, 'm? No, 'm. Dear me, there's no smell o' tobacco, is there?' said Mildred, who was always suspecting Tom of smoking slily in his crib under the stairs.

'Smell, no; but I smoke a pinch of tobacco now and again myself, the doctor says I must, and a breath just of opium when I want it. You can have a pipe of tobacco if you like, child, and you needn't be shy. Well?'

'Ho, Fau! No, ma'am, I thank ye.'

'Fau!' echoed the Dutchwoman, with a derisive, chilling laugh, which apprised old Mildred of her solecism. But the lady did not mean to quarrel.

'What sort of dress have you for Sundays, going to church, and all that?'

'An old dress it is now. I had the material, ye'll mind, when ye was here, long ago; but it wasn't made up till long after. It's very genteel, the folk all says. Chocolate colour – British cashmere – 'twas old Mrs Hartlepool, the parson's widow, made me a compliment o't when she was goin', and I kept it all the time, wi' whole pepper and camphor, in my box, by my bed, and it looked as fresh when I took it out to give it to Miss Maddox to make up as if 'twas just put new on the counter. She did open her eyes – that's nigh seven years gone – when I told her how old it was.'

'Heyday! Hi! I think I do remember that old chocolate thing. Why, it can't be that – that's twenty years old. Well, look in my box, here's the key. You'll see two books with green leather backs and gold. Can ye read? I'm going to make you a present.'

'I *can* read, ma'am; but I scarce have time to read my Bible.'

'The Bible's a good book, but that's a better,' said the lady, with one of her titters. 'But it ain't a book I'm going to give you. Look it out, green and gold – there are only two in the box. It is the one that has an I and a V on the back, *four*, the fourth volume. I have little else to amuse me. I have the news of the neighbours, but I don't like 'em, who could? A bad lot, they hate one another; 'twouldn't be a worse world if they were all hanged. They hate me because I'm a lady, so I don't cry when baby takes the croup, nor break my heart when papa gets into the "Gazette". Have you found it? Why, it's under your hand there. They would not cry their eyes out for me, so I can see the funny side of their adventures, bless them!'

'Is this is, ma'am?'

'There are but two books in the box. Has it an I and a V on the back?'

'V, O, L, I, V,' spelled out old Mildred, who was listening in a fever for the sounds of Charles Fairfield's arrival.

'That's it. That's the book you should read. I take it in, and I hire all the others, and a French one, from the Hoxton library. I make Molly Jinks, the little, dirty, starving maid, read to me two hours a day. She's got rather to like it. How are your eyes?'

'I can make out twelve or fourteen verses wi' the glasses, but not more, at one bout.'

'Well, get on your glasses. This is the "Magazine of the Beau-Monde, and Court and Vashionable Gazette", and full of pictures. Turn over.'

'La, ma'am, 'tis beautiful, but what have I to do with the like?'

'Well, look out for the puce *gros de Naples* walking dress, about page twenty-nine, and I'll show you the picture afterwards. Do be quick. I have had it four years – it's quite good though – only I'm grown a little fuller since, and it don't fit now. So read it, and you'll see how I'll dress you.'

And bending her head forward and knitting her brows, she listened absorbed, while old Mildred, helped, or corrected, at every second word, by her blind patroness, babbled and stuttered on with her in duet recitation.

'Walking dress,' said Mildred.

'Go on,' said the lady, who, having this like other descriptions in that cherished work pretty well by heart, led off energetically with her lean old companion, and together they read:–

'A *pelisse* of puce-coloured *gros de Naples*, the corsage made to sit close to the shape, with a large round pelerine which wraps across in front. The sleeve is excessively large at the upper part of the arm. The fulness of the lower is more moderate. It is confined in three places by bands and terminated by a broad wrist-band. The pelerine and bands of the sleeves are cased with satin to correspond, and three satin *rouleaus* are arranged *en tablier* on the front of the skirt. The bonnet is of rice straw of the cottage shape, trimmed under the brim on the right side, with a banal and *noeud* of gold-coloured ribbon. The crown being also ornamented with gold-coloured ribbon, and a sprig of lilac, placed perpendicularly. Half-boots of black *gros de Naples*, tipped with black kid.'

Here they drew breath, and Mildred Tarnley was silent for a minute, thinking how much more like a lady her mother used to dress than *she* was able, and what fine presents of old clothes old Mrs Fairfield used to send her now and then from Wyvern. For a moment an air of dignity, a sense of feminine vanity, showed itself in the face and mien of Mrs Tarnley.

'That rice straw bonnet, with the gold-coloured *noeud*, of course I haven't got, nor the *gros de Naples* boots – they're gone, of course, long ago; but it reads best, altogether, and I hadn't the heart to stop you, nor you to stop reading till we got to the end. And look at the pictures, you'll easily find it; and I'll write and have the pelisse sent here by the day coach. It will be here on Sunday. Do you like it?'

'It is a bit too fine for me, I'm afraid,' said Mildred, smiling in spite of herself, with a grim elation; 'my poor mother used to dress herself grand enough, in her day, and keep me handsome also when I was a young thing. But since the ladies come no more to Carwell the Grange has been a dull place, and gives a body enough to do to live, and little thought o' fine dresses, and few to see them, except o' Sundays, if 'twas here; not but 'twould be more for the credit o' the family if old Mildred Tarnley, that's known down here for housekeeper at the Grange of Carwell, wasn't turned out quite so poor and dowdy, and seeing them taking the wall o' me, which their mothers used to curtsey to mine, at church and market, and come up here to the Grange as humble as you please, when money was stirring at Carwell, and I, young as I was, thought more on, a deal more, than the best o' them.'

'I drink your health, Mildred; as you won't pledge me, I do it alone.'

'I thank ye, ma'am.'

'Ha, yes, that does me good; I'm tired to death, Mildred.'

'There's two on us so, ma'am; shall I get you to bed, please?'

'In a minute; give me your hand again, girl; come, come, come – yes, I have it. I think you are more friendly, eh? I *think* so; but the little goodwill I ever show you now is *nothing* to what I mean for you when I come to Wyvern – nothing.'

And she strengthened the present assurance with an oath, and grasped Mildred's hard brown hand very tight.

'And you'll be kind to me, Mildred, when I want it; and I *shall* want it, mind, and I'll never forget it to you; 'twill be the making of you. I'll show you how much I trust you, for I'll put myself in your power.'

And, hereupon, she shook her hand harder. Her face and manner were changed, and she looked horribly frightened for some minutes.

'I don't blame you, Mildred, but this thing must not go on – it must not be.'

Mildred in her own way looked disconcerted and even agitated at this odd speech. She screwed her mouth sharply to one side, and with her brow knit and turned a frightened gaze on her visitor.

'There's things as can't be undone, and things as can,' said she, after a pause, oracularly; 'best not meddle or make – worms that is, and dust that will be, and God over all.'

'God over all, why not?' repeated the old soldier vaguely, and stood up suddenly with a kind of terrified shudder – 'Take me, hold me, quick!'

'A fit? La bless us!' cried Tarnley, seizing her in her lean arms.

The lady answered nothing, but grasped her fast by the wrist and shoulder, and so she stood for a time, shuddering and swaying. 'Better at last,' she said, 'a little – put me in the chair.'

And she made a great shuddering sigh or two, and called for water and 'hartshorn', and the hysteria subsided. And now she seemed overpowered with languor, and answered faintly and in monosyllables to old Mrs Tarnley's uncomfortable inquiries.

'Now I shall get a sleep,' she said at last, in low drowsy tones, interrupted with heavy sighs, and she looked so ill that old Mildred more than ever wished her back again at Hoxton Old Town.

'Help me to my bed – support me – get off my things,' she moaned and mumbled, and at last lay down with a great groaning sigh.

'What am I to do with her now?' thought Mrs Tarnley, who was doubtful whether in this state she could be safely left to herself.

But the patient set her at ease upon the point.

'Get your ear down,' she whispered, 'near, *near*. You need not stay any longer – only – one thing – the closet with the long row of pegs and the three presses in it, that lies between *her* room and mine, I remember it well – it isn't open – I shouldn't like her to find me here.'

'No, ma'am, it ain't open; the doors were papered over, this room and hers, as I told you, when the rooms were done up.'

The old soldier sighed and whispered: 'My head is very bad – make no noise, dear – don't move the tray, don't touch anything – leave me to myself, and I'll sleep till eleven o'clock to-morrow morning; but go out softly, and then, no noise, for my sleep,' groaned this huge woman, 'is a bird's sleep – a bird's sleep, and a pin dropping wakes me, a mouse stirring wakes me – oh, –oh – oh! That's all.' Glad to be dismissed on these easy terms, Mildred Tarnley bid her softly good-night, having left her basket with her sal volatile, and all other comforts, on the table at her bedside.

And so, softly she stole on tiptoe out of the room, and closed her door, waiting for a moment to clear her head, and be quite sure that the 'Dutchwoman', whom they very much hated and feared, was actually established in her bedroom at Carwell Grange.

CHAPTER 31

NEWS FROM CRESSLEY COMMON

A pretty medley was revolving in old Mildred's brain as she stood outside the door on the gallery. The epileptic old soldier, the puce *gros de Naples*, Tom on outpost duty on Cressley Common – had he come back? Charles Fairfield, perhaps, in the house, and that foolish poor young wife in her room, in the centre, and herself the object of all this manoeuvring and conspiring; quite unconscious. Mildred had a good many wires to her fingers just now; could she possibly work them all and keep the show going?

She was listening now, wondering whether Master Charles had arrived, wondering whether the young lady was asleep, and wondering, most of all, why she had been fool enough to meddle in other people's affairs. 'What the dickens was it to her if they was all in kingdom come? If Mildred was a roastin' they wouldn't, not one of 'em, walk across the yard there, to take her off the spit – la, bless you, not a foot!'

Mildred was troubled about many things. Among others, what was the meaning of those oracular appeals of the Dutchwoman, in which she had seemed to know something of the real state of things?

Down went Mildred Tarnley, softly still, for she would not risk waking Alice, and at the foot of the second staircase she paused again.

All was quiet; she peeped into Tom's little room, under the staircase. It was still empty. Into the kitchen she went; nothing had been stirred there.

From habit she trotted about, and settled and unsettled some of the scanty ironmongery and earthenware, and peeped, with her candle aloft, into this corner and that, and she removed the smoothing iron that stood on the window stool, holding the shutters close, and peeped into the paved yard, tufted with grass, high over which the solemn trees were drooping.

Then, candle in hand, the fidgety old woman visited the back door; the latch was in its place, and she turned about and visited the panelled sitting-room. The smell of flowers was there, and on the little spider-table was Alice's workbox, and some little muslin clippings and bits of thread and tape, the relics of that evening's solitary work over the little toilet on which her pretty fingers and sad eyes were now always employed.

Well, there was no sign of Master Charles here; so with a little more pottering and sniffing, out she went, and again to the back door, which softly she opened, and she toddled across the uneven pavement to the back door, and looked out, and walked forth upon the narrow road, that, darkened with thick trees, overhangs the edge of the ravine.

Here she listened, and listened in vain. There was nothing but the soft rush of the leaves overhead in the faint visitings of the night air, and across the glen at intervals came that ghastliest of sounds, between a long-drawn hiss and shiver, from a lonely owl.

Interrupted at intervals by this freezing sound, the old woman listened and muttered now and again a testy word or two. What was to be done if, by any mischance or blunder of Tom's, the master should thunder his summons at the hall door? Down, of course, would fly his young wife to let him in, and be clasped in his arms, while from the low window of the Dutchwoman that evil tenant might overhear every word that passed, and almost touch their heads with her down-stretched hand.

A pretty scene it would lead to, and agreeable consequences to Mildred herself.

'The woman's insane; she's an evil spirit; many a time she would have brained me in a start of anger if I hadn't been sharp. The mark of the cut glass decanter she flung at my head is in the doorcase at the foot of the stairs this minute like the scar of a bill-hook, the mad beast. I thank God she's blind, though – there's an end o' them pranks, anyhow. But she's a limb o' the evil one, and where there's a will there's a way, and blind though she be, I would not trust her.'

She walked two or three steps slowly, towards Cressley Common, from which directions she expected the approach of Charles Fairfield.

No wonder Mildred was fidgeted; there were so many disasters on the cards. If she could but see Charles Fairfield something at least might be guarded against. This wiry old woman was by no means hard of hearing – rather sharp, on the contrary, was her ear. But she listened long in vain.

Fearful lest something might go wrong within doors during her absence, she was turning to go back, when she thought she heard the distant clink of a horseshoe on the road.

Her old heart throbbed suddenly, and, frowning as she listened, with eyes directed towards the point of approach, softly she said 'Hush,' as if to quiet the faint rustle of the trees.

Stooping forward she listened, with her lean arm extended, every wrinkled knuckle of her brown hand, and every black-rimmed nail distinct in the moonlight.

Yes, it was the clink of trotting horseshoes. She prayed heaven the blind woman might not hear it. There was a time when her more energetic misanthropy would possibly have enjoyed a *fracas* such as was now to be apprehended. But years teach us the value of quiet, the providential instincts of growing helplessness disarm our pugnacity, and all but quite reprobate spirits grow gentler and kinder as the hour of parting with earth approaches. Thus had old Mildred taken her part in this game, and as her stake became deeper and more dangerous, her zeal burnt intensely.

Nearer and sharper came the clink, and old Mildred in her anxiety walked on, sometimes five steps, sometimes twenty, to meet the rider.

It was Tom who appeared, mounted on the mule. I think he took Mildred for a ghost, for he pulled up violently more than twenty yards away, and said, 'Lord! who's that?'

'It's me, Tom – Mrs Tarnley; and is he comin'?'

'I hardly knowed you, Mrs Tarnley. No, I met him up near the stone.'

'Not a coming?' urged Mildred.

'No.'

'Thank God. Well, and what did you tell him?'

'I told him your message. He first asked all about the young lady, and then I told him how she was, and then I told him your message——'

'Ay?'

'Word for word, and he drew bridle and stood awhile, thinkin', and he wished to know whether the mistress had spoke with her – Mr Harry's friend, I mean – and I said I didn't know; and he asked was the house quiet, and no high words going, nor the new comer giving any trouble, and I said *no*, so far as I knowed. Then, says he, I think, Tom, I had best let Master Harry settle it his own way, so I'll ride back again to Darwynd, and you can come over to the old place for the horse to-morrow; and tell Mildred I thank her for her care of us, and she shall hear from me in a day or two, and tell no one else, mind, that you have seen me. Well, I asked was there anything more, and he paused a bit, and says he, no, not at present. And then again, says he, tell Mildred Tarnley I'll write to her, and let her know where I am, and mind, Tom, you go yourself to the post office, and be sure the letters go only to the persons they are directed to, your mistress's to her, and Mildred's to *her*, and don't you talk with that person that I hear has come to the Grange, and if by any chance she should get into talk with you, you must be wide awake, and tell her *nothing*, and get away from her as quick as you can. It's easy to escape her, for she's blind.'

'So she is,' affirmed Mildred, 'as that wall. Go on.'

'"Then," says he, "Good-night, Tom, get ye home again." So I wished him God speed, and I rode away, and when I was on a bit I threw a look back again over my shoulder, and I saw him still in the same spot, no more stirring than the stone at the roadside, thinking, I do suppose.'

'And that's all?' said Mildred.

'That's all.'

'Bring in the beast very quiet, Tom, unless you leave him in the field for the night, and don't be clappin' o' doors or jinglin' o' bridle bits. That one has an ear like a hare, and she'll be askin' questions; and when you've done in the stable, come you in this way, and I'll let you in softly, and don't you be talkin' within doors above a whisper. Your voice is rough, and her ear is as sharp as a needle's point.'

Tom gave her a little nod and a great wink, and got off the mule, and led him on the grass toward the stable-yard, and old Mildred at the same time got in softly by the other entrance, and in the kitchen awaited the return of Tom.

She sat by the fire, troubled in mind, with her eyes turned askance on the windows. What a small thing is a human body, and what a gigantic moral sphere surrounds that little centre! That blind woman lay still as death, on a six-foot-long bedstead, in a remote chamber. But the direful circuit of that sphere which radiated thence enveloped old Mildred Tarnley, go where she would, and outspread even the bourn of the road which Charles Fairfield was to travel that night. For Mildred Tarnley, something of molestation and horror was in it, which forbade her to rest.

Tom came into the yard, and Mildred was at the door, and opened it before he could place his hand on the latch.

'Put off them big shoes, and not a word above your breath, and not a stir, but get ye in again to your bed as still as a mouse,' said Mrs Tarnley in a hard whisper, giving him a shake of the shoulder.

'Ye'll gi'e me a mug o' beer, Mrs Tarnley, and a lump o' bread and a cut o' cheese wouldn't hurt me – I'm a bit hungry. If you won't I must even take a smoke, for I can't sleep as I am.'

'Well, I will give ye a drink and a bit o' bread and cheese. Did ye lock the yard door?'

'No,' said Tom.

'Well, no, never you mind – I'll do it,' said Mildred, stopping him; 'and go you straight to your room, and here's the lantern for you; and now get ye in, and not a sound, mind. You gi'e me your pipe here, for you sha'n't be stinkin' the house wi' your nasty tobaccy.'

So Tom was got quick to his bed.

And Mildred sat down again by the kitchen fire, to rest for a little, feeling too tired to undress.

'Well, I *do* thank God of His mercy he's *not* a comin' – I do. Who can tell what would be if he *was*? And now, if only Master Harry was sure to keep away all might go right – yes, all – might go right. Oh, ho, ho! I wish it was, and my old head at rest, for I'm worked worse than a horse, and wore off my feet altogether.'

And all this time she was looking through the kitchen window, with dismal eyes, from her clumsy oak chair by the fire, with her feet on the fender, and her lean shanks as close to the bars as was safe, shaking her head from time to time as she looked out on the black outlines of the trees which stood high and gloomy above the wall at the other side, against the liquid moonlit sky.

CHAPTER 32

AN UNLOOKED-FOR RETURN

In spite of her troubles, as she sat by the fire, looking out through the window, fatigue overcame Mildred, and she nodded. But her brain being troubled, and her attitude uneasy, she awoke suddenly from a sinister dream, and as still unconscious where she was, her eyes opened upon the same melancholy foliage and moonlit sky and the dim enclosure of the yard, the scenery on which they had closed. She saw a pale face staring in upon her through the window. The fingers were tapping gently on the glass.

Old Mildred blinked and shook her head to get rid of what seemed to her a painful illusion.

It was Charles Fairfield who stood at the window, looking wild and miserably ill.

Mildred stood up, and he beckoned. She signed toward the door, which she went forthwith and opened.

'Come in, sir,' she said.

His saddle, by the stirrup-leather, and his bridle were in his hand. Thus he entered the kitchen and dropped them on the tiled floor. She looked in his face, he looked in hers. There was a silence. It was not Mildred's business to open the disagreeable subject.

'Would you please like anything?'

'No – no supper, thanks. Give me a drink of water, I'm thirsty. I'm tired, and – we're quite to ourselves?'

'Yes, sir; but wouldn't ye better have beer?' answered she.

'No – water – thanks.'

And he drank a deep draught.

'Where's the horse, sir?' she asked, after a glance at the saddle which lay on its side on the floor.

'In the field – the poplar field, all right – *well?*'

'Tom told you my message, sir?' she asked, averting her eyes a little.

'Yes – where is she – *asleep?*'

'The mistress is in her bed – asleep, I do suppose.'

'Yes, yes, and quite well, Tom says. And where is the – the – you sent me word there was someone here. I know whom you mean. Where is she?'

'In the front bedroom – the old room – it will be over the hall door, you know – she's in bed, and asleep, I'm thinkin'; but best not make any stir – some folks sleep so light, ye know.'

'It's late,' he said, taking out his watch, but forgetting to consult it, 'and I dare say she *is* – she came to-night, yes – and she's tired, or ought to be – a long way.'

He walked to the window, and was looking, with the instinct which leads us always, in dark places, to look toward the light, above the dusky trees to the thin luminous cloud that streaked the sky.

'Pretty well tired myself, Mr Charles; you may guess the night I've put in; I was a'most sleepin' myself when ye came to the window. Tom said ye weren't a-comin'; 'tis a mercy the yard door wasn't locked – five minutes more and I'd have locked it.'

'It would not have mattered much, Mildred.'

'Ye'd 'a climbed, and pushed up the window, mayhap.'

'No – I'd have walked on; a feather would have turned me from the door as it was.'

He turned about and looked at her dreamily.

'On *where*?' she inquired.

'On, anywhere; on into the glen. If you are tired, Mildred, so am I.'

'You need a good sleep, Master Charles.'

'A long sleep, Mildred. I'm tired. I had a mind, as it was, to walk on and trouble you here no more.'

'Walk on – hoot! nonsense, Mr Charles. 'Tisn't come to that – giving up your house to a one like her.'

'I wish I was dead, Mildred. I don't know whether it was a good or an evil angel that turned me in here. I'd have been easier by this time if I had gone on, and had my leap from the scaur to the bottom of the glen.'

'None o' that nonsense, man!' said Mildred, sternly. 'Ye ha' brought that poor young lady into a doubtful pass, and ye must stand by her, Charles. You're come of no cowardly stock, and ye sha'n't gi'e her up, and your babe that's comin', poor little thing, to shame and want for lack of a man's heart under your ribs. I say, I know nowt o' the rights of it; but God will judge ye if ye leave her now.'

High was Mrs Tarnley's head, and very grim she looked, as with her hand on his shoulder, she shook up 'Master Charles' from the drowse of death.

'I won't, old Tarnley,' he said at last. 'You're right – poor little Alice, the loving little thing!'

He turned suddenly again to the window, and wept in silence strange tears of agony.

Old Tarnley looked at him sternly askance. I don't think she had much pity for him, she was in nowise given to the melting mood, and hardly knew what that sort of whimpering meant.

'I say,' she broke out, 'I don't know the rights of it – how should I? but this I believe, if you thought you were truly married to that woman that's come to-night, you'd never ha' found it in your heart to act such a villain's part by the poor young foolish creature upstairs, and make a sham wife o' her.'

'Never, never, by Heaven! I'm no more that wretched woman's husband than I'm married to you.'

'Mildred knew better than marry anyone; there's little I see but tears and wrinkles, and oftentimes rags and hunger comes of it; but 'twill be done, marryin' and givin' in marriage, says the Scriptures, 'tis so now, 'twas so when Noah went into the ark, and 'twill be so when the day of judgment breaks over us.'

'Yes,' said Charles Fairfield, abstractedly; 'of course that miserable woman sticks at no assertion; her idea is simply to bully her way to her object. It doesn't matter what she says, and it never surprised me. I always knew if she lived she'd give me trouble one day; but that's all – just trouble, but no more; not the slightest chance of succeeding – not the smallest; she knows it; I know it. The only thing that vexes me is that people who know all about it as well as I do, and people who, of all others, should feel for me, and feel with me, should talk as if they had doubts upon the subject now.'

'I didn't say so, Master Charles,' said Mildred.

'I didn't mean you – I meant others, quite a different person. I'm utterly miserable; at a more unlucky moment all this could not have happened by any possibility.'

'Well, I'm sure I never said it; I never thought but one thing of her, the foul-tongued wicked beast.'

'Don't you talk that way of her,' said Charles, savagely. 'Whatever she is she has suffered – she has been cruelly used, and I am to blame for all. I did not mean it, but it is all my fault.'

Mrs Tarnley sneered, but said nothing, and a silence followed.

'I know,' he said, in a changed way, 'you mean kindly to me.'

'Be kind to yourself. I hold it's the best way in this bleak world, Mr Charles. I never was thanked for kindness yet.'

'You have always been true to me, Mildred, in your own way, mind, but always true, and I'll show you yet, if I'm spared, that I can be grateful. You know how I am now – no power to serve anyone – no power to show my regard.'

'I don't complain o' nothing,' said Mildred.

'Has my brother been here, Mildred?' he asked.

'Not he.'

'No letters for me?' asked he.

'Nothing, sir.'

'You never get a lift when you want it – never,' said Charles, with a bitter groan; 'never was a fellow driven harder to the wall – never a fellow nearer his wits' ends. I'm very glad, Mildred, I have someone to talk to – one old friend. I don't know what to do – I can't make up my mind to anything, and if I hadn't you just now I think I should go distracted. I have a great deal to ask you. That lady, you say, has been in her room some time – did she talk loud – was she angry – was there any noise?'

'No, sir.'

'Who saw her?'

'No one but myself, and the man as drove her.'

'Thank God for that. Does she know about my – did she hear that your mistress is in the house?'

'I said she was Master Harry's wife, and told her – Lord forgive me – that he was here continually, and you hardly ever, and then only for a few hours at a time.'

'That's very good – she believed it?'

'Every word, so far as I could see. I ha' told a deal o' lies.'

'Well, well, and what more?'

'And the beginning of sin is like the coming in of waters, and 'twill soon make an o'er wide gap for itself, and lay all under.'

'Yes – and – and – you really think she believed all you said?'

'Ay, I do,' answered she.

'Thank God again!' said he, with a deep sigh. 'Oh, Mildred, I wish I could think what's best to be done. There are ever so many things in my head.'

She felt a trembling, she thought, in the hand he laid upon her arm.

'Take a drink o' beer – you're tired, sir,' said she.

'No, no – not much – never mind, I'm better as I am. How has your mistress been?'

'Well, middlin' – pretty well.'

'I wish she was quite well, Mildred – it's very unlucky. If the poor little thing were only quite well, it would make everything easy; but I daren't frighten her – I daren't tell her – it might be her death. Oh, Mildred, isn't all this terrible?'

'Bad enough – I can't deny.'

'Would it be better to run that risk and tell her everything?' he said.

'Well, it *is* a risk, an' a great one, and it might be the same as puttin' a pistol to her head and killin' her; 'tis a tryin' time with her, poor child, and a dangerous bed; and mind ye this, if there's any talk like that, and the crying and laughing fits mayhap that comes with it, don't ye think but the old cat will hear it, and then in the wild talk a's out in no time, and the fat in the fire; no, if she's to hear it, it can't be helped, and the will o' God be done; but if I was her husband I'd sooner die than tell her, being as she is.'

'No, of course, no – she must not be told; I'm sure you're right, Mildred. I wish Harry was here – he thinks of things sometimes that don't strike me. I wish Harry would come, he might think of something – he would, I dare say – he would, I'm certain.

'I wish that woman was back again where she came from,' said Mildred, from whose mind the puce *gros de Naples* was fading; for she has a profound distrust of her veracity, and the pelisse looked very like a puce-coloured lie.

'Don't, Mildred – don't, like a good creature – you won't, for my sake, speak harshly of that unhappy person,' he said, gently this time, and laying his hand on her shoulder. 'I'm glad you are here, Mildred – I'm very glad; I remember you as long as I can remember anything – you were always kind to me, Mildred – always the same – true as steel.'

He was speaking with the friendliness of distress. It is in pain that sympathy grows precious, and with the yearning for it returns something of the gentleness and affection of childhood.

'She's come for no good,' said Mildred. 'She's sly, and she's savage, and if you don't mind me saying so, I often thought she was a bit mad – folk as has them fits, ye know, they does get sometimes queerish.'

'We can talk of her by-and-bye,' said he; 'what was in my mind was about a different thing. For a thousand reasons I should hate a *fracas* – I mean a row with that person at present; you know yourself how it might affect the poor little thing upstairs. Oh, my darling, my darling, what have I brought you into?'

'Well, well, no help for spilled milk,' said Mildred. 'What was you a-thinking of?'

'Oh yes, thank you, Mildred – I was thinking – yes – if your mistress was well enough for a journey, I'd take her away from this – I'd take her away immediately – I'd take her quite out of the reach of that – that restless person. I ought to have done so at once, but I was so miserably poor, and this place here to receive us, and who could have fancied she'd have dreamed, in her state of health, and with her affliction – her sight, you know – of coming down here again; but I'm the unluckiest fellow on earth; I never, by any chance, leave a blot that isn't hit. Don't you think, Mildred, I had better not wake your mistress to-night to talk over plans?'

'Don't you go near her – a sight o' your face would tell her all wasn't right.'

'I had better not see her, you think?'

'*Don't* see her. So soon as you know yourself what you're going to do with her – and if you make up your mind to-night so much the better – write you to tell her what she's to do, and give me the letter, and I'll give it to her as if it came by a messenger; and take you my counsel –don't you stop here a minute longer than you can. Leave before daybreak, you're no use here, and if she finds you 'twill but make bad worse. When will ye lie down – you'll not be good for nothin' to-morrow if ye don't sleep a bit – lie down on the sofa in the parlour, and your cloak is hangin' in the passage, and be you out o' the house by daybreak, and I'll have a bit o' breakfast ready before ye go.'

'And there's Lady Wyndale, I didn't tell you, offered to take care of Alice, your mistress, and she need only go there for the present; but that might be too near, and I was thinking it might not do.'

'Best out o' reach altogether when ye go about it,' said Mildred. 'Sit there if you like it, or lie down, as I said, in the parlour, and if you settle your mind on any plan just knock at my door, and I'll have my clothes about me and be ready at all, and Tom's in his old crib under the stairs, if you want him to get the saddle on the horse, and I won't take down the fire – I'll have it handy for your breakfast; and now I can't stop talkin' no longer, for Mildred's wore off her feet – will ye take a candle, or will ye stop here?'

'Yes, give me a candle, Mildred – thanks – and don't mind the cloak, I'll get it myself, I will lie down a little and try to sleep – I wish I could – and if you waken shake me up in an hour or two. Something must be settled before I leave – something *shall* be settled, and that poor little creature out of reach of trouble and insult. Don't forget. Good-night, Mildred! and God bless you, Mildred – God for ever bless you!'

CHAPTER 33

CHARLES FAIRFIELD ALONE

Charles Fairfield talked of sleeping. There was little chance of that. He placed the candle on one of the two old oak cupboards, as they were still called, which occupied corresponding niches in the wainscoted wall, opposite the fireplace, and he threw himself at his length on the sofa.

Tired enough for sleep he was; but who can stop the mill of anxious thought into which imagination pours continually its proper grist? In his tired head its wheels went turning, and its hammers beat with monotonous pulsation and whirl – weariest and most wasting of fevers!

He turned his face, like the men of old, in his anguish, to the wall. Then he tried the other side, wide awake, and literally staring, from point to point, in the fear and fatigue of his vain ruminations. Then up he sat, and flung his cloak on the floor, and then to the window he went, and, opening the shutter, looked out on the moonlight, and the peaceful trees that seemed bowed in slumber, and stood, hardly seeing it – hardly thinking in his confused misery.

One hand in his pocket, the other against the window-case, to which the stalwart good fellow Harry had leaned his shoulder in their unpleasant dialogue and altercation. Harry, his chief stay, his confidant and brother – dare he trust him now? If he might, where could he find him? Better do his own work – better do it indifferently than run a risk of treason. He did not quite know what to make of Harry.

So with desultory resolution he said to himself: 'Now I'll think in earnest, for I've got but two hours to decide in.' There was a pretty little German village, quite out of the ordinary route of tourists. He remembered its rocks and hills, its ruined castle and forest scenery, as if he had seen them but yesterday – the very place for Alice, with her simple tastes and real enjoyment of nature. On that point, though under present circumstances by short journeys, they should effect their retreat.

In three hours' time he would himself leave the Grange. In the meantime he must define his plans exactly. He must write to Harry – he must write to Alice, for he was quite clear he would not see her; and, after all, he might have been making a great deal too much of this odious affair, which, rightly managed, might easily end in smoke.

Pen, ink, and paper he found, and now to clear his head and fix his attention. Luckily he had a hundred pounds in his pocket-book. Too hard that out of his miserable pittance, scarcely five hundred pounds a year, he should have to pay two hundred pounds to that woman, who never gave him an easy week, and who seemed bent on ruining him if she could. By the dull light of the mutton-fat with which Mildred had furnished him he wrote this note:–

'MY DARLING LITTLE WOMAN, – You must make Dulcibella pack up your things. Tom will have a chaise here at eleven o'clock. Drive to Wykeford and change horses there, and go on to Lonsdale, where I will meet you *at last*. Then and there your own, poor, loving Ry will tell you all his plans and reasons for this sudden move. We must get away by easy stages, and baffle possible pursuit, and then a quiet and comparatively happy interval for my poor little fluttered bird. I live upon the hope of our meeting. Out of reach of all trouble we shall soon be, and your poor Ry happy, where only he can be happy, in your dear presence. I enclose ten pounds. Pay *nothing and nobody* at the Grange. Say I told you so. You will reach Lonsdale, if you leave Carwell not later than eleven, before five. Don't delay to pack up any more than you actually want. Leave all in charge of old Mildred, and we can easily write in a day or two for anything we may want.

'Ever, my own, idolised little woman,
'Your own poor adoring
'Ry.'

So this was finished; and now for Harry:–

'MY DEAR HARRY, – How you must hate the sight of my hand! I never write but to trouble you. But, as you will perceive, I am myself in trouble more than enough to warrant my asking you again to aid me if it should lie in your way. You will best judge if you can, and how you can. The fact is that what you apprehended turns out to be too true. That person who, however I may have been at one time to blame, has certainly no right to charge me with want of generosity or consideration, seems to have made up her mind to give me all the annoyance in her power. She is at this moment *here* at Carwell Grange. I was absent when she arrived, and received timely notice, and perhaps ought to have turned about, but I could not do that without ascertaining first exactly how matters stood at Carwell. So I am here, without anyone's being aware of it except old Mildred, who tells me that the person in question is under the impression that it is *you* – and not *I* – who are married, and that it is your wife who is residing in the house. As you have been no party to this deception, pray let her continue to think so. I shall leave this before daybreak, my visit not having exceeded four hours. I leave a note for poor little Alice, telling her to follow me to-morrow – I should say *this* morning – to Lonsdale, where I shall meet her; and thence we get on to London, and from London my present idea is to make our way to some quiet little place on the Continent, where I mean to stay quite concealed until circumstances alter for the better. What I want you, and *beg* of you, to do for me at present is just this – to sell *everything* at Carwell that is salable – the horse, the mule, the two donkeys, the carts, plough, etc., etc. – in fact, everything out of doors; and let the farm to Mildred's nephew, who wanted to take it last year. It is, including the garden, nineteen acres. I wish him to have it, provided he pays a fair rent, because I think he would be kind to his aunt, old Mildred. He must stipulate to give her her usual allowances of vegetables, milk, and all the rest from the farm; and she shall have her room, and the kitchen, and her £8 a year as usual. Do, like a good fellow, see to this, and try to turn all you can into money for me. I shall have miserably little to begin with, and anything you can get together will be a lift to me. If you write under cover to J. Dylke, at the old place in Westminster, it will be sure to reach me. I don't know whether all this is intelligible. You may guess how distracted I am and miserable. But there is no use in describing. I ought to beg your pardon a thousand times for asking you to take all the trouble involved in this request. But, dear Harry, you will ask yourself who else on earth has the poor devil to look to in an emergency but his brother? I know my good Harry will remember how urgent the case is. Any advice you can spare me in my solitary trouble will be most welcome. I think I have said everything – at least all I can think of in this miserable hurry – I feel so helpless. But you are a clever fellow, and always were – so much cleverer than I, and know how to manage things. God bless you, dear Harry – I know you won't forget how pressed I am. You were always prompt in my behalf, and I never so needed a friend like you – for delay here might lead to the worst annoyances.

> 'Ever, dear Harry, your affectionate brother,
> 'CHARLES FAIRFIELD.
> 'Carwell Grange.'

It was a relief to his mind when, these letters were off it, and something like the rude outline of a plan formed.

Very tired was Charles Fairfield when he had folded and addressed his letters. No physical exertion exhausts like the monotonous pain of anxiety. For many nights he had had no sleep, but those wearying snatches of half-consciousness in which the same troublous current is still running through the brain, and the wasted nerves of endurance are still tasked. He sat now in his chair, the dim red light of the candle at his elbow, the window shutter open before him, and the cold serene light of the moon over the outer earth and sky.

Gazing on this, a weary sleep stole over his senses, and for a full hour the worn-out man slept profoundly.

Into this slumber slowly wound a dream, of which he could afterwards remember only that it was somehow horrible.

Dark and direful grew his slumber thus visited; and in a way that accorded well with its terrors he was awakened.

CHAPTER 34

AWAKE

In his dream a pale, frightened face approached him slowly, and, recoiling, uttered a cry. The scream was horribly prolonged as the figure receded. He thought he recognised someone – dead or living he could not say – in the strange, Grecian face, fixed as marble, that with enormous eyes had looked into his.

With this sound ringing in his ears he awoke. As is the case with other over-fatigued men, on whom, at length, slumber has seized, he was for a time in the attitude of wakefulness before his senses and his recollection were thoroughly aroused, and his dream quite dissipated. Another long shriek, and another, and another he heard. Charles recognised, he fancied, his wife's voice. Scared, and wide awake, he ran from the room – to the foot of the stairs – up the stairs. A tread of feet he heard in the room, and the door violently shaken, and another long, agonised scream.

Over this roof and around it is the serenest and happiest night. The brilliant moon, the dark azure and wide field of stars make it a night for holy thoughts, and lovers' vigils, so tender and beautiful. There is no moaning night-wind, not even a rustle in the thick ivy. The window gives no sound, except when the grey moth floating in its shadow taps softly on the pane. You can hear the leaf that drops of itself from the tree-top, and flits away from bough to spray to the ground.

Even in that gentle night there move, however, symbols of guilt and danger. While the small birds, with head under wing, nestle in their leafy nooks, the white owl glides with noiseless wing, a murderous phantom, cutting the air. The demure cat creeps on and on softly as a grey shadow till its green eyes glare close on its prey. Nature, with her gentleness and cruelty, her sublimity and meanness, resembles that microcosm, the human heart, in which lodge so many contrarieties, and the shabby contends with the heroic, the diabolic with the angelic.

In this still night Alice's heart was heavy. Who can account for those sudden, silent, but terrible changes in the spiritual vision which interpose as it were a thin coloured medium between ourselves and the realities that surround us – how all objects, retaining their outlines, lose their rosy glow and golden lights, and on a sudden face into dismallest grey and green?

'Dulcibella, do you think he's coming? Oh! Dulcibella, do you think he'll come to-night?'

'He may, dear. Why shouldn't he? Lie down, my child, and don't be sitting up in your bed so. You'll never go asleep while you're listening and watching. Nothing but fidgets, and only the wider awake the longer you watch. *Well* I know it, and many a long hour I laid awake myself expectin' and listenin' for poor Crane a-comin' home with the cart from market, long ago. He had his failin's – as who has not? poor Crane – but an honest man, and good-natured, and would not hurt a fly, and never a wry word out of his mouth, exceptin', maybe, one or two, which he never meant them, when he was in liquor – as who is there, Miss Ally, will not be sometimes? But he was a kind, handsome fellow, and sore was my heart when he was taken,' and Dulcibella wiped her eyes. 'Seven-and-twenty years agone last Stephen's Day I buried him in Wyvern Churchyard, and I tried to keep the little business agoin', but I couldn't make it pay nohow, and when it pleased God to take my little girl six years after, I gave all up and went to live at the vicarage. But as I was sayin', Miss, many a long hour I sat up a-watchin' for my poor Crane on his way home. He would sometimes stop a bit on the way, wi' a friend or two, at the "Cat and Fiddle" – 'twas the only thing I could ever say wasn't quite as I could ha' liked in my poor Crane. And that's how I came to serve your good mother, Miss, and your poor father, the good vicar o' Wyvern – there's not been none like him since, not one – no, indeed.'

'You remember mamma very well?'

'Like yesterday, Miss,' said old Dulcibella, who often answered that question. 'Like yesterday, the pretty lady. She always looked so pleasant, too – a smiling face, like the light of the sun coming into a room.'

'I wonder, Dulcibella, there was no picture.'

'No picture. No, Miss. Well, ye see, Miss Ally, dear, them pictures, I'm told, costs a deal o' money, and they were only beginnin', you know, and many a little expense – and Wyvern Vicarage is a small livelihood at best, and ye must be managin' if ye'd keep it – and good to the poor they was with all that, and gave what many a richer one wouldn't, and never spared trouble for them; they counted nothin' trouble for no one. They loved all, and lived to one another, not a wry word ever; what one liked t'other loved, and all in the light o' God's blessin'. I never seen such a couple – never; they doted on one another, and loved all, and they two was like one angel.'

'Lady Wyndale has a picture of poor mamma – very small – what they call a miniature. I think it quite beautiful. It was taken when she was not more than seventeen. Lady Wyndale, you know, was ever so much older than mamma.'

'Ay, so she was, ten year and more, I dare say,' answered Dulcibella.

'She is very fond of it – too fond to give it to me now; but she says, kind aunt, she has left it to me in her will. And oh! Dulcibella, I feel so lonely.'

'Lonely! why should you, darling, wi' a fine handsome gentleman to your husband, that will be squire o' Wyvern – think o' that – squire o' Wyvern, and that's a greater man than many a lord in Parliament; and he's good-natured, never a hard word or a skew look, always the same quiet way wi' him. Hoot, Miss! ye mustn't be talkin' that way. Think o' the little baby that's a-comin'. Ye won't know yourself for joy when ye see his face, please God, and I'm a-longin' to show him to ye.'

'You good old Dulcibella,' said the young lady, and her eyes filled with tears as she smiled. 'But poor mamma died when I was born – and oh, Dulcibella, do you think I shall ever see the face of the poor little thing? Oh! wouldn't it be sad! wouldn't it be sad!'

'Ye're not to be talkin' that nonsense, darling; 'tis sinful, wi' all that God has given you, a comfortable house over your head, and enough to eat, and good friends, and a fine, handsome husband that's kind to you, and a blessed little child a-comin' to make every minute pleasant to all that's in the house. Why, 'tis a sin to be frettin' like that; and as for this thing or that thing, or being afeard – why, everyone's afeard, it they'd let themselves, and not one in a thousand comes by any harm; and 'tis sinful, I tell ye, for ye know well ye're in the hands of the good God that's took care o' ye till now, and took ye out o' the little nursery of Wyvern Vicarage, when ye weren't the length o' my arm, and not a friend near but poor, foolish old Dulcibella, that did not know where to turn. And your aunt, that only went out as poor as your darling mamma, brought home well again from t'other end o' the world, and well to do, your own loving kith and kin, and good friends raised up on every side, and the old squire, Harry o' Wyvern, although he be a bit angered for a while, he's another good friend, that will be sure to make it up, whatever it is came between him and Master Charles. Hot blood's not the worst blood; better a blow in haste and a shake hands after than a smile at the lips and no goodwill wi' it. I tell you, they's not the worst, they hot-headed, hard-fisted, outspoken folk; and I'll never forget that day to him, when he brought you home that had no home, and me that was thinkin' o' nowt but the workhouse. So do or say what he will, God bless him for that day, say I, for 'twas an angel's part he did,' said old Dulcibella.

'So I feel, God knows; so I feel,' said Alice, 'and I hope it may all be made up; I'm sure it will; and, oh! Dulcibella, I have been the cause of so much sorrow and bitterness!'

She stopped suddenly, her eyes full of tears; but she restrained them.

'That's the way ye'll always be talking. I'd like to know where they'd be without you. Every man that marries will have care, more or less; 'tis the will o' God; and if he hadn't he'd never think o' Him; and 'tis a short life at the longest, and a sore pilgrimage at the best. So what He pleases to lay on us we must even bear wi' a patient heart, if we can't wi' a cheerful; for wi' His blessin' 'twill all end well.'

'Amen,' said Alice, with a cheerier smile, but a load still at her heart; 'I hope so, my good old Dulcibella. What should I do without you? *Wait!* hush! Is that a noise outside? No; I thought I heard a horse's tread, but there's nothing. It's too late now; there's no chance of him to-night. Do you think, Dulcibella, there is any chance?'

'Well, no, my dear; it's gettin' on too late – a deal too late; no, no, we must even put that clean out of our heads. Ye'll not get a wink o' sleep if you be listening for him. Well I know them fidgets, and many a time I lay on my hot ear – now this side, now that, listening till I could count the veins o' my head beating like a watch, and myself only wider and wider awake every hour, and more fool I; and well and hearty home wi' him, time enough, and not a minute sooner for all my watching. And mind ye, what I often told ye when ye were a wee thing, and ye'll find it true to the end o' your days, a watch-pot never boils.'

Alice laughed gently.

'I believe you are right, Dulcibella. No, he won't come to-night. It was only a chance, and I might have known. But perhaps, to-morrow? Don't you think to-morrow?'

'Very like, like enough, to-morrow – daylight, mayhap to breakfast – why not?' she answered.

'Well, I do think he may; he said, perhaps to-night, and I know, I'm sure he'll think how his poor wife is watching and longing to see him; and, as you advise, I'll put that quite out of my head; he has so many things to look after, and he only said *perhaps*; and you think in the morning. Well, I won't let myself think so, it would be too delightful; I won't think it. But it can't be many days, I'm sure – and – I won't keep you up any longer, dear old Dulcibella. I've been very selfish. So, good-night.'

And they kissed, as from little Allie's infancy they had always done, before settling for the night.

'Good-night, and God love it; it mustn't be frettin', and God bless you, my darling Miss Allie; and you must get to sleep, or you'll be looking so pale and poor in the morning he won't know you when he comes.'

So, with another hug and a kiss, they parted, and old Dulcibella, leaving her young mistress's candle burning on the table, as was her wont, being nervous when she was alone, and screened from her eyes by the curtain, with a final good-night and another blessing she closed the door.

Is there ever an unreserved and complete confidence after marriage? Even to kind old Dulcibella she could not tell all. As she smiled a little farewell on the faithful old soul her heart was ready to burst. She was longing for a good cry all to herself, and now, poor little thing, she had it.

She cried herself, as children do, to sleep.

An hour later the old Grange was silent as the neighbouring churchyard of Carwell. But there was not a household in the parish, or in the county, I suppose, many of whose tenants, at that late hour, were so oddly placed.

In his chair in the oak-panelled room, downstairs, sat Charles Fairfield, in that slumber of a tormented and exhausted brain which in its first profound submersion resembles the torpor of apoplexy.

In his forsaken room lay on the pillow the pale face of his young wife, her eyelashes not yet dry, fallen asleep in the sad illusion of his absence – better, perhaps, than his presence would have been, if she had known but all.

In her crib downstairs, at last asleep, lay the frightened Lilly Dogger, her head still under the coverlet, under which she had popped it in panic, as she thought of the possible return of the tall unknown, and the lobe of her ear still flaming from the discipline of her vice-like pinch.

Under his slanting roof, in the recess of the staircase, with only his coat off, stretched on the broad of his back, with one great horny hand half shut under his bullet head, and the other by his side, snored honest Tom, nothing the less soundly for his big mug of beer and his excursion to Cressley Common.

For a moment now we visit the bedside of good old Dulcibella. An easy conscience, a good digestion, and an easy place in this troublesome world are favourable to sound slumbers, and very tranquilly she slept, with a large handkerchief pinned closely about her innocent bald head, and a nightcap of many borders outside it. Her thick well-thumbed Bible, in which she read some half-dozen verses every night, lay, with her spectacles upon its cover, on the table by the brass candlestick.

Mildred Tarnley, a thin figure with many corners, lay her length in her clothes, her old brown stuff gown, her cap, and broad faded ribbons binding her busy head, and her darned black worsted stockings still on her weary feet, ready at call to jump up, pop her feet again into her misshapen shoes, and resume her duties.

In her own solitary chamber, at the deserted side of the house, the tall stranger, arrayed in a white woollen nightdress, lay her length, not stirring.

After Mildred Tarnley had got herself stiffly under her quilt, she was visited with certain qualms about this person, recollections of her abhorred activity and energy in old times, and fears that the 'grim white woman' was not resting in her bed. This apprehension grew so intense that, tired as she was, she could not sleep. The suspicion that, bare-footed, listening, that dreadful woman was possibly groping her way through the house made her heart beat faster and faster.

At last she could bear it no longer, and up she got, lighted her candle with a match, and in her stockings glided softly through the passage, and by the room where Charles Fairfield was at that time at his letters.

He recognised the step to which his ear was accustomed, and did not trouble himself to inquire what she was about.

So, softly, softly, softly – Mildred Tarnley found herself at the door of the unwelcome guest and listened. You would not have supposed old Mildred capable of a nervous tremble, but she was profoundly afraid of this awful woman, before whose superior malignity and unearthly energy her own temper and activity quailed. She listened, but could hear no evidence of her presence. Was the woman there at all? Lightly, lightly, with her nail, she tapped at the door. No answer. Then very softly she tried the door. It was secured.

But was the old soldier in the room still, or wandering about the house with who could fathom what evil purpose in her head?

The figure in white woollen was there still; she had been lying on her side, with her pale features turned towards the door as Mildred approached. Her blind eyes were moving in their sockets – there was a listening smile on her lips – and she had turned her neck awry to get her ear in the direction of the door. She was just as wide awake as Mildred herself.

Mildred watched for a time at the door, irresolute. Excuse enough, she bethought her, in the feeble state in which she had left her, had she for making her a visit. Why should she not open the door boldly and enter? But Mildred, in something worse than solitude, was growing more and more nervous. What if that tall, insane miscreant were waiting at the door, in a fit of revenge for her suspected perfidy, ready to clutch her by the throat as she opened it, and to strangle her on the bed? And when there came from the interior of the room a weary bleating 'Heigh-ho!' she absolutely bounced backward, and for a moment froze with terror.

She took a precaution as she softly withdrew. The passage, which is terminated by the 'old soldier's' room, passes a dressing-room on the left, and then opens, on the other side, upon a lobby. This door is furnished with a key, and having secured it, Mrs Tarnley, with that key in her pocket, felt that she had pretty well imprisoned that evil spirit, and returned to her own bed more serenely, and was soon lost in slumber.

CHAPTER 35

RESTLESS

Some lean, nervous temperaments, once fairly excited, and in presence of a substantial cause of uneasiness, are very hard to reduce to composure. After she had got back again, Mildred Tarnley fidgeted and turned in her bed, and lay in the dark, with her tired eyes wide open, and imagining, one after another, all sorts of horrors.

She was still in her clothes; so she got up again, and lighted a candle, and stole away, angry with herself and all the world on account of her fussy and feverish condition, and crept up the great stairs, and stealthily reached again the door of the 'old soldier's' room.

Not a sound, not a breath, could she hear from within. Gently she opened the door which no longer resisted. The fire was low in the grate; and, half afraid to look at the bed, she raised the candle and did look.

There lay the 'Dutchwoman,' so still that Mrs Tarnley felt a sickening doubt as she stared at her.

'Lord bless us! she's never quite well. I wish she was somewhere else,' said Mrs Tarnley, frowning sharply at her from the door.

Then, with a little effort of resolution, she walked to the bedside, and fancied, doubtfully, that she saw a faint motion as of breathing in the great resting figure, and she placed her fingers upon her arm, and then passed them down to her big hand, which to her relief was warm.

At the touch the woman moaned and turned a little.

'Faugh! what makes her sleep so like dead? She'd ha' frightened me a'most, if I did not know better. Some folks can't do nowt like no one else.' And Mildred would have liked to shake her up and bid her 'snore like other people, and give over her unnatural ways.'

But she did look so pale and fixed, and altogether so unnatural, that Mrs Tarnley's wrath was overawed, and, rather uneasily, she retired, and sat for a while at the kitchen fire, ruminating and grumbling.

'If she's a-goin' to die, what for should she come all the way to Carwell? Wasn't London good enough to die in?'

Mrs Tarnley only meant to warm her feet on the fender for a few minutes. But she fell asleep and wakened, it might be, a quarter of an hour later, and got up and listened.

What was it that overcame old Mildred on this night with so unusual a sense of danger of panic at the presence of this woman? She could not exactly define the cause. But she was miserably afraid of her, and full of unexplainable surmises.

'I can't go to bed until I try again – I can't. I don't know what's come over me. It seems to me – Lor' be wi' us! – as if the Evil One was in the house, and I don't know what I should do – and there's nowt o' any avail I can do; but quiet I can't bide, and sleep won't stay wi' me while she's here, and I'll just go up again to her room, and if all's right then I will lie down, and take it easy for the rest o' the night, come what, come may: for my old bones is fairly wore out, and I can't hold my head up no longer.'

Thus resolved, and sorely troubled, the old woman took the candle again and sallied forth once more upon her grizzly expedition.

From the panelled sitting-room, where by this time Charles Fairfield sat in his chair locked in dismal sleep, came the faint red mist of his candle's light, and here she paused to listen for a moment. Well, all was quite there, and so on and into the passage, and so into the great hall, as it was called, which seemed to her to have grown chill and cheerless since she was last there, and so again cautiously up the great stair, with its clumsy banister of oak, relieved at every turn by a square oak block terminating in a ball, like the head of a gigantic nine-pin. Black looked the passage through this archway, at the summit of this ascent; and for the first time Mildred was stayed by the sinking of a superstitious horror.

It was by putting a kind of force upon herself that she entered this dark and silent gallery, so far away from every living being in the house, except that one of whom secretly she stood in awe, as of something not altogether of this earth.

This gallery is pretty large, and about midway is placed another arch, with a door-case, and a door that is held open by a hook, and, as often happens in old houses, a descent of a couple of steps here brings you to a different level of the floor.

There may have been a reason of some other sort for the uncomfortable introduction of so many gratuitous steps in doorways and passages, but certainly it must have exercised the wits of the comparatively slow persons who flourished at the period of this sort of architecture, and prevented the drowsiest from falling asleep on the way to their bedrooms.

It happened that as she reached this doorway her eye was caught by a cobweb hanging from the ceiling. For a sharp old servant like Mrs Tarnley such festoonery has an attraction of antipathy that is irresistible; she tried to knock it with her hand, but it did not reach high enough, so she applied her fingers to loosen her apron, and sweep it down with a swoop of that weapon.

She was still looking up at the dusty cord that waved in the air, and as she did so she received a long pull by the dress, from an unseen hand below – a determined tweak – tightening and relaxing as she drew a step back, and held the candle backward to enable her to see.

It was not her kitten, which might have playfully followed her upstairs – it was not a prowling rat making a hungry attack. A low titter accompanied this pluck at her dress, and she saw the wide pale face of the Dutchwoman turned up towards her with an odious smile. She was seated on the step, with her shoulder leaning upon the frame of the door.

'You thought I was asleep under the coverlet,' she drawled; 'or awake, perhaps, in the other world – dead. I never sleep long, and I don't die easily – *see!*'

'And what for are ye out o' your bed at all, ma'am? Ye'll break your neck in this house, if he go walking about, wi' its cranky steps and stairs, and you blind.'

'When you go blind, old Mildred, you'll find your memory sharper than you think, and steps, and corners, and doors, and chimney-pieces will come to mind like a picture. What was I about?'

'Well, what *was* ye about? Sure I am I don't know, ma'am.'

'No, I'm sure you don't,' said she.

'But you should be in your bed – that I know, ma'am.'

Still holding her dress, and with a lazy laugh, the lady made answer:–

'So should you, old lass – a pair of us gadders; but I had a reason – I wanted you, old Mildred.'

'Well, ma'am, I don't know how you'd ha' found me, for I sleep in the five-cornered room, two doors away from the spicery – you'd never ha' found me.'

'I'd have tried – hit or miss – I would not have stayed where I was,' answered the old soldier.

'What, not in the state-room, ma'am – the finest room in the house, so 'twas always supposed!'

'So be it; I don't like it,' she answered.

'Ye didn't hear no noises in't, sure?' demanded Mildred.

'Not I,' said the Dutchwoman. 'Another reason quite, girl.'

'And what the de'il is it? It must be summat grand, I take it, that makes ye better here, sittin' on a hard stair, than lying your length on a good bed.'

'Right well said, clever Mildred. What is the state-room without a quiet mind?' replied the old soldier, with an oracular smile.

'What's the matter wi' your mind, ma'am?' said Mildred testily.

'I'm not safe there from intrusion,' answered the lady, with little pauses between her words to lend an emphasis to them.

'I don't know what you're afeard on, ma'am,' repeated Mrs Tarnley, whose acquaintance with fine words was limited, and who was too proud to risk a mistake.

'Well, it's just this – I won't be pried upon by that young lady.'

'What young lady, ma'am?' asked Mrs Tarnley, who fancied she might ironically mean Miss Lilly Dogger.

'Harry Fairfield's wife, of course, – what other? I choose to be private here,' said the Dutch dame, imperiously.

'She'll not pry – she don't pry on no one, and if she wished it she couldn't.'

'Why, there's nothing between us, woman, but the long closet where you used to keep the linen, and the broken furniture and rattle-traps' (raddle-drabs she pronounced the word), 'and she'll come and peep – every woman peeps and pries' (beebs and bries she called the words) – '*I* peep and pry. She'll just pretend she never knew anyone was there, and she'll walk in through the closet door, and start, and beg my pardon, and say how sorry she is, and then go off, and tell you next morning how many buttons are on my pelisse, and how many pins in my pincushion, and let all the world know everything about me.'

'But she can't come in.'

'Why?'

'Why? Because, ma'am, the door is papered over.'

'Fine protection – paper!' sneered the lady.

'I saw her door locked myself before 'twas papered over,' said Mildred.

'Did you, though?' said the lady.

'With my own eyes,' insisted Mildred.

'I'd rather see it with mine,' joked the blind lady. 'Well, see, we'll make a long story short. If I consent to stay in that room, I'll lock the door that opens into it. I'll have a room, and not a passage, if you please. I won't be peeped on, or listened to. If I can't choose my company, I'll be alone, please.'

'And what do you want, ma'am?' asked Mildred, whose troubles were multiplying.

'Another room,' said the lady, doggedly.

Mildred paused.

'Well, did I ever!' pondered Mrs Tarnley, reading the lady's features sharply as she spoke; but they were sullen, and, for aught she could make out, meaningless. 'Well, it will do if ye can have the key, I take it, and lock your door yourself?'

'Not so well as another room, if you'll give me one, but better than nothing.'

'Come along then, ma'am, for another room's not to be had at no price, and I'll gi'e ye the key.'

'And then, when you lock it fast, I may sleep easy. What's that your parson used to say – "the wicked cease from troubling, and the weary are at rest." Plenty of wicked people going, Mrs Tarnley, and weary enough am I,' sighed the great pale Dutchwoman.

'There's two on us so, ma'am,' said Mildred, as she led the lady back to her room, and, having placed her in her armchair by the fire, Mildred Tarnley took the key from a brass-headed tack, on which it hung behind the bedpost.

'Here it is, ma'am,' she said, placing the key in her groping fingers.

'What key is it?' asked the old soldier.

'The key of the long linen closet that was.'

'And how do I know that?' she inquired, twirling it round in her large fingers, and smiling in such a way as to nettle Mrs Tarnley, who began:–

'Ye may know, I take it, because Mildred Tarnley says so, and I never yet played a trick. I never tell lies,' she concluded, pulling up on a sudden.

'Well, I know that. I know you're truth itself, so far as human nature goes; but that has its limits, and can't fly very high off the ground. Come, get me up – we'll try the key. I'll lock it myself – I'll lock it with my own fingers. Seeing is believing, and I can't see; but feeling has no fellow, and, not doubting you, Mrs Tarnley, I'll feel for myself.'

She placed her hand on Mrs Tarnley's shoulder, and when she had reached the corner at the farther side of the bed, where the covered door, as she knew, was situated, with her scissors point, where the crevice of the door was covered over with the paper, she ripped it asunder (notwithstanding the remonstrances of Mildred, who told her she was 'leavin' it not worth a rag off the road') all round the door, which thus freed, and discovering by her finger-tips the point at which the keyhole was placed, she broke the paper through, introduced the key, turned it, and with very little resistance pulled the door partly open, with an ugly grimace and a chuckle at Mildred. Then, locking it fast, she said:–

'And now I defy madam, do all she can – and you'll clap the table against it, to make more sure; and so I think I may sleep – don't you?'

Mildred scratched above her eyebrow with one finger for a moment, and she said:–

'Yes, ye might ha' slept, I'm thinkin', as sound before if ye had a mind, ma'am.'

'What the dickens does the lass mean?' said the blind woman, with a sleepy laugh. 'As if people could sleep when they like. Why, woman, if that was so there would be no such thing as fidgets.'

'Well, I suppose, no more there wouldn't – no more there wouldn't. I may take away the tray, ma'am?'

'Let it be till morning – I want rest. Good-night. Are you going? Good-night.'

'Good-night, ma'am,' said Mildred, making her stiff little curtsey, although it was lost upon the lady, and a little thoughtfully she left the room.

The old soldier listened, sitting up, for she had lain down on her bed, and as she head the click-clack of Mildred's shoe grow fainter –

'Yes, good-night really, Mildred; I think you need visit no more to-night.'

And she got up, and secured the door that opened on the gallery.

'Good-night, old Tarnley,' she said, with a nod and an unpleasant smirk, and then a deep and dismal sigh. Then she threw herself again upon her bed and lay still.

Old Mildred seemed also to have come to a like conclusion as to the matter of further visiting for the night, for at the door, on the step of which the Dutchwoman sitting a few minutes before had startled her, she looked back suspiciously over her shoulder, and then, shutting the door noiselessly, she locked it – leaving that restless spirit a prisoner till morning.

CHAPTER 36

THROUGH THE WALL

Alice had slept quietly for some time. The old clock at the foot of the stairs had purred and struck twice since she had ceased listening and thinking. It was for all that time an unbroken sleep, and then she wakened. She had been half conscious for some time of a noise in the

room, a fidgeting little noise, that teased her sleep for a time, and finally
awoke her completely. She sat up in her bed, and heard, she thought, a
sigh in the room. Exactly from what point she could not be certain, nor
whether it was near or far.

She drew back the curtain and looked. The familiar furniture only met
her view. In like manner all round the room. Encouraged by which
evidence she took heart of grace, and got up, and, quite to satisfy herself,
made a search – as timid people will, because already morally certain that
there is no need of a search.

Happily she was spared the terror of any discovery to account for the
sound that had excited her uneasiness.

She turned again the key in her door, and, thus secured, listened there.
Everything was perfectly still. Then into bed she got, and listened to
silence, and in low tones talking to herself, for the sound of her own
voice was reassuring, she reasoned with her tremors, she trimmed her
light and made some little clatter on the table, and bethought her that
this sigh that had so much affrighted her might be no more than the
slipping of one fold of her bed-curtain over another – an occurrence
which she remembered to have startled her once before.

So after a time she persuaded herself that her alarm was fanciful, and
she composed herself again to sleep. Soon, however, her evil genius
began to worry her in another shape, and something like the gnawing
and nibbling of a mouse grated on her half-sleeping ear from the
woodwork of the room. So she sat up again, and said:–

'Hish!'

Now toward the window, now toward the fireplace, now toward the
door, and all again was quite still.

Alice got up, and, throwing her dressing-gown about her shoulders,
opened the window shutter and looked out upon the serene and
melancholy landscape which this old-fashioned window, with its clumsy
sashes and small panes, commanded. Sweet and sad these moonlit views that
so well accord with certain moods. But the cares at Alice's heart were real,
and returned as she quite awoke with a renewed pang – and the cold and
mournful glory of the sky and silvered woodlands neither cheered nor
soothed her. With a deep sigh she closed the shutter again, and by the dusky
candle-light returned to her bed. There at last she did fall into a quiet sleep.

From this she awoke suddenly and quite. Her heart was throbbing fast,
but she could not tell whether she awoke of herself or had been aroused
by some external cause.

'Who's there?' she cried, in a fright, as she started up and looked about
the room.

Exactly as she called she thought she heard something fall – a heavy
and muffled sound. It might have been a room or two away, it might have

been nearer, but her own voice made the sound uncertain. She waited in alarm and listened, but for the present all was again quiet.

Poor little Alice knew very well that she was not herself, and her reason took comfort from her consciousness of the excited state of her nerves.

'What a fool I am!' she whispered, with a sigh. 'What a fool! Everything frightens me now, I've grown such a coward. Oh! Charlie, Charlie – oh, Ry darling! – when will you come back to your poor wife – when shall this dreadful suspense be over and quiet come again?'

Then poor little Alice cried, after the manner of women, bitterly for a time, and then, as she used in all trouble, she prayed, and essayed to settle again to sleep. But hardly had she begun the attempt when it was terminated strangely.

Again she heard the same stealthy sound, as of something cutting or ripping. Again she cried, 'Hish, hish!' but with no effect. She fancied at the far corner of the room, about as high as she could easily reach, that she saw some glittering object. It might be a little bit of looking-glass pass slowly and tremulously along the wall, horizontally, and then with the same motion, in a straight line down the wall, glimmering faintly in the candlelight. At the same time was a slight trembling of that part of the wall, a slight, wavy motion, and – could she believe her eyes? – a portion of the wall seemed to yield silently, an unsuspected door slowly opened, and a tall figure wrapped in a flannel dress came in.

This figure crouched a little with its hand to its ear, and moved its head slowly round as if listening in all directions in turn. Then softly, with a large hand, it pushed back the door, which shut with a little snap, as with a spring-back.

Alice all this time was gazing upon the visitor, actually freezing with terror, and not knowing whether the apparition was that of a living person or not. The woollen-clothed figure, with large feet in stockings, and no shoes on, advanced, the fingers of one hand sliding gently along the wall. With an aspect fixed on the opposite end of the room, and the other hand a little raised in advance, it was such a fixed, listening look, and groping caution of motion as one might fancy in a person getting along a familiar room in the dark.

The feeling that she was not seen made Alice instinctively silent. She was almost breathless. The intruder passed on thus until she had reached the corner of the room, when she felt about for the doorcase, and having got her hand upon it she quickly transferred it to the handle, which she turned, and tried the door two or three times. Oh! what Alice would have given at this moment that she had not locked it, believing, as she now did, that the stranger would have passed out quietly from the room if this obstruction had not presented itself.

As if her life was concentrated in her eyes, Alice gazed still at this person, who paused for a few seconds, and, lowering her head, listened fixedly. Then very cautiously she with the tips of her fingers tried – was it to turn the key in the lock or to extricate it? At all events, she failed. She removed her hand, turned a little, stood still, and listened.

To Alice's horror, her business in the room was plainly not over yet. The woman stood erect, drawing a long breath, holding her underlip slightly in her teeth, with just a little nip. She turned her face toward the bed, and for the first time Alice now quite distinctly saw it – pale, seamed with small-pox, blind. This large face was now turned toward her, and the light of the candle, screened by the curtain from Alice's eyes, fell full upon its exaggerated and evil features. The woman had drawn in a long, full breath, as if coming to a resolution that needed some nerve.

Whatever this woman had come into the room for, Alice thought, with hope, that she, at all events, as she stood pallid and lowering before her, with eyes white with cataract, and brows contracted in malignant calculation, knew nothing, as she undoubtedly saw nothing, of her.

Still as death sat Alice in her terror, gazing into the sightless face of this woman, little more than two yards removed from her.

Suddenly this short space disappeared, and with two swift steps and an outstretched hand she stood at the bedside and caught Alice's nightdress, and drew her forcibly towards her. Alice as violently resisted. With a loud scream she drew back, and the nightdress tore. But the tall woman instantly grasped her nearer the shoulder, and, scrambling on the bed on her knees, she dragged her down upon it, and almost instantly struck at her throat with a knife.

To make this blow she was compelled to withdraw one hand, and with a desperate spring Alice evaded the stroke.

The whole thing was like a dream. The room seemed all a cloud. She could see nothing but the white figure that was still close, climbing swiftly over the bed, with one hand extended now and the knife in the other.

Not knowing how she got there, she was now standing with her back to the wall, in the farther corner of the room, staring at the dreadful figure in a catalepsy of terror.

There was hardly a momentary pause. She was afraid to stir lest the slightest motion should betray her to the search of this woman. Had she, as she stood and listened sharply, heard her breathing?

With sudden decision, long light steps, and her hand laid to the wall, she glided swiftly toward her. With a gasp Alice awoke, as it were, from her nightmare, and, almost wild with terror, fled round the bed to the door. Hastening, jostling by the furniture, gliding, on the whole, very adroitly after her, her face strained with a horrible eagerness and fear, came the blind woman.

Alice tried to pull open the door. She had locked it herself, but in her agitation forgot.

Now she seized the key and tried to turn it, but the strong hand of the stranger, in forcing it round a second time, had twisted it so that it was caught in the lock and would not turn.

Alice felt as people feel in dreams, when pursuit is urgent and some little obstruction entangles flight and threatens to deliver the fugitive into the hands of an implacable pursuer. A frantic pull, and a twist or two of the key in vain, and the hand of the pursuer was all but upon her. Again she sprang and scrambled across the bed, and it seemed enraged by the delay, and with a face sharpening and darkening with insanity, the murderess, guided by the sound, flung herself after her; and now, through the room and lobbies, pealed shrieks of murder, as Alice drew before the outstretched hand of the beldame, who, baulked of her prey, followed with reckless fury, careless now against what she struck or rushed, and clawing the air, as it seemed, within an inch of Alice's shoulder.

Unequal as it appeared, in this small pen, the struggle to escape could not have lasted very long. The old closet door, thinly covered with paper, through which the sharp knife had glided almost without noise, was locked, and escape through it as hopeless as through the other door. Through the window she would have thrown herself, but it was fastened, and one moment's delay would have been death. Had a weapon been in her hand, had she thought of it in this extremity of terror, her softer instincts might have been reversed, and she might have turned on her pursuer and fought, as timid creatures have done, with the ferocity of despair, for her life. But the chance that might have so transformed her did not come. Flight was her one thought, and that ended suddenly, for, tripping in the upturned carpet, she fell helplessly to the floor. In a moment, with a gasp, her pursuer was kneeling by her side, with her hand in her dishevelled hair, and drawing herself close for those sure strokes of the knife with which she meant to mangle her.

As the eyes of the white owl glare through the leaves on the awaking bird, and its brain swims, and its little heart bounces into a gallop, seeing its most dreadful dream accomplished, escape impossible, its last hour come – then the talons of the spectre clutch its throat, and its short harmless life is out, so might it have been with pretty Alice.

In that dreadful second of time all things that her eyes beheld looked strange, in a new reality – the room contracted, and familiar things were unlike themselves, and the certainty and nearness of that which she now knew – all her life before was but a dream to her – what an infidel, what a fool she had been – *here* it was, and *now* – death.

The helpless yell that burst from her lips, as this dreadful woman shuffled nearer on her knees, was answered by a crash from the door burst in, and a cry from a manly voice – the door flew wide, and Alice saw her husband pale as death; with a single savage blow he stretched her assailant on the floor – in another moment, Alice, wild with terror, half fainting, was in his arms.

And – did he *strike* her? Good God! – had he struck her! How did she lie there bleeding? For a moment a dreadful remorse was bursting at his heart – he would have kneeled – he could have killed himself. Oh, manhood! Gratitude! Charity! Could he, even in a moment of frenzy, have struck down any creature so – that had ever stood to him in the relation of that love? What a rush of remembrances and hell of compunction was there! – and for a rival! She the reckless, forlorn, guilty old love cast off, blasted with deformity and privation, and now this last fell atrocity! Alice was clinging to him, the words 'Darling, darling, my Ry, my saviour, my Ry,' were in his ears, and he felt as if he hated Alice – hated her worse even than himself. He froze with horror and agony as he beheld the ineffaceable image of that white, blood-stained twitching face, with sightless eyes, and on the floor those straggling locks of changed, grizzled hair, that once were as black as a raven's wing to which he used to compare them. Oh, maddening picture of degradation and cruelty! To what had they both come at last?

But an iron necessity was upon him, and with an energy of hypocrisy he said: 'Alice, my treasure, my darling, you're safe, aren't you?'

'Oh, darling, yes,' she gasped.

'Not here – you mustn't stay here – run down – she's mad – she's a mad woman – not here a moment.'

Half stunned and dreamy with horror, Alice glided down the stairs, passing honest Tom, who was stumbling up, half awake, but quite dressed excepting his coat.

'Run, Tom, help your master, for God's sake – there's something dreadful,' she said as she passed him with her trembling hands raised.

'Where, ma'am, may't be?' said Tom, pausing with a coolness that was dreadful, she thought.

'There, there, in his room – my room; go, for Heaven's sake!'

Up ran Tom, making a glorious clatter with his hob-nails, and down ran Alice, and just at the foot of the stair she met Mildred Tarnley's tall slim figure. The old woman drew to the banister, and stood still, looking darkly and shrewdly at her.

'Oh! good Mildred – oh, Mrs Tarnley, for God's sake don't leave me!'

'And what's the row, ma'am – what is it?' asked Mrs Tarnley, with her lean arm supporting the poor trembling young lady who clung to her.

'Oh, Mrs Tarnley, take me with you – take me out – I can't stay in the house – anywhere out of the house.'

'Well, well, come down, come along,' she said, more tenderly than was her wont, and watching her face hard from the corners of her eyes. She was convinced that the 'old soldier' was the cause of these horrors.

'Put your arm over my shouther, ma'am; there – that's it – an' I'll put mine round you, if you don't think I'm making too bold. There now, you're more easy, I think.'

And as they got on through the passage she asked:—

''Twas you that skritched, hey?'

'I? I dare say – did I?'

'Ay did ye, with a will, whoever skritched. Ye seen summat. What may ye have seen that frightened ye like that?'

'We'll talk by-and-bye. I'm ill – I'm horribly ill. Come away.'

'Come, then, if ye like best, ma'am,' said Mildred Tarnley, leading her through the kitchen, and by the outer door into the open air; but she had hardly got a step into the yard when the young lady, holding her fast, stopped short in renewed terrors.

'Oh, Mildred, if she follows us – if she overtook us out here?'

'Hoot, ma'am, who are ye afeard on? Is it that crazy blind woman, or who?'

'Oh, Mildred, yes, it is she. Oh, Mildred, where shall we go – where can I hide myself? There's nowhere safe.'

'Now, you're just drivin' yourself distracted, you be. What for need ye fear her? She's crazy, I'll not deny, but she's blind too, and she can't follow ye here, if she was so minded. Why, she couldn't cross the stile, nor follow ye through a spinnie. But see, ye've nowt but yer dressin' gown over yer night clothes, and yer bare feet. Odds, I'll not go wi' ye – ye'll come back, and if ye must come abroad, ye'll get yer cloaks and your shoon.'

'No, no, no, Mildred, I'll go as I am,' cried the terrified lady, at the same time hurrying onward to the yard door.

'Well,' said the old woman, following, 'wilful lass will ha' her way, but ye'll clap this ower your shouthers.'

And she placed her own shawl on them, and together they passed into the lonely woodlands that, spreading upward from the glen of Carwell, embower the deep ravine that flanks the side of the Grange, and, widening and deepening, enter the kindred shadows of the glen.

CHAPTER 37

A MESSENGER

Alice had not gone far when she was seized with a great shivering – the mediate process by which, from high hysterical tension, nature brings down the nerves again to their accustomed tones.

The air was soft and still, and the faint grey of morning was already changing the darkness into its peculiar twilight.

'Ye'll be better presently, dear,' said the old woman, with unaccustomed kindness. 'There, there, ye'll be nothing the worse when a's done, and ye'll have a cup o' tea when ye come back.'

Under the great old trees near the ivied wall which screens the court is a stone bench, and on this old Mildred was constrained to place her.

'There, there, there, rest a bit – rest a little bit. Hih! cryin' – well, cry if ye will; but ye'll ha' more to thank God than to cry for, if all be as I guess.'

Alice cried on with convulsive sobs, starting every now and then, with a wild glance to the yard gate, and grasping the old woman's arm. In a very few minutes this paroxysm subsided, and she wept quietly.

''Twas you, ma'am, that cried out, I take it – hey? Frightened, mayhap?'

'I was – yes – I – I'll wait a little, and tell you by-and-bye – horribly – horribly.'

'Ye needn't be afeard here, and me beside ye, ma'am, and daylight a-comin', and I think I could gi'e a sharp guess at the matter. Ye saw her ladyship, I do suppose? The old soger, ma'am – ay, that's a sight might frighten a body – like a spirit a'most – a great white-faced, blind devil.'

'Who is she? How did she come? She tried to kill me. Oh! Mrs Tarnley, I'm so terrified!'

And with these words Alice began to cry and tremble afresh.

'Hey! try to kill ye, did she? I'm glad o' that – right glad o't; 'twill rid us o' trouble, ma'am. But, la! think o' that! And did she actually raise her hand to you?'

'Oh yes, Mrs Tarnley – frightful. I'm saved by a miracle – I don't know how – the mercy of God only.'

She was clinging to Mrs Tarnley with a fast and trembling grasp.

'Zooks! the lass is frightened. Ye ha' seen sights to-night, young lady, ye'll remember. Young folk loves pleasure, and the world, and themselves ower well to trouble their heads about death or judgment, if the Lord in His mercy didn't shake them up from their dreams and their sins. "Awake thou that sleepest," says the Word, callin' loud in a drunken ear, at dead o' night, wi' the house all round a-fire, as the parson says. He's a good man, though I may ha' seen better, in old days in Carwell pulpit. So, 'tis all for good, and in place o' cryin' ye should be praisin' God for startlin' ye out o' your carnal sleep, and makin' ye think o' Him, and see yourself as ye are, and not according to the flatteries o' your husband and your own vanity. Ye'll pardon me, but truth is truth, and God's truth first of all; and who'll tell it ye if them as is within hearin' won't open their lips, and I don't see that Mr Charles troubles his head much about the matter.'

'He is so noble, and always my guardian angel. Oh, Mrs Tarnley, to-night I must have perished if it had not been for him; he is always my best friend, and so unselfish and noble.'

'Well, that's good,' said Mildred Tarnley, coldly. 'But I'm thinkin' something ought to be done wi' that catamountain in there, and strike while the iron's hot, and they'll never drive home that nail ye'll find – more like to go off when all's done wi' her pocket full o' money. 'Tis a sin, while so many an honest soul wants, and I'll take that just into my own old hands, I'm thinkin', and sarve her out as she would better women.'

'Isn't she mad, Mrs Tarnley?' asked Alice.

'And if she's mad, to the madhouse wi' her, an' if she's not, where's the gallows high enough for her, the dangerous harridan? For, one way or t'other, the fiend's in her, and the sooner judgment overtakes her, and she's in her coffin, the sooner the devil's laid, and the better for honest folk.'

'If she is mad, it accounts for everything; but I feel as if I could never enter that house again; and oh! Mrs Tarnley, you *mustn't* leave me. Oh, heavens! what's that?'

It was no great matter – Mrs Tarnley had got up, for the yard door had opened and someone passed out and looked round.

It was the girl, Lilly Dogger, who stood there looking about her under the canopy of tall trees.

'Hoot, ma'am, 'tis only the child Lilly Dogger – and well pleased I am, for I was thinkin' this minute how I could get her to me quietly. Here, Lilly – come here, ye goose-cap – d'ye see me?'

So, closing the door behind her, the girl approached with eyes very wide, and a wonderfully solemn countenance. She had been roused and scared by the sounds which had alarmed the house, huddled on her clothes, and, seeing Mrs Tarnley's figure cross the window, had followed in a tremor.

Mrs Tarnley walked a few steps towards her, and beckoning with her lean finger, the girl drew near.

'Ye'll have to go over Cressley Common, girl, to Wykeford. Ye know Wykeford?'

'Yes, please 'm.'

'Well, ye must go through the village, and call up Mark Topham. Ye know Mark Topham's house with the green door, by the bridge end?'

'Yes, please, Mrs Tarnley, ma'am.'

'And say he'll be wanted down here at the Grange – for *murder*, mind – and go ye on to Mr Rodney at t'other side o' the river – Squire Rodney of Wrydell. Ye know that house, too?'

'Yes 'm,' said the girl, with eyes momentarily distending, and face of blanker consternation.

'And ye'll tell Mr Rodney there's been bad work down here, and murder all but done, and say ye've told Mark Topham, the constable, and that it is hoped he'll come over himself to make out the writin's and send away the prisoner as should go. We being chiefly women here, and having to keep Tom Clinton at home to mind the prisoner – ye understand – and keep all safe, having little other protection. Now run in, lass, and clap your bonnet on, and away wi' ye; and get ye there as fast as your legs will carry ye, and take your time comin' back; and ye may get a lift, for they'll not be walkin', and you're like to get your bit o' breakfast down at Wrydell; but if ye shouldn't, here's tuppence, and buy yourself a bit o' bread in the town. Now, ye understand?'

'Yes 'm, please.'

'And ye'll not be makin' mistakes, mind?'

'No, ma'am.'

'Then do as I bid ye, and off ye go,' said Mrs Tarnley, despatching her with a peremptory gesture.

So, with a quaking heart, not knowing what dangers might still be lurking there, Lilly Dogger ran into the yard on her way to her bonnet, and peeped through the kitchen window, but saw nothing there in the pale grey light but 'still life'.

With a timid finger she lifted the latch, and stole into the familiar passage as if she were exploring a haunted house. She had quaked in her bed as thin and far away the shrill sounds of terror had penetrated through walls and passages to her bedroom. She had murmured 'Lord bless us!' at intervals, and listened, chilled with a sense of danger – associated in her imagination with the stranger who had visited her room and frighted away her slumbers. And she had jumped out of bed, and thrown on her clothes in panic, blessed herself, and pinned and tied strings, and listened, and blessed herself again; and seeing Mrs Tarnley cross the window accompanied by some one else whom she did not then recognise, and fearing to remain thus deserted in the house more than the risk of being blown up by Mrs Tarnley, she had followed that grim protectress.

Now, as on tiptoe she recrossed the kitchen with her straw bonnet in her hand, and she heard on a sudden cries of fury, and words, as doors opened and shut, reached her that excited her horror and piqued her curiosity.

She hastened, however, to leave the house, and again approached and passed by the lady and Mildred Tarnley, having tied her bonnet under her chin, and obeying Mildred's impatient beckon, and –

'Run, lass, run! Stir your stumps, will ye?'

She started at a pace that promised soon to see her across Cressley Common.

Old Mildred saw this with comfort. She knew that broad-shouldered, brown-eyed lass for a shrewd and accurate messenger, and, seeing how dangerous and complicated things were growing, she was glad that fortune had opened so short and sharp a way of getting rid of the troubler of their peace.

'Come in, ma'am, ye'll catch your death o' cold here. All's quiet by this time, and I'll make the kitchen safe against the world; and Mr Charles is in the house, and Tom Clinton up, and all safe – and who cares a rush for that blind old cat? Not I, for one. She'll come no nonsense over Mildred Tarnley in her own kitchen, while there's a poker to rap her ower the pate. Hoot! one old blind limmer; I'd tackle six o' her sort, old as I am, and tumble 'em one after t'other into the Brawl. Never ye trouble your head about that, ma'am, and I'll bolt the door on the passage, and the scullery door likewise, and lock 'em if ye like; and we'll get down old Dulcibella to sit wi' ye, and ye'll be a deal less like to see that beast in the kitchen than here. There's Miss Crane,' by which title she indicated old Dulcibella, 'a-lookin' out o' her window. Ho! Miss Crane, come down and stay a bit wi' your mistress?'

'Thank God! – is she down there?' exclaimed she.

'Come down, ma'am, please; she's quite well, and she'll be glad to see ye.'

Old Dulcibella's head disappeared from the window promptly.

'Now, ma'am, she'll be down, and when she comes – for ye'd like to ha' some one by ye – I'll go in and make the kitchen door fast.'

'And won't you search it well, Mrs Tarnley, and the inner room, that we may be certain no one is hid there? Pray do – may I rely on you – won't you promise?'

'There's nothin' there, that I promise ye.'

'But, oh! pray do,' urged Alice.

'I will, ma'am, just to quiet ye. Ye need not fear, I'll leave her no chance, and she'll soon be safe enough, she shall – safe enough when she gets on her doublet of stone; and don't ye be frightenin' yourself for nothin' – just keep yourself quiet, for there is nothing to fear, and if ye will keep yourself in a fever for nothin' ye'll be just making good for worms, mark my words.'

As she spoke old Dulcibella appeared, and with a face of deep concern waddled as fast as she could toward her young mistress, raising her hands and eyes from time to time as she approached.

As she drew nearer she made a solemn thanksgiving, and –

'Oh! my child, my child, thank God you're well. I was a'most ready to drop in a swound when I came into your room, just now, everything knocked, topsy-turvy, and a door cut in the wall, and all in a litter, I couldn't know where I was, and someone a-bleedin' all across the floor, and one of the big green-handled knives on the floor – Lord ha' mercy on us – with the blade bent and blood about it. I never was so frightened. I thought my senses was a-leavin' me, and I couldn't tell what I might see next, and I ready to drop down on the floor wi' fright. My darling child – my precious – Lord love it, and here it was, barefooted, and but half clad, and – come in ye must, dear, 'tis enough to kill ye.'

'I can scarcely remember anything, Dulcibella, only one thing – oh! I'm so terrified.'

'Come in, darling, you'll lose your life if you stay here as you are. And what was it, dear, and who did you see?'

'A woman – that dreadful blind woman, who came in at the new door; I never saw her before.'

'Well, *dear!* Oh, Miss Alice, darling, I couldn't 'a' believed, and thank God you're safe after all; that's she I heard a-screechin' as strong as a dozen – and frightful words, as well as I could hear, to come from any woman's lips. Lord help us!'

'Where is she now?'

'Somewhere in the front of the house, darlin', screechin' and laughin', I thought, but Heaven only knows.'

'She's mad, Mrs Tarnley says, and Mr Fairfield said so too. Master Charles is come – my darling Ry. Oh! Dulcibella, how grateful I should be! What could I have done if he hadn't?'

So Dulcibella persuaded her to come into the yard, and so, through the scullery door, at which Mildred stood, having secured all other access to the kitchen. So in she came, awfully frightened to find herself, again in the house; but was not her husband there, and help at hand, and the doors secured?

CHAPTER 38

UNREASONABLE BERTHA

Her husband was at hand – that is to say, under the same roof, and at that moment in the room in which the blind woman was now sitting, bleeding from head and hand, and smiling as she talked, with the false light of a malignant irony.

'So, husband and wife are met again! And what have you to say after so long a time?'

'I've nothing to say. Let my deeds speak. I've given you year by year fully half my income.'

She laughed scornfully, and exclaimed merely:–

'Magnificent man!'

'Miserable pittance it is, but, the more miserable, the harder the sacrifice for me. I don't say I have been able to do much; but I have done more than my means warrant, and I don't understand what you propose to yourself by laying yourself out to torment and embarrass me. What the devil do you follow me about for? Do you think I'm fool enough to be bullied?'

'A fine question from Charles Vairfield of Wyvern to his wife!' she observed with a pallid simper.

'Wife and husband are terms very easily pronounced,' said he.

'And relations very easily made,' she rejoined.

He was leaning with his shoulder against the high mantelpiece, and looking upon her with a countenance in which you might have seen disdain and fear mingling with something of compunction.

'Relations very easily made, and still more easily affected,' he replied. 'Come, Bertha, there is no use in quarrelling over points of law. Past is past, as Leonora says. If I have wronged you anything, I am sorry. I've tried to make amends; and though many a fellow would have been tired out long ago, I continue to give you proofs that I am not.'

'That is a sort of benevolence,' she said, in her own language, 'which may as well be voluntary for, if it be not, the magistrates will compel it.'

'The magistrates are neither fools nor tyrants. You'll make nothing of the magistrates. You have no rights, and you know it.'

'An odd country where a wife has no rights.'

'Come, Bertha, there is no use in picking a quarrel. While you take me quietly you have your share, and a good deal more. You used to be reasonable.'

'A reasonable wife, I suppose, gives up her position, her character, her prospects, whenever it answers her husband to sacrifice these trifles for his villanous pleasures. Your English wives must be meek souls indeed if they like it. I don't hear they are such lambs, though.'

'I'm not going to argue law points, as I said before. Lawyers are the proper persons to do that. You used to be reasonable, Bertha – where's the good in pushing things to extremes?'

'What a gentle creature you are!' she laughed; 'and how persuasive!'

'I'm a quiet fellow enough, I believe, as men go, but I'm not persuasive, and I know it. I wish I were.'

'Those whom you have persuaded once are not likely to be persuaded again. Your persuasions are not always lucky. Are they?'

'You want to quarrel about everything. You want to leave no possible point of agreement.'

'Things are at a bad pass when husband and wife are so.'

Charles looked at her angrily for a moment, and then down to the floor, and he whistled a few bars of a tune.

'What do you whistle for?' she demanded.

'Come, Bertha, don't be foolish.'

'You were once a gentleman. It is a blackguard who whistles in reply to a lady's words,' she said, on a sudden stretching out her hand tremulously, as if in search of someone to grasp.

'Well, don't mind. Stick to one thing at a time. For God's sake say what you want, and have done with it.'

'You must acknowledge me before the world for your wife,' she answered with resolute serenity, and, raising her face and shutting her mouth, she sniffed defiantly through her distended nostrils.

'Come, come, Bertha, what good on earth could come of that?'

'Little to you, perhaps.'

'And none to you.'

She laughed savagely. 'That lie won't do.'

'Bertha, Bertha, we may hate one another, if you will. But is it not as well to try whether we can agree upon anything? Let us just for the present talk intelligibly.'

'You tried to murder me, you arch-villain.'

'Nonsense!' said he, turning pale. 'How can you talk so – how can you? Could I help interposing? You may well be thankful that I did.'

'You tried to murder me,' she screamed.

'You know that's false. I took the knife down from your hand, and by doing so I saved two lives. It was you – not I – who hurt your hand.'

'You villain – you damned villain, I wish I could kill you dead.'

'All the worse for you, Bertha.'

'I wish you were dead and cold in your bed, and my hand on your face to be sure of it.'

'Now you're growing angry again. I thought we had done with storm and hysterics for a little, and could talk, and perhaps agree upon something, or at all events not waste our few minutes in violence.'

'Violence! – you wretch, who began it?'

'What can you mean, Bertha?'

'You've married that woman. Oh, I know it all – I your lawful wife living. I'll have you transported, double-dyed villain.'

'Where's the good of screaming all this at the top of your voice?' he said, at last growing angry. 'You wish you could kill me? I almost wish you could. I've been only too good to you, and allowed you to trouble me too long.'

'Ha, ha! – you would like to put me out of the way?'

'You'll do that for yourself. Can't you wait, can't you listen, can't you have common reason, just for one moment? What do you want – what do you wish? Do you want every farthing I possess on earth, and to leave me nothing?'

'I'm your wife, and I'll have my rights.'

'Now listen to me – that's a question I need not discuss, because you already know what I believe on the subject.'

'You know what your brother Harry thinks.'

'I know what it is his interest to think.'

'You daren't say that if he were here, you coward!'

'And I don't care a farthing what he thinks.'

'Ha, ha, ha!'

'But if it had been fifty times over, what it never was, a marriage, your own conduct, long ago, would have dissolved it.'

'And you allow you have married that woman?'

'I sha'n't talk to you about it; how I shall act, or may act, or *have* acted, is my own affair, and, rely upon it, I'll do nothing on the assumption that I ever was married to you.'

Up stood the tall woman, with hands extended toward him, wide open, with a slightly groping motion as if opening a curtain; not a word did she say, but her sightless eyes, which stared full at him, were quivering with that nervous tremor which is so pleasant to see.

She drew breath two or three times at intervals, long and deep, almost a sob, and then without speaking or moving more she sat down, looking awfully white and wicked.

For a long time the old soldier had lost the thread of her discourse. Charles heard a step not very far off. He thought his unreasonable Bertha was about to have a fit, and opening the door he called lustily to Mildred.

It *was* Mrs Tarnley.

'Will you get her some water, or whatever she ought to have – I think she is ill, and pray be quick.'

With a dark prying look Mildred glanced from one to the other.

'It's in a madhouse and not here the like of her should be, wi' them fits and frenzies,' she muttered, as she applied herself to the resuscitation of the Dutchwoman.

On her toilet was a little group of bottles labelled 'Sal-volatile', 'Asafoetida', 'Valerian'.

'I don't know which is the right one, but this can't be far wrong,' she remarked, selecting the sal-volatile, and dropping some into the water.

'La! so it was a sort of fit. See how stiff she was. Lor' bless us, I do wish she was under a mad doctor. See how her feet's stuck out, and her thumbs tight shut in her fists, and her teeth set,' and old Mildred applied the sal-volatile phial to the patient's nostrils, and gradually got her into a drowsy, yawning state, in which she seemed to care and comprehend little or nothing of where she was or what had befallen her.

'Tell her I stayed till I saw her better, if she asks, and that I'm coming back again. She says she is hurt.'

'So much the better,' said Mildred; 'that will keep her from prowling about the house like a cat or a ghost, as she did all night, and no good came of it.'

'And will you look to her wrist? She cut it last night, and it is very clumsily tied up, and I'll come again, tell her.'

So, with a bewildered brain and a direful load at his heart, he left the room.

Where was Alice? he thought. He went downstairs and up again by the back staircase to their room, and there found the wreck and disorder of the odious scene he had witnessed, still undisturbed, and looking somehow more shocking in the sober light of morning.

From this sickening record of the occurrences of last night he turned for a moment to the window, and looked out on the tranquil and sylvan solitudes, and then back again upon the disorder which had so nearly marked a scene of murder.

'How do I keep my reason?' thought he. 'Is there in England so miserable a man? Why should not I end it?'

Between the room where he stood and the angle of that bedroom in which at that moment was the wretch who agitated every hour of his existence with dismay, there intervened but eight-and-twenty feet, in that polyhedric and irregular old house. If he had but one tithe of her wickedness he had but to take up that poker, strike through, and brain her as she sat there.

Why was he not a little more or a little less wicked? If the latter, he might never have been in his present fix. If the other, he might find a short way out of the thicket – 'hew his way out with a bloody axe' – and none but those whose secrecy he might rely on be the wiser!

Avaunt, horrible shadows! Such beckoning phantoms from the abyss were not tempters, but simply terrors. No, he was far more likely to load a pistol, put the muzzle in his mouth, and blow his harassed brains out.

CHAPTER 39

AN ABDUCTION

So far as a man not very resolute can be said to have made up his mind to anything, Charles Fairfield had quite made up his, driven thus fairly into a corner, to fight his battle now, and decisively. He would hold no terms and offer no compromise. Let her do her worst. She had found out his secret. Oh! brother Harry, had *you* played him false? And she had quoted *your* opinion against him. Had you been inflaming this insane enemy with an impracticable confidence?

Well, no matter now; all the better, perhaps. There was already an end of concealment between that enemy and himself, and soon would be of suspense.

'God help me! at the eve of what an abyss I stand! That wretched woman, poor as she is, and nearly mad, in a place like London she'll be certain to find lawyers only too glad to take up her case, and force me to a trial – first, a trial to prove a marriage and make costs of me, and then, Heaven knows what more; and the publicity, and the miserable uncertainty; and Alice, poor little Alice! Merciful Heaven! what had she done to merit this long agony and possible ruin?'

He peeped into the dining-room as he passed, but all was there as he had left it. Alice had not been in it. So at the kitchen door he knocked.

'Who's there? Is anyone there?'

Encouraged by his voice, old Dulcibella answered from within. The door was opened, and he entered.

A few moments' silence, except for Alice's murmured and sobbing welcome, a trembling, close embrace, and he said, with a gentle look, in a faint tone:–

'Alice, darling, I have no good news to tell. Everything has gone wrong with me, and we must leave this. Let Dulcibella go up and get such things as are necessary to take with you; but, Dulcibella, mind you tell nobody your mistress is leaving this. And, Alice, you'll come with me. We'll go where they can neither follow nor trace us; and let fate do its worst. We may be happier yet in our exile than ever we were at home. And when they have banished me they have done their worst.'

His tenderness for Alice, frozen for a time, had returned. As she clung to him, her large, soft grey eyes looking up in his face so piteously moved him. He had intended a different sort of speech – colder, dryer – and under the spell of that look had come this sudden gush of a better feeling – the fond clasp of his arm, and the hurried kiss he pressed upon her cheek.

'I said, Alice, happier – *happier*, darling, a thousandfold. For the present I speak in riddles. You have seen how miserable I am. I'll tell you everything by-and-bye. A conspiracy, I do believe, an unnatural conspiracy, that has worn out my miserable brain and spirits, and harassed me to death. I'll tell you all time enough, and you'll say it is a miracle I have borne it as I do. Don't look so frightened, you poor little thing! We are perfectly safe; I'm in no real danger, but harassed incessantly – only harassed, and that, thank God, shall end.'

He kissed her again very tenderly, and again; and he said:–

'You and Dulcibella shall go on. Clinton will drive you to Hatherton, and there you'll get horses and post on to Cranswell, and I will overtake you there. I must go now and give him his directions, and I may as well leave you this note. I wrote it yesterday. You must have some money – there is some in it, and the names of the places, and we'll be there to-night. And what is it, darling? You look as if you wished to ask me something?'

'I – I was going to ask – but I thought perhaps I ought not until you can tell me everything – but you spoke of a conspiracy, and I was going to ask whether that dreadful woman who got into my room has anything to do with it.'

'Nonsense, child – that is a miserable mad woman!' he laughed dismally. 'Just wait a little, and you shall know all I know myself.'

'She's not to stay here, I mean, of course, if anything should prevent our leaving this to-day.'

'Why should you fancy that?' he asked, a little enigmatically.

'Mrs Tarnley said she was going to the madhouse.'

'We'll see time enough – you shall see her no more,' he said, and away he went, and she saw him pass by the window and out of the yard. And now she had leisure to think how ill he was looking, or rather to remember how it had struck her when he had appeared at the door. Yes, indeed, worn out and harassed to death. Thank God, he was now to escape from that misery, and to secure the repose which it was only too obvious he needed.

Dulcibella returned with such things as she thought indispensable, and she and her mistress were soon in more animated discussion than they had engaged in since the scenes of the past night.

Charles Fairfield had to make a call at Farmer Chubbs's to persuade him to lend his horse, about which he made a difficulty. It was not far up the glen towards Church Carwell, but when he came back he found the Grange again in a new confusion.

When Charles Fairfield, ascending the steep and narrow road which under tall trees darkly mounts from the Glen of Carwell to the plateau under the grey walls of the Grange, had reached that sylvan platform, he saw there, looking in the direction of Cressley Common, in that dim, religious light, Tom Clinton, in his fustian jacket, scratching his head and looking, it seemed, with interest, after some receding object. A little behind him, similarly engrossed, stood old Mildred Tarnley, with her hand above her eyes, though there was little need of artificial shade in that solemn grove, and again, a little to her rear, peeped broad-shouldered Lilly Dogger, standing close to the threshold of the yard door.

Tom Clinton was first to turn about, and, sauntering slowly toward the house, he spoke something to Mrs Tarnley, who, waiting till he reached her, turned about in the same direction, and talking gravely, and looking over their shoulders, as people sometimes do in the direction in which a runaway horse has disappeared, they came to a standstill at the door, under the great ash tree, whose columnar stem is mantled with thick ivy, and there again looking back, the little girl leaning and listening, unheeded, against the door-post, the group remained in conference.

Had Charles Fairfield been in his usual state of mind his curiosity would have been piqued by an appearance of activity so unusual in his drowsy household. As it was, he cared not, but approached, looking down upon the road with his hands in his pockets listlessly.

Mrs Tarnley whispered something to Tom and jogged him in the ribs, looking all the time at the approaching figure of Charles Fairfield.

The master of the Grange approached, looked up, and saw Tom standing near, with the air of one who had something to say. Mrs Tarnley had drawn back, a little doubtful, possibly, of the effect on his nerves.

'Well, Tom, Chubbs will lend the horse,' said Charles. 'We'll go round to the stable – I've a word to say.'

Tom touched his hat, still looking in his face with an inquiring and ominous expression.

'Do you want to say anything particular, Tom?' asked his master, with a sudden foreboding of some new ill.

'Nothing, sir, but Squire Rodney of Wrydell has come over from Wykeford.'

'He's here – is he?' asked Charles, paler on a sudden.

'He's gone, sir, please.'

'Gone, is he? Well, well, there's not much in that.'

''Twas only, sir, that he brought two men wi' him.'

'Do you mean? – you don't mean – what men did he bring?'

'Well, they was constable folk, I believe – they must 'a' bin, for they made an arrest.'

'A *what*, do you mean?'

'He made out a writin', and he 'ad me in, and questioned me, but I'd nowt to tell, sir, and he asked where you was, and I told him, as you ordered I was to say, you was gone, and he took the mistress's her story, and made her make oath on't, and the same wi' the others – Mrs Tarnley and the little girl, and the blind woman, she be took up for murder, or I don't know for what, only he said he could not take no bail for her, so they made her sure, and has took her off, I do suppose, to Wykeford pris'n.'

'Of course, that's right, I suppose, all right – eh?' Charles looked as if he was going to drop to the earth, so leaden was his hue, and so meaningless the stare with which he looked in Tom's face.

'But – but – who sent for him? I didn't. D——n you, who sent for him? 'Twasn't I. And – and who's master here? Who the devil sent for that meddling rascal from Wykeford?'

Charles's voice had risen to a roar as he shook Tom furiously by the collar.

Springing back a bit, Tom answered, with his hand grasping his collar where the squire had just clutched him.

'I don't know – I didn't, and I don't believe no one did. It's a smart run from here across the common. I don't believe no one sent from the Grange – I'm sure no one went from this – not a bit, not a toe, not a soul, I'm sure and certain.'

'What's this, what's this, what the devil's all this, Tom?' said the squire, stamping, and shaking his fist in the air, like a man distracted.

'Why did you let her go – why did you let him take her – d——n you? I've a mind to pitch you over that cliff and smash you.'

'Well, sir,' said Tom, making another step or two back, and himself pale and stern now, with his open hand raised, partly in deprecation, 'where's the good o' blamin' me? what could I do wi' the law again' me, and how could I tell what you'd think, and *'twarn't* no one from this sent for him – not one, but news travels apace, and who's he can stop it? – not me, nor *you*,' said Tom, sturdily, 'and he just come over of his own head, and nabbed her.'

'My God! It's done. I thought you would not have allowed me to be trampled on, and the place insulted; I took ye for a man, Tom. Where's my horse? By Heaven, I'll have him! I'll make it a day's work he'll remember. That d——d Rodney, coming down to my house with his catchpolls, to pay off old scores, and insult me!'

With his fist clenched and raised, Charles Fairfield ran furiously round to the stable yard, followed cautiously by Tom Clinton.

CHAPTER 40

PURSUIT

Having her own misgivings as to the temper in which her master would take this *coup* of the arrest, Mildred Tarnley prudently kept her own counsel, and retreated nearly to the kitchen door, while the *éclaircissement* took place outside. Popping in and out to see what would come of it, old Mildred affected to be busy about her mops and tubs. After a time, in came Tom, looking sulky and hot.

'Is he comin' this way?' asked Mildred.

'Not him,' answered Tom.

'Where is he?'

''Twixt this and Wykeford,' he answered – 'across the common he's ridin'.'

'To Wykeford, eh?'

'To Wykeford, every foot, if he don't run him down on the way; and when they meet – him and Squire Rodney – 'twill be hot and shrewd work between them, I tell ye. I'd 'a' rid wi' him myself if there was a beast to carry me, for three agin one is too long odds.'

'Ye don't mean to tell *me!*' exclaimed Mildred, planting her mop perpendicularly on the ground, and leaning immovably on this sceptre.

'Tell ye what?'

'There's goin' to be rough work like that on the head o't?'

'Hot blood, ma'am. Ye know the Fairfields. They folk don't stand long jawin'. It's like when the blood's up the hand's up too.'

'And what's he to fight for – not that blind beldame, sure?'

'I want my mug o' beer,' said Tom, turning the conversation.

'Yes, sure,' she said – 'yes, ye shall have it. But what for should Master Charles go to wry words wi' Squire Rodney, and what for should there be blows and blood spillin' between 'em? Nonsense!'

'I can't help 'em. I'd lend master a hand if I could. Squire Rodney's no fool neither – 'twill e'en be fight dog, fight bear – and there's two stout lads wi' him will make short work o't.'

'Ye don't think he's like to be hurt, do ye?'

'Well, ye know, they say fightin' dogs comes haltin' home. He's as strong as two, that's all, and has a good nag under him. Now gi'e me my beer.'

''Twon't be nothin', Tom, don't you think, Tom? It won't come to nothin'?'

'If he comes up wi' them 'twill be an up-and-down fight, I take it. 'Twas an unlucky maggot bit him.'

'Bit who?'

'What but the Divil brought Squire Rodney over here?'

'Who knows?' answered the dame, fumbling in her pocket for the key of the beer cellar – 'I'm goin' to fetch your beer, Tom.'

And away she went, and in a minute returned with his draught of beer.

'And I think,' she said, setting it down before him, ''twas well done, taking that beast to her right place, do it who might. She's just a bedlam Bess – clean out o' her wits wi' wickedness – mad wi' drink and them fits she has. We knows here what she is, and bloody work she'd 'a' made last night wi' that poor young lady, that'll never be the same again – the old limb – and master himself, though he's angered a bit because Justice Rodney did not ask his leave to catch a murderer, if ye please, down here at the Grange.'

'There's more in it, mayhap, than just that,' said Tom, blowing the froth off his beer.

'To come down here without with your leave or by your leave, to squat in the Grange here like gipsy would on Cressley Common, as tho'' she was lady of all – to hurt who she pleased, and live as she liked. More in't than that, ye say, – what more?'

'Hoot, how should I know? Mayhap she thinks she's as good a right as another to a bit and a welcome down here.'

'She was here before – years enough gone now, and long enough she stayed, and cost a pretty penny, too, I warrant you. Them was more tired of her than me – guest ever, welcome never, they say. She was a play-actor, or something, long ago – a great idle hussy, never would earn a honest penny, nor do nothing useful, all her days.'

'Ay, Joan reels ill and winds worse, and de'il a stomach she has to spin – that'll be the way wi' her, I swear – ha, ha, ha! She'll not be growin' richer, I warrant – left in the mud and found in the mire – they folk knows nowt o' thrift, and small luck and less good about 'em.'

'If ye heard her talk, Tom, ye'd soon know what sort she is, always cravin' – she would not leave a body a shillin' if she could help it.'

'Ay, I warrant, women, priests, and poultry have never enough,' said Tom. 'I know nowt about her, nor who she's a-lookin' after here, but she's safe enough now I take it; and bloody folks, they say, digs their own graves. But as I said, I knows nowt about her, and I say nowt, and he that judges as he runs may owertake repentance.'

''Tis easy judgin' here, I'm thinkin'. Killin' and murder's near akin, and when Mr Charles cools a bit he'll thank Squire Rodney for riddin' his house of that blind serpent. 'Tis somethin' to be so near losing his wife. So sure as your hand's on that mug it would 'a' bin done while the cat's lickin' her ear, if he had not bounced in on the minute, and, once dead, dead as Adam.'

'Who loseth his wife and sixpence hath lost a tester, they do say,' answered Tom, with a laugh.

'None but a born beast would say so!' said Mildred Tarnley, with a swarthy flush, and, striking her hand sternly on the table.

'Well, 'tis only a saying, ye know, and no new one neither,' said Tom, wiping his mouth with his sleeve, and standing up. 'But the mistress is a pretty lady, and a kind – and a gentle-born, and all may see, and I'd give or take a shrewd blow or two, or harm should happen her.'

'Ye'd be no man else, Tom, and I don't doubt ye. Little thought I last night what was in her head, the sly villain, when I left her back again in her bed, and the cross door shut and locked. Lord 'a' mercy on us! To think how the fiend works wi' his own – smooth and sly sometimes as if butter would not melt in her mouth.'

''Tis an old sayin'–

> When the cat winketh,
> Little wots mouse what the cat thinketh,'

said Tom with a grin and a wag of his head.

'She was neither sleek, nor soft, nor sly for that matter, when I saw her. I thought she'd 'a' had her claws in my chops; such a catamaran I never did see.'

'And how's the young lady?' asked Tom, clapping his greasy hat on his head.

'Hey! dear! I'm glad ye asked,' exclaimed the old woman – 'easier she'll be, no doubt, now *that* devil's gone. But, dearie me! all's in a jumble till Master Charles comes back, for she'll not know, poor thing, what's she's to do till he talks wi' her – now all's changed.'

And Mildred trotted off to see for herself, and to hear what the young lady might have to say.

CHAPTER 41

DAY – TWILIGHT – DARKNESS

In their homely sitting-room, with old Dulcibella in friendly attendance, Mildred Tarnley found Alice. It is not always that a dreadful impression makes itself immediately manifest. Nature rallies all her forces at first to meet the danger. A certain excitement of resistance sustains the system through a crisis of horror, and often for a long time after; and it is not until this extraordinary muster of the vital forces begins to dissolve and subside that the shattered condition of the normal powers begins to declare itself.

The scene which had just occurred was a dreadful ordeal for Alice. To recount, and with effort and minuteness, to gather into order the terrific incidents of the night preceding, relate them bit by bit to the magistrate as he wrote them down, make oath to their truth as the basis of a public prosecution, and most dreadful – the having to see and identify the spectre who had murderously assailed her on the night before.

Every step affrighted her, the shadow of a moving branch upon the wall chilled her with terror; the voices of people who spoke seemed to pierce the naked nerve of her ear, and to sing through her head; even for a moment faces, kind and familiar, seemed to flicker or darken with direful meanings alien from their natures.

In this nervous condition old Mildred found her.

'I come, ma'am, to know what you'd wish to be done,' said she, standing at the door with her usual grim little curtsey.

'I don't quite understand – done about what?' inquired she.

'I mean, ma'am, Tom said you asked him to be ready to drive you from here; but as Master ha'n't come back, and things is changed a bit here, I thought ye might wish to make a change, mayhap.'

'Oh, oh! thank you, Mrs Tarnley; I forgot, I've been so frightened. Oh, Mrs Tarnley, I wish I could cry – I'd be so much better, I'm sure, if I could cry – I feel my throat so odd and my head so confused – it seems so many days. If I could think of anything to make me cry.'

Mildred looked at her from the corners of her eyes darkly, as if with a hard heart, but I think she pitied her.

'That blind woman's gone, the beast – I'm glad she's away; and you'll be better o' that, ma'am, I'm thinkin'. I was afeard o' her a'most myself ever since last night; and Master Charles is gone, too, but he'll be back soon.'

'He'll come *to-day?*' she asked in consternation.

'To-day, of course, ma'am – in an hour or less, I do suppose; and it would not be well done, I'm thinking, ma'am, for you to leave the Grange till you see him again, for it's like enough he'll 'a' changed his plans.'

'I was thinking so myself. I'd rather wait here to see him – he had so much to distract him that he may easily think differently by this time. I'm glad, Mrs Tarnley, you think so, for now I feel confident I may wait for his return – I think I ought to wait – and thank you, Mrs Tarnley, for advising me in the midst of my distractions.'

'I just speak my mind, ma'am, and counsel's no command, as they say; and I never liked meddlers; and don't love to burn my fingers in other people's brewes; so ye'll please to mind, ma'am, 'tis for your own ear I speak, and your own wit will judge; and I wouldn't have Master Charles looking askew, nor like to be shent by him for what's kindly meant to you – not that I owe much kindness nowhere, for since I could scour a platter I ever gave work for wage. So ye'll please not tell Master Charles I counselled ye aught in the matter.'

'Certainly, Mrs Tarnley, just as you wish.'

'Would you please wish anything to eat, ma'am?' inquired Mildred, relapsing into her dry, official manner.

'Nothing, Mildred – no, thanks.'

'Ye'll lose heart, Miss, if ye don't eat – ye must eat.'

'Thanks, Mildred – by-and-bye, perhaps.'

Mrs Tarnley, like many worthy people, regarded eating as a simply mechanical process, and wondered why people affected a difficulty about it under any circumstances. Somewhat hard of heart, and with nerves of wire, she had no idea that a sufficient shock might rob one not only of appetite but positively of the power of eating for days.

Alone, for one moment, Alice could not endure to be – haunted unintermittingly by the vague but intense dread of a return of the woman who had so nearly succeeded in murdering her, and with nerves shattered in that indescribable degree which even a strong man experiences for a long time after a murder has been attempted upon him perfidiously and by a surprise. The worst panic comes after an interval of many hours.

As the day waned, more miserably nervous she became, and more defined her terror of the Dutchwoman's return. That straggling old house, with no less than four doors of entrance, favoured the alarms of her imagination. Often she thought of her kind old kinswoman, Lady Wyndale, and her proffered asylum at her snug house at Oulton.

But that was a momentary picture – no more. Miserable as she was at the Grange, until she had seen her husband, learned his plans, and knew what his wishes were, that loyal little wife could not dream of going to Oulton.

She remained there as the shades of evening darkened over the steep roof and solemn trees of Carwell Grange, and more and more grew the horror that deepened with darkness, and was aggravated and distracted by the continued absence of her husband.

In the sitting-room she stood, listening, with a beating heart. Every sound, which at another time would have been unheard, now thrilled her with hope or terror.

Old Dulcibella in the room was also frightened – more a great deal than she could account for. And even Mildred Tarnley – that hard and grim old lady – was touched by the influence of that contagious fear, and barred and locked the doors with jealous care, and even looked to the fastenings of the windows, and caught some faint shadows of that supernatural fear with which Alice Fairfield had come to regard the wicked woman out of whose hands she had escaped.

Now and then, when appealed to, she said a short word or two of reassurance respecting Charles Fairfield's unaccountably prolonged absence. But the panic of the young lady in like manner on this point began to invade her in uncomfortable misgivings.

So uneasy had she grown that at last she despatched Tom, when sunset had come without a sign of Charles Fairfield's return, riding to Wykeford. Tom had now returned. A bootless errand it had proved. At Wykeford he learned that Charles Fairfield had been there – had been at Squire Rodney's house and about the town, and made inquiries. His pursuit had been misdirected. At Wykeford is a House of Correction and reformatory, which institution acts as a prison of ease to the county gaol. But that gaol is in the town of Hatherton, as Charles would have easily recollected if his rage had allowed him a moment to think. Tom, however, made no attempt further to pursue him, on conjecture, and had returned to Carwell Grange, no wiser than he went.

CHAPTER 42

HATHERTON

Charles Fairfield, in true Fairfield wrath, had ridden at a hard pace, which helped to keep his blood up, all the way to the bridge of Wykeford. He had expected to overtake the magistrate easily before he reached that point, and, if he had, who knows what might have happened next?

Baulked at Wykeford, and learning there how long a ride interposed before he could hope to reach him, he turned and followed in a somewhat changed mood.

He would himself bail that woman. The question, felony or no felony – bailable offence or not bailable – entered not his uninstructed head. Be she what she might, assassin – devil, he could not and would not permit her to lie in gaol. Arrested in his own house, with many sufferings and one great wrong to upbraid him with – with rights, imaginary he insisted, but honestly believed in, perhaps, by her – with other rights, which his tortured heart could not deny, the melancholy rights which are founded on outlawry and disgrace, eleemosynary, but quite irresistible when pleaded with natures not lost to all good, and which proclaim the dreadful equity – that vice has its duties not less than virtue.

Baulked in his first violent impulse, Charles rode his hot horse quietly along the by-road that leads to Hatherton, over many a steep and through many a rut.

Yes, pleasant it would have been to 'lick' that rascal Rodney, and upset his dogcart into the ditch, and liberate the distressed damsel. But even Charles Fairfield began to perceive consequences and to approve a more moderate course.

At Hatherton was there not Peregrine Hincks, the attorney who carried his brother, Harry Fairfield – whose course, any more than that of true love, did not always run smooth – through the short turns and breaks that disturbed it?

He would go straight to this artist in all manner of quips and cranks in parchment, and tell him what he wanted – the most foolish thing perhaps in the world, to undo that which his good fortune had done for him, and let loose again his trouble.

Scandal! What did the defiant soul of a Fairfield care for scandal? Impulsive, reckless, affectionate, not ungenerous – all considerations were lost in the one compunctious feeling.

Two hours later he was in the office of Mr Peregrine Hincks, who listened to his statement with a shrewd inflexibility of face. He knew as much as Harry Fairfield did of the person who was now under the turnkey's tutelage. But Charles fancied him quite in the dark, and treated the subject accordingly.

'We'll send down to the gaol, and learn what she's committed for; but *two* will be necessary. Who will execute the recognisance with you?'

'I'm certain Harry will do it in a moment,' said Charles.

The attorney was very sure that Harry would do no such thing. But it was not necessary to discuss that particular point, nor to insinuate officiously his ideas about the county scandal which would follow his interposition in favour of a prisoner committed upon a charge involving an attempt upon the life of his wife, for the information brought back from the prison was such as to convince the attorney that bail could not be accepted in the case.

On learning this, Charles's wrath returned. He stood for a time at the chimney-piece, examining in silence a candlestick that stood there, and then to the window he went, with a haggard, angry face, and looked out for a while with his hands in his pockets.

'Very well. So much the worse for Rodney,' said he suddenly. 'I told you my sole motive was to snub that fellow. He chose to make an arrest in my house – his d——d impertinence! – without the slightest reference to me, and I made up my mind, if I could, to let his prisoner go. That fellow wants to be kicked – I don't care twopence about anything else, but it's all one – I'll find some other way.'

'You'd better have a glass of sherry, sir – you're a little tired – and a biscuit.'

'I'll have nothing, thanks, till I – till I – what was I going to say? Time enough; I have lots to do at home – a great deal, Mr Hincks – and my head aches. I *am* tired, but I won't mind the wine, thank you, my head is too bad. If I could just clear it of two or three things I'd be all right, and rest a little. I've been overworked, and I'll ride over here to-morrow – that will do, and we'll talk it over; and I don't choose the wretched, crazy woman to be shut up in prison, because that stupid prig Rodney pleases to say she's insane, and would like to hang her, just because she was arrested at Carwell; and – and as you say, of course, if she is insane she is best out of the way; but there are ways of doing things, and I won't be bullied by that vulgar snob. By – if I had caught him to-day I'd have broken his neck, I believe.'

'Glad you did *not* meet him, sir – a row at any time brings one into mischief, but an interference with the course of law – don't you see – a very serious affair indeed!'

'Well, see – yes, I suppose so, and there was just another thing. Believing, as I do, that wretched person quite mad – don't you see? – it would be very hard to let her – to let her half starve there where they've put her – don't you think? – and I don't care to go down to the place there, and all that; and if you'd just manage to let her have this – it's all I can do just now – but – but it's happening at my house – although I'm not a bit to blame, puts it on me in a way, and I think I can't do less than this.'

He handed a bank-note to the attorney, and was looking all the time on a brief that lay on the table.

Mr Hincks, the respectable attorney, was a little shy, also, as he took it.

'I'm to say you sent it to – what's her name, by the bye?' he asked.

'Bertha Velderkaust, but you need not mention me – only say it was sent to her – that's all. I'm so vexed, because, as you may suppose, I had particular reasons for wishing to keep quiet, and I was staying there at the Grange, you know – Carwell – and thought I might keep quiet for a few weeks; and that wretched maniac comes down there while I was for a few days absent, and in one of her fits makes an attack on a member of my family; and so my little hiding-place is disclosed, for of course, such a fracas will be heard of – it is awfully provoking – I'm rather puzzled to know where to go.'

Charles ceased, with a faint, dreary laugh, and the attorney looked at his bank-note, which he held by the corners, as the mate, in Mudford's fine story, might at the letter which Vanderdecken wished to send to his long-lost wife in Amsterdam.

It was not, however, clear to him that he had any very good excuse for refusing to do this trifling kindness for the brother of his quarrelsome and litigious client Harry Fairfield, who, although he eschewed costs himself, laid them prettily heavily upon others, and was a valuable feeder for Mr Hincks's office.

This little commission, therefore, accepted, the attorney saw his visitor downstairs. He had already lighted a candle, and in its light he thought he never saw a man upon his legs look so ill as Charles, and the hand which he gave Mr Hincks at the steps was dry and burning.

'It's a long ride, sir, to Carwell,' the attorney hesitated.

'The horse has had some oats, thanks, down here,' and he nodded towards the 'Plume of Feathers', at which he had put up his beast, 'and I sha'n't be long getting over the ground.'

And without turning about, or a look over his shoulder, he sauntered away, in the rising moonlight, toward the little inn.

CHAPTER 43

THE WELCOME

Charles rode his horse slowly homeward. The moon got up before he reached the wild expanse of Cressley Common, a wide sea of undulating heath, with here and there a grey stone peeping above its surface in the moonlight like a distant sail.

Charles was feverish – worn out in body and mind – literally. Some men more than others are framed to endure misery, and live on, and on, and on in despair. Is this melancholy strength better, or the weakness that faints under the first strain of the rack? Happy that at the longest it cannot be for very long – happy that 'man that is born of a woman hath but a short time to live,' seeing that he is 'full of misery.'

Charles was conscious only of extreme fatigue; that for days he had eaten little and rested little, and that his short snatches of sleep, harassed by the repetition of his waking calculations and horrors, tired rather than refreshed him.

When fever is brewing, just as electric lights glimmer from the sullen mask of cloud on the eve of a storm, there come sometimes odd flickerings that seem to mock and warn.

Every overworked man, who has been overtaken by fever in the midst of his toil and complications, knows well the kind of tricks his brain had played him on the verge of that chaos.

Charles put his hand to his breast, and felt in his pocket for a letter the appearance of which was sharp and clear on his retina as if he had seen it but a moment before.

'What have I done with it?' he asked himself – 'the letter Hincks gave me?'

He searched his pockets for it, a letter of which this picture was so bright – purely imaginary! He was going to turn about and search the track he had traversed for it; but he bethought him, 'To whom was the letter written?' No answer could he find. 'To whom?' To no one – nothing – an imagination. Conscious on a sudden, he was scared.

'I want a good rest – I want some sleep. Waking dreams – this is the way fellows go mad. What the devil can have put it into my head?'

Now rose before him the tall trees that gather as you approach the vale of Carwell, and soon the steep gables and chimneys of the Grange glimmered white among their boughs.

There in his mind, as unaccountably, was the fancy that he had met and spoken with his father, old Squire Harry, at the Catstone, as he crossed the moor.

'I'll give his message – yes, I'll give your message.'

And he thought what possessed him to come out without his hat, and he looked whiter than ever.

And then he thought, 'What brought him there?'

And then, 'What *was* his message?'

Again a shock, a chasm – his brain had mocked him.

Dreadful when that potent servant begins to mutiny, and instead of honest work for its master finds pastime for itself in fearful sport.

'My God! what am I thinking of?' he said, with a kind of chill; looking back over his shoulder.

His tired horse was plucking a mouthful of grass that grew at the foot of a tree.

'We are both used up,' he said, letting his horse, at a quicker pace, pursue its homeward path. 'Poor fellow, you are tired as well as I. It'll be all right, I dare say, in the morning, if I could only sleep. Something wrong – something a little wrong – that sleep will cure – all right to-morrow.'

He looked up as he passed toward the windows of his and Alice's room. When he was out a piece of the shutter was always open. But if so to-night there was no light in the room, and with a shock and a dreadful imperfection of recollection, the scene which occurred on the night past returned.

'Yes, my God! so it was,' he said, as he stopped at the yard gate. 'Alice – I forget – did I see Alice after that? did I – did they tell me – what is it?'

He dismounted, and felt as if he were going to faint. His finger was on the latch, but he had not courage to raise it. Vain was his effort to remember. Painted in hues of light was that dreadful crisis before his eyes; but how had it ended? Was he going quite mad?

'My God, help me!' he muttered again and again. 'Is there anything bad? I can't recall it. Is there anything very bad?'

'Open the door, it is he – I'm sure – I heard the horse,' cried the clear voice of Alice from within.

'Yes, I – it's I,' he cried in a strange rapture.

And in another moment the door was open, and Charles had clasped his wife to his heart.

'Darling, darling, I'm so glad! You're quite well?' he almost sobbed.

'Oh, Ry, my own, my own husband, my Ry, he's safe, he's quite well. Come in. Thank God, he's back again with his poor little wife; and oh, darling, we'll never part again. Come in, come in, my darling.'

Old Mildred secured the door, and Tom took the horse round to the stable; and as she held her husband clasped in her arms, tears, long denied to her, came to her relief, and she wept long and convulsively.

'Oh, Ry, it has been such a dreadful time; but you're safe, aren't you?'

'Quite. Oh! yes, quite, darling – very well.'

'But, oh, Ry, you look so tired. You're not ill, are you, darling?'

'Not ill, only tired. Nothing, not much – tired and stupid, want of rest.'

'You must have some wine, you look so very ill.'

'Well, yes, I'm tired. Thanks, Mildred, that will do,' and he drank the glass of sherry she gave him.

'A drop more?' inquired old Mildred, holding the decanter stooped over his glass.

'No, thanks, no, I – it tastes oddly – or perhaps I'm not quite well, after all.'

Charles now felt his mind clear again, and his retrospect was uncrossed by those spectral illusions of the memory that seem to threaten the brain with subjugation.

Better the finger of death than of madness should touch his brain, perhaps. His love for his wife, not dethroned, only in abeyance, was restored. Such dialogues as theirs are little interesting to any but the interlocutors.

With their fear and pain, agitated, troubled, there is love in their words. Those words, then, though, in him, troubled with inward upbraidings, in her with secret fears and cares, are precious. There may not be many more between them.

CHAPTER 44

THE WYKEFORD DOCTOR

A few days had passed, and a great change had come. Charles Fairfield, the master of the Grange, lay in his bed, and the Wykeford doctor admitted to Alice that he could not say what might happen. It was a very grave case – fever – and the patient could not have been worse handled in those early days of the attack, on which sometimes so much depends.

People went to and fro on tiptoe, and talked in whispers, and the patient moaned, and prattled, unconscious generally of all that was passing. Awful hours and days of suspense! The doctor said, and perhaps he was right, to kind Lady Wyndale, who came over to see Alice, and learned with consternation the state of things, that, under the special circumstances, her nerves having been so violently acted upon by terror, this diversion of pain and thought into quite another channel might be the best thing, on the whole, that could have happened to her.

It was now the sixth day of this undetermined ordeal.

Alice watched the doctor's countenance with her very soul in her eyes, as he made his inspection, standing at the bedside, and now and then putting a question to Dulcibella or to Alice, or to the nurse whom he had sent to do duty in the sick room from Wykeford.

'Well?' whispered poor Alice, who had accompanied him downstairs, and pale as death, drew him into the sitting room, and asked her question.

'Well, doctor, what do you think to-day?'

'Not much to report. Very little change. We must have patience, you know, for a day or two; and you need not be told, my dear ma'am, that good nursing is half the battle, and in better hands he need not be; I'm only afraid that you are undertaking too much yourself. That woman, Marks, you may rely on, implicitly; a most respectable and intelligent person; I never knew her to make a mistake yet, and she has been more than ten years at this work.'

'Yes, I'm sure she is – I like her very much. And don't you think him a little better?' she pleaded.

'Well, you know, as long as he holds his own and don't lose ground, he *is* better; that's all we can say; not to be worse, as time elapses, is, in effect, to be better; that you *may* say.'

She was looking earnestly into the clear blue eyes of the old man, who turned them kindly upon her, from under his shaggy white eyebrows.

'Oh! thank God, then you do think him better?'

'In that sense, yes,' he answered, cautiously, 'but, of course, we must have patience, and we shall soon know more, a great deal more, and I do sincerely hope it may all turn out quite right; but the brain has been a good deal overpowered; there's a tendency to a sort of state we call comatose; it indicates too much pressure there, d'ye see. I'd rather have him talking more nonsense, with less of that sleep, as you suppose it, but it isn't sleep – a very different sort of thing. I've been trying to salivate him, but he's plaguy obstinate. We'll try to-night what dividing the pills into four each, and shortening the intervals a little, will do; it sometimes does wonders – we'll see – and a great deal depends on our succeeding in salivating. If we succeeded in effecting that, I think all the rest would proceed satisfactorily – that's one of our difficulties just at this moment. If you send over your little messenger – the sooner the better, she shall have the pills, and let him take one the moment they come – pretty flower that is,' he interpolated, touching the petal of one that stood neglected in its pot, on a little table at the window. 'That's not a geranium: it's a pelargonium. I did not know there were such things down here – and you'll continue, I told her everything else, and go on just as before.'

'And you think he's better – I mean just a little?' she pleaded again.

'Well, well, you know, I said all I could, and we must hope – we must hope, you know, that everything may go on satisfactorily, and I'll go further. I'll say I don't see at all why we should despair of such a result. Keep up your spirits, ma'am, and be cheery. We'll do our duty all, and leave the rest in the hands of God.'

'And I suppose, Doctor Willett, we shall see you to-morrow at the usual hour?'

'Certainly, ma'am, and I don't think there will be any change to speak of till, probably, Thursday.'

And her heart sank down with one dreadful dive at mention of that day of trial that might so easily be a day of doom.

And she answered his farewell, and smiled faintly, and followed his steps through the passage, freezing with that fear, it seemed, that she did not breathe, and that her heart ceased beating, and that she glided like a spirit. She stopped, and he passed into the yard to his horse, turning his shrewd, pale face, with a smile and a nod, as he stepped across the door-stone, and he said —

'Good-bye, ma'am, and look out for me to-morrow as usual, and be cheery, mind. Look at the bright side, you know; there's no reason you shouldn't.'

She answered his smile as best she could, but her heart was full; an immense sorrow was there. She was frightened. She hurried into the homely sitting-room, and wept in an agony unspeakable.

The doctor, she saw, pitied and wished to cheer her; but how dreadful was his guarded language. She thought that he would speak to others in a different vein, and so, in fact, he did. His opinion was clear against Charles Fairfield's chance of ever being on his feet again. 'It was a great pity — a young fellow.' The doctor thought every one young whose years were ten less than his own. 'A tall, handsome fellow like that, and squire of Wyvern in a year or two, and a good-natured sort of fellow, he heard. It was a pity, and that poor little wife of his — and likely to be a mother soon — God help her!'

CHAPTER 45

SPEECH RETURNS

The dreaded day came and passed, and Charles Fairfield was not dead, but better. The fever was abating, but never did the vital spark burn lower in living man. Seeing that life was so low in his patient, that there was nothing between it and death, the doctor ordered certain measures to be taken.

'The fever is going, you see, but his strength is not coming, nor won't for a while. It's a very nice thing, I can tell you, to bring him to land with such fine tackle. I've brought a salmon ten pound weight into my net with a bit of a trout rod as light as a rush almost. But this is nicer play – not, mind you, that I'd have you in the dumps, ma'am, but it will be necessary to watch him as a cat would a mouse. Now, you'll have on the table by his bed three bottles – decanted all, and ready for use instantaneously. Besides that claret you'll have a bottle of port, and you must also have a bottle of brandy. He'll be always at his tricks, going to faint, and you mustn't let him. Because, ma'am, it might not be easy to get him out of such a faint, and a faint is death, ma'am, if it lasts long enough. Now, you're not to be frightened.'

'Oh no, Doctor Willett.'

'No, *that* would not do neither; but I want you clearly to see the importance of it. Let him have the claret to his lips constantly – in a tumbler, mind – you can't give him too much; and whenever you see him look faint, you must reinforce that with port; and no mincing of matters – none of your half-measures. I'd rather you made him drunk three times a day than run the least risk once of the other thing; and if the port doesn't get him up quick enough, you must fire away with the brandy; and don't spare it – don't be afraid – we'll get him round, in time, with jellies and other good things; but life must be maintained in the meanwhile any way – every way – whatever way we can. So mind, *three* – claret, port, brandy.'

He held up three fingers as he named them, touching them in succession.

'That's a fire it's better should burn a bit too fiercely for an hour than sink too low for a second; once out, out for ever.'

'Thanks, Doctor Willett, I understand quite; and you'll be here to-morrow, won't you, at the usual hour?'

'Certainly, ma'am, and it's high time you should begin to take a little care of yourself; you must, indeed, or you'll rue it; you're too much on your feet, and you have had no rest night or day, and it's quite necessary you should, unless you mean to put yourself out of the world, which would not do at all. We can't spare you, ma'am, we can't indeed – a deal too valuable.'

For some time Charles Fairfield continued in very much the same state. At the end of three or four days he signed faintly to Alice, who was in the room, with her large soft eyes gazing on the invalid, whenever she could look unperceived. She got up gently and came close to him.

'Yes, darling,' and she lowered her head that he might speak more easily.

Charles whispered:–

'Quite well?'

'You feel quite well? Thank God,' she answered, her large eyes filling with tears.

'Not I – you,' he whispered with querulous impatience; 'ain't you?'

'Quite, darling.'

His fine blue Fairfield eyes were raised to her face.

With a short sigh, he whispered:–

'I'm glad.'

She stooped gently and kissed his thin cheek.

'I've been dreaming so much,' he whispered. 'Will you tell me exactly what happened – just before my illness – something happened here?'

In a low murmur she told him.

When she stopped he waited as if expecting more, and then he whispered:–

'I thought so – yes.'

And he sighed heavily.

'You're tired, darling,' she said; 'you must take a little wine.'

'I hate it,' he whispered – 'tired of it.'

'But, darling, the doctor says you must – and – for my sake won't you?'

The faintest possible smile lighted his pale face.

'Kind,' he whispered.

And when she placed the glass of claret to his lips he sipped a little and turned away his head languidly.

'Enough. Bring me my dressing-case,' he whispered.

She did so.

'The key was in my purse, I think. Open it, Ally.'

She found the key and unlocked that inlaid box.

'Underneath there are two or three letters in a big envelope. Keep them for me; don't part with them,' he whispered.

She lifted a long envelope containing some papers, and the faintest nod indicated that they were what he sought.

'Keep it safe. Put the case away.'

When she came back, looking at her, he raised his eyebrows ever so little and moved his head. She understood his sign, and stooped again to listen.

'She mustn't be prosecuted, she's mad – Ally, mind.'

'Darling, whatever you wish.'

'Good Ally; that's enough.'

There was a little pause.

'You did not take enough claret, darling Ry. Won't you take a little more – for your poor little Ally?' whispered she, anxiously.

'I'm very well, darling; by-and-bye; sleep is better.'

So he laid his cheek closer to the pillow and closed his eyes, and Alice Fairfield stole on tiptoe to her chair, and, with another look at him and a deep sigh, she sat down and took her work.

Silent was the room, except for the low breathing of the invalid. Half an hour passed, and Alice stole softly to the bedside. He was awake, and said faintly:–

'Was it your mother?'

'Who, darling?'

'Talking.'

'No one was talking, darling.'

'I saw her; I thought I heard – *not* her – someone talking.'

'No, darling Ry, nothing.'

'Dreams, yes,' he murmured, and was quiet again.

Sad and ominous seemed those little wanderings. But such things are common in sickness. It was simply weakness.

In a little time she came over softly, and sat down by his pillow.

'I was looking down, Ally,' he whispered.

'I'll get it, darling. Something on the floor, is it?' she asked, looking down.

'No, down to my feet; it's very long – stretched.'

'Are your feet warm, darling?'

'Quite,' and he sighed and closed his eyes.

She continued sitting by his pillow.

'When Willie died, my brother, I was just fifteen.'

Then came a pause.

'Willie was the handsomest,' he murmured on.

'Willie was elder – nineteen, very tall. Handsome Willie, he liked me the best. I cried a deal that day. I used to cry alone, every day in the orchard, or by the river. He's in the churchyard at Wyvern. I wonder shall I see it any more. There was rain the day of the funeral – they say it is lucky. It was a long coffin – the Fairfields, you know———'

'Darling Ry, you are talking too much, it will tire you; take ever so little claret, to please your poor little Ally.'

This time he did quite quietly, and then closed his eyes, and dozed.

CHAPTER 46

HARRY DRINKS A GLASS AND SPILLS A GLASS

About an hour after, old Dulcibella came to the door and knocked. Charles Fairfield had slept a little, and was again awake. Into that still darkened room she came to whisper her message.

'Mr Harry's come, and he's downstairs, and he'd like to see you, and he wanted to know whether he could see the master.'

'I'll go down and see him; say I'll see him with pleasure,' said Alice. 'Harry is here, darling,' she said gently, drawing near to the patient; 'but you can't see him, of course.'

'I must,' whispered the invalid, peremptorily.

'Darling, are you well enough? I'm sure you ought not. If the doctor were here he would not allow it. Don't think of it, darling Ry, and he'll come again in a few days, when you are stronger.'

'It will do me good,' whispered Charles. 'Bring him – you tire me; *wait, she* can tell him. I'll see him alone; go, go, Ally, go.'

She would have remonstrated, but she saw that in his flushed and irritated looks which warned her against opposing him further.

'You are to go down, Dulcibella, and bring Mr Harry to the room to see your master; and, Dulcibella, like a dear good creature, won't you tell him how weak Master Charles is?' she urged, following her to the lobby; 'and beg of him not to stay long.'

In a minute or two more the clank of Harry Fairfield's boot was heard on the stair. He pushed open the door, and stepped in.

'Hullo! Charlie – dark enough to blind a horse here – all right, now. I hear you'll be on your legs again – I can't see you, upon my soul, not a stim a'most – before you see three Sundays – you mustn't be tiring yourself. I'm not talking too loud, eh? Would you mind an inch or two more of the shutter open?'

'No,' said Charles, faintly. 'A little.'

'There, that isn't much. I'm beginning to see a bit now. You've had a stiff bout this time, Charlie – 'twasn't typhus, nothing infectious, chiefly the upper storey; but you had a squeak for it, my lad. I'd 'a' come over to look after you, but my hands was too full.'

'No good, Harry; could not have spoken, or seen you. Better now.'

'A bit shaky still,' said Harry, lowering his voice. 'You'll get o'er that, though, fast enough. Keeping your spirits up, I see,' and Harry winked at the decanters. 'Summat better than that rot-gut claret, too. This is the stuff to put life in you. Port, yes.' He filled his brother's glass, smelled to it, and drank it off. 'So it is, and right good port. I'll drink your health, Charlie,' he added, playfully filling his glass again.

'I'm glad you came, Harry – I feel better,' said the invalid, and he extended his thin hand upon the bed to his brother.

'Hoot! of course you do,' said Harry, looking hard at him, for he was growing accustomed to the imperfect light. 'You'll do very well, and Alice, I hear, is quite well also. And so you've had a visit from the old soldier, and a bit of a row – eh?'

'Very bad, Harry. Oh! God help me!' moaned Charles.

'She ain't pretty, and she ain't pleasant – bad without and worse within, like a collier's sack,' said Harry, with a disgusted grimace, lifting his eyebrows and shaking his head.

'She's headlong and headstrong, and so there has been bad work. I don't know what's to be done.'

'The best thing to be done's to let her alone,' said Harry. 'They've put her up at Hatherton, I hear.'

'That's one thing,' murmured Charles, with a great sigh. 'I'm a heart-broken man, Harry.'

'That's easy mended. Don't prosecute, that's all. Get out o' the country when you're well enough, and they must let her go, and maybe the lesson won't do her no great harm.'

'I'm glad I have you to talk to,' murmured Charles, with another great sigh. 'I can't get it out of my head. You'll help me, Harry?'

'All I can – 'tain't much.'

'And, Harry, there's a thing that troubles me.' He paused, it seemed, exhausted.

'Don't mind it now, you're tirin' yourself. Drink a glass o' this.'

And he filled the glass from which he had been drinking his port.

'No, I hate wine,' he answered. 'No, no – by-and-bye, perhaps.'

'You know best,' he acquiesced. 'I suppose I must drink it myself,' which necessity he complied with accordingly. 'I heard the news, you know, and I'd 'a' come sooner but I'm taking an action next 'sizes on a warranty about the grey filly against that d——d rogue Farmer Lundy, and had to be off t'other side o' Wyvern wi' the lawyer. 'Tain't easy to hold your own wi' the cheatin' chaps that's goin' now, I can tell you.'

'I'm no good to talk now, Harry. You'll find me better next time, only, Harry, mind, remember, I mayn't be long for this world, and – I give you my honour – I swear, in the presence of God, who'll judge me, I never was married to Bertha. It's a lie. I knew she'd give me trouble some day; but it's a lie. Alice is my wife, by G——d Almighty! That other's a lie. Don't you know it's a lie, Harry?'

'Don't be botherin' yourself about that now,' said Harry, coldly, with rather a sullen countenance, looking askance through the open space in the window shutter to the distant horizon. 'Long heads, my lad, and lawyer's lear for the quips and cranks o' law. What should I know?'

'Harry, I know you love me; you won't let wrong be believed,' said Charles Fairfield, in a voice suddenly stronger than he had spoken in before.

'I won't let wrong be believed,' he answered coolly, perhaps sulkily; and he looked at him steadily for a little with his mouth sullenly open.

'You know, Harry,' he pleaded, 'there's a little child coming; it would not do to wrong it. Oh! Harry, don't you love your poor, only brother?'

Harry looked as if he was going to say something saucy, but instead of that he broke into a short laugh.

'Upon my soul, Charlie, a fellow'd think you took me for an affidavit man. When did I ever tell nowt but the truth? Sich rot! A chap like me, that's faulted always for bein' too blunt and plain-spoken; and as for likin', I'd like to know what else brings me here. Of course I don't say I love anyone, all out, as well as Harry Fairfield. You're my brother, and I stand by you according; but as I said before, I love my shirt very well, but I like my skin better. Hey! And that's all fair.'

'All fair, Harry – I'll – I'll talk no more now, Harry. I'll lie down for a little, and we'll meet again.'

Harry was again looking through the space of the open shutter, and he yawned. He was thinking of taking his leave.

In this 'brown study' he was interrupted by a sound. It was like the beginning of a little laugh. He looked at Charlie, who had uttered it; his thin hand was extended toward the little table at the bedside, and his long arm in his shirt-sleeve. His eyes were open, but his face was changed. Harry had seen death often enough to recognise it. With a dreadful start, he was on his feet, and had seized his brother by the shoulder.

'Charlie, man – Charlie! look at me – my God!' and he seized the brandy bottle and poured ever so much into the open lips. It flowed over from the corners of the mouth, over cheek and chin; the throat swallowed not; the eyes stared their earnest stare, unchanging into immeasurable distance. Charles Fairfield was among the Fairfields of other times; hope and fear, the troubles and the dream, ended.

CHAPTER 47

HOME TO WYVERN

When a sick man dies he leaves his bed and his physic. His best friend asks him not to stay, and sweetheart and kindred concur in putting him out of doors, to lie in a bed of clay, under the sky, come frost or storm or rain; a dumb outcast from fireside, tankard, and even the talk of others.

Tall Charles Fairfield, of the blue eyes, was, in due course, robed in his strange white suit, boxed up and screwed down, with a plated inscription over his cold breast, recounting his Christian and surnames, and the tale of his years.

If from that serene slumber he could have been called again, the loud and exceeding bitter cry, the wild farewell of his poor little Ally would have wakened him; but her loving Ry, her hero, slept on, with the unearthly light on his face till the coffin-lid hid it, and in the morning the athlete passed downstairs on men's shoulders, and was slid reverently into a hearse, and went away to old Wyvern churchyard.

At ten o'clock in the morning, Charles Fairfield was on the ground. Was old Squire Harry there to meet his son, and follow his coffin to the aisle of the ancient little church, and thence to his place in the churchyard? Not he.

'Serve him right,' said the squire, when he heard it. 'I'm d——d if he'll lie in our vault; let him go to Parson Maybell, yonder, under the trees; I'll not have him.'

So Charles Fairfield is buried there under the drip of those melancholy old trees, close by the gentle vicar and his good and pretty wife, over whom the grass has grown long, and the leaves of twenty summers have bloomed and fallen, and whose forlorn and beautiful little child was to be his bride, and is now his widow.

Harry Fairfield was there, with the undertaker's black cloak over his well-knit Fairfield shoulders. He nodded to this friend and that in the crowd, gruffly. His face was lowering with thought, his eyes cast down, and sometimes raised in an abstracted glare to the face of some unobserved bystander for a few moments. Conspicuous above other uncovered heads was his. The tall stature, and the statuesque proportions of his race would have marked him without the black mantle for the kinsman of the dead Fairfield.

Up to Wyvern House, after the funeral was over, went Harry. The old man, his hat in his hand, was bareheaded, on the steps; as he approached he nodded to his last remaining son. Three were gone now. A faint sunlight glinted on his old features; a chill northern air stirred his white locks. A gloomy but noble image of winter the gaunt old man presented.

'Well, that's over; where's the lad buried?'

'Just where you wished, sir, near Vicar Maybell's grave, under the trees.'

The old squire grunted an assent.

'The neighbours was there, I dare say?'

'Yes, sir – *all*, I think.'

'I shouldn't wonder – they liked Charlie – they did. He's buried up there alone – well, he deserved it. Was Dobbs there, from Craybourne? He was good to Dobbs. He gave that fellow twenty pun' once, like a big fool, when Dobbs was druv to the wall, the time he lost his cattle; *he* was there?'

'Yes, I saw Dobbs there, sir – he was crying.'

'More fool Dobbs – more fool he,' said the squire, and then came a short pause. 'Cryin', was he?'

'Yes, sir.'

'He's a big fool – Dobbs is a fool.'

'A man cryin' always looks a fool, the rum faces they makes when they're blubbin',' observed Harry. 'Some o' the Wykeford folk was there – Rodney was at his funeral.'

'Rodney? He didn't like a bone in his skin. Rodney's a bad dog. What brought Rodney to *my* son's funeral?'

'He's took up wi' them preachin' folk at Wykeford, I'm told, and he came down, I s'pose, to show the swaddlers what a forgivin', charitable chap he is. Before he put on his hat, he come over and put out his hand to me.'

'And ye took it! ye know ye took it.'

'Well, the folk was lookin' on, and he took me so short,' said Harry.

'Charlie wouldn't 'a' done that; he wouldn't 'a' took his hand over your grave; but you're not like us – never was; you were cut out for a lawyer, I think.'

'Well, the folk would 'a' talked, ye know, sir.'

'Talked, sir, would they?' retorted the squire, with an angry leer. 'I never cared the crack o' a cart whip what the folk talked – let 'em talk, d——n 'em. And ye had no gloves, Dickon says, nor nothin', buried like a dog a'most, up in a corner there.'

'Ye told me not to lay out a shillin', sir,' said Harry.

'If I did I did, but angry folk don't always mean all they says; no matter, we're done wi' it now – it's over. He was worth ye all,' broke out the squire, passionately; 'I could 'a' liked him, if he had 'a' liked me – if he had 'a' let me, but he didn't, and – there it is.'

So the squire walked on a little hastily, which was his way when he chose to be alone, down the steps with gaunt, stumbling gait, and slowly away into the tall woods close by, and in that ancestral shadow disappeared.

Future – present – past. The future – mist, a tint, and shadow. The cloud on which fear and hope project their airy phantoms, living in imagination, and peopled by romance – a dream of dreams. The present only we possess man's momentary dominion, plastic under his hand as the clay under the potter's – always a moment of the present in our absolute power – always that fleeting, plastic moment speeding into the past – immutable, eternal. The metal flows molten by, and then chills and fixes for ever. So with the life of man – so with the spirit of man. Work while it is called day. The moment fixes the retrospect, and death the character, for ever. The heart knoweth its own bitterness. The proud man looks on the past he has made. The hammer of Thor can't break it; the fire that is not quenched can't melt it. His thoughtless handiwork will be the same for ever.

Old Squire Harry did not talk any more about Charlie. About a month after this he sent to Craybourne to say that Dobbs must come up to Wyvern. Dobb's heart failed him when he heard it. Everyone was afraid of old Squire Harry, for in his anger he regarded neither his own interest nor other men's safety.

'Ho, Dobbs! you're not fit for Craybourne, the farm's too much for you, and I've nothing else to gi'e ye.' Dobb's heart quailed at these words. 'You're a fool, Dobbs – you're a fool – you're not equal to it, man. I wonder ye didn't complain o' your rent. It's too much – too high by half. I told Cresswell to let you off every rent day a good penn'orth, for future, and don't you talk about it to no one, 'twould stop that.' He laid his hand on Dobb's shoulder, and looked not unkindly in his face.

And then he turned and walked away, and Dobbs knew that his audience was over.

And the old squire was growing older, and grass and weeds were growing apace over handsome Charlie Fairfield's grave in Wyvern. But the old man never sent to Carwell Grange, nor asked questions about Alice. That wound was not healed, as death heals some.

Harry came, but Alice was ill, and could not see him. Lady Wyndale came, and her she saw, and that good-natured kinswoman made her promise that she would come and live with her so soon as she was well enough to leave the Grange.

And Alice lay still in her bed, as the doctor commanded, and her heart seemed breaking. The summer would return, but Ry would never come again. The years would come and pass – how were they to be got over? And, oh! the poor little thing that was coming! – what a sad welcome! It would break her heart to look at it. 'Oh, Ry, Ry, Ry, my darling!'

So the morning broke and evening closed, and her great eyes were wet with tears – 'the rain it raineth every day.'

CHAPTER 48

A TWILIGHT VISIT

In the evening Tom had looked in at his usual hour, and was recruiting himself with his big mug of beer and lump of bread and cheese at the kitchen table, and now, the keen edge of appetite removed, he was talking agreeably. This was what he called his supper. The flush of sunset on the sky was fading into twilight, and Tom was chatting with old Mildred Tarnley.

'Who'd think it was only three weeks since the funeral?' said Tom – 'three weeks to-morrow.'

'Ay, to-morrow. 'Twas a Thursday, I mind, by the little boy comin' from Gryce's Mill, for the laundress's money, by noon. Two months ago, to look at him, you'd 'a' said there was forty years' life in him; but death keeps no calendar, they say. I wonder Harry Fairfield isn't here oftener. Though she might not talk wi' him nor see him, the sound o' his voice in the house would do her good – his own brother, you know.'

'Dead men, 'tis an old sayin', is kin to none,' said Tom. 'They goes their own gate, and so does the livin'.'

'There's that woman in gaol. What's to be done wi' her, and who's to talk wi' the lawyer folk?' said Mildred.

'Ill luck came wi' her to Carwell,' said Tom. 'Pity he ever set eyes on her; but chances will be, and how can cat help it if maid be a fool? I don't know nothin' o' that business, but in this world nowt for nowt is the most of our wages, and I take it folks knows what they are about, more or less.'

Mildred Tarnley sniffed at this oracular speech, and turned up her nose, and went over to the dresser and arranged some matters there.

'The days is shortening apace. My old eyes can scarce see over here without a candle,' she said, returning. 'But there's a many a thing to be settled in this house, I'm thinkin'.'

Tom nodded an acquiescence, and stood up and stretched himself, and looked up to the darkening sky.

'The crows is home in Carwell Wood; 'twill be time to be turning keys and drawing of bolts,' said Tom. 'Ay, many a thing 'll want settlin', I doubt, down here, and who's to do it?'

'Ay, who's to do it?' repeated Mildred. 'I tell ye, Tom, there's many a thing – *too* many a thing – more than ye wot of – enough to bring him out o' his grave, Tom – as I've heerd stories, many a one, wi' less reason.'

As she ceased, a clink of a horseshoe was heard in the little yard without, and a tall figure leading a horse, as Charles Fairfield used often to do, on his late return to his home, looking in at the window – in that uncertain twilight, in stature, attitude, and, as well as she could see, in face, so much resembling the deceased master of Carwell Grange, that Mrs Tarnley gasped:–

'My good lord! Who's that?'

Something of the same momentary alarm puzzled Tom, who frowned wildly at it, with his fists clenched beside him.

It was Harry Fairfield, who exhibited, as sometimes happens in certain lights and moments, a family resemblance, which had never struck those most familiar with his appearance.

'Lawk, it's Mr Harry; run out, Tom, and take his nag, will ye?'

Out went Tom, and in came Harry Fairfield. He looked about him. He did not smile facetiously and nod, and take old Mildred's dubious hand, as he was wont, and crack a joke, not always very welcome or very pleasant, to the tune of:–

> Nobody coming to marry me –
> Nobody coming to woo.

On the contrary, he looked as if he saw nothing there but walls and twilight, and as heavy laden with gloomy thoughts as the troubled ghost she had imagined.

'How is Miss Ally? how is your mistress?' at last he inquired abruptly. 'Only middling?'

'Ailing, sir,' answered Mildred, dryly.

'Tell her I'm here, will ye? and has something to tell her and talk over, and will make it as short as I can. Tell her I'd ha' come earlier, but couldn't, for the sessions at Wykeford, and dined wi' a neighbour in the town; and say I mayn't be able to come for a good while again. Is she up?'

'No, sir, the doctor keeps her still to her bed.'

'Well, old Dulcey Crane's there; ain't she?'

'Ay, sir, and Lilly Dogger too. Little good the slut's to me these days.'

Harry was trying to read his watch at the darkened window.

'Tell her all that – quick, for time flies,' said Harry.

Harry Fairfield remained in the kitchen while old Mildred did his message, and she speedily returned to say that Alice was sitting up by the fire, and would see him.

Up the dim stairs went Harry. He had not been up there since the day he saw the undertakers at Charlie's coffin, and had his last peep at his darkening face. Up he strode with his hand on the banister, and old Mildred gliding before him like a shadow. She knocked at the door. It was not that of the room which they had occupied, where poor Charles Fairfield had died, but the adjoining one, hurriedly arranged, with such extemporised comforts as the primitive people of the household could manage – homely enough, but not desolate, it looked.

Opening the door, she said –

'Here's Master Harry, ma'am a-comin' to see you.'

Harry was already in the room. There were candles lighted on a little table near the bed, although the shutters were still open, and the faint twilight mingling with the light of the candles made a sort of purple halo. Alice was sitting in a great chair by the fire in her dressing-gown, pale, and looking very ill. She did not speak; she extended her hand.

'Came to see you, Ally. Troublesome world; but you must look up a bit, you know. Troubles are but trials, they say, and can't last for ever; so don't you be frettin' yourself out o' the world, lass, and makin' more food for worms.'

And with this consolation he shook her hand.

'I would have seen you, Harry, when you called before − it was very kind of you − but I could not. I am better now, thank God. I can't believe it still, sometimes,' and her eyes filled with tears.

'Well, well, well!' said Harry: 'where's the good o' cryin'? Cryin' won't bring him back, you know. There, there! And I want to say a word to you about that woman that's in gaol, you know. 'Tis right you should know everything. He should 'a' told you more about that, don't you see, else ye might put your foot in it.'

Paler still turned Alice at these words.

'Tell them to go in there,' said he in a lower tone, indicating with his thumb over his shoulder a sort of recess at the far end of the room, in which stood a table with some work on it.

At a word from Alice old Dulcibella called Lilly Dogger into that distant 'alcove', as Mildred termed it.

'It's about that woman,' he continued, in a very low tone, 'about that one − Bertha. That woman, you know, that's in Hatherton Gaol, you remember. There's no good prosecuting that one. Poor Charles wouldn't have allowed it at no price.'

'He said so. I wouldn't for the world,' she answered very faintly.

'No, of course; he wished it, and we'd like to see his wishes complied with, poor fellow, now he's gone,' acquiesced Harry with alacrity. 'And you know about her?' he added, in a *very* low tone.

'Oh no, no, Harry; no, please,' she answered imploringly.

'Well, it wouldn't do for you, you know, to be gettin' up in the witness-box at the 'sizes to hang her, ye know.'

'Oh, dear Harry; no, I never could have thought of it.'

'Well, you are not bound, luckily; nor no one. I saw Rodney to-day about it; there's no recognisances − he only took the informations − and I said you wouldn't prosecute; nor *I* won't, I'm sure; and the Crown won't take it up, and so it will fall through, and end quietly − the best way for you; for, as I told him, you're not in health to go down there to be battlin' wi' lawyers, and all sorts; 'twould never answer *you*, ye know. So here's a slip o' paper I wrote, and I told him I knew you'd sign it − only sayin' you have no notion of prosecutin' that woman, nor moving more in the matter.'

He placed it in her hand.

'I'm sure it's quite right; it's just what I mean. Thank you, Harry; you're very good.'

'Get the ink and pen,' said Harry aloud to Dulcibella.

''Tis downstairs,' answered she. 'I'll fetch it.'

And Dulcibella withdrew. Harry was poking about the shelves and the chimney-piece.

'This is ink,' said he, 'ain't it?' So it was, and a pen. 'I think it will write – try it, Ally.'

So it was signed; and he had fairly described its tenor and effect to his widowed sister-in-law.

'I'll see Rodney this evening and show him this, to prevent his bothering you here about it. And,' he almost whispered, 'you know about that woman? or you don't – do you?'

Her lips moved, but he could hear no words.

'She was once a fine woman – ye wouldn't think – a devilish fine woman, I can tell you; and she says – ye know 'twas more than likin' – she says she has the whip hand o'er ye – first come, first served. She's talkin' o' law, and all that. She says – but it won't make no odds now, you know, what she says – well, she says she was his wife.'

'Oh, God! – it's a lie!' whispered the poor lady, with white lips, and staring at him with darkening eyes.

'Well, maybe it is, and maybe it ain't,' he answered. 'But it don't much matter now; and I dare say we'll hear nothing about it, and dead men's past fooling, ye know. Good-night, Ally, and God bless you; and take care o' yourself, and don't be crying your eyes out like that. And I'll come again as soon as I can; and any business, you know, or anything, I'll be always ready to do for you – and good-night, Ally, and mind all I said.'

Since those terrible words of his were spoken she had not heard a syllable. He took her icy hand. He looked for a puzzled moment in her clouded eyes, and nodded, and he called to the little girl in the adjoining room.

'I'm going now, child, and do you look after your mistress.'

By a coincidence of association – something suggested by Harry Fairfield's looks, was it? – old Mildred Tarnley's head was full of the Dutchwoman when Dulcibella came into the kitchen.

'You took out the ink, Tom, when you was weighin' them oats to-day,' said she, and out went Tom in search of that always errant and miching article.

'I was sayin' to Tom as ye came in, Mrs Crane, how I hoped to see that one in her place. I think I'd walk to Hatherton and back to see her hanged; the false jade, wi' her knife, and her puce pelisse, and her devilry. Old witch!'

'Lawk, Mrs Tarnley, how can ye?'

'Well, now Master Charles is under the mould, I wouldn't spare her. What for shouldn't Mrs Fairfield make her pay for the pipe she danced to. It's her turn now –

> When you are anvil, hold you still,
> When you are hammer, strike your fill.

And if I was Mrs Fairfield, *maybe* I wouldn't make her smoke for all.'

'I think my lady will do just what poor Master Charles wished, and I know nothing about the woman,' said Dulcibella, 'only they all say she's not right in her head, Mrs Tarnley, and I don't think she'll slight his last word, and punish the woman; 'twould be the same as sacrilege a'most; and what of her? Much matter about a wooden platter! and it's ill burning the house to frighten the mice.'

Harry Fairfield here sauntered into the kitchen, rolling unspoken thoughts in his mind. The conversation subsided at his approach; Dulcibella made her curtsey and withdrew, and said he to Tom, who was entering with the ink-bottle:–

'Tom, run out, will ye, and get my nag ready for the road; I'll be off this minute.'

Tom departed promptly.

'Well, Mildred,' said he, eyeing her darkly from the corners of his eyes, 'sorrow comes unsent for.'

'Ay, sure, she's breakin' her heart, poor thing.'

''Twon't break, I warrant, for all that,' he answered; 'sorrow for a husband, they say, is a pain in the elbow, sharp and short.'

'All along o' that ugly Dutch beast. 'Twas an ill wind carried her to Carwell,' said Mildred.

He shut his eyes and shook his head.

'That couldn't do nowhere,' said he:–

> 'Two cats and one mouse,
> Two wives in one house.'

'Master Charles was no such fool. What for should he ever 'a' married such as that? I couldn't believe no such thing,' said Mrs Tarnley, sharply.

> 'Two dogs at one bone
> Can never agree in one.'

repeated Harry, oracularly. 'There's no need, mind, to set folk's tongues a-ringin', nor much good in tryin' to hide the matter, for her people won't never let it rest, I lay ye what ye please – never. 'Twill be strange news up at Wyvern, but I'm afeard she'll prove it only too ready; 'twill shame us finely.'

'Well, let them talk – "As the bell clinks, so the fool thinks" – and who the worse. I don't believe it nohow. He never would 'a' brought down the Fairfields to that, and, if he had, he could not 'a' brought the poor young creature upstairs into such trouble and shame. I won't believe it of him till it's proved.'

'I hope they may never prove it. But what can we do? You and I know how they lived here, and I have heard her call him husband as often as I have fingers and toes, but, bless ye, we'll hold our tongues – you will, eh? won't ye, Mildred? ye mustn't be talkin'.'

'Talkin'! I ha' nowt to talk about. Fudge! man, I don't believe it – 'tis a d——d lie, from top to bottom.'

'I hope so,' said he.

'A shameless liar she was, the blackest I ever heard talk.'

'Best let sleepin' dogs be,' said he.

There was some silver loose in his trousers pocket, and he was fumbling with it, and looking hard at Mildred as he spoke to her. Sometimes, between his finger and thumb, he held the shilling – sometimes the half-crown. He was mentally deciding which to part with, and it ended by his presenting Mildred with the shilling, and recommending her to apply this splendid 'tip' to the purchase of tea.

Some people experience a glow after they have done a great benevolence; as he walked into the stable yard, Harry experienced a sensation, but it wasn't a glow – a chill rather. Remembering the oblique look with which she eyed the silver coin in her dark palm, and her scant thanks, he was thinking what a beast he was to part with his money so lightly.

Mildred Tarnley cynically muttered to herself in the kitchen:–

> 'Farewell frost,
> Nothing got nor nothing lost.

Here's a gift! Bless him! I mind the time a Fairfield would 'a' been ashamed to give an old servant such a vails. Hoot! what's the world a-comin' to? 'Tis time we was a-goin'. But Master Harry was ever the same – a thrifty lad he was, that looked after his pennies sharply,' said old Mildred Tarnley, scornfully; and she dropped the coin disdainfully into a little tin porringer that stood on the dresser.

And Tom came in, and the doors were made sure, and Mildred Tarnley made her modest cup of tea, and all was subsiding for the night.

But Harry's words had stricken Alice Fairfield. Perhaps those viewless arrows oftener kill than people think of. Up in her homely room Alice now lay very ill indeed.

CHAPTER 49

THE HEIR OF THE FAIRFIELDS

At dead of night Alice was very ill, and Tom was called up to ride across Cressley Common for the Wykeford doctor. Worse and worse she grew. In this unknown danger – without the support of a husband's love or consolation – 'the pains of hell gat hold of her,' the fear of death was upon her. Glad was she in her lonely terrors to hear the friendly voice of Doctor Willett as he came up the stairs, with a heavy booted step, in hurried conversation with old Dulcibella Crane, who had gone down to meet him on hearing the sound of his arrival.

In lower tones the doctor put his questions when he had arrived in his patient's room, and his manner became stern, and his measures prompt, and it was plain that he was very much alarmed.

Alice Fairfield was in danger – in so great danger that he would have called in the Hatherton doctor, or any other, to share his responsibility if the horse which Tom drove had not had as much as he could do that night in the long trot – and partly canter – to Wykeford and back again to the Grange.

Alice's danger increased, and her state became so alarming that the doctor was afraid to leave his patient, and stayed that night at the Grange.

In the morning he sent Tom to Hatherton with a summons for his brother physician, and now this quaint household grew thoroughly alarmed.

The lady was past the effort of speaking, almost of thinking, and lay like a white image in her bed. Old Dulcibella happily had charge of the money, not much, which Alice had for present use; so the doctors had their fees, and were gone, and Doctor Willett, of Wykeford, was to come again in the evening, leaving his patient, as he said, quieter, but still in a very precarious state.

When the Wykeford doctor returned he found her again too ill to think of leaving her. At midnight Tom was obliged to mount and ride away to Hatherton for the other doctor.

Before the Hatherton doctor had reached the Grange, however, a tiny voice was crying there – a little spirit had come, a scion of the Fairfield race.

Mrs Tarnley wrote to Harry Fairfield to Wyvern to announce the event, which she did thus:–

'SIR, – Master Harey, it has came a sirprise. Missis is this mornin' gev burth to a boy and air; babe is well, but Missis Fairfield low and dangerous.

'Your servant,
'MILDRED TARNLEY.'

Dulcibella, without consulting Mildred, any more than Mildred did her, wrote also a letter, gentler and more gracious, but certainly no better spelled. When these reached Wyvern, Harry was from home.

It was not till four days had passed that Harry Fairfield arrived in the afternoon.

He had thrown his horse's bridle to Tom in the stable yard, and appeared suddenly before Mildred Tarnley in the kitchen door.

'Well, how's the lady in the straw?' inquired Harry, looking uncomfortable, but smiling his best. 'How is Miss Alice?'

'Mrs Fairfield's very bad, and the doctor ha'n't much hope of her. She lies at God's mercy, sir.'

'She'll be better, you'll find. She'll be all right soon. And when was it – you put no date to your note?'

'On Friday, I think. We're so put about here I scarce know one day from t'other.'

'She'll be better. Is anyone here with her?'

'A nurse from Hatherton.'

'No one else? I thought Lady Wyndale might ha' come.'

'I was goin' to send over there, but Doctor Willett said no.'

'Did he? Why?'

'Not yet a bit; he says she'd be in his way and no use, and maybe worrit her into a fever.'

'Very like,' said Harry; 'and how's the boy – isn't it a boy?'

'Boy – yes, sir, a fine thumpin' baby – and like to do well, and will prove, belike, a true, open-handed Fairfield, and a brave Squire o' Wyvern.'

'Well, that's as it may be. I'll not trouble him. I have more than enough to my share as it is – and there's some things that's better never than late, and I'll live and die a bachelor. I've more years than my teeth shows.'

And Harry smiled and showed his fine teeth.

'There's Fairfields has took a wife later than you,' said she, eyeing him darkly.

'Too wise, old girl. You'll not catch me at that work. Wives is like Flanders mares as the squire says, fairest afar off.'

'Hey?' snarled old Mildred, with a prolonged note.

'No, lass, I don't want, nohow, to be squire o' Wyvern – there's more pains than gains in it; always one thing or t'other wrong – one begs and t'other robs, and ten cusses to one blessin'. I don't want folks to say o' me as they does of some – Harry's a hog, and does no good till he dies.'

'Folk do like an estate, though,' said Mildred, with another shrewd look.

'Ay, if all's straight and clear, but I don't like debts and bother, and I 'a' seen how the old boy's worried that way till he's fit to drown himself in the pond. I can do something, buyin' or sellin'; and little and often, you know, fills the purse.'

Mildred was silent.

'They do say – I mean, I knows it for certain, there is a screw loose – and you know where, I think – but how can I help that? The Dutchwoman, I know, can prove her marriage to poor Charlie, but never you blab – no more will I. There was no child o' that marriage – neither chick nor child, so, bein' as she is, 'tis little to her how that sow's handled. 'Twould be a pity poor Charlie's son should lose his own; and ye may tell Alice I'm glad there's a boy, and that she'll ha' no trouble from me, but all the help I can, and that's a fact, and that's God's truth.'

'Well, well, that *is* queer! – I never heard man speak as you speak.'

There was a cynical incredulity in Mildred Tarnley's tone.

'Listen, now – here we be alone, eh?' said he, looking round.

'Ye may say so,' she said, with a discontented emphasis.

'I'd tell you a thing in a minute, old Tarnley, only they say old vessels must leak. Will you be staunch? Will ye hold your tongue on't if I tell you a thing?'

'Ay,' said Mildred.

'Because one barking dog sets all the street a-barking, ye know,' he added.

'Ye know me well, Master Harry. I could hold my tongue always when there was need.'

'And that's the reason I'm going to talk to you,' said Harry, 'and no one knows it, mind, but yourself, and if it gets out I'll know who to blame.'

''Twon't get out for me,' said Mildred, looking hard at him.

'One devil drubs another, they say, and if the young squire upstairs has a foot in the mud I've one in the mire,' said Harry. 'If his hat has a hole, my shoe has another. And 'tis a bad bargain where both are losers.'

'Well, I can't see it nohow. I don't know what you're drivin' at; but I think you're no fool, Master Harry; ye never was that, and it's a cunning part, I've heerd, to play the fool well.'

And Harry did look very cunning as she cited this saw, and for a moment also a little put out. But he quickly resumed, and, staring in her face surlily, said he:–

'Well, I *am* cunnin'; I hope I am; and you're a little bit that way yourself, old Mildred; no fool, anyhow, that ever I could see.'

'Crafty I may be – I ha' lived years and seen folk enough to make me, but my heart weren't set never on pelf.

> 'A thousand pounds and a bottle of hay
> Is all one at doom's-day.'

'So it is,' said he, 'but there's a good many days 'twixt this and doom's-day yet, and money'll do more than my lord's letter, any place, and I'll not deny I'd like Wyvern well enough if my hand was free to lay on it. But I ha' thought it well over, and it wouldn't fit me nohow. I can't.'

'Ye're the first Fairfield I ever heerd say that Wyvern wouldn't fit him,' said she.

'Is that beer in the jug?' he asked, nodding towards a brown jug that stood on the dresser.

'Yes, sir. Would ye like a drink?'

'Ay, if it bain't stale.'

'Fresh drew, just as you was coming in, sir,' said she, setting it down on the table. 'I'll fetch ye a glass.'

'Never mind a glass – a rantin' dog like me can drink out of a well-bucket, much less a brown jug,' and clutching it carelessly by the handle he quaffed as long and deep a draught as his ancestor and namesake might after his exhausting flight from Worcester a couple of hundred years before.

'You are puzzled, old girl, and don't know whether I be in jest or earnest. But, good or bad, wives must be had, you know, and you never heard of a Fairfield yet that was lucky in a wife, or hadn't a screw loose sometime about they sort o' cattle; and ye're an old servant, Mildred, and though you be a bit testy, you're true, and I may tell ye things I wouldn't tell no one, not the governor, not my little finger; I'd burn my shirt if it knew; and ye won't tell no one, upon your soul, and as ye hope to be saved.'

'I can keep counsel, I'm good at that,' said Mildred.

'Well, I need not say no more than this; there's them that's quiet enough now, and will be, that if they thought I was Squire o' Wyvern I'd make the world too hot to hold me. I'd rather be Harry Fairfield at fair and market than archbishop of hell, I can tell ye, havin' no likin' for fine titles and honour, and glory, wi' a tethered leg and a sore heart; better to go your own gait, and eat your mouthful where ye find it, than go in gold wi' a broken back, that's all, and that's truth. If 'twas otherwise I'd be down in the mouth, I can tell you, about the young genman upstairs, and I'd ha' liked his birthday no better than a shepherd loves a bright Candlemas; but as it is – no matter, 'tis better to me than a pot o' gold, and I drink the little chap's health, and I wish she had a sieve full o' them, and that's God's truth, as I stand here,' and Harry backed the declaration with an oath.

'Well, I believe you, Harry,' said Mildred. 'And I'm glad o't,' she added after a pause. 'I'm very glad – there has been ill blood o'er much in the family,' she resumed; 'it's time there should be peace and brotherhood, God knows – and – I'm glad to hear you speak like that, sir.'

And, so saying, she extended her dark, hard palm to him, and he took it, and laughed.

'Every man knows where his own shoe pinches,' said he; ''tis a shrewish world, old girl, and there's warts and chilblains where no one guesses, but things won't be for ever; 'tis a long lane, ye know, that has no turning, and the burr won't stick always.'

'Ay, ay, Master Harry, as I've heard the old folks say, "Be the day never so long, at last cometh evensong."'

'And how is the lady herself?' said he.

'As bad as can be, a'most,' answered Mildred.

'Who says so?' he asked.

'The doctor; he has no opinion of her, I'm afeard, poor little thing!'

'The doctor – does he? – but is he any good?'

'It's Doctor Willett, of Wykeford. He's thought a deal of by most folk down here. I don't know, I'm sure, but he seems very nice about her, I think, and kind, and looks after the baby too.'

'That's right; I'm glad of that. I'd pay something myself rather than it should be neglected; and what does he say o' the boy?'

'Doin' very well – nothin' against him; but, you know, 'tis only a few days, and o'er soon to judge yet a bit.'

'I wonder could she see me for a minute?'

'Hoot, man! How came that in your head? Why, the room's dark, and she never speaks above a whisper, and not five words then, and only, maybe, thrice in a day. Ye don't know what way she is; 'tis just the turn of a halfpenny whether she'll live till mornin'.'

'That's bad. I didn't think she could be that bad,' said he.

'She is, then.'

''Twould do her no harm to know that there's some rent – about thirty pounds – due from Riddleswake. I'll give Tom a bit of a note to Farmer Wycraft, and he'll pay it. It's settled to her for her life – I know that – and she'll be wantin' money; and see you that the child wants nothing. I have lots o' reasons why that child should do well. This ain't bad beer, I can tell you. Another mug of it wouldn't hurt me, and if you can make me out a mouthful of anything – I'm beastly hungry.'

A bit of cold corned beef, some cheese, and a loaf Mildred Tarnley produced, and Harry made a hearty meal in the kitchen, not disturbing that engrossing business by conversation, while old Mildred went to and fro, into the scullery and back again, and busied herself about her saucepans and dishes.

'Now get me a pen and ink and a bit o' paper. There's no one in the house will be the worse of a little money, and I'll write that note.' And so he did, and handed it to Mildred with the air of a prince who was bestowing a gift.

'*There!* That will make the mare go for a while longer; and, look ye, where's old Dulcibella Crane? I'd like to shake hands wi' her before I go.'

'Upstairs, wi' her mistress.'

'Tell her to come down and see me for a minute; and mind, old Tarnley, ye must write to me often – to-morrow and next day – and – where's my hat? – on my head, by Jove! – and so on; for if anything should happen – if little Alice should founder, you know – there should be someone, when she's off the hooks, to look after things a bit; and the governor won't do nothing – put that out o' yer head – and 'twill all fall on my shoulders; and send her down to me – old Dulcibella Crane, I mean – for I'm going, and unless I'm wanted I mayn't see ye here for many a day.'

Thus charged, Mildred Tarnley went away, and in a few minutes old Dulcibella appeared.

From her, after he had examined her as to the state of the lady upstairs, and of her baby, he exacted the same purpose as that which Mildred had made him – a promise to write often to Wyvern.

He did not mind making her the same odd confidence which he had made to Mildred. There was no need, he thought, for Dulcibella was soft-hearted, and somewhat soft-headed too, and by no means given to suspicion; and as she had not the evil that attends shrewdness, neither had she the reliability, and she was too much given to talking, and his secret would then become more public than he cared to make it.

'And tell the mistress I wish her joy, do you mind, and I'd like to stand godfather to the boy whenever the christenin' is, and to put me to any work she thinks I'm fit for; and tell her I wrote about a handful o' rent that's coming to her, and good-bye, and take care o' yourself; and who's nursing the baby?'

'We feeds it wi' goat's milk and sich like, by direction of the doctor. Wouldn't ye like to see it?'

'Not this time – I'm off – but – who's taking charge of him?'

'Among us the poor little darling is, but mostly me.'

'Well, that's right, and look after it well, and I'll give ye a bit o' money – when – when it's on a little, and don't forget to write; and ye needn't say nowt to old Mildred, for she's goin' to write too, and might take huff if she knew that you was writin' also, do you see?'

'Yes, Master Harry, surely none shall know, and I'm thinkin' ye *would* like to see it, and it won't be nothin' the worse, ye'll find, and it *is* such a darlin'.'

'And so like its poor papa that's gone, eh? But I haven't no time, dear, this bout, and you may give his worship my kind regards, and tell him the more he thrives the better I'm pleased, and old chimneys won't stand for ever, and he won't be long kept out of his own, and I'll keep them aloof that would make or meddle or mar – and good-bye, old Dulcie Crane, and mind what I said.'

And, clapping her on the shoulder with his strong hand, he smiled after his fashion and wagged his head and strode into the yard, mounted his horse, and was soon far away on the road from Carwell Grange.

CHAPTER 50

BERTHA VELDERKAUST

Harry Fairfield, when, crossing Cressley Common, he reached the road that diverges eastward, took that turn, and rode towards Hatherton.

Surely enough he looked when he slackened his pace to a walk at the foot of the long low hill that interposes between the common and that town.

He had a short pipe in his pocket, with a big bowl, and a metal cover to it, into which he stuffed some pinches of tobacco – a shilling went a good way in that sort of smoking, and Harry was economical – and soon his pipe was in full play.

This narcotic helped his cogitative powers, and he had a good deal to think about. He was going to see his old friend Bertha Velderkaust, in her new situation, and he was considering how best to approach her.

From such ruminations – too vague and irregular to be reduced to logical sequence and arrangement – there arise, nevertheless, conclusions by no means unimportant, and quite distinct enough. By this time he had smoked his pipe out, and looked down from the summit of this rising ground upon the pretty town spreading among the trees, with its old tower and steeple, its court-house, its parsonage, and that high-walled stronghold on the right in which the object of his visit was at present secluded.

When, having complied with all formalities, he obtained an entrance and obtained permission to visit that person, it was her pleasure to keep him waiting for some time for his audience. Harry grew cross and impatient, the more so as he heard that she had a friend with her, drinking tea, and reading the newspaper to her.

As Harry Fairfield was one of those persons who are averse to sacrificing themselves without a good consideration, the reader will conclude that his object was not altogether to serve the old soldier. If it had been only that, I think he would have left the town of Hatherton *re infecta*. As it was, he waited, and at last was admitted.

This lady, Bertha Velderkaust, chose to be known among her

neighbours in misfortune as Madame Bertha Fairfield of Wyvern, which style and title she preferred to that by which she had been committed to the safe keeping of the gaoler.

When Harry Fairfield stepped into her small apartment he found her dressed and bedizened in a way that a little surprised him.

She had on a sky-blue satin dress, caught up at one side with a bunch of artificial flowers. She had a lace scarf and a lace coiffure lying flat across her head, with a miniature coronet of Roman pearl in the centre, and lappets depending at each side. She had a double necklace of enormous Roman pearls about her throat, and a pair of pink velvet slippers, embroidered with beads and bugles, and this tawdry figure sat on the side of her truckle-bed to receive him, with the air of a princess in a pantomime. She accumulated her finery in this way, I think, for the purpose of impressing the people about the prison with a due sense of her position and importance. It may not have been quite without its effect.

'Hullo! madame, I came to tell you some news,' said he, as soon as the door was closed. 'But, by the makins! you 'most took my breath away at first sight o' ye.'

'Pity to have so nice a man breathless – deplorable pity!' – or *biddy*, as she pronounced it. 'Suppose you go away – I did not ask you to come – and get your breath again in the air of my place.'

'What place may that be – not Hoxton Old Town, hey?'

'Not at all – Wyvern, dear child!' she said, with a quiet sneer.

'Oh, thank ye – yes – well, I will, I think, take a mouthful there, as you are so good.'

As he concluded this speech Master Harry put out his tongue at the blind lady with a grimace that was outrageous.

'I'll hide my name no longer,' she said. 'I'm Mrs Fairfield of Wyvern.'

'That's as it may be,' he answered, serenely.

'I say, I'm Mrs Fairfield of Wyvern,' repeated she.

'Boo!' answered Harry.

'Beast! By that noise what do you mean?'

'I'll tell ye, by-and-bye. Come, you mustn't be cross, it wastes time.'

'More time than we know what to do with in this house,' she sneered.

'Well, that's true for some, I'll not deny; but there's some as is pretty well worked, I hear – eh? – and, so long as we bain't, we may endure the leisure, for, as bad as that is, business here, I'm told, is a deal worse,' and Harry laughed.

'Pleasant was my Harry always,' again sneered the lady.

'And ye heard of poor Charlie, of course?' he asked.

'Yes, of course. Everyone is not like you. I did hear. I don't thank you,' she answered tartly, and turned her pale, malignant face toward him.

'But, dear girl, I could not. There was difficulties, eyes a-watchin' on all hands, and ears cocked, and I knew you could not be long without knowing. So you heard; but mayhap you haven't heard this – there's a child born o' that marriage.'

'Marriage!' and with an oath the big Dutchwoman burst into a discordant laugh.

For a moment Harry was alarmed, but the laugh was not hysterical – purely emotional, and an escape for pent-up scorn and fury.

'Well, anyhow, there's a child – a boy – and a fine hale little chap, wi' a big bald head and a bawlin' mouth as ever a mother hugged – the darlin'.'

'Well, let the brat lie on the dungheap – you'll not lift him,' said the lady.

'I'll not meddle or make. I'm not over-hot about Wyvern. I'd rather have a pocketful of money than a house full o' debts any day; and, anyhow, there he is, and four bones that's to walk off with my share o't.'

'I should have got mourning,' said Bertha Velderkaust, speaking from some hidden train of thought.

'Bah! No one to see you here,' said Harry.

'If I had money or credit, I'd have got it,' she said.

'That's very affectionate of you,' said Harry; 'but why do you dress like that – why do you dress like the lady wi' the glass slipper, Cinderella, at the king's ball, in the story book?'

'I should dress, you think, like Cinderella over the coal-shuttle?'

'Well, I wouldn't set the folk a-laughing when I was in no laughing humour myself – not that it makes much odds, and I do suppose it don't matter – not it.'

'It does matter something, perhaps, and perhaps nothing; but I know who I am, and I won't let myself down,' said she. 'I don't want to lose myself among these people; I'll keep myself distinct, I'm too high to put my foot in the mud.'

'Too high to put your foot in the mud – too high to put your foot on the pavement,' said Harry, mischievously, with his eyes on this impulsive lady, and hitching his chair off a little to secure a fair start. 'You'll be too high, I'm thinkin', to get your foot to ground at all, one o' these days, if you don't look sharp. It's too high a flight, I'm told, to touch *terra firma* wi' the top o' your toe – the gallows, I mean – and that's what you're coming to quick, I'm afeard.'

As Harry concluded, he stood up, intending to get out, if possible, without the indignity of coming to hand-grips with a woman.

The Herculean lady, in sky-blue satin and Roman pearls, leaned forward with sharpened features, but neither extended her arm nor attempted to rise. Then she sighed deeply, and leaned with her shoulders to the wall.

'Off in a coach for this bout,' thought Harry.

'Thank you, kind lad, always the same,' she sneered, quietly. 'You wish it, no doubt, but – no, you don't think it. I know better.'

'Why the devil should I wish you hanged, Bertha? Don't be a fool! You're not in my way, and never can be. There's that boy, and, for reasons of my own, I'm glad he is – I'm *glad* he's where he is – and Wyvern will be for him and not for me – never!'

'Harry, dear, you know quite well,' she drawled, softly, with a titter, 'you'll poison that boy if you can.'

'You lie!' said Harry, turning scarlet, and then as suddenly pale.

'You *lie!* – and so that's answered.'

Here followed a silence. The woman was not angry, but she tittered again and nodded her head.

'Wyvern's out o' my head. I never cared about it. I had my own reasons. I never did,' he swore, furiously, striking his hand on the table. 'And I won't see that boy ruined – my flesh and blood – my own nephew. No, no, Bertha, that would never do; the boy must have his own. I'll see you made comfortable, but that lay won't do – you'll find it won't pay nohow.'

'Speak out man   what do you mean?' said Bertha.

'Come, come, come, Bertha, you're no fool,' wheedled he; 'there isn't a sounder head from this to London; and though you be a bit hot-headed, you're not as bad as you'd have us believe – 'tain't the worst, always, that has an o'er-hasty hand. Why, bless ye, girl, I'd be sorry ye were hurt, and I'll help to get ye out o' this, without scathe or scorn, if you'll let me.'

'Well, come; what's in your mind, Harry Vairfield?' she asked.

'I tell ye what it is, it can do you no good nohow, bein' hard on that boy, and I know, and you know, you never were married to poor Charlie.'

'You lie!' cried the lady, bitterly. So they were quits on the point of honour.

'Now, Bertha, lass, come now – reason, reason; don't you be in a hurry, and just listen to reason, and I'll make it better to you than fifty marriages.'

'Don't you think I have no advice – I've engaged Mr Wynell, the best attorney in Hatherton; I know what I'm about.'

'The better you know it, the better I'm pleased; but the lawyer folk likes always a bit of a row – they seldom cries kiss and be friends until their hands be well greased, and their clients has a bellyful o' law; therefore it's better that friends should put their heads together and agree before it comes to that sort o' milling, and I tell ye, ye shall be cared for; I'll see to it, if ye don't be kickin' up no rows about nothing.'

She laughed a quiet, scornful laugh. 'O-ho! Master Harry, poor little fellow! he's frightened, is he?'

'You're damnably mistaken,' said he. 'Frightened, indeed! I'll see whose frightened. I know there was no marriage − I *know* it, and it won't do tryin' it on me − you'll just get yourself into the wrong box. Where's the use of runnin' your head into a cotton bag?'

'Cotton bag your own head. Who's to do it?'

'They'll be clumsy fingers that can't tie that knot, lass. Come, you're a clever girl, you're not to be talking − not like a fool. I know everything about it. If you try that on, it will turn out bad. 'Tain't easy to green Harry Fairfield; I don't think he was ever yet fooled, and it's pretty well allowed there's no use trying to bully him.'

'I ought to like you, if all that be so,' said she, 'for you are very like my own self.'

'I'm not tryin' to bully you, girl, nor to sell ye, neither; ye were always a bit rash, and too ready wi' your hand; but them's not the worst folk goin'. We Fairfields has a touch o' it, and we shouldn't be o'er hard on quick-tempered folk like that. There was no lass that ever I met, gentle or simple, that could match ye for good looks and pleasant talk, and ye dress so beautiful, and if ye had but your eyes this minute, you'd have who ye liked at your feet.'

And Harry Fairfield repeated this view of her charms with an oath.

'"If ifs an' ans were pots an' pans,"' repeated the lady, with a sigh of gratification, and with that foreign accent and peculiar drawl which made the homely proverb sound particularly odd; 'I forget the end − there would be no use in tinkers, I think.'

'Well said, Bertha! but there's none like ye, not one, this minute, so handsome,' exclaims he.

'Not that chit down at Carwell Grange, I dare say − eh?'

'Alice! Not fit to stand behind your chair. If ye could but see her, and just look in the glass, ye'd answer that question yourself,' he replied.

'There it is again − *if* I could look in the glass − it is fourteen years since I did that − *if* I could see that fool of a girl − if − if − *if!*' she said, with an irrepressible simper − 'the old proverb again − ifs and ans were pots and pans − 'twas old Mistress Tarnley used to say that − a d——d old witch she always was,' she broke out, parenthetically, 'and should be broke alive on the wheel.'

'Bang away wi' the devil's broomstick, and break her to smash for me,' said Harry. 'But I'd sooner talk o' yourself. Hang me, if you ever looked better − there's no such figure! and, by the law, it's looking up − it *is* − better and better every day. I like a tall lass, but ye beat them all, by the law, and ye shows off a dress so grandly.'

'Now don't think, foolish thing, I like compliments − in at one ear and out of the other,' she said, with the same smirk, shaking her great head.

'Hoot, lass! Compliments, indeed! Why should I? Only this, that, knowing you so long, I just blurts out everything that comes uppermost, and it's a pity ye shouldn't have money to dress as ye should.'

'I never had that,' said the lady.

'Never – I know that well – and if ye won't be said by me, ye'll have less,' said Harry.

'I don't think you know much about it,' said Bertha, serenely.

'Now, Bertha, child, you mustn't keep contradictin' me. I do know a deal about it – *everything*. There was no marriage, *never*.'

'As long as Charlie lived, ye never said that – you always backed me.'

'I'm not going to tell lies for no one,' said he, sulkily.

'Not going! Why, you have been lying all your life – you'd lie for a shilling any day – all lies, you mean, miserly liar!'

'Come, Bertha, draw it mild, won't ye? Did you never hear say o' the Fairfields that they were a quick-tempered folk? and it's an old saying, don't knock a mad horse over the head.'

'It's true all I said,' she laughed; 'and that's why it stings.'

'And did ye never hear that true jests breed bad blood?' he laughed. 'But no matter – I'm not a bit riled, and I won't. I like ye better for speaking out; I hate that mealy mouthed talk that fine-spoken folk goes on wi'. I likes a bit of a rub now and then; if ye were too civil I couldn't speak my own mind neither, and that would never do.'

'Get along with ye! Have you any more to say?'

'Shall I say it out, plain and short, and will ye hear it through?' he asked.

'Ay.'

'Well, here it is; if ye don't sign that, I think ye'll be hanged.'

'No, you don't,' she said, more quietly.

'I do, by——!' he swore.

'No, you don't,' she repeated in the same tone. 'Who is to do it? Charlie's gone, and, vilely as he used me, he never would have done that; and Alice won't – she told you so. I'm better informed, I believe, than you fancied. So don't you suppose I am at all anxious.'

'I wanted to take you off in a coach, and you won't let me,' said he.

'Thanks, simple Harry,' she sneered.

'And I'm coming this day week, and then it will be within ten days o' the 'sizes.'

'And I'll be discharged; and I'll bring separate actions against every soul that had a hand in putting me here. Ask my attorney,' said the lady, with a pale, angry simper.

'And Judge Risk is coming down, and you'd better ask your attorney, as you talk of him, whether he's a hangin' judge or no.'

'Cunning beast! all won't do,' she said, sarcastically.

'Well, Bertha, this day week I'll be here, and this day week will be your last chance, for things will begin that day, and no one can stop them.'

'Lord have mercy upon us!' she whined, with an ugly mockery and an upturning of her sightless eyes.

'You may be saying something like that in the press-room yet, if you won't take the trouble to think in earnest before it's too late. Now, listen, once for all, for it's the last words I'll say. That's all true you say: Charlie's gone, and if he was here, instead of in kingdom come, 'twould ha' been all one, for he wouldn't never ha' moved a hand in the matter, nor ha' suffered it; and as for Alice, she won't neither. But if you don't sign that paper by this day week, and make no bones about it' – here he swore a hard oath – 'blind as you be, I'll open your eyes – and I'll prosecute the indictment myself. Good-bye, ma'am, and *think* between this and then.'

Harry Fairfield strode from the room, and was still full of the grim emotion which had animated the close of the interview, when he reached the little inn at which but a few weeks before his brother Charles had stabled his horse, when making his last visit to Hatherton.

CHAPTER 51

SERGEANT-MAJOR ARCHDALE

Harry Fairfield was a captain in his county militia. It was right that the House of Fairfield should be represented in that corps. Charlie, who was of an easy, compliant temper, would have taken the commission and the light duties, if that dignity had been put upon him. But Harry chose it. It extended his acquaintance, added to his opportunities of selling his horses, and opened some houses, small and great, to him, in a neighbourly fashion, when making his circuits to fair and market. He knew something of games, too, and was shrewd at whist and draughts, and held a sure cue at billiards. On the whole, his commission turned him in something in the course of a year.

It was upon some regimental business that Sergeant-Major Archdale was awaiting his return at Wyvern.

Harry Fairfield, as it happened, was thinking of the sergeant as he rode into the yard in gloomy rumination.

'Well, Archdale, what's the news?' said he, as he dismounted.

The news was not a great deal. After he had heard it Harry paused for a time, and said he:–

'Quite well, Archdale, I hope?'

'Well, sir, I thank you.'

Again Harry paused.

'How did you come, Archdale?'

'Walked, sir.'

'Walked, oh! very well.'

Here was another pause.

'Archdale, you must go in. Here, Clinton, get some luncheon for Sergeant-Major Archdale. A drink of beer and a mouthful won't do you no harm; and, Archdale, before you go let me know; I may have a word, and I'll say it walking down the avenue. Get Mr Archdale some luncheon, Clinton, and some sherry.'

'I thank you, sir,' said the sergeant-major. ''Tis more like a supper for me; I've had my dinner, sir, some time.'

And with a stiff military step the sergeant followed Clinton into the house.

The sergeant-major was above the middle size, and stout of body, which made him look shorter. His hair was closely cut, and of a pale blue iron grey. His face was rather pale, and smooth as marble; full and long, with a blue chin, and a sort of light upon his fixed lineaments, not exactly a smile, but a light that was treacherous and cruel. For the rest his military coat, which was of the old-fashioned cut, and his shako, with all the brasses belonging on them, and his Wellington boots, were natty and brilliant, and altogether unexceptionable, and a more perfectly respectable-looking man you could not have found in his rank of life in the country.

Without a word, with a creak in his boots, he marched slowly in, with inflexible countenance, after Clinton.

The squire met Harry in the hall.

'Hollo! it's a week a'most since I set eye on ye – ye'll look out some other place for that mad filly ye bought of Jim Hardress; she's broke a boy's arm this morning in the stable; I'll not look after him, I promise ye; 'tis your affair, mind, and you better look sharp, and delay may cost ye money. Ye're over clever. The devil owes ye a cake this many a day, and he's a busy bishop, and he'll pay ye a loaf yet, I promise you. She sha'n't be kicking my men – and she bites the manger besides. Get her away, mind, or, by my soul, I'll sell her for the damage.'

So old Squire Harry stalked on, and the last scion of his stock grinned after him, sulkily, and snarled something between his teeth so soon as he was quite out of hearing.

'Whose arm's broke, Dick, or is it all a d——d lie o' the governor's?' inquired Harry of a servant who happened to be passing at that moment.

'Well, yes, sir, Jim Slade's arm was broke in the stable. 'Twas a kick, sir.'

'What kicked him?'

'The new horse that came in on Thursday, sir.'

'*Mare*, ye mean. Why, that thing's a reg'lar lamb; she never kicked no one. A child might play wi' her. More like 'twas the governor kicked him. And what did he do wi' his arm?'

'The doctor, down in the town, set it, and bound it up wi' splints, sir.'

'Well, *I* didn't tell him, mind that – I wasn't here, ye know – good-natured of the doctor, I'll not deny, but he sha'n't be sending in no bills to me. And how's Jim since – gettin' on nicely, I'll swear.'

'I don't know, sir; I didn't see him since.'

'Hoot! then it's all right, I warrant ye, and ye can tell old Slade, if he likes it, I'll get him a bit of a writin' to the hospital for Jim; but it won't be nothin' – not a bit.'

And with this economical arrangement Harry dismissed the subject for the present, and took his stand upon the hall-door steps, and smoked his pipe, awaiting the close of Sergeant-Major Archdale's repast.

The long shadows and lights of golden sunset faded before the guest appeared, and twilight and the moths were abroad.

Almost as the servant informed Harry Fairfield that Mr Archdale was coming round to the hall door to receive his commands, the sergeant-major appeared in front of the house, and Harry Fairfield stepped down to the court, and was received by the militiaman with a military salute.

'I'll walk a bit wi' you, Archdale; I want a word about another matter – not regimental business. We'll walk down towards the gate.'

Stiffly and silently the sergeant-major marched beside the smoking gentleman, who, having got a little way from the house, knocked the ashes out of his pipe, and dropped it into his pocket.

'That militia sogerin' is beggarly pay for a man like you, Archdale; and I'll want a clever fellow, by and bye – for when the squire goes off the hooks, and that can't be a long way off – I'll have a deal o' trouble lookin' after things; for there's a young chap to succeed, and a plaguy long minority 'twill be, and, one way or another, the trouble will fall to my share, bein' uncle, ye see, to the little fellow. Am I making it plain what I mean?'

'Quite plain, sir,' said the cold voice of the sergeant-major.

'Well, there's the property down at Warhampton, a devilish wide stretch o' land for the rental. There's good shootin' there, and two keepers, but I doubt they makes away wi' the game, and *they* want lookin' after; and there's the old park o' Warhampton – ye know that part o' the country?'

'Yes, sir, well.'

'I know you do. Well, it should turn in a good penny more than the governor gets. I can't bring it home to them, but I know what I think. Where the horse lies down, the hair will be foun', and I doubt the park book's doctored. There'll be a sort o' steward wanted there, d'ye see. D'ye know Noulton Farm?'

'Yes, sir.'

'Well, it's a nice thing, a snug house, and as many acres as you'd want to begin wi'; the tenant's going after harvest – you'd be the very man for't, and I'll tell them I'll do all I can to serve my nephew, but I must live myself too. I've nowt but my time and my wits to turn a penny by, and if I try to manage for him I'll want the best help I can get, d'ye see? and *you're* the man I want; I've got no end o' a character o' ye, for honesty and steadiness and the like; and ye're a fellow can use his eyes, and hold his tongue; and ye'd have the farm and the house – ye know them – rent free; and the grazing of three cows on the common, and it's none o' your overstocked, bare commons, but as sweet a bit o' grass as ye'd find in the kingdom; and ye shall ha' fifty pounds a year beside; and the farm's nigh forty acres, and it's worth close on a hundred more. And – if ye do all we want well, and I'm sure you will – I'll never lose sight o' ye while grass grows and you and me lives.'

'I thank you, sir,' said the cold, clear voice of Archdale.

'And there's a little bit of a secret – I wouldn't tell another – about myself, Archdale. I'll tell *you*, though,' said Harry, lowering his voice.

'Yes, sir,' said Archdale, in the same cold, stern way, which irritated Harry.

'Well, I'm not talking, mind, to Sergeant-Major Archdale, if you like the other thing, at Noulton, best.'

'Noulton best, sir, certainly; thank you.'

'But to Mr Archdale of Noulton, and steward of Warhampton, mind ye, and 'twill be settled next harvest.'

'I thank you, sir.'

'Don't walk so quick, we're gettin' over the ground too fast. Well, there's a thing you'll have to keep dark for me.'

'You'll find me confidential, sir; my superior officers did.'

'I know that well – I know you, Archdale, and that is why I chose you out o' a thousand, and it's a confidential fellow – d——d confidential – I want, for the country's all one as the town for talk, and tongues will keep goin' like the bells on a sheep-walk, and there's many a bit o' nonsense, that's no great odds when all's told, that a chap wouldn't like to have made the laugh or the talk o' the country side.'

'Yes, sir,' said the inflexible sergeant-major.

'You held the same rank in the line, sergeant-major, didn't you?'

'Yes, sir,' said the sergeant-major, and saluted from habit.

'I thought so, and that says a deal for you, Mr Archdale; and I remember one of your papers says you were the youngest sergeant ever made in your regiment.'

'Yes, sir.'

'Well, that says a lot too, and a very responsible office that is. Egad, from all I ha' seen, I'd say the sergeants has more to do with the state of a regiment than all the other officers, commissioned or non-commissioned, put together.'

'There's a good deal depends on 'em, sir.'

'You keep to yourself, Archdale; that's the way to rise.'

'I was a man of few acquaintances, sir, and confidential with my superior officers, and few words, but I meant 'em, sir, and made the men do their duty.'

'That's the man for my money,' said Harry. 'Will ye be ready for Noulton Farm by the middle o' next month?'

'Yes, sir, I expect.'

'I'll settle that for ye, then, and the pay and the commonage, I'll settle that wi' my father to-morrow, and we'll get the writings drawn.'

'I thank you, sir.'

'And, wait a bit. I told you,' said Harry, perhaps a little embarrassed, 'there's another little thing you must manage for me.'

'Yes, sir.'

He almost wished Mr Archdale to ask questions and raise difficulties. This icy surface, beneath which he saw nothing, began to embarrass him.

'Every fellow's a fool once or twice in his life, you know, Archdale; and that's the way rogues make money, and honest chaps is sold –

> 'No fools at the fair,
> No sale for bad ware,

you know?'

He looked for sympathy in the face of the sergeant-major, but he found there neither sympathy nor ridicule, but a serene, dignified, supercilious composure.

'Well, I'm not married, and more's the pity,' he said, affecting a kind of jocularity, uneasily; 'but among 'em they've made me a present of a brat they calls my son, and I must just put him to nurse and provide for him, I do suppose; and keep all quiet, and ye look out some decent poor body that lives lonely and won't ask no questions nor give no trouble, but be content wi' a trifle, and I'll gi'e't to you every quarter for her, and she'll never hear my name, mind, nor be the wiser who owns it or where it came from. I'd rayther she thought 'twas a poor body's – if they think a fellow's well-to-do it makes 'em unreasonable, and that's the reason I pitched on you, Archdale, because you're a man o' sense, and won't be talkin' like the pratin' fool that's goin' – and is it settled? is it a bargain?'

'Yes, sir, I thank you, quite,' said Archdale.

'Well, then, ye shall hear from me by the end o' the week, and not a word, mind – till all's signed and sealed – about Noulton Farm, and about t'other thing – *never*. The stars is comin' out bright, and the sunset did ye mind; we'll ha' frost to-night; it's come dark very sudden; sharp air.'

He paused, but the non-commissioned officer did not venture a kindred remark, even an acquiescence in these meteorological speculations.

'And I heard the other day you made an organ for Mr Arden. Is it true?' said Harry, suddenly.

'Just a small thing, three stops, sir – diapason, principal, dulciana.'

'Well, I don't know nothing myself about such gear, except to hear the old organ o' Wyvern o' Sundays. But it's clever o' you. How did ye learn?'

''Prenticed, sir, two years to an organ builder in Westminster – Mr Lomas – and he died, and I was put to the army,' said Archdale.

'Well, I may give ye a lift that way, too. They were talkin' of an organ for Warhampton Church. We'll see. I'll not forget.'

'I thank you, sir,' repeated Archdale. 'Any more commands for me, sir?'

Mr Archdale stood stiffly at the gate, drawn up, as it were, at right angles to Harry Fairfield.

'No, nothing, Archdale. I'm glad the thing suits you, and it may lie in my way yet to make them better than you think for. Good-night, Archdale; good-night, sergeant-major.'

'Good-night, sir.'

And Archdale wheeled to his left, and, with his back toward the village of Wyvern, marched away at so stiff and regular a quick march that you could have fancied the accompaniment of the drums and fifes.

Harry stood at the iron gate, one half of which was open, and he kicked a stone listlessly into the road, and, leaning on the old iron arabesques, he looked long after that portly figure receding in the distance and melting in twilight.

'Night's the mother o' thought, I've heard say,' said Harry, rousing himself, and swinging the great valve into its place with a clang. 'But thought won't do to dine on. Hallo! Gate! gate! Jorrocks, anyone,' he shouted. 'Lock the gate, some of you, and make all sure for the night.'

And with these orders to Jorrocks he marched back under the ancestral trees to the old hall of Wyvern. Who was to keep the hearth of the Fairfields aglow? The light of the old squire's life was flaring low in the socket, a tiny taper was just lighted in darksome Carwell, and Harry Fairfield – was he ever to take his turn and illuminate the Wyvern world?

CHAPTER 52

A TALK WITH THE SQUIRE

Harry proved how hungry he was by eating a huge dinner. He had the old dining-room to himself, and sipped his brandy and water there by a pleasant fire of coal and spluttering wood. With a button or two undone, he gazed drowsily into the fire, with his head thrown back and his eyes nearly closed; and the warmth of the fire and the glow of the alcohol flushed his cheeks and his nose and his forehead to a brilliant crimson.

Harry had a hard day's riding. Some agitations, great variety of air, and now, as we have seen, a hearty dinner and many glasses of brandy and water, and a hot fire before him. Naturally he fell asleep.

He dreamed that the old squire was dead and buried. He forgot all about the little boy at Carwell, and fancied that he, Harry Fairfield, draped in the black mantle with which the demure undertaker hangs the mourners in chief, had returned from the funeral, and was seated in the old 'oak parlour', just in all other respects as he actually was. As he sat there, Master of Wyvern at last, and listening, he thought, to the rough tick of the old clock in the hall, old Tom Ward seemed to him to bounce in, his mulberry-coloured face turned the colour of custard, his mouth agape, and his eyes starting out of their sockets. 'Get up, Master Harry,' the old servant seemed to say, in a woundy tremor, 'for may the devil fetch me if here bain't the old master back again, and he's in the blue room callin' for ye!'

'Ye lie!' gasped Harry, waking up in a horror.

'Come, ye, quick, Master Harry, for when the squire calls it's ill tarrying,' said now the real voice of Tom Ward.

'Where?'

'In the blue chamber.'

'Where – where am I?' said Harry, now on his feet and looking at Tom Ward. 'By jingo, Tom, I believe I was dreaming! You gave me a hell of a fright, and is he there really? Very well.'

And Harry walked in and found the old squire of Wyvern standing with his back to the fire, tall, gaunt, and flushed, and his eyes looking large with the glassy sheen of age.

'Well, why didn't ye tell me the news, ye fool?' said the squire, as he entered. 'D——n ye, if it hadn't a bin for Tom Ward I shouldn't a heerd nowt o' the matter. So there's a brat down in Carwell Grange – ha, ha! – marriage is honourable, I've heerd tell, but housekeepin's costly. 'Tis the old tune on the bagpipe. That's the way to beggar's bush. When marriage gets into the saddle repentance gets up at the crupper. Why the devil didn't ye tell me the news? Why didn't ye tell me, ye d——d wether-head?'

'So I would ha' told ye to-night, but I fell asleep after dinner. It's true enough, though, and there's doctors, and nurses, and caudles, and all sorts.'

'Well for Charlie he's out of the way – dead mice feels no cold, you know, and she's a bad un – Alice Maybell's a bad un. The vicar was a thankless loon, and she's took after him. She went her own gait, and much good it did her. Sweetheart and honey bird keeps no house, and the devil's bread is half bran. She'll learn a lesson now. I was too good to that huzzy. Put another man's child in your bosom, they say, and he'll creep out at your sleeves. She's never a friend now. She's lost Charlie and she's lost me. Well might the cat wink when both her eyes were out. She'd like well enough to be back here again in Wyvern – d——n her. She knows who was her best friend by this time. Right well pleased wi' herself, I'll be bound, the day she gi'ed us the slip and ran off with the fool Charlie – down in the mouth, I warrant her now, the jade. I dare say the parson's down at the Grange every day to pray wi' my lady and talk o' resignation. When all their rogueries breaks down they take to cantin' and psalm singin', and turns up their eyes, the limmers, and cries the Lord's will be done. Welcome death, quoth the rat, when the trap fell. Much thanks to 'em for takin' what they can't help. Well, she's a bad un – a black-hearted, treacherous lass she proved, and Charlie was a soft fellow and a mad fellow, and so his day's over, and I was just a daft old fool, and treated accordin'. But time and thought tames all, and we shall all lie alike in our graves.'

'And what's the boy like?' the old man resumed. 'Is he like Charlie?'

'He was asleep, and the room dark, so there was no good trying to see him,' said Harry, inventing an excuse.

'Not a bit, dark or light, not a bit; he's Ally's son, and good won't grow from that stock – never. As the old bird crows, so crows the young, and that foreign madam, I hear, swears she was married first to poor Charlie, and what's that to me? – not that spoonful of punch. She's up in limbo, and if her story be true, why then that boy of Ally's ain't in the runnin', and his mother, bless her heart, needn't trouble her head about Wyvern, nor be wishin' the old squire, that was good to her, under the sod, to make way for her son, and then there's you to step in and claim my shoes, and my chair, and cellar key, and then Madame – what's her name – Van Trump, or something, will out wi' a bantling, I take it, and you'll all fight it out, up and down – kick, throttle, and bite – in the Court of Chancery, or where ye can, and what is't to me who wins or who loses? Not that bit o' lemon-peel, and if ye think I'm going to spend a handful o' money in law to clear up a matter that don't concern me, no more than the cat's whisker, you're a long way out in your reckonin' – be me soul ye are, for I'll not back none of ye, and I won't sport a shillin' – and I don't care a d——n. Ye'll fight the battle o'er my grave, and ye'll take Wyvern who can, and 'twill cost ye all round a pretty penny. Ye'll be sellin' your shirts and your smocks, and you're

pretty well in for it, and ye can't draw back. Well lathered is half shaved, and
it won't break my heart, I promise you.'

And the old man chuckled and hooted, and wagged his head fiercely as
he declaimed, in his own way, upon the row that was coming.

'Don't ye spare one another for my sake. Take Wyvern who can. I'll
keep my hands in my pockets, I promise ye. What have I to do wi' other
folks' windmills?'

So the old squire stormed on more serenely than he had done for a
long time.

'Make another tankard o' that thing, Tom; make a big one, and brew it
well, and fetch a rummer for yourself, lad.'

'Beggar's breed for rich men to feed,' resumed the squire. 'A son at the
Grange o' Carwell, no less! Well, I ha' taken enough, and too much on
my shoulders in my day, and 'tis often the least boy carries the biggest
fiddle. She's a sly lass – Alice. She'll find fools enough to help her. I ha'
done wi' her – she's a bad un. Look at that harpsichord thing there she
used to play on,' he pointed to the piano. 'I got that down from Lunnon
for her to jingle tunes at as long as she liked, and I'd ha' had it smashed
up and pitched in the river, only 'twould ha' made her think I cared
enough about her to take that trouble about her lumber. She turned her
back on me when she liked, and I'll not turn my face on her when she
lists. A graceless huzzy she was and is, and grace lasts but beauty blasts,
and so let it be for me. That's enough. I take it there's no more to tell. So
take ye a candle if ye're sleepy, man, no use dawdlin' sluggard's guise,
loath to bed, and loath to rise,' and so, with a gruff nod, he dismissed
him, and in came Tom Ward with the punch before very long.

'That's good, Tom; that'll warm yer ribs. How long ha' you been here?
Wyvern always, but a long time in the house, Tom, a long time wi' the
family. 'Tis sixty years ago, Tom. I remember you in our livery, Isabel and
Blue – them's the old colours. They don't know the name now – *salmon*,
they calls it. We ha' seen Christmas pretty often in the old house. We'll not
see many more, I'm thinking. The tale's nigh done. 'Twasn't bad times wi' ye
here, Tom; we can't complain; we ha' had our share, and after cheese comes
nothing, as the old folks used to say. Take the rummer and sit ye down by
the door, Tom. There's Master Harry. I'd rather ha' a glass wi' you, Tom,
than a dozen wi' him, a d——d pippin' – squeezing rascal. Tom, ain't he a
sneak, and no Fairfield, Tom, ain't he, ain't he, d——n ye?'

'I won't say that all out, sir. He's a tall, handsome lad, and Master
Harry can sit down and drink his share like a man.'

'Like a beast, ye mean. He never tells ye a pleasant story, nor laughs
like a man, and what liquor he swallows, it goes into a bad skin, Tom.
He's not hot and hearty in his cups, like a Fairfield; he has no good
nature, Tom; he's so close-fisted and cunnin'. I hate them fellows that

can't buy at the market and sell at the fair, and drink when he's drinkin';
d——n him, he's always a-watching to *do* ye, just like his mother; a screw
she was, and her son's like her, crooked to sell, and crooked to buy. I hate
him sober, Tom, and I hate him drunk. Bring your glass here, old lad; a
choice mug-full ye've brewed to-night. Hold it straight, you fool!

'What was I sayin'? The old things is out o' date, Tom; the world's
changin', and 'tain't in nature, Tom, to teach old dogs tricks. I do
suppose there's fun goin', though I don't see it, and the old folks
beginning to be in the way, as they were always, and things won't change
for us. We were brave lads, we Fairfields, but there's no one to come
now. There won't be no one after me in Wyvern house. To the wrestlin'
on Wyvern Fair Green when I was a boy, I mind the time when lords
and ladies 'd come ridin' down for twenty miles round, and all the old
stock o' the country, some on horseback, and some in coaches, and silks
and satins, to see the belt played for and singlestick and quarter-staves.
They were manly times, Tom, and a Fairfield ever first in the field, and –
what year is this? ay, I was twenty the week before that day – 'tis sixty-
four years ago – when I threw Dick Dutton over my shoulder and broke
his collar-bone, and Dutton was counted the best man they ever brought
down here, and Meg Weeks – ye'll mind Meg Weeks wi' the hazel eyes –
was lookin' on; and the wrestlin's gone, and not a man in the country
round that could tell a quarter-staff from a flail; and when I'm gone to
my place in the churchyard, there's not a Fairfield in Wyvern no longer,
for I don't count Harry one, he's not a Fairfield, by no chance, and never
was. Charlie had it in him, handsome Charlie. I seen many a turn in him
like me, I did; and that Captain Joliffe's died only t'other day that he shot
in the arm at Tewkesbury only twenty years ago for sayin' a wry word o'
me; old Morton read it yesterday, he says, in the Lunnon paper. But it's
all over wi' Charlie, and – stand up, Tom, and fill yer glass, and we'll
drink to him.'

Old Tom Ward was the first to speak after.

'Hot blood and proud, sir, and a bit wild, when he was young; more
than that, there's nowt to be said by any. A brave lad, sir, and the good-
naturedest I ever see. He shouldn't be buried where he is, alone. I don't
like that, nohow. He wouldn't ha' done so by you, squire; he liked ye
well; he liked everyone that was ever kind to him. I mind well how he
cried after poor Master Willie. They two was very like and loving.
Master Willie was tall, like him, and handsome.'

'Don't be ye talkin' o' them at all, ye fool,' broke in the squire,
violently, 'stop that, and hold your tongue, Tom. D——n you, do you
think I'm foolish? Light my candle, and get ye to bed, the tankard's out;
get ye to bed, ye d——d old fool,' and he shook the old servant hard by
the hand as he spoke.

CHAPTER 53

HARRY FAIRFIELD GROWS UNEASY

A few days later Harry Fairfield rode from Wyvern into the picturesque little town of Wykeford, and passing the steep, narrow bridge, pulled up near the church, at the door of Dr. Willett. Harry had something to say to the doctor, but, like a good diplomatist, that shrewd dealer in horses preferred letting the doctor talk a bit on his own account first.

He found him in slippers and dressing-gown, clipping the evergreens that grew in front of his house, the hour of his forenoon excursion not having yet arrived.

'Woodman, spare that tree,' said Harry, quoting a popular song, facetiously.

The doctor looked up.

'And how is Doctor Willett this morning?' said Harry.

'Oh! oh! Is that you?' said the doctor, straightening his back with a little effort, for he had been stooping for his task, and old backs don't unbend in a moment.

'Quite well, thank you – so are you, I see.'

'Can't complain.'

'And how's the old squire?' said the doctor.

'How's the old house?' answered Harry; 'staunch and straight, and like to stand for ever. I see no change in him. And all well over at Carwell?'

'Far from it,' said the doctor.

'And who's sick?'

'The poor young mother – very ill indeed,' said he, 'nervous, low, and feverish, when I saw her, it was plainly fever – quite declared.'

'What sort of fever?' asked Harry.

'Well, the nerves are very much engaged,' began the doctor –

'Take care it ain't typhus,' said Harry. 'The baby ha'n't got it, I hope?'

'No, the child's all safe.'

'There's typhus down at Gryce's Mill, and a child in scarlatina in the glen, I hear.'

'Is there? ha! It has been going a good deal at that side, I'm told,' said Dr Willett. 'There's Lady Wyndale at Oulton – very good-natured she seems to be – wouldn't she take the child and nurse it for a while? It's a nice place, well enclosed, and lies high – not likely to get in there. I attended a patient there in dropsy, once, when it was let, and the Wyndales away in India.'

'Ay, she's good-natured; she'd have the mother and child together, with a welcome, but she says she won't take no one's babby to nurse away from its people, and she's right, I think, so the young chap must stand his ground, and bide the fortune o' war, you know. What time shall you be there to-day?' he inquired.

'Three o'clock.'

'Very well, then, I'll be passin' at the mill end o' the glen about that time, and I'll ride up, and look in, just to hear what you have to say, and I'll get home by Cressley Common. It will do me as well as t'other way. I turned aside a bit to reach you, and hear the news, and I must be joggin' again. Good-bye, doctor. Is your church clock right?' said Harry, looking up at the old tower and pulling out his watch to compare.

'"The clock goes as it pleaseth the clerk," the old saw tells us, but we all go by the clock here, and it does keep right good time,' said old Dr Willett, with his hand over his eyes, reading its golden hands and figures, as Harry was.

'Well, then, doctor, good-bye, and God bless ye,' said Harry, and away he rode, without hearing the doctor's farewell.

At Carwell Grange, at three o'clock, there was the gloom and silence of a sick house.

The tiptoe tread of old Dulcibella, and her whisperings at the door, were scarcely audible, and now and then a weary moan was heard in the darkened room, and the wail and squall of a little child from another room not far off.

Old Mildred Tarnley had undertaken the charge of the child, while Dulcibella, with the aid of a neighbour brought in for the occasion, took charge of the sick lady.

Before three o'clock came, to the surprise of this sad household, Harry Fairfield arrived. He did not come riding; he arrived in a tax-cart. He had got through more real work that day than many men who were earning their bread by their labour.

'Give this one a feed, Tom; and how's all here?' said he, throwing the apron off and jumping down.

'Bad enough, I'm afraid, sir.'

'*Worse?*'

'I don't know, sir, till the doctor comes; but can't be no better, for I heard Mrs Crane say she didn't close an eye all night.'

'I hope they're not forgetting the child in the hurry?' said Harry.

'Mrs Tarnley and Lilly Dogger looks after it, turn about.'

'That wouldn't do nohow, you know,' said Harry – 'and give her a good feed, Tom; good dog, good bone. She came at a good lick, I can tell you, up the glen. The doctor will be here soon.'

'Ay, sir.'

'Well, I'll stay till I hear what he says; and there's sickness in Carwell Glen here, I'm told.'

'I dessay, sir; there's a good deal going, I hear.'

'Ye needn't take her out of the shafts, Tom. Fix her head in a halter by the gate – in the ring there, if he have a nosebag at hand – and come in here. She's as quiet as a lamb; I want to talk to you a bit. I'm going to buy two or three fillies, and think of any you may have seen down about here. Old Tarnley's in the kitchen now, is she?'

'I think she is, sir.'

'Well, think of them fillies if you can; there's business to be done if I can get 'em to suit.'

So in marched Harry, and tapped at the kitchen window, and nodded and smiled to Mrs Tarnley.

'So you're all sick down here, I'm told; but sickness is better than sadness. That's all I can say, lass,' said Harry, pacing, much in his usual way, into the kitchen, and clapping his big hand down on Mildred's shoulder.

'Sick, sore, and *sorry* we be, sir. Your brother's not that long buried that there should be no sadness in the Grange, his own house that was, and his widow's that is – sickness may well be better than sadness, but 'tain't turn about wi' them here, but one and t'other, both together. And that slut upstairs, Miss Dogger, if you please, out of the scullery into the bedchamber, she's no more use to me than the cock at the top o' Carwell steeple. I never knew such times in Carwell Grange; I'm wore off my old feet – I can't stan' it long, and I wish twenty times in a day I was quiet at last in my grave.'

'A gruntin' horse and a grumblin' wife, they say, lasts long. Never you fear, you won't die this time, old girl, and I wouldn't know the Grange if *you* wasn't here. 'Twill all be right again soon, I warrant – no wind blows long at the highest, ye know, and we'll hear what the doctors says, just now.'

'Hoot! what can the doctor say but just the old thing? The leech to the physic and God to the cure, and death will do as God allows, and sickness shows us what we are, and all fears the grave as the child does the dark. I don't know much good he's doin', or much he did for Master Charles – but not he's as good as another, and better than many a one, maybe – but he costs a deal o' money, and only Lady Wyndale came over here yesterday – poorly though she is, and not able to get out o' her coach – and saw Mrs Crane, and lent a fifty-pun note to keep all straight till the young lady, please God, may be able to look about her, and see after 'em herself, we'd a bin at a sore pinch before the week was out. Pity's good, but help's better. 'Tis well in this miserly world there's a kind one left here and there, that wouldn't let kindred want in the midst of plenty. There's Squire Harry o' Wyvern and his own little grandson lyin' up in the cradle there, and look at you, Master Harry. I wonder you hadn't the thought.'

Harry laughed, perhaps the least degree awkwardly.

'Why, chick-a-biddy——' began Harry.

'I'm none o' yer chick-a-biddies. I'm old Mildred Tarnley, o' the Grange o' Carwell, that's in the service o' the family – her and hers – many a long year, and I speaks my mind, and I shouldn't like the family to be talked of as it will for meanness. If there's a want o' money here in times of sickness, 'tis a shame!'

'Well, ye know there's no want, but the governor's riled just now, and he'll come round again; and as for me, I'm as poor a dog as is in the parish. Take me and turn me round and round, and what more am I than just a poor devil that lives by horses, and not always the price of a pot o' stout in my pocket –

'Four farthings and a thimble
Makes the tailor's pocket jingle.

Your tongue's a bit too hard, Mildred; but ye mean well, and there's kindness at the bottom o' the mug, though the brew be bitter.'

'I think I hear the doctor,' said Mildred, placing her palm behind her ear and listening.

'Ay,' said Harry; 'I hear him talkin'.'

And forth he strode to meet him.

Before he went up, Harry and the doctor talked together for a little in the panelled sitting-room, with which we are familiar.

'I'm sure to see you here, eh?'

'Before I go? Yes. I shall look in here.'

'All right,' said Harry, and the doctor walked up the stairs on his exploration.

CHAPTER 54

A DRIVE TO TWYFORD

In less than ten minutes the doctor came down.

'Well?' said Harry, over his shoulder, turning briskly from the window.

'No material change,' replied the doctor. 'It's not a case in which medicine can do much. The most cheering thing about it is that her strength has not given way, but you know it is an anxious case – a *very* anxious case.'

'I hope they are taking care of the child. Old Dulcibella Crane would be a deal better for that sort of thing than that dry old cake, Mildred

Tarnley. But then Ally would half break her heart if ye took old Dulcibella from her; always used to her, you know. And what's best to be done? It would be bad enough to lose poor Ally, but it would be worse to lose the boy, for though I'm willing to take my share of work for the family, there's one thing I won't do, and that's to marry. I'm past the time, and d——n me if I'd take half England to do it. I'd like to manage and nurse the estate for him, and be paid, of course, like other fellows, and that's what would fit my knuckle. But, by Jove, if they kill that boy among them there will be no one to maintain the old name of Wyvern; and kill him they will, if they leave him in the hard hands of that wiry old girl, Mildred Tarnley. She's a cast-iron old maid, with the devil's temper, and she has a dozen other things to mind beside, and I know the child will die, and I don't know anything to advise, d——n me if I do.'

'The house is in confusion, and very little attention for the child, certainly,' said Doctor Willett.

'And that d——d scarlatina, beyond a doubt, is in the glen there.'

The old doctor shrugged and shook his head.

'I talked to the governor a bit,' said Harry, 'thinking he might have the child over to Wyvern, where it would be safe and well looked after, but he hates the whole lot. You know it was a stolen match, and it's no use trying in that quarter. You're going now, and I'll walk a little bit beside you; maybe you'll think of something, and I haven't no money, ye may guess, to throw away; but rather than the child shouldn't thrive I'd make out what would answer.'

'That's very kind of you, sir,' said Doctor Willett, looking at him, admiringly. 'They certainly have their hands pretty full here, and a little neglect sometimes goes a long way with a child.'

So they walked out together, talking, and when the doctor got on his horse Harry walked beside him part of the way towards Cressley Common.

When he came back to the Grange Harry asked to see old Dulcibella, and he told her, standing on the lobby, and talking in whispers:–

'The doctor says she's not able to understand anything as she is at present.'

'Well, the doctor says she's wandering just now, but she may clear up a bit for a while by and bye.'

'Well, the doctor says she's not to be told a word that can fret her, and particularly about the child, for he says this is no place for it, and he won't be answerable for its life if it's left longer here, and there's scarlatina and fever all round, and ye have as much as ye can well manage here already, so few as there is, without nursing children; and Doctor Willett says he'll have it well attended to by a person near Wykeford, and I'll bring old Mildred over with it to the place this evening, and we'll get it out o' reach o' the sickness that's goin'.'

'Please God!' said Dulcibella, after a pause.

'Amen,' added Harry, and walked down, whistling low, with his hands in his pockets, to tell the same story to old Mildred Tarnley.

''Tis a pity,' she said, darkly, 'the child should be sent away from its home.'

'Especially with scarlet fever and typhus all round,' said Harry.

'And away from its mother,' she continued.

'Much good its mother is to it.'

'Just now she mayn't be able to do much.'

'Oh! but she can though,' interrupted Harry; 'she may give it the fever she's got, whatever that is.'

'Well, I can't say nothin' else, but it's a pity the child should be took away from its natural home, and its own mother,' repeated Mrs Tarnley.

'And who's takin' care o't *now?*' demanded Harry.

'Lilly Dogger,' answered she.

'Lilly Dogger! Just so; the slut! you said yourself to-day, you wouldn't trust a kitten with!'

Mrs Tarnley couldn't deny it. She sniffed and tossed up her chin a little.

'Ye forget, lass, 'twas never a Wyvern fashion nursin' the babbies at home. *I* wasn't, nor Charlie, poor fellow! nor Willie, nor none of us. 'Twas a sayin' with the old folk, and often ye heered it, "one year a nurse, and seven years the worse;" and we all was tall, well-thriven lads, and lives long, without fever or broken bones or the like, floors us untimely; and, anyhow, the doctor says, so it must be. There's no one here, wi' all this sickness in the house, has time to look after it, and the child will just come to grief unless his orders be followed. So stick on your bonnet and roll up the young chap in blankets, and I'll drive ye over to the place he says. It brings me a bit out o' my way, but kith and kin, ye know; and I told the doctor if he went to any expense, I'd be answerable to him myself, and I'll gi'e ye a pound for good luck. So ye see I'm not sich a screw all out as ye took me for.'

'I thank you, Master Harry, and I'll not deny but 'twas always the way wi' the family to send out the children to nurse.'

'And what Mr Charles would ha' done himself if he was alive, as everyone of us knows; and for that reason what the lady upstairs would ha' done if she had ha' bin able to talk about anything. I'm sorry I have to drive ye over, but I'll bring ye back to-night, and ye know I couldn't drive and manage the babby, and the folk would be wonderin' when the child set up the pipes in the tax-cart, and I'd soon have the hue-and-cry behind me.'

'Hoot! I wouldn't allow no such thing as let the poor little thing be druv so, all alone, like a parcel o' shop goods. No, no. The family's not come to that yet a bit, I hope,' cried Mrs Tarnley.

'Gi'e me a lump o' bread and cheese and a mug o' beer. I don't think I ever was here before without a bit and a sup, and it wouldn't be lucky, ye know, to go without enough to swear by, anyhow; but there's no hurry, mind – ye needn't be ready for a good hour to come, for Willett won't have no nurse there sooner.'

Harry went out and had a talk with Tom Clinton, and smoked his pipe for half an hour; and Tom thought that the young squire was dull and queerish, and perhaps he was not very well, for he did not eat his bread and cheese, but drank a deal more beer than usual instead.

'Bring a lot of lolly-pops and milk, or whatever it likes best, wi' ye, to keep it quiet. I can't abide the bawlin' o' children.'

Lilly Dogger, with red eyes and an inflamed nose, blubbered heartbroken, and murmured to the baby – lest old Mildred should overhear and blow her up – her leave-takings and endearments, as she held it close in her arms.

Beautiful though to us men, utterly mysterious is the feminine love of babies. Lilly Dogger had led a serene, if not a very cheerful life, at Carwell Grange up to this. But now came this parting, and her peace was shivered.

Old Mildred had now got up, with her threadbare brown cloak, and her grizzly old bonnet, and had arranged the child on her lap; so, at last, all being ready, the tax-cart was in motion.

It was late in the autumn now. The long days were over. They had dawdled away a longer time than they supposed before starting. It turned out a long drive, much longer than Mildred Tarnley had expected. The moon rose, and they had got into a part of the country with which she was not familiar.

They had driven fourteen miles or upward through a lonely and somewhat melancholy country. It was, I suppose, little better than moor, but detached groups of trees, possibly the broken and disappearing fragments of what had once been a forest, gave it a sad sort of picturesqueness.

Mildred Tarnley was not a garrulous person, and had not spent her life at Carwell Grange without learning the accomplishment of taciturnity, but she remarked and resented the gloomy silence of Master Harry, who had never once addressed a word to her since they started.

Toward the close of their journey she observed that Harry Fairfield looked frequently at his watch, and hurried the pace of the mare, and altogether seemed to grow more and more anxious. They had been obliged to pull up twice to enable her to feed the baby, who was now fast asleep.

''Tis right,' she thought, 'he should look ahead and mind the driving, while we're getting on, though a word now and then would not have troubled him much. But when we stopped to feed the child there was no excuse. He got down and settled the buckle at the horse's head. He got up again and drew the rug over his knees, and he leaned on his elbow back upon the cushion, and he never so much as asked was me or the baby alive!'

They now reached a gentle hollow, in which a shallow brook crossed the road, and some four or five habitations of a humble sort stood at either side; one under the shade of two gigantic ash trees had a sign depending in front, being a wayside inn of the humblest dimensions.

A village this could hardly be termed; and at the near end Harry pulled up before a building a little above the rank of a cottage, old and quaint, with a large-leafed plant that, in the moonlight, looked like a vine, growing over the prop of a sort of porch that opened under the gable.

If the mare was quiet at the Grange, you may be sure that her run to Twyford had not made her less so.

Harry helped old Tarnley down, with her little charge in her arms, and led her silently into the neat little room, with tiers of delf ornaments, in brilliant colours, on the cupboard, and a Dutch clock ticking in the nook by the fire where some faggots crackled, and a candle was burning on the table in a bright brass candlestick.

Mrs Tarnley's experienced eye surveyed the room and its belongings. She descried, moreover, a ladder stair which mounted to a loft, from whose dormant window, as she looked from her seat in the tax-cart, she had observed the light of a candle.

Very humble it undoubtedly was, but nothing could be more scrupulously clean. It had an air of decency, too, that was reassuring. There was a woman there in a cloak and bonnet, who rose as they entered and curtseyed.

Harry set a lumbering arm-chair by the fire, and beckoned Tarnley to occupy it. Then he asked:–

'How soon is the Warhampton 'bus expected?'

'Twenty-five minutes, please, sir,' answered the woman, with another curtsey and a glance at the clock.

'That woman from Willett's is coming by the 'bus,' he said gruffly, to Mildred. ''Tis a snug little place this, and as clean as a bone after a hungry dog. Would you mind,' he continued, addressing the stranger or hostess, whichsoever she might be, 'tellin' Archdale, if he's here, I want a word wi' him at the door?'

'He's over the way, I think, sir, with the horse. I'll call him, please, sir.'
So off she went.

'This is where poor Charles said he'd like to have his child nursed – Twyford; 'tis sweet air about here, considered. He was expectin' a babby, poor fellow, and he talked a deal wi' me about it the day he was took.

Wouldn't ye like a bit to eat and a glass o' beer, or somethin'? They have lots over the way, for as poor as it looks; and here's the pound I promised ye, lass, for luck, ye know, when we was leaving the Grange.'

He drew forth the hand with which he had been fumbling in his pocket and placed the piece of gold in hers.

'Thank you, Master Harry,' she said, making a little instinctive effort to rise for the purpose of executing a curtsey. But Harry, with his hand on her shoulder, repressed it.

'Sit ye quiet, and rest yourself, after joggin' all this way; and what's that bundle?'

'The baby's things, sir.'

'All right. Well, and what will ye have?'

'I feel a bit queerish, Master Harry, I thank ye. I'd rather not eat nothin' till I gets home, and I'll get my cup o' tea then.'

'Not eat!'

'Nothin', sir, I thank ye, Master Harry.'

'Well,' said Harry, so far forth relieved, but resolved, cost what it might, to make Mildred happy on this particular occasion, 'if ye won't eat, I'm hanged but ye shall drink some. I tell ye what it shall be, a jug of sherry negus. Come, ye must.'

'Well, Master Harry, as so ye will have it, I'll not say ye nay,' consented Mildred, graciously.

Harry went himself to the little pot-house over the way, and saw this nectar brewed, and brought it over in his own hand – the tankard in one hand and the glass in the other.

'Devilish good stuff it is, Mildred, and I'm glad, old lass, I thought of it. I remember you liked that brew long ago, and much good may it do you, girl.'

He was trying to be kind.

He had set it down on the table, and now, as he spoke, he laid his hand on her shoulder, and she thought she might have wronged Master Harry with his rough jests, and shrewd ways, and that he had more of the Fairfield in his nature than she had always given him credit for.

Out he went again, and talked with Archdale, who was in plain clothes, and a round hat, with a greatcoat buttoned up to his smooth blue chin, and a gig-whip in his hand. Archdale, as usual, was severely placid and brief, and as Harry talked with him outside, Mildred Tarnley thought she heard a step in the loft over her head, and another sound that excited her curiosity. She listened, but all was quiet again.

Harry returned in comparatively high spirits.

'Well, Mrs Tarnley,' said he, 'the 'bus is a bit late, I'm thinkin', but anyhow, he can't wait,' and he pointed over his shoulder at Mr Archdale who stood at the door; 'he'll drive you back again, and he knows the road as far as Cressley Common, and you can show him the rest – and you'll want to be back again with poor Alice – and the doctor will look in here, often in the week – almost every day – and tell you how the little chap's going on. And see, here's a very respectable woman – what's her name? – she was here this minute, and she won't be leaving till after the 'bus comes in, and you leave her the baby, and I'll wait here till I see it in charge of the nurse that's coming from Wykeford. Come in, will ye? – not *you* – the woman, I mean. Now, Mildred, give her the baby.'

The woman had a gentle, cheerful, and honest face; and looked down with the angelic light of a woman's tenderness on the sleeping face of the little baby.

'Lord love it,' she murmured, smiling. 'What a darling little face!'

Mildred Tarnley looked down on it, too. She said nothing. She bit her lips hard, and her old eyes filled up with tears that welled over as she surrendered the baby, without a word, and then hastily she went out, mounted to her seat in the tax-cart, and was driven swiftly away by a companion as silent as he who had conveyed her there.

CHAPTER 55

HOW FARES THE CHILD?

Dr Willett called regularly at the Grange, and kind Lady Wyndale was daily there, taking the doctor's directions about jellies, wines, and such other good things as the depressed state of the patient called for, notwithstanding her fever.

In a few days more he changed this treatment. The patient, in fact, could not be got to swallow these things. Dr Willett became more perplexed. It was not exactly gastric fever, but he thought it more resembled that flickering treacherous fire than any other fever with which he was acquainted.

There are sicknesses that will not be cured through the body. The mind diseased, which is the parent of these impracticable maladies, of which, when people die, they are said to have died of a broken heart – disdains the apothecary's boxes and bottles – knows nothing of them. The heart-ache, of which it is no more than an unusually protracted fit, has its seat in that which no apothecary can hear, see, feel, or understand. When the immortal, and in this life, inscrutable, spirit, which is the unseen lodger, the master, of the body, sickens, all sickens. In its pain all below it writhe and wither, and the body, its ultimate expression, reflects but cannot mitigate its torment.

Dr Willett, too, complained that the child was ill, and that it must have been ill before it left the Grange.

On this point he and Mildred Tarnley had a sharp battle.

When both parties had cooled a little he admitted that possibly the symptoms might not have been sufficiently developed to have excited the attention of an uninstructed observer.

The Grange was growing all this time more awful. Death seemed to have made his abode there, and the shadow of the hearse plumes seemed to rest upon the windows. Courage flagged, despair, supervened, and Mrs Tarnley's temper grew all but insupportable. A day in such situations seems very long, and many had passed since the baby had made his journey to Twyford. The doctor seemed desponding, and stood longer silent by his patient's bed this day than usual. His questions were briefer, and he was less communicative than usual when he was going.

Mildred Tarnley was making up her mind that the blow was inevitable, and was secretly wishing it might come soon, since come it must.

The father buried but two months since, the mother sinking into an untimely grave, and the poor little baby also dying! Was this family accursed? What a blight was this!

The doctor had said that he would return by Gryce's Mill. It had been dark some time and was now about seven o'clock. Tom was down at the forge, Dulcibella and Lilly Dogger both upstairs, and she quite alone in the kitchen. She was more uncomfortable than she had ever been before about Alice that night.

She had seen in the doctor's countenance that day, as he told her he would look in again on his return up the glen, that which had profoundly alarmed her, and now, sitting alone in this dark kitchen, she was infested by gloomy forebodings and terrible fancies.

She went upstairs to the sick lady's door. At that hour no amendment was probable, and there certainly was none. Down again she went. The idea had got into her head that the patient would die that night, and she grew nervous, and tired of listening for death-watches, and picking incipient winding sheets off the candle. 'I wonder Master Harry doesn't come here, if 'twas only to ask whether his sister was dead or alive, and why old Willett don't come. Smelt out a good supper somewhere, and he's stuffin' his gut, I'll warrant, while the poor lady's takin' the rattles.'

Mildred Tarnley could stand this no longer, and she went out and down the dark road that leads to the Glen of Carwell, close by, down which, with the uselessness of impatience, she went to look for a sight of the absent doctor, and listen for the tread of his horse.

Nothing cheered by that darksome walk, and the solemn and solitary view down the Carwell road, she stood gazing down towards distant

Gryce's Mill, until she tired of that too, and in dismay and bitterness retraced her steps towards the Grange.

On entering the yard she saw a man's figure approaching her from the kitchen door. She thought it was the doctor's for a moment, but it was not, and with a 'Lord! who's that?' gasped in fear that sounded like fury, she stood fixed as the old pump.

'Bah! don't you know me, woman?' said Harry Fairfield, surlily; 'I have only a few minutes. Ye'll have to come wi' me in the morning over to Twyford.'

'To Twyford?'

'Ay, to Twyford; and why the devil do ye leave the yard-door open; I walked into the kitchen and right up the stairs, lookin' for ye, and knocked at Ally's door. I think ye're cracked.'

'And what's to fear here, down in the Grange? Hoot! If 'twern't for form's sake we need never draw bolt from one Christmas to another.'

'There was a woman found her throat cut by the Three Pollards, between this and Hatherton, on Tuesday. If you likes it down here, 'tis little to me. I'll come here at eight o'clock in the morning to fetch ye.'

'Is the child sick?'

'Not it. It was, but it's gettin' all right; that is, if it *be* the child.'

'What the de'il d'ye mean, Master Harry?'

'I was lookin' at the child this mornin', and d——n me, if I think it's the same child we left there!' said Harry.

'Why, sir – Mr Harry, what's this?'

'I say I misdoubt it's not the same child, and ye must come over and look at it. Don't ye say a word o' the matter to no one; no more did I; if you do we'll never come to the bottom of it.'

'My good Lord!' exclaimed old Mildred, turning paler, and frowning very hard.

'I won't stop. I won't eat anything. I can't delay to-night; my nag's by the bridle, there, beside the scale, and – any message to Wykeford? I'll be passing Willett's house.'

'Well! well!' repeated Mildred, gaping at him still, with scarcely a breath left her, 'sin is sin, be it seen or no; judgment follows. God has feet of wool and hands of iron.'

'Sweep before your own door, lass; ye're a bit daft, bain't ye?' said Harry, with a sudden glare in his face.

'God forgive us all!'

'Amen,' said Harry.

And there came a pause.

'Women and fools will be meddlin',' he resumed. 'Lord love ye! For mad words, deaf ears, they say. 'Pon my soul! 'twould make a cow laugh, and if he don't mind ye may run your head against the wall.'

'I *will* go to-morrow and look at the child,' said Mildred, with sullen emphasis, clapping one lean hand down on the other.

'That's all I want ye. Come, what mischief can ye make o' that? Clear yer head!'

'There's two things shouldn't anger ye; what ye can help and what ye can't,' said Mildred. 'I'll go wi' ye in the mornin', Master Harry.'

'That's the least we can do and the most. How's Ally?'

'Dyin', I think; she'll be gone before daybreak, I'm thinkin'.'

'That's bad,' said Harry.

'Good hap or ill hap, as God awards. I know nowt against her.'

'Poor little thing,' said Harry.

'I blame myself; but what could I do? If aught's gone wrong wi' the child, poor lady! 'tis well she were gone too.'

'There's many a fellow'd knock ye on the head for less,' replied Harry, with a very black look; 'you women has a hintin', funkin' way wi' ye. Ye like to ladle the drippin' over a fellow's legs, and say ye meant the mutton. Can't ye speak out and say what ye mean, and get it off yer stomach, and let me know, and I'll answer it straight like a man and a Fairfield, d——n me!'

'I'll go wi' ye to-morrow; and I take it that's what ye want.'

'Well, this I'll say. If ye suppose I'd hurt that poor baby to the value of a pin's point, you're a stupider and a wickeder witch than I took ye for, and I wish poor Ally could hear me, and I'd swear to her on my knees, at her dying bed, by the Creator that made me, that I'll work for that boy as if he was my own, till I make him safe in Wyvern. And can't ye see, woman, d——n ye, that I can have but the boy's good in my mind when I ask ye to come over on such an errand to Twyford?'

'Well, I do suppose – I do suppose. Eight o'clock, and there's two feet will be cold ere then, I'm afeard.'

'Don't be a fool no more, and I forgive ye, Mildred,' said he, extending his hand; 'and don't ye mind a lick wi' the rough side o' my tongue – 'tis a way wi' us Fairfields – and there wasn't many on 'em would ha' stood to let ye rile them as ye did me. And bolt yer doors, mind; and, poor Ally! I hope she may do yet, and mind ye – eight o'clock sharp.'

So Harry departed.

Mildred stood and looked after him for a time.

'There's nothin' ever goes right at the Grange,' she said with a short, hard sigh; 'nor never did, nor never will.'

And after a pause, with another sigh, she said:–

'No, no; I won't think it – I couldn't think it – 'tain't in one o' them. They might be fickle wi' a lass, or hot tempered wi' a man, and a bit too hard wi' tongue or hand, but the like o' that – I can't believe it – never, and I wish I hadn't ha' heard that. I'm 'most sure I heard the child cry in the loft there; I'm sorry I didn't say so then. I don't know why, and I don't know now, what it should be no more than another, but I didn't like it. It looked summat *hid* – I can't say. But my heart misgave me.'

Old Mildred walked into the house. She had other thoughts now than the poor lady upstairs. They were remorseful, though she could hardly say for what she could blame herself. Perhaps she overrated her authority, and fancied she could have prevented the baby's being taken away.

But it might be all quite right – men were so stupid about babies. A pretty hand a Fairfeld man would make of a nursery! At all events the morrow would clear a great deal up.

The morning came. The doctor had looked in, and, as often happened, had surprised the lookers-on by pronouncing positively that the patient was *not* worse.

With a qualm at her heart, Mildred asked him when he had seen the child; and watched his face hard while he answered, quite frankly, that he had seen it the day before – that it was decidedly better, and might possibly do well.

When should he see it again?

There was nothing alarming, probably to-morrow; certainly not later than the next day. There was nothing urgent – the chances were rather in favour of its recovery, but, of course, there were the risks, and we weren't to hollo till we were out of the wood.

With this cheer Mildred was much comforted, so much reassured that when eight o'clock came next morning and brought no Harry Fairfield, she felt rather relieved of a bore than disappointed.

Two days later Dr Willett reported more favourably than he had yet done on Alice. His account of the boy, however, was by no means so cheery.

Harry looked in still later, and talked the matter over with Mildred.

'I thought, ye see, I might just be makin' a fool o' myself – and another o' you, so I went over there quietly next day, and I'm sure it *was* a mistake. The child's thinner a deal, and its colour gone, and it was dark a'most when I saw it, and she held the candle too low and cast a shadow from its nose, by Jove, across its face. You never see so queer a monkey as it looked, and so I held my tongue, but made over here to put our heads together and make sure o' the matter. But when I went next day and saw it in the daylight, by Jove it was all right – the child and no mistake. But it is grown awful thin and wry-faced, only you couldn't take it for any other, and the doctor sees it every second day, and I'm glad to hear that poor little Alice is getting on so well. She'll be on her legs again in no time, I'm thinking.'

After Harry had gone, Dr Willett arrived with a very ill account of the baby.

'Dying, poor little thing. Its heart wrong, and all the organs; but you mustn't tell poor Mrs Fairfield. It may cost her her life, if she begins to fret about it, and just tell her it's quite well, for it's true, you know – it's nearer heaven, and best of all when it gets there. So tell her, when she asks, that it was sent in charge of careful people to get it out of the reach of the infection that is in the neighbourhood, and keep her mind quiet.'

A few days later the news of its death arrived in the kitchen, and Lilly Dogger, who was afraid to give way to her emotions before Mrs Tarnley, abruptly rose and ran out, and throwing her apron over her head, broke into absolute screams of crying under the great old trees that stand by the scales.

Here there was a sad secret to disclose when the time came, and poor Alice was strong enough to bear the story.

In the meantime Harry Fairfield came and had a stormy interview with old Mildred. The doctor, he swore, didn't know his business. The women at Twyford had neglected the child. He'd see to it. He'd be a devil among the tailors. He'd open their eyes for them. He had often got fifty pounds for a less neglect of a filly. They should smoke all round for it. And there now was Wyvern without an heir, for, d——n him if he'd ever marry; he wouldn't for Saint Peter! It wouldn't do – it couldn't be, at no price; and there was old Wyvern, and never a Fairfield to see tankard filled or faggot fired in the old house.

Harry was not married, although he had insinuated some matrimonial ambiguities in his talk with old Mildred. But I believe he swore truly when he vowed that he never would marry. He had quite made up his mind on that point for some time.

For the rest, his threatenings ended in the noise they began in. In truth there was no ground for complaint, and both nurse and doctor had done their duty.

Alice recovered. I do not attempt to describe the long mourning that followed, the sweet, the bitter, and the terrible recollections that ever after tinted the image of Carwell Grange in her memory.

As soon as she could bear removal to her kind kinswoman, Lady Wyndale insisted on taking her to Oulton. After a time they travelled, and finally returned to Oulton, where they lived on together in the happiness of great and tried affection.

A difference of five-and-thirty years did not separate them any more than the interval of a generation did Naomi and Ruth. Lady Wyndale, being one of those gifted women in whom the girlish spirit burns high and bright so long as life itself continued, full of sympathy and gaiety, with a strong vein of romance, and a pleasant sense of the ridiculous, and also fine immovable affections, was to one who had suffered calamities so dire as had befallen Alice Fairfield a more delightful companion than any of her own age could have been. For, when it was needed, there was the graver charm of a long and sad experience, and there was also the grander teachings of religion, and these were not obtruded or vaunted in anywise, but rather toned her thoughts and feelings, with their peculiar sublime and melancholy lights, in which all things are subdued and also glorified.

CHAPTER 56

THE OLD SQUIRE LEAVES WYVERN

The old folk can't go on living always. The King's messenger had called at Wyvern, and the old squire must needs get up and go.

Sickness was a cross he had never been used to bear, and now that it was laid on his shoulders he knew that he could not keep his feet very long.

He had the Wyvern lawyer, who did the business of the estate, up to his room, and the parson and his own son, Harry Fairfield. He made the attorney read the will, which he had told him to bring up with him, and the squire listened as it was read slowly.

After the clergyman had gone:—

'Have ye ought to say to that, son Harry?' said the old squire.

''Tis an old will, father,' said Harry.

'It ain't,' said the squire.

'Eight years less two months,' said the lawyer.

'About the age rum's fit to drink,' said the old squire. 'What say ye to it – now's your time, son?'

'Priests, women, and poultry, they say, has never enough. There's bin changes since, and I don't see why Wyvern should be charged so heavy?'

'There's three hundred a year to Alice, that's what ye mean!' said the old squire.

His son was silent.

'Well, I don't owe her nothin', that's true, but I'll let it stand, mind. And Harry, lad, the day ye do a good thing there will be seven new moons.'

'What was parson a whisperin' about in the window wi' ye?' he asked of the attorney after a time.

'Some claim upon the vicarage which he thought you said you meant to remit by will.'

'I ha' thought upon it, and I won't. *Paternoster* built churches, and Our Father pulled 'em down. There's o'er many parsons for the churches, and o'er many churches for the people – tell him I won't.'

'What the devil made ye talk about that to him?' said Harry, with a dark look, when he and the attorney had got out of the room.

'My dear sir,' said the lawyer, 'we must be true to our clients, and beside, don't you remember the clergyman said he'd be here to-morrow at one to administer the Lord's Supper, and he'll be certain to speak of it then to our client.'

At nightfall the squire grew worse, and his head wandered.

'Tell that white-faced Vicar Maybell, there's never a one but the thankless in hell – I'll not sit under none o' his sermons – Ay, he frowns at that.'

'Hey, dear?' whispered the housekeeper, gazing at him from the hearth where they were sitting.

'And who does he mean, ma'am?' asked the nurse.

'God knows – old times, I suppose,' she answered.

'There's a glass broke, Tom; who's kicking up the row?' mumbled the squire. 'Play, women, and wine undoes men, laughin'. – Ay, light it, I'm very dark. – Who's he, ye fool? – Joan and my lady's all one in the dark.'

'That's Tom Ward he's thinkin' on?' said the nurse.

'Ay, he liked Tom ever. He wouldn't think 'twas Wyvern without Tom,' answered the housekeeper.

In a little time he said, more distinctly and sternly:–

'The dead should do nothing. – So that's the bishop. – Ay – ay. – The devil, mind ye, isn't always at one door. – If there was a good man here he'd put a clout over that face. – Ye'll never do it.'

Then it would sink into mumbling and then again grow more distinct.

At last the morning came, and the squire so many hours nearer death, was, nevertheless, now like himself.

In due course the clergyman arrived, and the housekeeper, and serious Jim Hopper of the mill, close by, attended to make up a little congregation with whom the dying squire was to receive that most 'comfortable' Sacrament, before setting out on his long journey.

'You're distinctly a Church of England man?' inquired the clergyman gently.

'Ay, what do you take me for?'

'I make it a rule, dear sir, to inquire. I have once or twice found Presbyterians and other Dissenters among the attendants at my church at Nottingham before I came here, and I am happy to hear so clear an answer to my inquiry,' said the clergyman with a gracious solemnity.

'The crow thinks her own bird fairest – go on,' said Squire Harry.

After these rites were over, the squire needed rest.

Then, after an hour or so, he called for Tom Ward.

'Well, Tom, we ha' lived a long while together – here in Wyvern – you and me, and "be the day never so long, at last cometh evensong," as they say, and now the doctor thinks my time be come, and I sent for ye to shake hands, Tom, and bid ye good-bye.'

Tom was drying his eyes hastily, and his old face was more puckered than ever.

'Yer honour was always kind to me——'

'Come, Tom, ye mustn't be cryin', man. Penny in pocket's a merry companion, and I wrote ye down for somethin' in my will, and ye ha' brewed me many a tankard, Tom – ye'll never brew me another – and I wouldn't go without a word and a shake by the hand.'

When this was over, the nurse signed to Tom to go.

I wonder how the grim old man, with near a week's white stubble on his chin, felt as he saw Tom Ward glide away softly, with tears on his rugged cheeks. For Tom, it was the breaking up and foundering of old Wyvern in the deep. He was too old to live in the new Wyvern that was coming, mayhap.

'I'll never get the old days out o' my head, nor ever like the new, and 'twon't be long, I'm thinkin', before I follow him down the ashtree road to Wyvern churchyard.'

And so for the old squire it came, the last day of light, and the first of death.

It was a stately funeral in the old-fashioned way. All the good old houses of the county were represented there. The neighbours, great and small, mustered; the shops in the town were all shut, and the tenants attended in masses.

This solemn feast and pageant over, the fuss subsided, and Harry entered upon his reign with a gravity becoming his new prerogative and responsibilities.

Sergeant-major Archdale was an influential, and prosperous, and reserved minister under the new *régime*. He had a snug berth at Warhampton, as Harry Fairfield had promised, and from that distant legation he was summoned every now and then to Wyvern, and there conferred with the squire. I have called him sergeant-major, but he was so no longer. He had retired some time before from the militia, and was now plain Mr Archdale.

CHAPTER 57

MARJORY TREVELLIAN

In order to throwing a light upon the nature of some of the duties of Mr Archdale, we must convey the reader, in spirit, to some little distance.

In the sequestered country, about twelve miles south of Twyford, in a pretty nook formed by a wooded hollow close by the old by-road to Warhampton, stands an antique cottage, with a loft and two little windows peeping through the very steep thatched roof and high narrow gable – gable and wall alike streaked and crossed with those black oak beams which formed the cage into whose interstices our ancestors built their brick and plaster. The steep roof runs out over a little porch which has a bench in one side of it. Another stone bench stands under the lattice window, the woodwork of which casement, as well as the black spars crossed and morticed in the walls, and even the curved brick chimney, look shrunk and warped by time, by which too, the hatch at the door is rounded and furrowed, and the stone seat and window stones worn into curves and hollows, and such and so venerable is the air of the structure, with its ivy-bound porch, that one might fancy it the very farmhouse in which Anne Hathaway passed her girlhood.

Here dwelt good Mrs Marjory Trevellian, some fifty years old and upward, with, I think, the kindest face and pleasantest laugh in that part of the country; a widow for many years; not very happy in her marriage, and quite content with her experience of the wedded state; quiet, cheerful, very industrious; with a little farm of three acres and a cow; spinning sometimes, knitting at others, and, when she could, taking in washing, and in all things approving herself diligent, cheerful, and honest.

With this kind, cheery, honest dame lived a little boy, the son of a Mr Henry – that was all she knew distinctly about his people. She called him her Fairy, and her Prince, and, when curious people questioned her closely, she said that his father was a merchant, 'unfortunate in business,' as the phrase is; that he was living perhaps in concealment, and in distressed circumstances, or possibly was dead. All she could say for certain was that she received a very small allowance for maintaining him, which was paid punctually every three months in advance, and that as to the name of the boy, his Christian name was William and his surname Henry, and that she called him her 'Prince' or her 'Fairy,' and he called her 'Granny.'

She idolised this pretty boy, and he loved her with the tenderness which a child bestows upon a loving nurse, something more than filial.

The boy remembers no other home but this, and no other friend but 'Granny.' He was now a little past eleven. His life had been solitary, but cheerful. Was there not the pond only thirty yards away from their door-step, in which he sailed his fleet of ships, made of corks, which old Peter Durdon gave him? He was a cousin of Marjory Trevellian's, and lived in the village two miles away. He used to call every Sunday and to bring these corks in his pocket, and a bit of such lead as tea is wrapped in, to make the keels of their navy. He was dressed in a blue 'swallow-tailed' coat with brass buttons; his drab trousers were very short; his stockings faded sky blue; and his shoes clumsy and clouted, and highly polished. He wore a chestnut wig of a long and lank cut, and his forehead slanted back very much, and his nose came forward, and a perpetual smile expanded his cheeks, which were as red and smooth as a ripe apple. His countenance was not wise, though very good-natured – rather silly, I'm afraid – and I think he took more interest in this sort of shipping than was quite compatible with strength of mind.

As these ships glided with thin paper sails across the pond, while Master Henry watched them in grave absorption, Peter's raptures expressed themselves in continuous peals of laughter.

These were great occasions in the solitary life of Fairy.

There were a set of big boxwood ninepins – skittles, I suppose, with balls – battered and discoloured – I never knew how they got into the cottage, but they looked a hundred years old if a day. Many a game with these on the smooth patch of sward at the other side of the pond had pleasant old Marjory with her darling.

In its seclusion its life was monastic, but not in its liberty. The boy was, on the whole, very happy.

Looking on honest Marjory as mistress of all she surveyed, it never struck him that in the points in which her dietary differed from his she was practising a compulsory economy. The article of meat was not often found in her bill of fare. But conscientiously she placed the little fellow's bit of broiled meat before him every day, and told him when he inquired why she had none for herself that she did not like it, and that it did not agree with her, which he accepted as undoubted truths, and wondered and regretted secretly.

On winter evenings their tea was very cosy. A wheaten cake baked on the griddle, a new-laid egg each, and a cup of tea from the many-coloured delf teapot – a good deal burnt on the side next the fire. With the door barred and the window carefully closed, the fire burning cheerfully, and their candle lighting the party – who so happy? And was there not the old Robinson Crusoe, with binding black with age, and a frontispiece showing the hero with his grave countenance and beard, his tall cap and goat-skin dress, his musket over one shoulder and his umbrella over the other, and recounting his marvellous life in the quaint old type of Queen Anne? And was there not that other literary treasure, the old folio of Captain Cook's, Commodore Anson's, and other seafaring worthies' voyages round or up and down the world, with no end of careful old copperplates, showing Pacific islands, curious volcanoes, flotillas of armed canoes, thick-lipped miscreants with rings in their noses and birds' tails enlivening their foreheads, and long processions of official people, priests, etc, with a small white pocket-handkerchief by way of dress? But better far than these, which, together with her Bible and Prayer-Book, constituted Marjory's library, was that good creature's inexhaustible collection of fairy tales, received traditionally and recounted *viva voce*, and prefaced with the rhyme which even at this distance recalls me to the nursery fireside with the far-off tones of a kindly voice that I shall hear no more.

> Once upon a time there was a king and a queen,
> As many have been,
> But few I have seen,
> Except in pictures!'

And starting with this little trumpeting and summons to attention – the 'oyes-oyes-oyes' and immutable prelude of an ever-varying sequel, good Marjory, the herald of ever new wonders, would tell her tale of dwarfs and castles, of god-mother fairies, and malignant enchantresses, broken-hearted princes and persecuted princesses, and enchanted palaces and awful forests, till the hour came for the little fellow to get to his bed and enter the no less wonderful land of dreams.

Another person who contributed to the regular entertainment of the boy was Tom Orange.

Tom Orange called at the cottage sometimes at intervals of three months, sometimes, for perhaps half a year, on the first of every month, and was always made welcome by Marjory Trevellian, and feasted with rashers and whatever else her humble larder afforded, and on going had established a mysterious right to a shilling 'tip,' which he always made it a point should be an honourable secret among them.

What might be the nature of his business the little boy neither knew nor cared, but Tom Orange was in the boy's eyes the ideal and epitome of all that was enchanting, brilliant, and exhilarating.

Tom was somewhat long and lean, with a face also long and always smiling, except when it was making a grimace, an art in which he excelled almost every other blackguard I have heard of. His clothes and hat were seedy, and, for so merry a person, he was wonderfully poor.

Tom Orange's accomplishments were infinite. He could dance a hornpipe with all the well-known airs and graces of a sailor; he could protrude his mouth till it assumed a shape quite unknown to physiognomists, and with a delicate finger, turning his eyelids inside out, make the pupils of these organs quiver strangely, while he uttered a sound like the call of a jackdaw. He could sing a variety of comic songs, with refrains delivered with a volubility which distances admiration, and made his very audience breathless, and some of these were relieved with occasional dialogue of matchless character and humour. He could swallow any number of pennies you pleased, and take them all out at different angles of his body; he could put several potatoes under his hat, and withdraw them all without touching either the hat or the potatoes.

He could keep three balls always in the air together, and he could balance two chairs upon his chin.

In short, as I have said, his accomplishments were innumerable and extraordinary, and the only wonder was how so universal a genius could possibly possess so few shillings and so many seedy articles of dress.

Tom Orange, too, was great at skittles, and gave his pupil wonderful new lights.

He taught him also how to guard, stop, and strike according to the principles of 'the noble art of self-defence.' In fact, it would have been difficult to discover a more fascinating companion and instructor of youth. Possibly it was as well, however, that his visits were so far between, and as brief as fortune ordained them to be. It was no wonder, however, that these visits were looked for by the boy, as the return of the life and excitement of an annual fair might have been by the ingenious youth of some other rural district.

There was but one point on which Marjory was obliged to impose a prohibition upon the child. It seemed a trifle, but in reality was a gigantic privation.

'No, darling, you mustn't talk to any other boys, nor play with them, nor go near them; if you do you'll be took away by your friends, and I'll never see you again; and what will poor Granny do then without her darling?'

And Granny's eyes filled with tears, and the boy cried and hugged her passionately, and this little agony gave place to wild affection and a glow of unspeakable delight and happiness, and was celebrated by a hot cake that evening, and new-laid eggs and a great tea, and stories to no end.

And she found her darling that night crying in his sleep, and was sure he was dreaming of leaving the old cottage, and she wakened him with kisses, herself crying.

So these two persons, notwithstanding some disparity of years, were wonderfully happy in one another's society, and if they had each their will would have fixed things as they were, and neither grown older nor younger, but just gone on living so for ever.

CHAPTER 58

THE ENCHANTED GARDEN

Marjory Trevellian was what is accounted among her class 'a good scholar,' and she had taught the little boy to read and write, to 'say his tables,' and to 'cypher,' as she termed the initiatory arithmetical exercises.

It was plain, however, that the boy was not abandoned to chance, but that an eye was upon him, and some friendly, if not conscientious direction controlling his destiny.

In one of his visits Tom Orange handed her a letter, written in the same neat clerk's hand in which the short memorandum that accompanied each remittance was penned. Having read the letter she was thoughtful.

When Tom had gone away, she said:—

'You are to be taught like a gentleman, as you are, my darling, and you're not to be sent to school for three or four years, and in the meantime Mr Wharton — he's a kind, good gentleman — is to teach you for two hours every evening after the school is over. You know his house. It is about a mile away from this; just half-way on the road to the grammar school.'

'But I'm to live at home, Granny, all the same?' inquired the boy in great trepidation.

'Lord love it, to be sure he is,' she answered, beaming on him with great affection. 'Only two hours, and everyone likes Mr Wharton, and I'm desired to go to his house to take his orders to-morrow.'

So she did, and the new order of things was established with very little disturbance of the old.

The narrow road which the boy every afternoon passed to and from Doctor Wharton's house makes, about half-way, a sudden curve. It is a wooded road, not without little ups and downs, and formidable ruts, and blocks of worn old stone, so large as to shock all the rules of modern road-making.

Upon this curve, so as nearly to front the boy's line of march, is a very old fruit garden, with a discoloured ivy-grown wall, on which are growing moss and house-leek, and here and there tufts of grass and wall-flower. Over the wall are seen ancient standard plum and cherry and pear-trees, and beyond them the upper windows, and the steep grey roof and slender chimneys of a house as much out of date as the garden.

In the garden-wall is a tall door with worn fluted pilasters corresponding in antiquity with the rest of the building and its belongings. This stone framework has an iron door, old-fashioned and fancifully wrought into arabesques of spikes, leaves, and stars, facing the quiet road, and within this a strong wooden door.

Fruit trees are, of course, always interesting to boys, but quite another interest mingled in the feeling with which little Willie viewed such glimpses of the old grey house and its background of dark and towering timber as his approach afforded, and he often wished, as he passed, that a hole in the wall might afford him a peep into the old garden and a glimpse of its owners. He sometimes heard their voices.

A clear, childish laugh he had heard more than once, from among the tall fruit trees and climbing roses that over-topped the wall, and a sweet female voice also faintly prattling with the child.

One evening, as he returned from Doctor Wharton's, with his books buckled in his strap swinging from his hand, having slackened his pace as usual when he found himself under the garden wall, to his infinite delight the inner wooden door, which had always obstructed his curiosity, was open. The outer gate of iron rails and foliage was locked, but through its bars he could see at last the garden. Its trees were old and overgrown. It was wonderfully dark, with roses and other flowers growing here and there, and one straight walk leading up to the house, and continuing the line of the narrow bridge which, at the iron door, crossed what seemed a sort of moat, whose banks were overgrown with docks and nettles. He could see part of the steps leading up to the door of the house, and a portion of one of its windows. The rest was concealed by the thick foliage, and the effect of this little glimpse was increased by the deep shadow of the foreground.

It was not very far from sunset, and the small birds were already singing among the boughs, and the deep shadow – the antique and neglected air and the silence of the place – gave it, in his romantic eyes, a character of monastic mystery and enchantment.

As he gazed straight up the dark walk towards the house, suddenly a man turned the corner of the yew hedge that met the bridge's parapet close to him, and walking straight up to the door, shut and locked the wooden door in his face.

So all was gone for the present. He knew there was no good in looking through the keyhole, for envious fortune had hung a spray of sweetbriar so as effectually to intercept the view, and nothing remained but the dingy chocolate-coloured planks before him, and the foliage and roses trembling over the old wall.

Many a time again he passed and repassed the door without a like good hap.

At length, however, one evening he found the envious wooden door once more open, and the view again disclosed through the iron bars.

A very pretty little girl, with golden hair, was standing on tip-toe near, and with all her soul was striving to reach an apple with a stick which she held in her tiny fingers.

Seeing him she fixed her large eyes on him, and said, with an air of command:–

'Come, and climb up the tree and get me that apple.'

His heart beat quick – there was nothing he liked better.

'But I can't get in,' he said, blushing; 'the door is locked.'

'Oh! I'll call mamma – she'll let you in. Don't you know mamma?'

'No, I never saw her,' answered the boy.

'Wait there, and I'll fetch her.'

And so she was gone.

The first flutter of his excitement was hardly over when he heard steps and voices near, and the little girl returned, holding the hand of a slight, pale lady, with a very pretty face, dressed all in black. She had the key in her hand, and smiled gently on the little boy as she approached. Her face was kind, and at once he trusted her.

'Oh! he has left the inner door open again,' she said, and with a little nod and smile of welcome she opened the door, and the boy entered the garden.

Both doors were now shut.

'Look up, little boy,' said the lady in black, with a very sweet voice.

She liked his face. He was a very handsome little fellow, and with an expression earnest, shy, and bright, and the indescribable character of refinement too in his face. She smiled more kindly still, and placing just the tip of her finger under his chin she said:–

'You are a gentleman's son, and you are nicely dressed. What is your name?'

'My papa's name is Mr Henry,' he answered.

'And where do you go to school?'

'I don't go to school. I say lessons to Mr Wharton – about half a mile from this.'

'It is great fun, I suppose, playing with the little boys – cricket, and all that?'

'I'm not allowed to play with the little boys.'

'Who forbids you?'

'My friends won't allow me.'

'Who are your friends?'

'I never saw them.'

'Really! and don't you live with your papa?'

'No, I live with Marjory.'

'Do you mean with your mamma?'

'Oh, no. She died a long time ago.'

'And is your papa rich – why aren't you with him?'

'He was rich, Granny says, but he grew poor.'

'And where is he now?'

'I don't know. I'm to go to school,' he said, acquiring confidence the more he looked in that sweet face. 'My friends will send me in three years, Granny says.'

'You are a very nice little boy, and I'm sure a good little fellow. We'll have tea in a few minutes – you must stay and drink tea with us.'

The little fellow held his straw hat in his hand, and was looking up in the face of the lady, whose slender fingers were laid almost caressingly on his rich brown hair as she looked down smiling, with eyes in which 'the water stood'. Perhaps these forlorn childhoods had a peculiar interest for her.

'And it is very polite of you taking off your hat to a lady, but put it on again, for I'm not a bit better than you; and I'll go and tell them to get tea now. Dulcibella,' she called. 'Dulcibella, this little friend is coming to drink tea with us, and Amy and he will play here till it comes, and don't mind getting up, sit quiet and rest yourself.

And she signed with her hand, smiling, to repress her attempt to rise.

'Well, darling, play in sight o' me, till your mamma comes back,' said the rheumatic old woman, addressing the little girl; 'and ye mustn't be pulling at that great rolling-stone; ye can't move it, and ye may break your pretty back trying.'

With these and similar injunctions the children were abandoned to their play.

He found this pretty young lady imperious, but it was pleasant to be so commanded, and the little boy climbed trees to gather her favourite apples, and climbed the garden wall to pluck a bit of wallflower, and at last she said:–

'Now, we'll play ninepins. There's the box – set them up on the walk. Yes, that's right; you *have* played; who taught you?'

'Granny.'

'Has Granny ninepins?'

'Yes, ever so much bigger than these.'

'Really! So Granny is rich, then?'

'I think so.'

'As rich as mamma?'

'Her garden isn't so big.'

'Begin, do *you*; ah, ah! you've hit one – and who plays best?'

'Tom Orange does; does your mamma know Tom Orange?'

'I dare say she does. Dulcibella, does mamma know Tom Orange?'

'No, my dear.'

'No, she doesn't,' echoed the little girl – 'who is he?'

What, not know Tom Orange! How could that be? So he narrated on that brilliant theme.

'Tom Orange must come to tea with mamma, I'll tell her to ask him,' decided the young lady.

So these little wiseacres pursued their game, and then had their tea, and in about an hour the little boy found himself trudging home, with a sudden misgiving, for the first time, as to the propriety of his having made these acquaintances without Granny's leave.

The kind voice, the beloved smile of Granny received him before the cottage door.

'Welcome, darlin', and where was my darlin', and what kept him from his old Granny?'

So they hugged and kissed, and then he related all that had happened, and asked, 'Was it any harm, Granny?'

'Not a bit, darlin' – that's a good lady, and a grand lady, and a fit companion for ye, and see how she knew the gentle blood in your pretty face; and ye *may* go, as she has asked you, to-morrow evening again, and as often as she asks ye; for it was only the little fellows that's going about without edication or manners, that your friends, and who can blame them, doesn't like ye to keep company with – and who'd blame them, seeing they're seldom out of mischief, and that's the beginning o' wickedness, and you're going, but oh, darlin', not for three long years, thank God, to a grand school where there's none but the best.'

So this chance acquaintance grew, and the lady seemed to take every week a deeper interest in the fine little boy, so sensitive, generous, and intelligent, and he very often drank tea with his new friends.

CHAPTER 59

AN OLD FRIEND

I am going now to describe the occurrences of a particular evening on which my young friend drank tea at Stanlake Farm, which was the name of the house with the old garden to which I have introduced the reader.

A light shower had driven the party in from the garden, and so the little boy and Amy were at their ninepins in the great hall, when, the door being open, a gentleman rode up and dismounted, placing the bridle in the hand of a groom who accompanied him.

A tall man he was, with whiskers and hair dashed with white, and a slight stoop. He strode into the hall, his hat on, and a whip still in his hand.

'Hollo! So there you are – and how is your ladyship?' said he. 'Skittles, by the law! Brayvo! Two down, by Jove! I'd rather that young man took you in hand than I. And tell me – where's Ally?'

'Mamma's in the drawing-room,' said the young lady, scarcely regarding his presence. 'Now play, it's your turn,' she said, addressing her companion.

The new arrival looked at the boy and paused till he threw the ball.

'That's devilish good, too,' said the stranger – 'very near the nine. Eh? But a miss is as good as a mile; and I don't think he's quite as good as you – and she's in the drawing-room; which is the drawing-room?'

'Don't you know the drawing-room! Well, *there* it is,' and the young lady indicated it with her finger. 'My turn now.'

And while the game was pursued in the hall, the visitor pushed open the drawing-room door and entered.

'And how is Miss Ally?'

'Oh, Harry! Really!'

'Myself as large as life. You don't look half pleased, Ally. But I have nowt but good news for you to-day. You're something richer this week than you were last.'

'What is it, Harry? Tell me what you mean?'

'So I will. You know that charge on Carwell – a hundred and forty pounds a year – well, that's dropped in. That old witch is dead – ye might ha' seen it in the newspaper, if you take one in – Bertha Velderkaust. No love lost between ye. Eh?'

'Oh, Harry! Harry! *don't*,' said poor Alice, pale, and looking intensely pained.

'Well, I *won't* then; I didn't think 'twould vex you. Only you know what a head devil that was – and she's dead in the old place, Hoxton. I read the inquest in the *Times*. She was always drinkin', I think she was a bit mad. She and the people in the back room were always quarrelling; and the father's up for that and forgery. But 'twasn't clear how it came about. Some swore she was out of her mind with drink, and pitched herself out o' the window; and some thought it might ha' bin that chap as went in to rob her, thinkin' she was stupid; and so there was a tussle for't – she was main strong, ye know – and he chucked her out. Anyhow she got it awful, for she fell across the spikes of the area rails, and she hung on them with three lodged in her side – the mad dog-fox, she was!'

'Oh, Harry! How shocking! Oh! pray don't!' exclaimed Alice, who looked as if she was going to faint.

'Well, she lay there, without breath enough to screech, twistin' like a worm – for three hours, it's thought.'

'Oh! Harry – pray don't describe it; don't, I implore. I feel so ill!'

'Well, I won't, if you say so, only she's smashed, and cold in her wooden surtout; and her charge is reverted to you, now; and I thought I'd tell ye.'

'Thank you, Harry,' she said, very faintly.

'And when did you come here? I only heard this morning,' asked Harry.

'Five weeks ago.'

'Do you like it; ain't it plaguy lonesome?'

'I like the quiet – at least for a time,' she answered.

'And I'm thinkin' o' gettin' married – upon my soul I am. What do you think o' that?'

'Really!'

'Sure as you're there, but it won't be none of your love-matches.

> 'Bring something, lass, along wi' thee,
> If thou intend to live wi' me.

That's my motto. Sweetheart and honey-bird keeps no house, I've heard say. I like a body that can look after things, and that would rather fund fifty pounds than spend a hundred.

> 'A nice wife and a back door
> Hath made many a rich man poor,

as they say; and besides, I'm not a young fellow no longer. I'm pushin' sixty, and I should be wise. And who's the little chap that's playin' skittles wi' Amy in the hall?'

'Oh, that's such a nice little boy. His father's name is Henry, and his mother had been dead a long time. He lives with a good old woman named Marjory Trevellian. What's the matter, Harry?'

'Nothing. I beg your pardon. I was thinkin' o' something else, and I didn't hear. Tell me now, and I'll listen.'

So she repeated her information, and Harry yawned and stretched his arms.

> 'For want o' company,
> Welcome trumpery,

and I must be goin' now. I wouldn't mind drinkin' a glass o' sherry, as you're so pressing, for I've had a stiff ride, and dust's drouthy.'

So Harry, having completed his visit characteristically, took his leave, and mounted his nag and rode away.

CHAPTER 60

TOM ORANGE

Little Miss Amy had a slight cold, and the next tea-party was put off for a day. On the evening following Harry's visit at Stanlake Farm, Marjory Trevellian being at that time absent in the village to make some frugal purchases, who should suddenly appear before the little boy's eyes, as he lifted them from his fleet upon the pond, but his friend, Tom Orange, as usual in high and delightful spirits.

Need I say how welcome Tom was? He asked in a minute or two for Marjory, and took her temporary absence with great good humour. Tom affected chilliness, and indeed the evening was a little sharp, and proposed that they should retire to the cottage, and sit down there.

'How soon do you suppose, youngster, the old hen will come home?'

'Who?'

'Marjory Daw, down the chimney.'

'Oh, Granny?'

This nickname was the only pleasantry of Mr Orange which did not quite please the boy.

Tom Orange here interpolated his performance of the jackdaw, with his eyelids turned inside out and the pupils quivering, which, although it may possibly have resembled the jackdaw of heraldry, was not an exact portraiture of the bird familiar to us in natural history; and when this was over he asked again – 'How soon will she be home?'

'She walked down to the town, and I think she can't be more than about half-way back again.'

'That's a mile, and three miles an hour is the best of her paces if she was runnin' for a pound o' sausages and a new cap. Heigh ho! and alas and alack-a-day! No one at home but the maid, and the maid's gone to church! I wrote her a letter the day before yesterday, and I must read it again before she comes back. Where does she keep her letters?'

'In her work-box on the shelf.'

'This will be it, the very identical fiddle!' said Tom Orange, playfully, setting it down upon the little deal table, and opening it, he took out the little sheaf of letters from the end, and took them one by one to the window, where he took the liberty of reading them.

I think he was disappointed, for he pitched them back again into their nook in the little trunk-shaped box contemptuously.

The boy regarded Tom Orange as a friend of the family so confidential, and as a man in all respects so admirable and virtuous, that nothing appeared more desirable and natural than that excellent person's giving his attention to the domestic correspondence.

He popped the box back again in its berth. Then he treated the young gentleman to Lingo's song with the rag-tag-merry-derry-perry-wig and hat band, etc., and at the conclusion of the performance admitted that he was 'dry,' and with a pleasant wink, and the tip of his finger pushing the end of his nose a good deal to the left, he asked him whether he could tell him where Mrs Trevellian, who would be deeply grieved if she thought that Tom was detained for a drink till her return, kept her liquor.

'Yes, I can show you,' said the boy.

'Wait a minute, my guide, my comforter, and friend,' said Tom Orange; and he ascertained from the door-stone that no one was inconveniently near.

The boy was getting a teacup off the shelf.

'Never mind sugar, my hero, I'll sweeten it with a thought of Marjory Daw.'

The boy explained, and led him into the dark nook by the hall door. Tom Orange, well pleased, moved almost on tiptoe, and looked curiously and spoke under his breath, and he groped in this twilight.

'Here it is,' said the boy, frankly.

'Where?'

'Here.'

'This!' said Tom, for his friend had uncovered a crock of water.

Tom Orange glared at him and at the water with grotesque surprise, and the *bona fides* of the boy and the simplicity of the situation struck Tom comically, and, exploding good-humouredly, he sat down in Marjory's chair and laughed hilariously.

Having satisfied himself by a confidential dialogue that Marjory Daw had no private bottle of comfort anywhere, this agreeable fellow so far forgot his thirst that he did not mind drawing water from the crock, and talked on a variety of subjects to the young gentleman. In the course of this conversation he asked him two topographical questions. One was –

'Did you ever hear of a place called Carwell Grange?'

And the other resembled it.

'Did you ever hear of a place called Wyvern?'

'No.'

'Think, lad. Did you never hear Mrs Trevellian speak of Wyvern? or of Carwell Grange?'

'No.'

'Because there is the tallest mushroom you ever saw in your life growing there, and it is grown to that degree that it blocks the door so that the squire can't get into his own house, and the mushroom is counted one of the wonders of the world, upon my little word of honour as a gentleman! And

> 'Since there's neither drink nor victuals,
> Suppose, my lord, we play at skittles?

And if she's not back by the end of the game, tell her I had to go on to the bridge to see lame Bill Withershins, and I'll be back again this evening, I think, or in the morning at latest.'

The game was played, but Marjory did not appear, and Tom Orange, entertaining his young friend with a ludicrous imitation of Bill

Withershins' knock-knees, took his departure, leaving his delighted companion in the state which Moore describes as being usual –

> When the lamp that lighted
> The traveller at first goes out.

So, having watched Tom till he was quite out of sight, he returned to his neglected navy on the pond, and delivered his admirable Crichton's message to Marjory Daw on her return.

CHAPTER 61

THE HOUR AND THE MAN

Supper-time came, and Tom Orange did not return. Darkness closed over the old cottage, the poplar trees and the town, and the little boy said his prayers under the superintendence of worthy Marjory, and went to his bed.

He was disturbed in his sleep by voices talking in the room. He could only keep his eyes open for a little time, and he saw Tom Orange talking with mammy. He was at one side of the little table and she at another, and his head was leaning forward so as to approach uncomfortably near to the mutton-fat with a long snuff in the middle. Mammy, as he indiscriminately called 'Granny', was sobbing bitterly into her apron, and sometimes with streaming eyes, speaking so low that he could not hear, to Tom Orange.

Interesting as was the scene, slumber stole him away, and when he next wakened Tom was gone, and mammy was sitting on the bed, crying as if her heart would break. When he opened his eyes, she said:–

'Oh, darlin'! darlin'! My man – my own, own blessed man – my darlin'!' and she hugged him to her heart.

He remembered transports similar when two years ago he was very ill of a fever.

'I'm not sick, mammy, indeed; I'm quite well,' and with these assurances and many caresses, he again fell asleep.

In the morning his Sunday clothes, to his wonder, were prepared for him to put on. The little old faded crimson carpet-bag, which she had always told him, to the no small content of his self-importance, was his own, stood plump and locked on the little table under the clock. His chair was close beside mammy's. She had all the delicacies he liked best for his breakfast. There was a thin little slice of fried bacon, and a new-laid egg, and a hot cake, and tea – quite a grand breakfast.

Mammy sat beside him very close. Her arm was round him. She was very pale. She tried to smile at his prattle, and her eyes filled up as often as she looked at him, or heard him speak.

Now and then he looked wonderingly in her face, and she tried to smile her old smile, and nodded, and swallowed down some tea from her cup.

She made belief of eating her breakfast, but she could not.

When the wondering little man had ended his breakfast, with her old kind hands she drew him towards her.

'Sit down on my lap, my precious – my own man – my beautiful boy – my own angel bright. Oh, darlin' – darlin' – darlin'!' and she hugged the boy to her heart, and sobbed over his shoulder as if her heart was bursting.

He remembered that she cried the same way when the doctor said he was safe and sure to recover.

'Mammy,' he said, kissing her, 'Amy has birthdays – and I think this is my birthday – is it?'

'No, darlin'; no, no,' she sobbed, kissing him. 'No, my darlin', no. Oh, no, 'tain't that.'

She got up hastily, and brought him his little boots that she had cleaned. The boy put them on, wondering, and she laced them.

With eyes streaming she took up one of the little cork boats, which he kept on the window stool floating in a wooden bowl.

'You'll give me one of them, darlin' – to old mammy – for a keepsake.'

'Oh, yes. Choose a good one – the one with the gold paper on the pin; that one sails the best of all.'

'And – and' – she cried bitterly before she could go on – 'and this is the little box I'll put them in,' and she picked them out of the bowl and laid them in a cardboard box, which she quickly tied round. 'And this is the last day of poor mammy with her bright only darlin' – for your friends are sending for you to-day, and Mr Archdale will be here in ten minutes, and you're to go with him. Oh, my precious – the light o' the house – and to leave me alone.'

The boy stood up, and with a cry, ran and threw his arms round her, where she stood near the clock.

'Oh! no, no, no. Oh! mammy, you wouldn't, you couldn't, you couldn't.'

'Oh, darlin', you're breaking my heart. What can I do?'

'Don't let me go. Oh, mammy, don't. Oh, you couldn't, you couldn't.'

'But what can I do, darlin'? Oh, darlin', what can I do?'

'I'll run away, mammy, I'll run away; and I'll come back when they're gone and stay with you.'

'Oh, God Almighty!' she cried, 'here he's coming. I see him coming down the hazel road.'

'Hide me, mammy; hide me in the press. Oh, mammy, mammy, you wouldn't give me to him!'

The boy had got into this large old painted press, and coiled himself up between two shelves. There was hardly a moment to think; and yielding to the instinct of her desperate affection, and to the child's wild appeal, she locked the door, and put the key in her pocket.

She sat down. She was half stunned by her own audacity. She scarcely knew what she had done. Before she could recover herself, the door darkened, a hand crossed the hatch and opened it, and ex-Sergeant-major Archdale entered the cottage.

In curt military fashion he announced himself, and demanded the boy.

She was looking straight in this formidable man's face, and yet it seemed as if he were vanishing from before her eyes.

'Where's the boy?' inquired the chill, stern voice of the sergeant.

It seemed to her like lifting a mountain this effort to speak. She felt as if she were freezing as she uttered the denial.

'He ain't here.'

'Where is he?' demanded the sergeant's imperturbably clear, cold voice.

'He's run away,' she said with an effort, and the sergeant seemed to vanish quite away, and she thought she was on the point of fainting.

The sergeant glanced at the breakfast table, and saw that two had taken tea together; he saw the carpet-bag packed.

'H'm!' intimated Archdale, with closed lips. He looked round the cottage room, and the sergeant sat down wonderfully composed, considering the disconcerting nature of the announcement.

The ex-sergeant-major had in his time commanded parties in search of deserters, and he was not a bad slaught-hound of that sort.

'He breakfasted with you?' said he, with a cool nod toward the table.

There was a momentary hesitation, and she cleared her voice and said:–

'Yes.'

Archdale rose and placed his fingers on the teapot.

'That's hot,' said the sergeant with the same inflexible dignity.

Marjory was awfully uneasy.

'He can't be far. Which way did he go?'

'Out by the door. I can't tell.'

The ex-sergeant-major might have believed her the goddess of truth itself, or might have thought her the most impudent liar in England. You could not have gathered in the least from his countenance toward which view his conclusions tended.

The sergeant's light cold grey eye glided again round the room, and there was another silence awfully trying to our good friend Marjory.

CHAPTER 62

THE MARCH TO NOULTON FARM

'I think, ma'am, the boy's in the house. You'd best give him up, for I'll not go without him. How many rooms have you?'

'Three and a loft, sir.'

The sergeant stood up.

'I'll search the house first, ma'am, and if he's not here I'll inform the police and have him in the "Hue-and-Cry"; and if you have had anything to do with the boy's deserting, or had a hand in making away with him anyhow, I'll have you in gaol, and punished. I must secure the door, and you can leave the house first, if you like best.'

'Very well, sir,' answered she.

But at this moment came a knocking and crying from within the press.

'Oh! no – 'twasn't mammy; 'twas I that did it. Don't take mammy.'

'You see, ma'am, you give useless trouble. Please open that door – I shall have to force it, otherwise,' he added, as, very pale and trembling, she hesitated.

Standing as he might before his commanding officer, stiff, with his heels together, with his inflexibly stern face, full before her, he extended his hand, and said simply, 'The key, ma'am.'

In all human nature – the wildest and most stubborn – there is a point at which submission follows command, and there was that in the serenity of the ex-sergeant-major which went direct to the instinct of obedience.

It was quite idle any longer trying to conceal the boy. With a dreadful ache at her heart she put her hand in her pocket and handed him the key.

As the door opened the little boy shrank to the very back of the recess, from whence he saw the stout form of the sergeant stooped low, as his blue, smooth fixed countenance peered narrowly into the dark. After a few seconds he seemed to discern the figure of the boy.

'Come, you sir, get out,' said the commanding voice of the visitor, as the cane which he carried in his hand, paid round with wax-end for some three inches at the extremity, began switching his little legs smartly.

'Oh, sir, for the love of God!' cried Marjory, clinging to his hand. 'Oh, sir, he's the gentlest little creature, and he'll do whatever he's bid, and the lovingest child in the world.'

The boy had got out by this time, and looking wonderingly in the man's face, was unconsciously, with the wincing of pain, lifting his leg slightly, for the sting of the cane was quite new to him.

'If I catch you at that work again I'll give you five dozen,' said his new acquaintance.

'Is this his?' said he, touching the carpet bag with his cane.

'Yes, sir, please.'

He took it in his hand, and glanced at the boy – I think it was in his mind to make him carry it. But the child was slender, and the bag, conscientiously packed with everything that had ever belonged to him, was a trifle too heavy.

'Anything else?' demanded the sergeant-major.

'This – this, God bless him.'

It was the little box with his ships.

'And this;' and she thrust the griddle cake, broken across and rolled up in brown paper, into the boy's pocket.

'And these;' and three apples she had ready she thrust after them.

'And ho! my blessed darlin', my darlin', darlin', darlin'.'

He was lifted up against her, folded fast, and hugging her round the neck, they kissed and cried and cried and kissed, and at last she let him down; and the sergeant-major, with the cane under his arm, the carpet bag in one hand, and the boy's wrist firmly held in the other, marched out of the door.

'That's enough – don't follow, woman,' said he, after they had gone about twenty yards on the path; 'and I'll report you,' he added with a nod which, with these pleasant words, she might take as a farewell or not as she pleased.

She stood on the little rising ground by the hawthorn tree, kissing her hands wildly after him, with streaming eyes.

'I'll be sure to see you soon. I'd walk round the world barefoot to see my pretty man again,' she kept crying after him; 'and I'll bring the ninepins, I'll be sure. Mammy's comin', my darlin'.'

And the receding figure of the little boy was turned toward her all it could. He was gazing over his shoulder, with cheeks streaming with tears, and his little hand waving yearningly back to her until he was out of sight. And after a while she turned back, and there was their ninepins' ground, and the tarn, and her sobs quickened almost to a scream; and she sat down on the stone bench under the window – for she could not bear to enter the dark cottage – and there, in Irish phrase, she cried her fill.

In the meantime Archdale and his companion, or prisoner – which you will, pursued their march. He still held the boy's wrist, and the boy cried and sobbed gently to himself all the way.

When they had come down to the little hamlet called Maple Wickets he hired a boy to carry the carpet bag to Wunning, four miles further on, where the Warhampton 'bus passes, as everybody knows, at half-past twelve o'clock daily.

They resumed their march. The sergeant was a serenely taciturn man. He no more thought of addressing the boy than he did of apostrophising the cane or the carpet bag. He let him sob on, and neither snubbed nor consoled him, but carried his head serene and high, looking straight before him.

At length the novelty of the scene began to act upon the volatility of childhood.

As he walked by the sergeant he began to prattle, at first timidly, and then more volubly.

The first instinct of the child is trust. It was a kind of consolation to the boy to talk a great deal of his home, and Tom Orange was of course mentioned with his usual inquiry, 'Do you know Tom Orange?'

'Why so?'

Then followed the list of that facetious and brilliant person's accomplishments.

'And are we to go near a place called Wyvern or Carwell Grange?' asked the boy, whose memory, where his fancy was interested, was retentive.

'Why so?' again demanded the sergeant, looking straight before him.

'Because Tom Orange told me there's the biggest mushroom in the world grown up there, and that the owner of the house can't get in, for it fills up the door.'

'Tom Orange told you that?' demanded the sergeant in the same way.

And the boy, supposing it incredulity on his part, assured him that Tom, who was truth itself, *had* told him so only yesterday.

The sergeant said no more, and you could not have told in the least by his face that he had made a note of it and was going to 'report' Tom Orange in the proper quarter. And, in passing, I may mention that about three weeks later Tom Orange was peremptorily dismissed from his desultory employments under Mr Archdale, and was sued for stealing apples from Warhampton orchard, and some minor peccadilloes, and brought before the magistrates, among whom sat, as it so happened, on that occasion, Squire Fairfield of Wyvern, who was 'precious hard on him,' and got him in for more than a month with hard labour. The urchin hireling with the carpet-bag trudged on in front, as the sergeant-major had commanded.

Our little friend, with many a sobbing sigh, and a great load at his heart, yet was looking about him.

They were crossing a moor with beautiful purple heather, such as he had never seen before. The sergeant had let go his wrist. He felt more at his ease every way.

There were little pools of water here and there which attracted the boy's attention, and made him open his box of cork boats and peep at them. He wondered how they would sail in these dark little nooks, and at last, one lying very conveniently, he paused at its margin, and took out a ship and floated it, and another, and another. How quickly seconds fly and minutes.

He was roused by the distant voice of the sergeant-major shouting, 'Hullo, you sir, come here.'

He looked up. The sergeant was consulting his big silver watch as he stood upon a little eminence of peat.

By the time he reached him the sergeant had replaced it, and the two or three seals and watch-key he sported were dangling at the end of his chain upon his paunch. The sergeant was standing with his heels together and the point of his cane close to the side of his boot.

'Come to the front,' said the sergeant.

'Give up that box,' said he.

The boy placed it in his hand. He uncovered it, turned over the little navy with his fingers, and then jerked the box and its contents over the heath at his side.

'Don't pick one of 'em up,' said he.

'Move half a pace to the right,' was his next order.

His next command was:—

'Hold out your hand.'

The boy looked in his face, surprised.

The sergeant's face looked not a bit angrier or a bit kinder than usual. Perfectly serene.

'Hold out your hand, sir.'

He held it out, and the cane descended with a whistling cut across his fingers. Another. The boy's face flushed with pain, and his deadened hand sunk downward. An upward blow of the cane across his knuckles accompanied the command, 'Hold it up, sir,' and a third cut came down.

The sergeant was strong, and could use his wrist dexterously.

'Hold out the other;' and the same discipline was repeated.

Mingled with and above the pain which called up the three great black weals across the slender fingers of each hand, was the sense of outrage and cruelty.

The tears sprang to his eyes, and for the first time in his life he cried passionately under that double anguish.

'Walk in front,' said the sergeant, serenely.

And squeezing and wringing his trembling hands together, the still writhing little fellow marched along the path, with a bitterer sense of desolation than ever.

The 'bus was late at Wunning; and a lady in it, struck by the beauty and sadness of the little boy's face, said some kind words and seemed to take to him, he thought, with a tenderness that made his heart fuller; and it was a labour almost too great for him to keep down the rising sobs and the tears that were every moment on the point of flowing over. This good Samaritan bought a bag of what were called 'Ginger-bread nuts' – quite a little store; which Archdale declined leaving at the boy's discretion. But I am bound to say that they were served out to him, from day-to-day, with conscientious punctuality by the sergeant-major, who was strictly to be depended on in all matters of property; and would not have nibbled at one of those nuts though his thin lips had watered and not a soul had been near. He must have possessed a good many valuable military virtues, or he could not, I presume, have been where he was.

Noulton Farm is a melancholy but not an ugly place. There are a great many trees about it. They stand too near the windows. The house is small and old, and there is a small garden with a thick high hedge round it.

The members of the family were few. Miss Mary Archdale was ill when they arrived. She was the only child of the ex-sergeant, who was a widower; and the new inmate of the house heard of her with a terror founded on his awe of her silent father.

They entered a small parlour, and the boy sat down in the chair indicated by the sergeant. That person hung his hat on a peg in the hall, and placed his cane along the chimney-piece. Then he rang the bell.

The elderly woman, who was the female staff of the kitchen, entered. She looked frightened, as all that household did in their master's presence, and watched him with an alarmed eye.

'Where's Miss Mary?'

'A-spitting blood, sir, please.'

'Bring in supper,' said the sergeant.

The boy sat in fear at the very corner of the table. His grief would not let him eat, and he sipped a cup of tea that was too hot, and had neither milk nor sugar enough. The sergeant snuffed his candle, and put on a pair of plated spectacles, and looked through his weekly paper.

While he was so employed there glided into the room a very slight girl, with large eyes and a very pale face. Her hair was brown and rich.

The hand with which she held her shawl across was very thin; and in her pale face and large eyes was a timid and imploring look that struck the little boy. She looked at him and he at her silently; her sad eyes lingered on his face for a moment, and he felt that he liked her.

She took a chair very softly and sat down without saying a word.

In a little while the sergeant laid down his paper and looked at her. Her large eyes were raised toward him with timid expectation, but she did not speak.

'Not well just now?'

'No, sir.'

'You take the bottle regularly?'

'Yes, sir.'

'You'll be better in the morning, belike.'

'I'm sure I shall, sir.'

He lighted a candle that stood on a side table, and his dog Bion got up to attend him. It was a large pug-dog, gambouge-coloured, with a black nose. The boy often afterwards wished to play with Bion, and make his acquaintance. But he did not know how the attempt would be taken either by the dog or his master, and so he did not venture.

No caresses passed between the dog and the sergeant. Each did his duty by the other, and they understood one another, I suppose, but no further signs of love appeared.

The sergeant went out and shut the door, and the girl smiled very sweetly on the little guest, and put out her hand to welcome him.

'I'm very glad you are come here. I was very lonely. My father is gone to the work room; he's making an organ there, and he won't come back till a quarter to nine. That's an hour and three-quarters. Do you hear – listen.'

She raised her finger and looked toward the partition as she spoke, and he heard a booming of an organ through the wall.

'Tony blows the organ for him.'

Tony was a little boy from the workhouse, who cleaned knives, forks, shoes, and made himself generally useful being the second servant, the only male one in their modest establishment.

'I wish I was better, I'm so out of breath talking. We'll be very happy now. That's tuning the pipes – that one's wolving. I used to blow the bellows for him, but the doctor says I must not, and indeed I couldn't now. You must eat something and drink more tea, and we'll be great friends, shan't we?'

So they talked a great deal, she being obliged to stop often for breath, and he could see that she was very weak, and also that she stood in indescribable awe of her father. But she said, 'He's a very good man, and he works very hard to earn his money, but he does not talk, and that makes people afraid of him. He won't be back here until he comes here to read the Bible and prayers at a quarter to nine.'

So she talked on, but all the time in an undertone, and listening every now and then for the boom of the pipes, and the little boy opened his heart to her and wept bitterly, and she cried too, silently, as he went on, and they became very near friends. She looked as if she understood his griefs. Perhaps her own resembled them.

The old woman came in and took away the tea-things, and shortly after the sergeant entered and read the chapter and the prayers.

CHAPTER 63

A SILENT FAREWELL

At Noulton Farm each day was like its brother. Inflexible hours, inflexible duties, all proceeded with a regimental punctuality. At meals not a word was spoken, and, while the master of the house was in it, all conversation was carried on, even in remote rooms, in an undertone.

Our little friend used to see the workhouse boy at prayers, morning and evening, and occasionally to pass his pale, disquieted face on the stairs or lobbies when his duties brought him there. They eyed one another wistfully, but dared not speak. Mr Archdale had so ordained it.

The workhouse boy – perhaps he was inefficient, perhaps too much was expected from him – but he had the misfortune perpetually to incur – I can hardly say his master's displeasure, for the word implies something emotional, whereas nothing could be at all times more tranquil and cold than that master – but his correction.

These awful proceedings occurred almost daily, and were conducted with the absolute uniformity which characterised the system of Noulton Farm. At eleven o'clock the cold voice of the sergeant-major called 'Tony!' and Tony appeared, writhing and whimpering by anticipation.

'My cane,' said the master, stepping into the room which he called the workshop, where the organ, half finished, stood, stop-diapason, dulciana, and the rest in deal rows, with white chips, chisels, lead, saws, and glue-pots, in industrious disorder, round. Then Tony's sad, miserable face was seen in the 'parlour', and Miss Mary would look down on the floor in pale silence, and our little friend's heart would flutter over his lesson-book as he saw the lank boy steal over to the chimney-piece, and take down the cane, and lingeringly disappear.

Then was heard the door of the workshop close, and then very faint the cold clear voice of the master. Then faint and slow the measured cut of the cane, and the whine of the boy, rising to a long hideous yell, and, 'Oh, sir – dear – oh, sir, dear; oh, Mr Archdale, oh, master, dear, oh, master, dear!' And this sometimes so protracted that Mary used to get up and walk round the room in a kind of agony, whispering, 'Oh, poor boy! Oh, poor Tony! Oh mercy – oh goodness! Oh! my good Lord, when will it be over!' And, sitting apart, the little boy's eyes as they followed her would fill with tears of horror.

The little fellow said lessons to Mr Archdale. There was nothing unreasonable in their length, and his friend Mary helped him. It was well for him, however, that he was a bright little fellow, with a good memory, for the sergeant was not a teacher to discriminate between idleness and dulness.

No one ever heard Mr Archdale use a violent expression, or utter a curse. He was a silent, cold, orderly person, and I think the most cruel man I ever saw in my life.

He had a small active horse, and a gig, in which he drove upon his outdoor business. He had fixed days and hours for everything, except where he meditated a surprise.

One day the sergeant-major entered the room where the boy was reading at his lessons, and, tapping him on the shoulder, put the county newspaper into his hand; and, pointing to a paragraph, desired him to read it, and left the room.

It was a report of the proceedings against Tom Orange, and gave a rather disreputable character of that amusing person. There was a great pain at the boy's affectionate heart as he read the hard words dealt to his old friend, and, worse still, the sentence. He was crying silently when the sergeant returned. That stern man took the paper, and said in his cold, terrible tones:–

'You've read that?'

'Yes, sir.'

'And understand it?'

'Yes, sir.'

'If I find you speaking to Thomas Orange, I'll tie you up in the workshop, and give you five dozen,' and with this promise he serenely left him.

Children are unsuspicious of death, and our little friend, who every night used to cry in his bed silently, with a bursting heart, thinking of his mammy and old happy times, till he fell asleep in the dark, never dreamed that his poor friend Mary was dying – she, perhaps, herself did not think so any more than he, but everyone else said it.

They two grew to be great friends. Each had a secret, and she trusted hers to the little friend whom God had sent her.

It was the old story – the troubled course of true love. Willie Fairlace was the hero. The sergeant-major had found it all out, and locked up his daughter, and treated her, it was darkly rumoured, with cruel severity.

He was proud of his daughter's beauty, and had ambitious plans, I dare say; and he got up Willie's farm, and Willie was ruined, and had enlisted and was gone.

The sergeant-major knew the post-office people in the village, and the lovers dared not correspond directly. But Willie's cousin, Mrs Page, heard from him regularly, and there were long messages to Mary. His letters were little else. And *now at last* had come a friend to bear her messages to trusty Mrs Page, and to carry his back again to Noulton Farm.

After her father had gone out, or in the evening when he was at the organ in the 'workshop', and sometimes as, wrapped in her cloak, on a genial evening, she sat on the rustic seat under the great ash tree, and the solemn and plaintive tones of the distant organ floated in old church music from the open window through the trees and down the fragrant field toward the sunset sky, filling the air with grand and melancholy harmony, she would listen to that whispered message of the boy's, looking far away, and weeping, and holding the little fellow's hand, and asking him to say it over again, and telling him she felt better, and thanking him, and smiling and crying bitterly.

One evening the sergeant was at his organ pipes as usual. The boy as he stood in the garden at his task, watering the parched beds, heard a familiar laugh at the hedge, and the well-known refrain:–

'Tag-rag-merry-derry-perrywig and hatband-hic-hoc-horum-genetivo!'

It was Tom Orange himself!

In spite of his danger the boy was delighted. He ran to the hedge, and he and Tom, in a moment more, were actually talking.

It became soon a very serious conversation. The distant booming of the organ pipes assured him that the light grey eye and sharp ear of the sergeant were occupied still elsewhere.

Tom Orange was broaching a dreadful conspiracy.

It was no less than that the boy should meet him at the foot of the field where the two osiers grow, at eleven o'clock, on the night following, and run away with him, and see mammy again, and come to a nice place where he should be as happy as the day is long, and mammy live with him always, and Tom look in as often as his own more important business would permit.

'I will, Tom,' said the boy, wildly and very pale.

'And oh! Tom, I was so sorry about the trial, and what lies they told,' said the boy, after they had talked a little longer; 'and saying that you had been with gipsies, and were a poacher; and oh! Tom, is mammy quite well?'

'Yes.'

'And all my ships were lost on the moor; and how is little Toozie the cat?'

'Very well; blooming – blushing.'

'And, Tom, *you* are quite well?'

'Never better, as I lately told Squire Harry Fairfield; and mind ye, I'll be even yet with the old boy in there,' and he indicated the house with a jerk of his thumb.

'I don't hear the organ, Tom. Good-bye.'

And Tom was off in a moment, and the boy had resumed his watering-pot. And that evening he sat down with, for the first time, a tremendous secret at his heart.

There was one grief even in the hope of his liberation. When he looked at poor Mary, and thought how lonely she would be. Oh! if poor Mary could come with him! But some time or other he and Tom would come and take her away, and she would live with him and mammy, and be one of that happy family.

She did not know what thoughts were in the boy's mind as his sad earnest eyes were fixed on her, and she smiled with a little languid nod.

But he need not have grieved his gentle heart on this account. There was not to be a seeming desertion of his friend; nor anything she could mistake for a treacherous slight.

That morning, at two o'clock, Mary died.

About ten minutes before, an alarm from the old servant, who slept in the room, called up her father.

Her faithful little friend was on his knees sobbing beside the bed, with her wasted hand in his, as the sergeant-major, hastily dressed, walked in, and stood by the curtain looking down into those large, deep eyes. She was conscious, though she could not speak. She saw, as she looked up her last look, a few sullen drops gather in those proud eyes, and roll down his cheeks. Perhaps the sad, wondering look with which she returned these signs of tenderness smote him, and haunted him afterwards. There was a little motion in her right hand as if she would have liked him to take it – in sign of reconciliation – and with those faint tokens of the love that might have been, the change of death came, and the troubled little heart was still, and the image of Willie Fairlace was lost in the great darkness.

Then the little boy cried aloud wildly:–

'Oh! Mary, pretty Mary. Oh! Mary, are you dead? Oh! isn't it a pity; isn't it a pity! Oh! is she dead?'

The sergeant dried his eyes hastily. He hoped, I dare say, that no one had seen his momentary weakness. He drew a long breath. With a stern face he closed the pretty eyes that Willie Fairlace, far away now, will never forget; and closed the little mouth that never will complain, or sigh, or confess its sad tale more.

'You had better get to your room, boy. Get to your bed,' said the sergeant, not ungently laying his hand on the boy's shoulder. 'You'll take cold. Give him a candle.'

CHAPTER 64

THE MARCH BY NIGHT

The next day the sergeant was away in his gig to Wyvern, a long journey, to report to the squire, and obtain leave of absence from his duties for a day or two. He was to spend that night at Hatherton, there to make arrangements about the funeral.

It was a relief to all at Noulton Farm, I need hardly say, when the master of the house was away.

A very sad day it was for the boy – a day whose gloom was every now and then crossed by the thrill and fear of a great excitement.

As evening darkened he went out again to the garden in the hope of seeing Tom Orange. He would have liked that cheer at the eve of his great venture. But Tom was not there. Neither counsel nor encouragement to be heard; nothing but the song of the small birds among the leaves, and the late flowers, soon to close, peeping from among the garden plants, and the long quiet shadows of the poplars that stood so tall and still against the western sky.

The boy came in and had his lonely cup of tea in the 'parlour', and a little talk with the somewhat sour and sad old servant. He was longing for the night – yearning to see Tom's friendly face and to end his suspense.

At last the twilight was gone. The night had indeed come, and the moon shone serenely over the old grey roof and the solemn trees; over the dead and the living.

The boy lay down in his bed at the accustomed early hour. The old woman had taken away his candle and shut the door. He lay with his eyes wide open listening with a palpitating heart for every sound.

The inflexible regularity which the absent master had established in his household was in the boy's favour. He heard the servant shut and bar the outer door at the wonted hour. He saw the boy's candle in his window for a while and then put out. Tony was in his bed, and for tired Tony to lie down was generally to be asleep.

Peeping stealthily from his lattice he saw the old servant's candle glimmering redly through the window on the juniper that stood near the wall in the shadow; and soon that light also disappeared, and he knew that the old woman had gone into her room. It was half-past ten. She would be asleep in a quarter of an hour, and in another fifteen minutes his critical adventure would have commenced.

Stealthily, breathlessly, he dressed. His window looked toward the osier trees, where Tom was to await him. It opened, lattice fashion, with a hinge.

Happily, the night was still, and the process of preparing to descend perfectly noiseless. The piece of old rope that lay in the corner he had early fixed on as his instrument of escape. He made it fast to the bed-post, and began to let himself down the wall. The rope was too short, and he dangled in air from the end of it for a second or two, and then dropped to the ground. The distance of the fall, though not much, was enough to throw him from his feet, and the dog in the lock-up yard at the other side of the house began to bark angrily. For a minute the boy gave himself up.

He lay, however, perfectly still, and the barking subsided. There was no other alarm, and he stole very softly away under cover of the trees, and then faster down the slope toward the appointed osiers.

There indeed was Tom Orange in that faint light, more solemn than he ever remembered to have seen him before. Tom was thinking that the stealing away this boy might possibly turn out the most serious enterprise he had yet engaged in.

He had no notion, however, of receding, and, merely telling the boy to follow him, he got into a swinging trot that tried the little fellow's endurance rather severely. I think they ran full three miles before Tom came to a halt.

Then, more like himself, he inquired how he was, and whether he thought he could go on fifteen miles more that night.

'Oh yes, he could do anything that night. Quite well.'

'Well, walk a bit that you may get breath, and then we'll run again,' said Tom, and so they set forward once more.

They had now accomplished about four miles more. The little fellow was not so fresh as at starting. A drizzling rain, too, had commenced, with a cold change of wind, and altogether the mere adventure of running away was not quite so pleasant, nor even Tom's society quite so agreeable on the occasion, as he had fancied.

'You have done four out of the fifteen; you have only eleven of the fifteen before you now. You have got over seven altogether up to this. Not so bad. You're not tired, youngster?'

'Not the least.'

'That's right. You're a good soldier. Now, come, we'll stand close under this hedge and eat a bit.'

They supped very heartily on great slices of bread and corned beef, which bore ample traces of the greens in which it had been served when hot.

'And now, boy, you must get on to Hatherton by yourself, for I'm known about here, and there's a fair there in the morning, and there will be people on the way before light. You must go a mile beyond the town, to the "George" public. Mrs Gumford keeps it, and there I'll meet you.' Then he detailed the route and the landmarks for the boy's guidance. 'Take a drink of this,' said he, pulling a soda-water bottle full of milk out of his coat pocket.

And when he had done:–

'Take a mouthful of this, my hero, it will keep you warm.'

And he placed a flask of brandy to the boy's lips, and made him swallow a little.

'And here's a bit more bread, if you should be hungry. Good-night, and remember.'

After about an hour's solitary walking, the boy began to grow alarmed.

Tom's landmarks failed him, and he began to fear that he had lost his way. In half an hour more he was sure that he was quite out of his reckoning, and as his spirits sank he began to feel the cold wind and drenching rain more and more.

And now he found himself entering a town not at all answering Tom's description of Hatherton.

The little town was silent, its doors and windows shut, and all except a few old-fashioned oil-lamps dark.

After walking listlessly about – afraid to knock and ask anywhere for shelter – worn out, he sat down on a door-step. He leaned back and soon fell fast asleep.

A shake by the shoulder roused him. A policeman was stooping over him.

'I say, get up out o' that!' said the imperious voice of the policeman.

The boy was not half awake; he stared at him, his big face and leather-bound chimney-pot looked like a dream.

'I say,' he continued, shaking him, but not violently, 'you must get up out o' that. You're not to be making yourself comfortable there all night. Come, be lively.'

Comfortable! Lively! – all comparative – all a question of degrees.

The boy got up as quickly as the cold and stiffness of his joints would let him.

Very dutifully he got up, and stood drenched, pale, and shivering in the moonlight.

The policeman looked down, not unkindly now, at the little wayfarer. There was something piteous, I dare say. He looked a grave, thoughtful man, of more than fifty, and he put his hand on the child's shoulder.

'Ye see, boy, that was no place to sleep in.'

'No, sir, I'll never do it again, sir, please.'

'You're cold; you'd get pains in your bones.'

'I'll not any more, sir, please.'

'Come with me, my boy, it's only a step.'

He brought the boy into his house down the lane close by.

'There's a fire. You warm yourself. There's my little one in fever, so you can't stop long. Sit down, child, and warm yourself.'

He gave him a drink of hot milk and a piece of bread.

'You don't get up, you know; there's no need,' he added.

I think he was afraid of his pewter spoons. He kept the little fellow nearly half an hour, and he lent him an old bottomless sack to wrap about his shoulders, and charged him to bring it back in the morning. I think the man thought he might be a thief. He was a kind man – there was a balancing of great pity and suspicion.

The boy returned the sack with many thanks, in the first faint twilight

of morning, and set forth again for Hatherton. It was, the fellow who
directed him said, still five miles on.

At about a mile from Hatherton, cold and wet, and fearing to be too
early at the "George Inn", the rendezvous agreed on, the tired little
fellow crept in, cold and wet, to a road-side pot-house.

At the fire of the ale-house three fellows were drinking beer. Says one
who had now and then had his eye on the boy:–

'That boy there has run away from school.'

I cannot describe the terror with which the little fellow heard those
words. The other two looked at him. One was a fat fellow in breeches
and top boots, and a red cloth waistcoat, and a ruddy good-humoured
face; and after a look they returned to their talk; and in a little while the
lean man, who seemed to find it hard to take his eyes off him, said,
'That's a runaway, that chap; we ought to tell the police and send him
back to school.'

'Well, that's no business of ours; can't you let him be?' said the red
waistcoat.

'Come here,' said the lean man, beckoning him over with his hard eye
on him.

He rose and slowly approached under that dreadful command.

I can't say that there was anything malevolent in that man's face.
Somewhat sharp and stern, with a lean inflexibility of duty. To the boy at
this moment no face could have been imagined more terrific; his only
hope was in his fat companion. He turned, I am sure, an imploring look
upon him.

'Come, Irons, let the boy alone, unless ye mean to quarrel wi' me,
d——n me, ye *shall* let him alone! And get him breakfast of something
hot, and be lively,' he called to the people; 'and score it up to me.'

So, thanks to the good Samaritan in top boots and red waistcoat, the
dejected little man pursued his way comforted.

As he walked through Hatherton he was looking into a shop window
listlessly, when he distinctly saw, reflected in the plate glass, that which
appalled him so that he thought he should have fainted.

It was the marble, blue-chinned face of the sergeant-major looking
over his shoulder, with his icy grey eyes, into the same window.

He was utterly powerless to move. His great eyes were fixed on that
dreadful shadow. He was actually touching his shoulder as he leaned over.
Happily the sergeant did not examine the reflection, which he would
have been sure to recognise. The bird fascinated by the cold eye of a
snake, and expecting momentarily, with palpitating heart, the spring of
the reptile, may feel, when, withdrawing the spell, it glides harmlessly
away, as the boy did when he saw that dreaded man turn away and walk
with measured tread up the street. For a moment his terror was renewed,

for Bion, that yellow namesake of the philosopher, recognising him, stood against the boy's leg, and scratched repeatedly, and gave him a shove with his nose, and whimpered. The boy turned quickly, and walking away the dog left him, and ran after his master, and took his place at his side.

CONCLUSION

At the 'George Inn', a little way out of Hatherton, the boy, to his inexpressible delight, at last found Tom Orange.

He told Tom at once of his adventure at the shop window, and the occurrence darkened Tom's countenance. He peeped out and took a long look towards Hatherton.

'Put the horse to the fly and bring it round at once,' said Tom, who put his hand in his pocket and drew forth a rather showy handful of silver.

I don't pretend to say, when Tom was out of regular employment, from what pursuits exactly he drew his revenue. They had rather improved than otherwise; but I dare say there were anxious compensations.

The boy had eaten his breakfast before he reached Hatherton. So much the better; for the apparition of the sergeant-major would have left him totally without appetite. As it was, he was in an agony to be gone, every moment expecting to see him approach the little inn to arrest him and Tom.

Tom Orange was uneasy, I am sure and very fidgety, till the fly came round.

'You know Squire Fairfield of Wyvern?' said the hostess, while they were waiting.

'Ay,' said Tom.

'Did you hear the news?'

'What is it?'

'Shot the night before last in a row with poachers. Gentlemen should leave that sort o' work to their keepers; but they was always a fightin', wild lot, them Fairfields; and he's lyin' now a dead man – all the same – gave over by Doctor Willett and another – wi' a whole charge o' duck-shot lodged under his shoulder.'

'And that's the news?' said Tom, raising his eyes and looking through the door. He had been looking down on the ground as Mrs Gumford, of the "George", told her story.

'There's sharp fellows poachers round there, I'm told,' he said; 'next time he'd ha' been out himself with the keepers to take 'em dead or alive. I suppose that wouldn't answer *them*'

''Tis a wicked world,' said the lady.

'D——d wicked,' said Tom. 'Here's the fly.'

In they got and drove off.

Tom was gloomy, and very silent.

'Tom, where are we going to?' asked the boy at last.

'All right,' said Tom. 'All right, my young master. You'll find it's to none but good friends. And, say now – haven't I been a good friend to you, Master Harry, all your days, sir? Many a mile that you know nothing about has Tom Orange walked on your business, and down to the cottage and back again; and where would you or her have been if it wasn't for poor Tom Orange?'

'Yes, indeed, Tom, and I love you, Tom.'

'And now, I've took you away from that fellow, and I'm told I'm likely to be hanged for it. Well, no matter.'

'Oh, Tom; poor Tom! Oh, no, no, no!' and he threw his arms round Tom's neck in a paroxysm of agonised affection, and in spite of the jolting, kissed Tom, sometimes on the cheek, on the eyebrow, on the chin, and in a great jolt violently on the rim of his hat, and it rolled over his shoulder under their feet.

'Well, that is gratifyin',' said Tom, drying his eyes. 'There is some reward for *prenciple*, after all, and if you come to be a great man some o' these days, you'll not forget poor Tom Orange, that would have spent his last bob and spilt his heart's blood, without fee or reward, in your service.'

Another explosion of friendship from the boy assured Tom of his eternal gratitude.

'Do you know this place, sir?' asked Tom, with a return of his old manner, as making a sudden turn the little carriage drove through an open gate, and up to a large old-fashioned house. A carriage was waiting at the door.

There could be no mistake. How delightful! And who was that? Mammy! at the hall door, and in an instant they were locked in one another's arms, and 'Oh! the darlin',' and 'Mammy, mammy, mammy!' were the only words audible, half stifled in sobs and kisses.

In a minute more there came into the hall – smiling, weeping, and with hands extended toward him, the pretty lady dressed in black, and her weeping grew into a wild cry, as coming quickly she caught him to her heart. 'My darling, my child, my blessed boy, you're the image – oh! darling, I loved you the moment I saw you, and now I know it all.'

The boy was worn out. His march, including his divergence from his intended route, had not been much less than thirty miles, and all in chill and wet.

They got him to his bed and made him thoroughly comfortable, and with mammy at his bedside, and her hand, to make quite sure of her, fast in his, he fell into a deep sleep.

Alice had already heard enough to convince her of the boy's identity, but an urgent message from Harry, who was dying, determined her to go at once to Wyvern to see him, as he desired. So, leaving the boy in charge of 'mammy', she was soon on her way to the old seat of the Fairfields.

If Harry had not known that he was dying, no power could ever have made him confess the story he had to tell.

There were two points on which he greatly insisted.

The first was, that believing that his brother was really married to Bertha Velderkaust, he was justified in holding that his nephew had no legal right to succeed.

The second was, that he had resolved, although he might have wavered lately a little, never to marry, and to educate the boy better than ever he was educated himself, and finally to make him heir to Wyvern, pretending him to be an illegitimate son of his own.

Whether the sergeant-major knew more than he was ordered or undertook to know, he never gave the smallest ground to conjecture. He stated exactly what had passed between him and Harry Fairfield. By him he was told that the child which was conveyed to Marjory Trevellian's care was his own unacknowledged son.

On the very same evening, and when old Mildred Tarnley was in the house at Twyford, was a child taken, with the seeds of consumption already active in it, from a workhouse in another part of England and placed there as the son of Charles Fairfield and Alice. It was then, contrary to all assurances, this child appeared for a few days to rally, and the situation consequent on its growing up the reputed heir to Wyvern alarmed Harry, that he went over, in his panic, to the Grange, and there opened his case, that the child at Twyford was a changeling, and not his brother's son.

When, however, the child began to sink, and its approaching death could no longer be doubtful, he became, as we have seen, once more quite clear that the baby was the same which he had taken away from Carwell Grange.

Dr Willett's seeing the child so often at Twyford also prevented suspicion, though illogically enough, for had they reflected they might easily have remembered that the doctor had hardly seen the child twice after its birth while at the Grange, and that, like everyone else, he took its identity for granted when he saw it at Twyford.

Alice returned greatly agitated late that evening. No difficulty any longer remained, and the boy, with ample proof to sustain his claim, was accepted as the undoubted heir to Wyvern, and the representative of the ancient family of Fairfield.

The boy, Henry Fairfield, was as happy as mortal can be, henceforward. His little playmate, the pretty little girl whom Alice had adopted, who called her 'mamma', and yet was the daughter of a distant cousin only, has now grown up, and is as a girl even more beautiful than she was as a child. Henry will be of age in a few months, and they are then to be married. They now reside at Wyvern. The estate, which has long been at nurse, is now clear, and has funded money beside.

Everything promises a happy and a prosperous reign for the young Fairfield.

Mildred Tarnley, very old, is made comfortable at Carwell Grange.

Good old Dulcibella is still living, very happy, and very kind, but grown a little huffy, being perhaps a little over petted. In all other respects, the effect of years being allowed for, she is just what she always was.

Tom Orange, with a very handsome sum presented by those whom he had served, preferred Australia to the old country.

Harry Fairfield had asserted, in his vehement way, while lying in his last hours at Wyvern, that the fellow with the handkerchief over his face who shot him was, he could all but swear, his old friend Tom Orange.

Tom swore that had he lived he would have prosecuted him for slander. As it is, that eccentric genius has prospered as the proprietor of a monster tavern at Melbourne, where there is comic and sentimental singing, and some dramatic buffooneries, and excellent devilled kidneys and brandy.

Marjory Trevellian lives with the family at Wyvern, and I think if kind old Lady Wyndale were still living the consolations of Alice would be nearly full.

OTHER BOOKS IN THIS SERIES

(ALL THE TITLES IN THIS SERIES ARE PAPERBACK)

W N P BARBELLION

0 86299 098 X	Journal of a Disappointed Man, The	3.99

ARNOLD BENNETT

0 7509 0667 7	Man from the North, A	3.99

CHARLOTTE BRONTË

0 7509 0481 X	Unfinished Novels	3.99

E G E BULWER-LYTTON

0 7509 0823 8	Coming Race, The	4.99

COLLINS AND DICKENS

0 86299 836 0	No Thoroughfare and other Stories	4.95

WILKIE COLLINS

0 7509 0654 5	Black Robe, The	5.99
0 7509 0841 6	Evil Genius, The	4.99
0 7509 0659 6	Fallen Leaves	4.99
0 7509 0010 5	Guilty River, The	3.99
0 7509 1045 3	"I Say No"	5.99
0 7509 0453 4	Legacy Of Cain	5.99
0 7509 0454 2	Miss or Mrs?	3.99
0 7509 0455 0	New Magdalen, The	4.99

A DUMAS

0 7509 1467 X	Masked Ball and other Stories, A	6.99

THOMAS HARDY

0 86299 093 9	Group of Noble Dames, A	3.99
0 86299 069 6	Life's Little Ironies	5.99

HENRY JAMES

0 7509 1409 2	Watch and Ward	5.99

J SHERIDAN LE FANU

0 86299 913 8	House by the Churchyard, The	7.99

WILLIAM MORRIS

0 7509 1207 3	The Well at the World's End	7.99

ANN RADCLIFFE

0 7509 0691 X	Castles of Athlin and Dunbayne, The	3.99

L T C ROLT

0 7509 1157 3	Sleep No More	4.99

BRAM STOKER

0 7509 0947 1	Jewel of Seven Stars, The	5.99
0 7509 0689 8	Lady of the Shroud, The	5.99
0 7509 1468 8	Mystery of the Sea, The	6.99

FANNY TROLLOPE

| 0 86299 086 6 | Domestic Manners of the Americans | 4.99 |

HUGH WALPOLE:

	THE HERRIES CHRONICLE	
0 7509 1042 9	Bright Pavilions, The Vol.V	6.99
0 7509 0803 3	Fortress, The Vol.III	6.99
0 7509 1043 7	Katherine Christian Vol.VI	6.99
0 7509 0668 5	Rogue Herries Vol.I	6.99
0 7509 0804 1	Vanessa Vol.IV	6.99
0 7509 1559 5	Secret City, The	6.99

HUGH WALPOLE & J B PRIESTLEY

| 0 7509 1047 X | Farthing Hall | 4.99 |

HENRY WILLIAMSON

	A CHRONICLE OF ANCIENT SUNLIGHT	
0 7509 2157 9	A Solitary War	7.99
0 7509 0819 X	Dark Lantern, The Vol.I	5.99
0 7509 0818 1	Donkey Boy Vol.II	5.99
0 7509 1214 6	Fox Under my Cloak, A Vol.V	5.99
0 7509 2155 2	Gale of the World	7.99
0 7509 1215 4	Golden Virgin, The Vol.VI	6.99
0 7509 0955 2	How Dear is Life Vol.IV	5.99
0 7509 1977 9	Innocent Moon, The vol. ix	7.99
0 7509 1978 7	It was the Nightingale vol. x	7.99
0 7509 1471 8	Love and the Loveless Vol.VII	6.99
0 7509 2156 0	Lucifer Before Sunrise	8.99
0 7509 2152 8	Phoenix generation, The Vol XiI	7.99
0 7509 2153 6	Power of the Dead, The Vol XI	7.99
0 7509 1470 X	Test to Destruction, A VolVIII	6.99
0 7509 0956 0	Young Phillip Maddison Vol.III	5.99

ÉMILE ZOLA

| 0 86299 216 8 | Fortune of the Rougons, The | 5.99 |
| 0 7509 0451 8 | Rome | 5.99 |

To order any of the titles listed above please contact:

LITTLEHAMPTON BOOK SERVICES, FARADAY CLOSE,
DURRINGTON, WEST SUSSEX, BN13 3RB

TEL: 01903 828500
FAX: 01903 828801